MW00778364

The Worship of Walker Judson

Also By
Janice Strubbe Wittenberg

Non Fiction:

The Rebellious Body: Reclaim Your Life From Environmental
Illness or Chronic Fatigue Syndrome

My Husband is Under Here Somewhere: Clutter, Pack Rats and
Pathological Hoarders
(forthcoming)

The Worship of Walker Judson

Janice Strubbe Wittenberg

Spiral Publishing
Aptos, California, U.S.A.
2013

Spiral Publishing
P.O. Box 2054, Aptos, CA, 95001-2054

Published in the United States by Spiral Publishing
Strubbe-Wittenberg.com

Library of Congress Cataloging-in-Publication Data
Strubbe Wittenberg, Janice
The Worship of Walker Judson: a novel / Janice Strubbe Wittenberg

ISBN 978-0-9895623-0-0
Library of Congress Control Number 2013954854

Printed in the United States of America on acid-free paper

First edition

Cover design by William Strubbe.
Cover painting by Dante Gabrielle Rosetti, titled *Beata Beatrix*.
Template images: Leonardo DaVinci's Vitruvian Man, artistic license
adaptation, source unknown.
Photograph of the author by Michael Paris,
mikeparisphotography.com

The Worship of Walker Judson is a work of fiction. Names,
characters, places, and incidents are the products of the author's
imagination and are used fictitiously. All resemblance to actual events,
locales, or persons, alive or dead, is entirely coincidental.

This book is dedicated to my siblings:

The most gorgeously fierce sister, Anne Strubbe Wallace, for having the courage to get up each day and face multiple challenges.

My trusty beacon, Richard (Dick) Strubbe, for the comfort his presence brings with every breath I've ever taken.

My amazing, William (Bill) Strubbe, for the incredible adventure that's been his entire life and for his unique vision of this world.

The sweetest brother ever, John Adrian Strubbe, for his unconventional role co-raising three unique children.

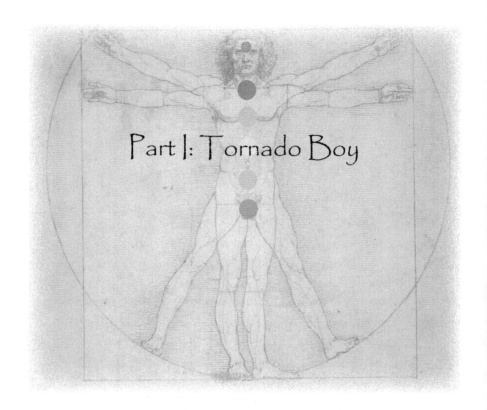

Part I: Tornado Boy

Chapter One: Walker

Years of hard-slog on foot to thank, he called himself *Walker*...and *Judson* because the saying created a most pithy tang. *Walker Judson*— the vibrations formed nicely in his mouth to move smoothly over tongue and lips. *Walker Judson*—he liked to say it. And renaming himself had been a thing of great comfort.

With no further need to walk, countryside speeding by, on this day he drove a big rig. Country and western tunes blaring, sky dropping rain, *whump-shump* went the windshield wipers as Walker whistled away. Yet with each passing mile, his chest crimped tighter.

Rounding a bend, spotting a seersucker-suited man in the roadway, he swerved, eased the rig on past, parked, jumped out and ran back to ask, "You OK?"

The fellow tried to point; his arm, half-lifted, twisted, oddly. "Help! I can't. Someone...," the gent mustered.

Eying the curve, Walker envisioned a vehicle barreling round it. "It's not safe here."

Good arm raised, the man indicated a smashed guardrail; skid marks ranged over its top. Down the embankment, chrome glinting, a car lay on its side, wheels spinning.

"I'll go check," Walker said, returning, "but first you must move." The man failed to budge. "OK then..." Walker dragged him from harm. "I'll be back."

Rain thumping earth, guardrail vaulted, branches smacking his face and ribs, Walker crouched to avoid taking a tumble, but slid out anyhow.

Chug-a, chug, the car's engine rattled. He scooted over to peer inside. Nobody within. Mud sucking his boots, rocks shifting, giving way underfoot, he skidded further, grabbed an upturned root and glanced about.

Blood scenting the air, legs cocked at immodest angles, there she lay.

Full-up with dread, moved adjacent, Walker shed his coat to cover her thighs.

Lips, arms, legs—all flesh a perfect match to the indigo of her dress; with his ear to her mouth, he could not detect breath. Fingertips at her neck. No throb, either.

Glass embedded the woman's skin and hair. A fist-size shard nearly cleaved her throat. Blood gushed around it. Given the extreme bend of her neck, it appeared broken.

Guidance whisked his ears—*take her pulse.* He gripped her wrist and felt the tiniest flicker. Faint, waining flutterings trickled beneath flesh: the woman hovered at death's lip.

"Lord," he implored, "what next?" He sat back on haunches to wait.

As if an epileptic, his body took up with the shivers and quakes. Try as he might, he could not contain them. Tremors intensifying, he shut his eyes.

Eyes open again, inquiring hand upon the woman's chest; still no breath.

But then...spasmodic articulations, barely perceptible, sparked beneath his fingertips.

Light visible to his eyes now—mostly at the woman's elbow and knee joints, thin murky streamers leached out.

Walker pulled back. *Is this the egress of her life force?*

Deep inhale, then exhale, calm descending, filament-like tentacles trickled from his spine's base. As if he'd taken root, they sunk, twisting, wending, to anchor him within the soft spongy earth.

Something primal birthed within, heat passed upward to fill every cell and crevice of his being, but then spewed, mightily, out from his skull's top. Overtaken by a rolling surge, breathless, amazed, Walker gazed down from above. Palms, fingertips aglow, no longer himself, but something other, he metamorphosed into ethereal mist to comprise *All that Sees and Knows, All that Has Ever Been.*

Shrunk to dot size, imperceptibly small, he entered the woman's psyche to witness the crash replay itself. Rubber screeched. He felt the car flip, dive into free-fall, hit rock with an immense *whump* as metal crumpled.

A body, hers, suspended, weightless—soft *woof*, it thudded back to earth. Air sucked inward, chest imploded, breath gone, she departed her body.

"God, a little help here!" Walker called out.

Motes of confusion whirring about, inexplicably foreign to his usual self, he heard himself coo and burble.

Touch her head and then her heart, came the command.

His hands obeyed; her body sparked slightly.

Rush, rush. Intuiting the precise means to create a circuit, he touched the woman's neck, arms, and chest. Hands roving, he massaged her temples, stroked her chin, brushed fingers through her hair—anything to gain purchase—to call back a life.

Blood gush ebbing, the woman's pulse throbbed softly. Heartbeats rippling hair follicles, gradually those pulsations expanded outward in layers, steadily strengthening.

Walker gripped the woman's head, positioned her neck, and yanked, grinding bone against bone, twisting. Gagging, he wretched, then leaned back, applying steady traction.

Eyes blurted open, the woman convulsed, then flailed. Walker tapped her brow. She lay back, becalmed.

Long suck of air, pain—her pain—swept through to overwhelm. Yet, never had he known such joy.

Stink of mud swarmed round as Walker paced the hospital corridor. Doors swung open, a doctor emerged, scruffing his chin to announce, "We're treating the gent for a broken arm and for shock. The woman has cracked ribs. She bled so bad, the trauma alone could've killed her. Don't know what to make of it; she also suffered a recent spinal fracture that seems to be on the mend. Judging from its location and severity, she should be dead, but isn't. And"—he eyed Walker—"her companion claims you slid his ulna and radius back inside and closed up the hole with a flash of light. Likely, trauma and shock altered his mind." The doctor paused, expectant.

"Imagine that," Walker muttered, noncommittal. Inwardly, however, he grinned.

Chapter Two: Young Walker

Many a time the boy spied Ma, lips moving, soundless, sniffing air as if an apron-wearing hound dog. His take, this meant she'd departed and...that she kept secrets.

Would she disappear altogether?

Often, he feared she just might.

"Does Ma plan to leave us?" he'd once asked Pa.

"Ask yer Ma," Pa practically hollered, "see if she'll say!"

The boy had a secret of his own—a pretty good one. He saw things invisible to others; light emanated from and surrounded folks. First time it happened, Pa caught fire. No one else saw. Not Pa, nor Ma.

Late one night, just turned ten, he came upon his parents, faced-off in the kitchen. "You lost your mind?" Pa hissed, barely audible. "Where'd you put it, then?" Sorrow, confusion, permeated his question.

Ma jutted her chin. "I cannot tell, Hollis." Air highly charged, sparked and sizzled.

"I suppose you'll say," Pa growled, "Almighty God gave you the right? But, I say, go git it!"

An expectant hum clung in the air as Ma shifted, warily. "I can't." Pa made fists.

Tiny pricks stabbing at innards, closer, the boy inched.

Pa tried a pleasant tone, "Who'd you give it to, then?"

Ma's eyes darted, blinking fast. "It's not like that."

Pa tensed again. "Git it back tomorrow, first thing. Hear?"

"It's gone. I..." Ma wavered. "I won't—can't—get it. Not now—not ever."

"Do as I say!" Pa's balled fist shot out, colliding with Ma's jaw.

Ma flew backward, but kept right on, in the exact same tones she used to calm the chickens, "You can't make me obey."

"Hush, Ma!" the boy blurted.

Ma whipped round. "Get to bed, son. This is no matter of yours."

"Show you who's in charge! Sure as hell, it ain't your God!" Grin insanely wide, arm unfurled, Pa whapped Ma's belly. Ma doubled over, then stumbled.

"Pa don't!" the boy yelped and wrung his hands.

Pa punched again. Ma teetered, then toppled, tangling legs in a chair as she went. Pa kept coming. Quick, hard kicks. Boots collided with Ma's bones, teeth, and skull.

Despite darkness, the boy saw all. Drops of sweat laced Pa's brow. Spray arced from punches. Ma's flesh took blows, then caved in. Smells—hot, rank—sickened.

Ma tried to stand. Pa slammed her to the wall.

"Stay down, Ma!" The boy pushed between them. "Stoppit, Pa!"

Scooted back, Ma cast her son a quick, wild glance.

"Mind me, woman," Pa menaced. "Return what's mine. Else, I pound you to bits!"

Full-up with feeling, unable to catch breath, the boy saw himself charge, headlong, pummeling with windmilled fists. Heard himself howl, saw himself grab the frying pan, swing it, braining Pa a doozy. Hands at his sides, feet glued to floor, he emitted a mere puny croak, "Stop knocking Ma!"

"Git outta here, son!" Pa gave him a shove. The boy stumbled, cracked his head on counter's edge, tried to stand, but his legs slid out.

Slumped, dazed, blood whooshing his ears, he looked to Ma.

Nightgown hiked up, moonlight illumined her thighs, as Pa loomed above her. "No more prayin' to your Almighty God. If he knows all, no need botherin'—is there? Like I said," Pa enunciated real slow, "git it back tomorrow, else I'll whup you good."He then swiveled to bark, "You try my patience, boy!"

Fumbled upright, the boy stepped out of reach.

Then it came...

Soft flames, comprised of light and variegation, drifted up, then off from Pa's hulking frame.

Blink, blink—the boy worked to clear his vision.

The flames remained.

Mouth shaped to give warning, instead the boy stared transfixed.

Pa smoothed hands down his shirtfront; smoky puffs unfurled from his fingertips.

"Clean up this mess," Pa directed Ma; murky streamers blurted forth from his lips. "Then come to bed." Pa hadn't noticed anything amiss.

Blink, blink—the boy stared again.

"Git a move on!" Smoke frothed out Pa's nostrils.

Even this, Pa failed to catch. "What're you starin' at, boy?" Vaporous trail retracted, it then disappeared.

Had Ma seen? The boy checked.

Eyes looking dully out from swelling flesh, Ma slumped, panting. *No, she couldn't have.*

Pa yanked Ma to her feet. Then they leaned together as if to whispering endearments; the boy hoped they might make up.

Pa grunted, then gave Ma a shove. "Second thought, don't bother comin' to bed. I'm sick of the sight of ya." Ma stumbled, let out a yip, then gripped the sink rim.

Senses swarmed the boy: murder, rage, prominent amongst them. Yet, feet smarting on floorboards, off he scurried to bed.

Sunup next morning, Ma shuffled about, painfully slow. Care taken not to bang pots, she shut cupboards with most deliberate intent, and seemed scarcely present at all.

Pa hovered at the radio, absorbing the weather report as he chomped away at his grits. Coffee slurped down, he stood, wiped his mouth, and went out.

On her way to the sink, as Ma caught his stare, crimson blotches swept up from her collar to overtake her cheeks. Heart jolted at sight of the night's ravages, the boy too went blotchy.

If asked, she'd claim a wayward hoe fell off its peg, whacked her up-side the head, gashed her cheek, swelled her eye and split her lip.

But he knew different.

Why'd she defy Pa? And why not just go get It?

It—he guessed, referred to one of their cows, sheep, goats, or chickens. Ma could fix the problem if she wanted; easy-peasy. Go get *It* back, and peace would be restored.

Napkin fretted to tatters, he hoped she'd do just that.

But Ma never left the farm that day. She never shed her apron, never combed her hair, or donned her town-going hat to fetch back what had gone missing.

Ma *did* grope her way onto the porch to sit in her rocker. Occasionally, she moaned, swayed, and clutched at herself. The boy couldn't tell if she prayed or wept, but there she stayed till day's end.

And *It* stayed gone. As if arm or leg had been hacked off to leave an ugly scar, always, the boy felt *Its* absence as a familiar clench in his heart.

Subsequent months, voices—high, pressing, insistent—mostly Pa's, echoed the house.

"Can't trust you, Bethel," Pa liked to shout. "You betrayed me!" He pounced, pounded. "And I can tell you how to keep the peace—just stop praying." Heedless as to consequence, grainy whispers frothing from lips, onward Ma communed.

Naturally, this provoked Pa all the more.

As if blows were kisses, Ma permitted Pa's fists to meet her face, ribs, thighs, shins and gut. Yells, silence, followed by a thud; repeatedly she fell undefended. Pa near-to killed her.

One episode, Pa smacked every tooth clean out from her head. Caved in about the cheeks and mouth, she seemed kin to a wizened apple-headed doll. Although still young, Ma wore ill-fitting dentures ever after.

Formerly ramrod straight, she grew stooped. Her hands trembled as if volts of electricity ran through them. A black eye or a gashed cheek was common. Bruises purpled her neck where Pa's fingers indented.

Despite abuse, Ma seemed ever so smug. Chin up, nostrils flaring, arched poise to her neck, she leaned in to the blows. Each split lip, every bruise seeming treasured, unspeakable illumination, outright joy, arose from her suffering.

Fascinated, repulsed, the boy's breath came ragged from watching.

Inwardly fuming at being forced to witness, he tucked away his colossal hatred of Pa and his yearning for Ma. See, he understood enough to keep such matters hidden.

Daily, he walked off his fury and guilt for his impotence. Trudging through pastures and into ravines, he hurled vile oaths at Pa, promised to wreak vengeance, contrived diatribes and affronts, and imagined acts of extreme violence.

No violence on his part ever *did* transpire. Yet his heart cleaved with anguish. And his exertions allowed him to pass through days without the public humiliation of tears, howls, or vomiting.

Outwardly, he tried to help. Raucous, quick, darting movements made Ma flinch. So he spoke in low tones and moved with slow, fluid grace, careful not to bump, trip, or tumble—manners unlike lads his age. Always, he came when called, did chores when bidden, and never lollygagged or sassed.

Hoping a tidy appearance might organize his inner tumult, the boy traded natty coveralls and work shirt for a moth-eaten business suit and yellowed dress shirt found in the attic. Untroubled that his limbs shot out from the cuffs several inches; by his estimation he looked downright snappy. Moreover, without the garment's tight press of snugness to swaddle him, he feared he might sproing apart, going every which way.

Faithfully, he wore this get-up while slopping mush for the hogs— even while chasing down calves. Hottest days, heat unbearable, he luxuriated by undoing the topmost button.

"What's this?" Pa came along, limp-wristed, mincing steps, first time he saw the attire. "Too high and mighty for the likes of us?" Humiliation tumbled through. Ma laid eyes on him, gargled a bit, but offered no protection.

Schoolmates called him Preacher Man, snickering behind hands. Kids teased. Pa scoffed. Everyone poked fun. Still, Ma said nothing.

Using the look to separate himself, he proudly suffered the fuss. See—the greater the unease he caused, the gladder he felt.

"You think Pa's a monster?" Ma asked one day. The boy glanced up from chopping vegetables.

A long moment shimmered past.

Of late, hands pressed firmly to ears, he'd acquired the habit of crouching within confined spaces: in cupboards, beneath beds, under tables, mostly inside Ma's closet. Calm best achieved therein, he liked to bury his face in her clothes, soaking up the smell of her and her soaps. Even still, he heard his parent's wince-making groans and shouts.

One time, when she came upon him, he claimed, "I'm inspecting the innards of things."

"I'm the monster," she now announced, emphatic.

"Why's that, Ma?"

"Fights between me and Pa are my fault." She motioned him close. "Really, Pa's a decent man."

Briefly, the boy considered this, but found it hard to fathom.

"After Pa hits, he's terribly sorry. I...I just can't obey."

"Aw, Ma—" The boy tried to shush her; she talked right over him.

"Mustn't hold a grudge, son. Ma deserves all of it."

Maybe, he reasoned, *she did!* Ma's prayers posed an appeal to God. But for the boy, prayer meant loss—that she abandoned him. And all that praying...for what net result?

Ma risked Pa's temper and ignored her son, praying for help that never seemed to come. Yet for her, prayer meant everything.

His take: prayer meant empty conversation and seemed just plain dumb. "Why not stop praying, least not so Pa knows?"

"It's not my choice. Besides, that's not the crux of our troubles."

"What is?" The boy leaned in. Raised cleaver in hand, Ma paused, considering.

"I can't explain." Knife set down, she turned away.

Nearly as strong as Pa, Ma could tote two full apple sacks and was as nimble as you please. *It would be so easy,* he thought, *for her to defend herself. And then Pa would leave her be.*

Plainly though, Ma lets Pa have at her as penance for wrongdoing.

"We're done here; you can go." Ma gave him a nudge.

Out he went, crossed over to the barn, climbed up to the hayloft, flung open the baling doors, flopped onto the straw, and gazed out.

Shortly, Ma came onto the porch. Eyes cast upward, hands primly folded, she took up her rocker, immersed herself in a force mighty powerful, and slid off to that far-away place yet again. Face ecstatic, polished sheen to cheeks, clutter abounding, potted plants—some vibrant hued, others crispy leafed—surrounding, there she swayed and hummed. A doorless refrigerator stood nearby. Waist-high newspaper stacks ran the porch length. No vacant space remained.

Hugely fascinated, sight of so much praying and swaying turned the boy light-headed. Root of his tongue achy with longing, sweet plum-like tartness surged his mouth.

Cows' warmth radiating from below, their familiar grunts and snuffles comforted as he tried to imagine being slurped up inside Ma's brain to have a look-see.

Ezra, a most resplendent rooster, batted wings, hopping up the ladder to root through the boy's hair and poke his pockets for edibles. Barnyard animals as his only pals, his recent friend-making venture had sorely failed.

Hank Stedum, a grade ahead in school, possessed an admirable talent for hawking and spitting. So the boy took up walking with a hitch and greased his hair into a perfect pompadour, same as Hank.

Hank, certain such mimicry was meant to poke fun, had socked him, hard.

On the porch now, as Ma moaned, wagged her head, blurted a giggle, nodded, shimmied about, acting ever so strange—the eeriest notion cropped up: *Ma was loony! Crazy! Gone round the bend!*

Except that very morning, at Bixby's Dry Goods, Mr. Bixby slid his glasses down his nose, eyed their egg flats, and announced, "Them eggs is pretty scrawny. Eight cents or nothing."

Anyone who cares, knows; eggs fetch a dime a dozen.

So Ma had set her jaw, crossed arms, and affixed herself, firmly, to the spot. Seemed a surety she had nothing better to do: that she'd block the register all day if she had to as customers, begging her pardon, reached past to pay for wares.

"Chrissake, Bixby," crabbed an old lady, "don't be a cheapskate; pay the woman!"

"OK, OK!" Mr Bixby had counted six dimes into Ma's outstretched palm.

No word of thanks, Ma had huffed out.

Not exactly the act of a loon!

Breezes picked up, creaking the barn. Across the way, Ma rocked some more.

Dark came early those days. Stars pocked the sky. The moon—a sliver—passed behind the trees.

Hunched to pluck burrs from his socks, shame engulfed the boy. Pa wasn't too nice. Ma made some mysterious mistake; for this she kept paying.

Much more lurked, hidden. And, although he only grasped the tiniest speck, he too was tainted.

But then, heart lifted, he'd seen Pa on fire—seen it for real!

Chapter Three: Walker

Walker departed the hospital and headed home. Gone three weeks hauling, he imagined his wife, Delia, rushing out to greet him, and then smiled all over, not just with a grin, but with his toenails, nostrils, and hair follicles.

Two people could not have been more opposite. Walker was a neatnik. Delia was a slob.

She'd attempt a meal, try to decipher a recipe's hieroglyphics, pile meats and foodstuffs, mix a few items, laugh at her ineptitude, and then give up, leaving food splatters on the floor, where they'd crust up, harden, and remain. Likewise with his shirts; she'd give them a half-hearted iron-over, neglect the collar and entire back panel.

Walker was solitary, whereas Delia was social. They had no friends in common. The one time she convinced him to play poker with her friends, she cheated so outrageously, bent rules to suit herself, all the fun got sucked from the event.

Hard as he worked to see her foibles as adorable, a single incident changed all of it.

Walker stopped to pick her up at Shop 'N Save; she'd stormed out, cheeks aflame. "Royal Canadian Mountie, my ass!" she'd huffed, slamming the truck door, hard.

A pencil-necked fella—the manager—Walker guessed—marched out and glared. A beefy gent trotted at his heels, hollering, "Don't ever come back. We'll arrest you if you do!"

Delia sat rigid, fuming. "So?" he'd carefully probed.

"They insist that I swiped a pack of Salems," she spluttered. "That big one says he's a Mountie—on vacation, no less—says he saw me stick 'em in my purse! Ha—Salems aren't even my brand!" Jerky moves, cigarette extracted from handbag, she'd lit up, inhaled, then exhaled, fiercely.

"Did you..." Walker inquired. "Ahem...take them?"

"Course not!" she'd snapped.

Plainly visible within purse confines snuggled a Salem pack.

A bad feeling overtook him. He'd cast his wife a sidelong glance, opened his mouth, formed a word; no sound came.

Something essential began to crack. *My lovely wife*, he'd realized, *is reckless with the truth!*

Would that he could have erased that revelation! Distress within heartbeats, he'd longed to gently touch her; all his muscles had ached with it. Trying to calm himself, then, just then, he'd glimpsed further to see the grave crimes they'd commit against each other.

Only there, that afternoon, they'd merely sat poised, waiting.

As Walker sped homeward, contemplating the man whose arm he'd just fixed and the woman whose life he'd saved, he also grasped that Delia, unable to tolerate anything that happened to him without her sanction, would not approve. *Therefore*, he resolved, *that event must remain mine alone to savor.*

Walker pulled up outside his cottage and set the brake.

Delia, wearing pedal pushers and blouse, slid off her shoulders, came to lean at the door frame. Buttery skin a sharp contrast to her blood red lips, she gave the appearance of a hot-house plant.

Climbed down from the cab, dust clapped off, he came up the walk calling, "Hey there!"

Spun on heel, Delia disappeared inside but then poked her head back. "We gotta talk." He went to kiss her; she pushed him off.

Walker stepped back, mystified. "What's up?" Eager to keep on her good side, he'd phoned daily, sometimes twice, and sent a steady stream of cards, baubles, and roses.

"That's what..." Delia pointed and pouted. "It's been here all week. I don't appreciate it blocking my way."

An immense crate loomed to fill much of the living room. Sense-memory triggered, heart off at a gallop, Walker heard humming; couldn't tell if it came from the crate or if his own throat made it. He felt like grinning but prudently refrained. "What is it?"

"How would I know!"

Should've attended to Delia, fussed over her a bit. Instead he circled the box, eying it, perplexed.

His name, in unfamiliar scrawl, bore no return address, only a New York routing stamp.

Crowbar in hand, he broke down slats and yanked away packing.

Wings protruded. Blue, then gold ceramic patches visible, a statue emerged—his very own angel— The Angel's face trumpeted love.

Room air highly charged—an exchange of sorts—surged and expanded to enfold him.

Walker fell to his knees and tenderly stroked its base.

Astonished by her husband's theatrics, Delia kept uncharacteristically silent.

"It's come," he whispered.

"If it's for me…" Delia brightened, but then scrunched her face—"I don't want it."

"A minute, please." Walker tried to figure.

Crate so huge, The Angel so immense, how'd Ma manage to ship it? "I..." he stammered, "had nothing to do with its arrival, but may know who did." *Surely, Ma hadn't purchased the statue. Seemed unlikely she'd stolen it. And why now, after all these years?*

Abrupt laughter welled up. He strove to squelch it, but then unleashed a blurt. "Thanks, Ma."

"Ma?" Delia repeated, incredulous.

Not ready to yield, ignoring his wife, thoughts turned to Ma—her relationship with Pa, her comings and goings between the worlds, and his own longing—his eyes moistened up.

"In time you'll help many," Ma had once asserted.

Would that he'd inquired precisely what she'd meant.

But the statue's arrival, coupled with saving the woman earlier, heralded great changes—of that he felt certain.

An image arose: Ma living nearby, he envisioned her admiration as to the good he'd do. Theirs would be an odd relationship. Always, they'd stay safely tethered to the present. Never would they discuss the harm Pa had caused. No questions, much silence, they'd find peace in it.

Yet Ma, wedded to impossible misery, would refuse to come. Delia too would refuse to have her.

Furthermore, no matter how many miles he traveled, no matter how life improved, rage still sundered him. Try as he might to put it behind him, he seethed with it.

"Get up," Delia interrupted, "you make me nervous." Walker, who usually went to great appeasing lengths, ignored her.

She persisted, "Get that monstrosity outta here." Walker paid no heed.

Delia grabbed her purse, slammed out, revved the car engine, and sped off.

Shakily, Walker got to his feet and kissed The Angel's fingertips. "Thank you so much for coming!"

Chapter Four: Young Walker

On a day "hotter'n Hades," as Pa liked to say, the boy heard rustling in the brush, crept up, and spied Shamus, the family mutt, take an object in his teeth. Quick snap, Shamus flung the object aloft, rushed forth, retrieved, and tossed the thing again.

A bird!

"No, Shamus, stop!"

Dog shooed off, the boy found the bird, a macaw, wedged between rocks.

How a macaw might arrive in the Midwest—he couldn't quite figure.

Sometime back he'd read about macaws in a tattered *National Geographic.* Awestruck by their vibrant turquoise, yellow, and red-throated feathers, he'd given thanks for the invention of such radiance.

Just now, bird given a cautious poke, its eyes stayed shut. Scooped up, he held it close and began to turn in tight circles. Careful not to trip, gathering momentum, faster, faster, he spun. Imagined Ma looking out, mistaking him for a pint-sized tornado, and hoped she'd join him.

Tornado-boy—a whirling funnel of human flesh—a surge came. Body lifted, swirling ever-upward, a heavenly chorus rippled through him.

Fiery rays shot out from his eyes and arced from fingertips.

How can I be burning and not hurt?

Didn't hurt, though. Actually, it felt grand!

Compared to the smoke that had bloomed from Pa, this was a whole lot different! What happened to Pa was the ooze of evil. This smoke—this fire—seemed cleansing.

Slowed to a halt, world still swirling, he called out, "Please, someone...Fix this bird!"

His mind's eye saw the macaw's feathers lift and fluff; its eyeballs darting open to place an unwavering fix upon him. He envisioned his own startled reflex as its talons flicked, clawing to be freed.

Bird set down, he imagined it hopping once, twice. Wings spreading, it would then take off, circle, caw, and head south.

Nudged with his boot, neck wobbling, it flopped onto its side. And so he buried it beneath a heap of dirt and leaves.

Dizzying pulses still thrumming, he lifted his hands to examine them; each digit opalescent, appeared lit from within. The surrounding field, luminous as well, light radiated from rocks, weeds— even from their shoddy farmhouse.

Gradually, that illumination seeped out, till the smoky radiance faded.

Subsequent to seeing Pa all lit up that night, the boy had tried, mightily, to replicate the experience. Eyelids pulled taught, he'd taped his outer eye's edges into a squint, hoping for wondrous sights, but nothing came of it. Also, he'd tried pretending the light into existence.

Nothing happened there either.

Full up with feeling, he began to run, enormous grin plastered upon his face.

Never mind that he'd failed to revive the bird, the attempt alone changed everything.

Chapter Five: Walker

Two weeks subsequent to The Angel's arrival, Walker and Delia awoke to frantic banging on their door. Delia donned her robe, then returned shortly. "There's a man; I can barely understand him. He says he needs help—that it's urgent."

Dressed in haste, Walker went to inquire, "Can I help you?"

"Please, meester..." The brown man wrung his hat. "My bambina ess sick." Stepped aside, he indicated a woman cradling a bundle. "You please to fix?"

Walker gripped the ashen-faced infant the man thrust in his arms. "Ish," it gasped. "Ish," it gasped again.

He moved to hand the baby back. "Sorry, you need a doctor."

Abrupt recollection sundered: *Here's the path of courage Ma had once mentioned.* "Come in...please." Walker flung the door wide, spotted folks milling about The Angel—at Delia's insistence it had been moved into the yard. —*Must be family*, he surmised.

Inside, the couple shifted, foot-to-foot. Delia looked on, uncertain. Uncertain as well and infant still clasped, Walker passed a silent plea heavenward. The couple shot each other questioning looks. Hands on hips, Delia readied to grin or to spit. Slowly, Walker rolled onto the balls of his feet, then rolled back down again.

The lungs—touch the chest—intuition advised.

Hand cupped atop the baby's bubbly lungs, Walker envisioned light streaming from his fingertips, entering, healing. Next, he palmed her belly then palpated the neck and armpits.

Deep within, the infant emitted a resolute click. "Put her to bed, she should be fine." He handed her back.

Bundle held at arm's length, the father examined it. "Isss that all?"

Steadily, Delia held her eyes on Walker. "Uh, I think so," he affirmed. Should've felt elated; instead his innards went rubbery. The man tried to pay. Walker waved him away. "No need."

As the couple departed, the crowd in the yard swarmed, begging, beseeching. "Gimme a blessing," a smelly old woman demanded. Lifting Walker's hands, she set them atop her head, rotated them about as if he were a hairdresser giving a scrub, proceeded to jabber inanely, and then stepped back.

Mouth crusted in froth, a reed-thin man hopped and whistled, taking repeated swipes at air. Walker touched his arm. Bent double, the fellow barked into his kneecaps, then shuttled off.

A wheelchair-bound girl-child, chin mashed to chest, came forth, propelled by a sad-faced mother. "Whatever you can do," begged the parent, "we'll be grateful." At a loss, Walker caressed the girl's cheek.

Sudden strength gained, the child lifted her head to beam at him.

More bodies surged.

Mortified to be the focus of such fuss, Walker patted and reassured anyhow. Beneath the surging tumult of needy souls, certainty came to him. Several claimed to feel tingles or heat. One asthmatic laughingly announced, "Birdies chirp when you touch me!"

Crowd dissipated, Walker went inside. Delia sat on the sofa, arms crossed, foot wagging. "I'm a healer," he announced, figuring an explanation to be called for. Delia stared, mouth agape. "Since when?"

"Since forever, I guess."

"Why not say so?"

"Ah…" Walker wracked his brain.

Softly, the radiator hissed.

"Ahem." He undid his topmost shirt button. *Say something for God sakes!*

Delia detested this about him. Silence, she claimed, he meted out as punishment.

He took a stab. "Only recently did the mantle of responsibility descend upon me. The Angel's arrival was my prompt to begin."

"The Angel causes this?"

"Not exactly, but it's part of the"—he stirred a hand—"plan. It helps me do this work."

"So..." Delia regarded him cautiously. "What about our life?"

"We go on as we have."

First, people came in a slow trickle. Then word spread. As if guided by The Angel's invisible beacon, sunup to sundown, needy souls converged round it to wait politely. Rare times, an aggressive sort pounded their door, begging for help.

All manner of ill and suffering folk—the lame, the diseased, the sickly—the healthy too—arrived, asking Walker to fix them. Some even brought animals.

After crowds departed, human misery, pungent within his pores, still clung to him. Convulsed with unstoppable sorrow, he pawed his temples, squelched throaty howls, and screeched, inwardly, *God, why do you permit such suffering?*

"People," Delia noted, as they shared a rare quiet moment, "go so gooey-eyed around you; it's way-creepy." Indeed, folks clambered, shouting his praises. Some fell prostrate, others kissed him.

"Yup," he mused, "I find such reverence troubling." How he longed to fully share his burden, yet feared Delia would not accept it.

He tried anyhow. "This is not about me. This is about God's Will. I merely serve as a conduit to jump-start the healing process." Never would he claim these acts as his own. It was God. *Always!*

Delia came up to face him. "Saintly as you seem, you're so withdrawn, you actually seem cold. It's like, deep down, you don't really give a hoot about anyone or anything."

"But I *do* care." His frozen nature would frustrate many, himself included, but most of all his wife.

Chapter Six: Walker

Donated crates of apples, a rusty washing machine, and a garden hose coiled at his feet as Walker waved off an ancient, puckered woman who tried to pay cash for a healing. Consistently, he refused to accept money for healing services, so non-cash reimbursement came faster than manageable.

Dark of night, offerings got deposited at their doorstep. Come morning, Walker and Delia tripped over flour sacks, pinto beans, and produce. Tethered goats munched away, and crated, scratching chicks got left. One day a mooing cow awoke them. Later, a Steinway blocked the driveway. Eventually, their tiny cottage, fortressed behind heaps of sundry items, disappeared from sight.

Fearing Ma's penchant for hoarding, Walker disposed of these gifts as swiftly as he acquired them.

"Don't let them inflict their rubbish on us," chafed Delia. "Make them pay." This, a minor inconvenience for Walker, would bloom into a major rift between them.

With Delia unemployed and money scarce, Walker still did long distance hauling. Not that he minded; it afforded alone-time, a scarcity he dearly craved.

Regarding healings themselves: crediting The Angel's presence for the guidance to perform them, he didn't much care to part from it.

Regardless as to our juxtaposition, be you near or far, The Angel saw fit to announce, *I oversee all.* Resisting the urge to lash it to his truck as if a gigantic hood ornament, he reluctantly left it behind.

His eighteen-wheeler had lousy suspension. Each rut hit, the truck screamed, banshee loud. Come to a new town, with a yowling rig to herald his arrival, folks bounded out to see the fuss, gaped at the oddity of this business-suit-garbed truck driver. Figuring him to be a person of import, they then stepped in line to be touched.

Other times, barely settled into a motel room, there'd come a knock, signaling he'd been discovered. A lifetime spent lost, it pleased him to be found.

Small towns to cities, folks graciously loaned workspace: boarded-up shops, empty office buildings, an abandoned gas station, a church here and there. Volunteers, mostly women, dotted his routes. They spread word of his arrival, placed fliers on bulletin boards and blurbs in newsprint. Bolder ones even helped with healings.

Two years passed. One June day, several men thundered into his cottage toting neighbor, Harice Clems, on a stretcher. "Set him down, careful," Walker coached.

"Help me." Harice gasped and gulped as they eased him onto the kitchen table.

Skin parchment yellow, belly watermelon size, the man reeked a sour smell. His tight lipped wife, Alice, hovered nearby. "I'll try, but can't promise." Walker lifted the blanket. "Mind if I touch you?" Harice assented. "Let me know if this hurts." Probing, he palpated the boggy growth.

What causes disease? he pondered. *Is it the life we lead: our goodness or evil quotient? And what gives me the power to fix one person and not another?* In the case of his neighbor, long-festering unhappiness seemed to have bloomed into disease.

But perfectly happy people became ill as well. An ornery cuss lost his arthritis, whereas the sweetest old lady stayed infirmed. Rare ones claimed to feel ecstasy when he touched them but died nonetheless. Some treasured their infirmities, actually gripped them tight. To Walker's mind, illness served such folk. Yet, in time their infirmed selves tugged stronger than their healthy aspect to eventually consume them. Much of it would remain a mystery; he was at a loss to make sense of it.

Mostly, success rebuffed him. For that, he blamed his limited ideas as to what seemed possible.

Recently, a Vietnam vet brought his Siamese twins. Woven together from sternum to hip, both bore flippers instead of hands, courtesy,

Walker guessed, of the chemical defoliant, Agent Orange. "Sorry," he'd informed the dad, "I can't make structural changes." But perhaps his belief merely lacked vigor.

And, no—the stupid did not automatically become smart. Re-grow an amputated limb or repair a busted heart, although he tried to do so, he never really could.

Healings of late assumed lives all their own. Pure feeling overtook him; nothing else existed as he worked. Walker was not even slightly in control.

Remedy feeble mindedness? *Touch the forehead between the eyes*, came the directive, *cup the skull, then link and balance cranial hemispheres.* Final touch to the base of the neck, and the patient flushed with vigor and clarity.

Link skin together without a stitch to heal fragmented, torn tissue, realign smashed limbs; those were simple tasks. Fix a rheumatic hip? Small potatoes! Reach inside to rewire lymph and bloodflow?Easy-peasy!

Attention returned to the dying man, Walker continued to probe. All present waited, expectant.

Healthy humans vibrate at a fierce pace. Harice, on the other hand, lacking such vigor, seemed nearly gone. "Sorry to say, your tumor's far too advanced."

"That so?" Harice grimaced and slumped back.

Gently, Walker cradled him. "It would be a privilege, however, to assist your release."

Mouth shaped to form a perfect O, the wife reached to interfere. "I'm ready," Harice interrupted. "Except one thing..." Face mashed to the side, he lifted into a snarl, "I've been one mean son of a bitch! Hated all my life." Alice nodded, bit her lip.

"OK, then"—Walker turned to the wife—"take his hand." She hesitated, then took it, ever so careful. "Do you forgive your husband?"

The wife glared, indignant. "Of course!"

"Don't just say so; really mean it."

"Well…" She gulped. "Uh, yes...I do."

"With all your heart?" Eyes red-rimmed, tenderly she gazed upon Harice.

"Yes, definitely." Gently she stroked her husband's face.

Air rushed out in a push; Harice's jaw bagged. Color leached from his cheeks as he folded and collapsed into himself. Yet, even still, his eyes shone like beacons, till, gradually, their light dimmed.

Pleased to be witness, Walker's heart throbbed, bittersweet.

For a long time after he would be known as The Angel's Servant: an appellation he so thoroughly savored.

Chapter Seven: Young Lauren

Reek of piss in the doorway, a teen, Lauren, paused, impressed with herself, amazed actually, that she'd come.

What if he can fix me so people no longer stare, so nobody shouts "Freak," or trips me, or hurtles spit wads at my head?

Hope had drawn her to this rundown storefront. So, resolute inhale, door swung wide, she stepped inside to behold the space.

Candlelight shimmered upon all surfaces, walls included. Tiny cup crouched atop his head, a be-whiskered Chinese gentleman's portrait hung on a sidewall. Anyone else in such a hat would've caused a snicker, but this gent's dignified air made that impossible.

More pictures graced a makeshift altar: Jesus, St. Francis of Assisi, the Virgin Mother and a plump bald guy whom she failed to recognize. An angel, bedecked in gold and blue robes, dangled above. Wings fluttering, shifting with room air currents, it seemed to address her: *Always, I have known and loved you.*

Flooded with feeling, barely able to catch breath, first time ever, she felt totally accepted, flaws and all.

Surrounding the altar's front sat a dozen or so people, who watched a shirtless man moan and mash his face into his palms. Another man, she took for the healer, kneaded the shirtless man is if he were a wad of dough.

Do all these people struggle with pains or disfigurement, same as I do?

Click of the tongue—the healer signaling—a woman, his assistant, stepped up to scoop air. An abrupt image—the helper's hair, single, fat braid wagging (the intertwining of good and evil)—locked into sharp focus, as the healer's hands hovered, cupped flesh, then held perfectly still. Slowly, the helper circled the ill man, fanning him.

Despite the distance, the healer's gorgeous hands mesmerized.

Light as dancers, they tapped and slid across the shirtless man's flesh. Ceaseless now, the healer touched the patient: stroked the man's throat, eyelids, neck, and shoulders. Mostly, he pressed flesh at the regions of lungs and heart.

Excruciating catch of breath, chest heaving, the ailing man gasped out horrid, sucking sounds, "Ah-eeeeeee, ah-eeee…"

Suffocation—Lauren knew just how he felt!

See…the brace she wore, gripping at her neck, slowly strangled.

Stance adjusted, the pressure at her throat eased up a bit.

"Bring it up," the healer reassured the patient. "Set it free. You'll feel better shortly."

Longing truncated, the sensible lobe of Lauren's brain reengaged: *A few kind words, arms flapping, hands tenderly cuddling flesh…Then what?*

The body refashions, brand-spanking new, and runs across the school yard, pain-free, no hunching?

Not likely!

The shirtless fellow breathed with greater ease, even sighed, seemingly content.

Limbs turned heavy, a wave of relaxation rippled through Lauren as well. Eyelids drooping, a quick snooze would've been swell.

Fighting wooziness, the harder she resisted, the more floaty she felt.

Brisk uptick, as if swarming bees invaded, something, someone—the healer, perhaps—vibrated her innards.

Suction bore down. Flurry of images, mind making impossible, expansive shifts, she felt herself fly outward.

Can this guy control what I see, think, and feel? Is he a con man, or a hypnotist, or…has he cast a spell?

Scared, confused, she tried to focus.

Silvery particles glimmering about, the healer, his actual being, surged, then flew into the ailing man. And then…and then…The healer, the ailing man, the braid-haired woman, the angel, the onlookers, the entire room's contents merged to become one.

Lauren's body went rubbery; it seemed to stretch, and then she too joined them.

Full up with buoyancy, she—all of them—lifted to float about.

Not uncomfortable, just way freaky!

Get a grip! she willed herself.

Breath caught, she reclaimed her body, bumped a chair, and clattered it to the floor.

Eyes swiveled round to stare; someone called out, "You OK?"

"Fine," she croaked. "Didn't mean to interrupt." She caught the healer's gaze.

Totally overgroomed, first he seemed ancient, except he wasn't so old, about a decade older than she. His eyes, same as the angel's, seemed all knowing. As light came into them, they bored into her, and the room fell away.

Alone, just him and her.

The healer chuckled, a dry throaty laugh. She got that her clumsiness did not cause his mirth. Boundless kindness: that's what she saw.

And...What did he see?

Ugly mug. Hulking body. Crooked spine. Horrid brace.

Sorry for herself?

You betcha!

Desperate for help, any help she could find—that's why she'd come.

Trying for nonchalance, hand raised, fingers frilled, she grinned.

I know you, she wanted to blurt. *I feel you in my bones.*

Still grinning, she dropped the hand.

"Come." The healer beckoned.

Mind a-chatter, Lauren zigzagged through the audience. *Will he heal me? Can he? What if he can't?* Scarier yet: *What if he can?*

The healer took Lauren's hands—his smells, tobacco and mint, soothed—as he set them atop the patient's shoulders.

But then her heart sunk.

You've made a mistake—she bit back a blurt—*I too need your touch.*

Conscious of eyeballs watching, hands kept as he'd set them, she waited, wondering.

Minutes passed.

Nothing happened.

She counted rose petals strewn about, wondered as to their function. Really, she could not concentrate!

Being an obedient sort, she stayed put anyhow.

Maybe, just maybe, my submission will prove my worth.

Time slid along. Noises fell away.

Gradually, bit by bit, the finest feeling seeped in.

Stronger, warmer, it bloomed.

Her hands grew huge, elongated, then disappeared, sinking into the ailing man's body.

Rush, rush—as before, silvery sparkles flooded the room. Later she'd learn: this haze signaled the thinning of the veils between the worlds.

Mind's eye periscoped inside the sick man, her hands burrowed into ailing flesh. She felt his pulses and his very heartbeat as blood rhythmically whisked past.

Hands searing hot, she yanked them up to inspect. Palms glowing, lighted filaments streamed out from each fingertip. "What's this?" she demanded, fighting panic.

"Trust me," the healer instructed. "Put them back."

Mind a-jumble, sweating rivulets, she wanted to believe. Oddly, and most important, she wanted his respect. *Does he really think I can help this man?*

Hands resettled; the healer placed his hands on the patient, as well. Fingertips sending out healing rays, they blasted away at sickly cells. Tissue evaporated, shriveling, sizzling, leaving pink, new-formed flesh.

I know this stuff, it's totally amazing!—Except...How can this be? Lauren stared at the healer, saucer eyed.

"Yes, you're causing this."

Wildness churning inside, endless possibilities zoomed before her.

Hands lifted, the healer stepped away. "You can stop now."

Reluctantly, she drew hands back.

Patient's flesh no longer dusky, the man basked, grinning.

Crowd muttering approval, all looked on in rapt awe. Lauren too basked in the thrall and envisioned grabbing the palsied woman up-front to remove her tremors.

"I don't...I..." Flooded with exuberance, longing...and loss, she struggled to comprehend. "It's so strange!"

"That's just a sample. There's much more but"—the healer gave a regretful head shake— "you've come too soon."

Lauren cast about, but then noticed the angel.

Calm, wise, it soothed, *You too have The Touch, dearest.*

Impossible, it spoke!

Checking to see if others had heard; no one reacted.

She inspected her hands. Long tapered digits and man-size palms, normal as ever, fingers flicked, no lit filaments shot out.

Quick glance at the healer; he beamed back.

Sorrow and relief hit. Sad that the heady rush had ceased. Glad she hadn't turned more freakish than she already was.

Grief that she hadn't been fixed overtook her.

Overwhelmed by all of it, she announced, "I'll be going now."

Backed up to the exit, door pushed open, she glanced at the healer.

"I'm glad you've come." Pain, sharply etched, wracked his face, which surprised her.

Back she marched to pump his hand. Would that she were brazen enough to shove her nose into the bristly curve of his jaw and sniff—naturally, there'd be aftershave—in truth, she ached to know the scent of a saint. "I haven't a clue...," she groped, "what just happened, but it's the most amazing thing ever!"

"Someday, you'll return." He gazed fondly, sadly, upon her.

"You promise?" Cheeks a-gleam, she quivered with happiness.

"God promises."

Why she'd been summoned that day, vulnerability of the brace aside, took years to digest, but it shaped all that would come later.

Chapter Eight: Walker

Endless tragic stories weighed Walker down like a grief-imbued sponge. Human suffering, the dependence of others, their intense, cloying need, rubbed off and clung to him. Repeatedly, his heavy-laden heart tore open as a result.

To protect himself, to counter the pain, be it a demanding patient or a perfectly pleasant one, Walker stole fragments—their laughter, their joy, the loving connection common to most—all things he craved.

Hand to an elderly gent's heart, other hand cradling the man's skull, he burrowed into those warm, yielding places, broke off snippets, and secreted them away.

Later when alone, he allowed that fellow's memories to surface so as to savor them. The man's hike in the woods while gripping his grandson's damp, sticky hand; the child's awe at the slant of light through the trees as it hit ferns; the damp smell of moss; a joyous family picnic after.

Ripe memories released from fingertips, Walker scooped and drank of them.

What harm did he do, really?

Time, again, he absorbed their pain. And, without this taking, to his mind, he could not give. So that which he snatched from them served as his true recompense.

Besides...No one noticed a thing missing; of this, he felt confident. Oh, the extractions *did* leave the donor a smidge lighter, perhaps, but they claimed to feel better overall.

It seemed so divine, so oddly glorious to cross this invisible, ethical boundary. And, given that God permitted it, surely it was acceptable.

Three years into his healing practice, Walker set off one day to see about hauling a load of pea gravel. He'd promised Delia they'd take in a matinée later, but as often happened, he got waylaid by endless requests for help.

Home now, too late for movie-going, as he made his way past the crowd out front, billowing garments, carelessly strewn atop low-lying shrubs, arrested his attention.

Acting the unflappable butler, his favorite coat had been settled about The Angel's shoulders, his briefs draped in her outstretched arms. Walker plucked a note from its chest and tried the front door; it refused to budge. Key used; the door's lock held. "I'm back," he called, rattling the handle. "Delia, open up."

No Delia.

Dropped onto the porch, Walker read the missive:

Sainted One,

We live in a freakin' fishbowl! Day and night, people intrude. I've got no privacy. We have no married life. Trouble is, for you this is fine. But while you're off saving lives, your own wife is dying. I'm sick of sharing you and want my old life back. Be gone when I return.

Your Ever-loving, Former Wife,

Odelia Garcia

He tried to feel, knew he'd hurt her. Should have felt sad; relief bathed him instead.

First, Delia had basked in the limelight, congratulating herself for landing such a man. As he grew in renown, fellow healers, even medical professionals, flocked to him for advice. At this, Delia fluffed up all the more.

But, as Walker pursued his work with grim vehemence and labored, ceaselessly, enveloped, drowned by it, he scarcely ate or slept and felt that he had no right to turn anyone away. Without a moment to himself, little attention paid to his spouse, life's niceties—time alone together, raucous sex—disappeared. And so, Delia's pleasure soured.

Walker needed Delia. They shared a bond. Yet, companion of his soul, one who accepted and understood him best, she was not.

Heartfelt, soul-searing connection eluding, her insatiable need also troubled him. Once, she'd come home bawling that a diamond ring she'd coveted had sold from a jeweler's window, insisted life lacked meaning without it.

So, much as Walker wanted her, he felt imprisoned by her, which conflicted and confused him. With healing others as his life's calling, when forced to chose, he did not choose his wife.

"Come, Walker." Rosalee Soo, his best and only friend, waved him over.

Pushed off the step, he went to her. "Hey Rosalee. What's up?"

Rosalee grabbed his lapels, stood on tiptoe to kiss his cheeks: a move he adored. "I have a proposition..." Sunflower seeds dropped into her mouth, she offered him a fistful, which he declined. "Pfft, pfft..." Discards spit into her fist, Walker marveled that she made an art of shucking.

"One dollar," she finally announced. "You pay one dollar, I rent you, The Sullivan Hotel, my old oarhouse." She meant whorehouse.

"Very kind. I should pay the going rate, but as it stands, can't afford to."

"If I rent, you must charge for your work. It will help your clinic grow and prosper."

"Much as I appreciate the offer, I can't sell what God gives as a gift."

"Paying helps people get well. For free robs them of self-respect."

"But you give away herbs and teas. Isn't that the same?"

"Yes, but they buy a movie ticket too—that is fair exchange. Besides, giving myself away is not my life lesson. It *is* yours, though."

"Well...OK. I accept, but refuse to turn anyone away for lack of funds."

"Good! One condition, you must promise to keep Sherman."

"Understood."

Long resided at The Sullivan, as a living, breathing work of art, face aside, every inch of Sherman Moncrief's flesh—bald head included—was inked. Tattoos slithered and waltzed across his chest, arms, hands, legs, even feet. And the fellow possessed a most girly flute-like laugh, so much so that heads whipped around to check. Walker never quite got used to it.

"I have a condition, as well," countered Walker. "We make space there for you to dispense herbs."

Face twitching, Rosalee Soo struggled, mightily, to squelch a giggle. "Okey-dokey!"

High-five, they sealed the deal.

Joyous burbles overtook Rosalee. Walker laughed too, very pleased.

Crowd helping, they gentled The Angel onto Walker's truckbed. Then, belongings packed, he moved to The Sullivan.

Chapter Nine: Young Walker

Trudging home from school, the boy caught sight of their farm. Overgrown brush encircling the house seemed to hold it aloft. For economy's sake, only the road-facing side had been painted; even that side had peeled and grayed. And sorrow, impossible to miss, emanated.

That others might detect his family's business greatly shamed him.

Screen shut softly behind, there Ma sat humming, methodically stroking an object's surfaces. Eyes a-sparkle, her face shone splendid, relaxed, worry-free.

Sensing a presence, she slid the thing into her apron pocket. "I didn't hear you come in!"

"Whatcha doin'?" The boy sidled close.

"Ah—well—these are my treasures. See…" Object brought back out, Ma extended it.

Ordinarily, stuff that didn't wriggle or writhe held no sway, but Ma's fervor piqued the boy's interest. "Seashells…" Ma made a grand sweep. "Miraculous demonstrations of God's perfection!"

Surveying the scene, the boy nodded solemnly. Wadded newspapers, nested with seashells, scattered the kitchen floor and tabletops. "Can I?" he ventured.

Shell handed over, he hefted the sieve-like bowl.

"That's an abalone."

Fluted holes ran along its lipped edge. On closer inspection, he noted majestic whoops and swirls. "It's like rainbow's melted."

"I've never seen the ocean," Ma said, wistful, "but someday hope to.—Here are the rest…" Tenderly, she unwrapped each shell.

Careful hands slid across cool surfaces—some shells bore knobby spines and whorls, others were creamy smooth; it confounded the boy how seashells might arrive on Midwestern soil, when geography taught the nearest oceans to be over a thousand miles east and west. "How'd you get them?"

"They just come, sometimes by parcel post. Other times, they materialize on my rocking chair as if just set there."

On that first day, a hatbox contained them. As their numbers grew, Ma settled them into a packing crate. Display only possible when Pa was away, shells overflowed counter tops and windowsills.

The boy fit the pointy pilot shell in his palm. "This is my favorite."

"I adore them all, but this one—" Ma lofted a chunk, "the conch...I favor best." Luscious pink lip, insides spread to lighter shades, she put its scalloped edge to his ear.

"What's that sound?" He inserted a finger into its opening, quizzical.

"The ocean, silly! Take a whiff; that's salt sea air!" Head thrown back, she chortled, truly happy. The boy laughed along with her.

"The ocean's immense, deep, and dark. It's teeming with fish, and full of mystery." Silent a moment, briny air, waves pummeling rocks, glinting water, frothed the boy's brain.

Ma reached to ruffle his hair.

Would that the moment could last forever!

Ma never tossed out a thing. Boxes and newspapers lined walls, overflowed the pantry and all closets. Crates, stacked high in every room, bulged with assorted broken bits. Seven toasters marched across the kitchen countertop, their cords hopelessly tangled. Never mind that all were on the fritz, keeping them was crucial.

Tin pie plates, empty oat boxes, got saved by the dozens. Light bulbs, burnt filaments jangling, were interspersed between cracked plates and broken furniture. An ornate sideboard, copper hat stand, crystalline light fixture, assorted demitasse cups, and jewelry by the handful—probably worth a tidy sum—lay buried beneath heaped debris.

Ma's position on the aggregation was straightforward, "Never know when I might need the very thing I've tossed out, so I save the worry and keep all of it. And...when I die," she proudly informed, "all of this'll be yours."

"Yess-um," the boy tried to enthuse.

"Why, the other day, you threw out a pair of moccasins." Said slippers slid before him; she eyed him shrewdly.

"But, Ma, they're worn clear through!"

How had she known? He'd buried them five feet under.

"It's wasteful. Besides, God turns his back on a sneak, so promise you won't do that again."

Hand held, pledge-style, the boy appeased, "Promise."

Ma nodded, clicking dentures softly.

A sneak! Secret soul set a-tremble, truly, that's how he saw himself.

Livingroom brimmed with an artless array of mismatched furniture—a smelly sofa as its centerpiece—there Pa sat one hot day, yelling, "Woman...Bring ice tea!"

Ma rushed to serve him.

No word of thanks, Pa, pressing the moist glass to his brow, spotted his son.

Whump! Cushions smacked, he invited, "Come sit, boy!"

Warily, the boy sat at sofa's edge.

"Hot and dry, thunder and lightning," the radioman announced. "Two inches of precip the next three days." Brow furrowed, Pa drummed fingers and leaned into the console.

At sight of those thick grooved hands, big as frying pans, sweat prickled the boy's neck.

Pa swung round to grin at him. "How's school? Getting on with the girls?"

"School's OK, I guess. I don't know any girls, though, sir."

Pause. Stout silence; the refrigerator rattled and hummed.

Pa blanched. "Got something against me?"

The boy reared back, fretted fingers through his hair as if the proper reply might reside there. "Ah...I just...I...don't have anything to say, sir."

Time and again, the boy envisioned rescuing Ma from Pa's beatings, jumping Pa, braining him silly, and Pa begging forgiveness.

My face, the boy supposed, *is etched with such imaginings.*

Not exactly a big man, Pa was nearly as wide as he was tall and solid as a tree trunk. A ropy scar gouged his hairline, traversing his left eyelid, then ran from cheek to chin.

Given Pa's constant frown, the boy never dared ask how that mark came to reside there.

Recently, there'd been a close call.

Pa sat down, whooshing upholstery. The boy leaned from sofa's backside, sniffed his father's hair, smelt dust and grease, and then spied Pa's carefully combed, meager hair wisps. Each strand sought to cover over a bald spot, yet pink defenseless gaps remained.

Sight of Pa's vulnerability; inexplicable sorrow overtook him. And so, aching to give comfort, he ventured round in front, "Pa?"

"What?" Pa had barked.

"I was wondering..."

Pa sat, attentive.

"Does it hurt to be bald?"

"Why you...!" Pa flew up, yanked him close—Pa had dog breath, terrible bad—then shook his son. Out from the kitchen flew Ma. She wrung her hands, shot her son a warning glance, but did not interfere. "Mockin' me, are you?"

Abruptly released, the boy nearly tripped. "Lucky for you I'm feeling first-rate. Else I'd whup you, good. Tell you what, though... early to bed, no supper."

Pa wasn't always foul tempered. At times he tried to be friendly, kind even. Months back, he brought home a baseball mitt: one the boy had his eye on. Evenings, after chores, they tossed balls. Hooted. Had fun.

Returned to the present, guard firmly up, there the boy sat. "Want me to get the cows in before the storm hits, Pa?"

Radio broadcast crackling, Pa reached to adjust the dial. The boy winced, trying not to. Pa shot him an off-kilter smile. "Let's get to it."

Feeling safer than he had moments prior, the boy exhaled.

Daily, the boy clapped eyes on his parents but knew nothing, whatsoever, about them. No relatives visited or wrote, and neither parent shared biographical details.

One night, Ma tucked him in, smoothing covers without affection, and the boy tried for more, "Please, Ma, say about when you were little."

"Let's see..." Chair scooted up, Ma sat primly. "Deary me!" Flustered, she fanned herself. "When I was little, I was small." Knee slapped as if she'd made an immense joke, she tittered.

"No...really tell me!"

"Sleep now," she insisted, getting up.

She never told. Always, she eluded.

He liked to imagine Ma, much beloved among a dozen boisterous siblings, hearty farm-fed parents. Aunts, uncles, gobs of cousins, welcoming, encircling with open arms.

What little he *did* know, he'd cobbled from gossip. Then Odette Potter passed word she knew something.

Odette, ever surrounded by a clutch of girls, bigger boys trailing after, the boy spent subsequent weeks angling to speak with her, till he finally caught a moment alone.

"Hey, Odette."

"Hey yourself."

He cleared his throat. "They say you know about my ma. I wondered what?"

Her dress several sizes too small, washed into transparency, revealed tiny, pink nipples; the boy blushed madly. "You don't know?" Odette winked and did a hubba-hubba with her hips.

Toe scuffed in dirt, he bluffed, "Yeah, I know things." Up an octave his voice pitched to betray him. "I just wasn't sure what you'd heard."

"My mama says your mama usta be a nun. You know...from a convent. That she was bad and got throwed out."

"Naaa," the boy brayed.

"Cross my heart. My mama also says your mama is touched."

"Touched, how so?"

"You know..." Finger twirled at her temple, eyes crossed, she lolled her tongue. "Mental."

"Shush, Odette Potter!" Whirled on heel, the boy marched off, angry at himself, angry at matters he worked to grasp.

"Odette Potter's Ma says you used to be a nun," he queried as Ma readied supper that night.

Ma yanked off silken corn tassels, dropped the ear of corn into a pot, and then tore away at another.

"Ma?"

Wrapped up in that familiar far-away look, Ma paused, but said nothing.

Unsure how to interpret this detail, the boy shut his mind against it. But for certain, Ma had secrets!

Chapter Ten: Lauren

Elevator taken to the third floor, Lauren keyed in, stomped her feet to take off the chill, and began her workday.

Oswell Nothnagel, who paced before the nursing station, spanked together his wrist backs as if a seal lion, then inquired, "How's the weather up there?" His pontoon-size feet were impossible not to admire.

"Dandy, thanks." Imposingly tall, not much to look at otherwise, Lauren endured constant comment. Always a head taller than her peers, she liked to imagine going to bed her usual stature to awake the next day, all dainty and precious.

Extreme height wasn't her real problem though: her crooked spine was. Although she no longer wore the back brace, her spine still curved to such an extreme even polite folk had to stare.

Clipboard in hand, she greeted co-workers and took off to make rounds. Environment so refined, so restful, footfall muted by dense carpet, Brahms lullabies wafting over the intercom, this was The Croft Foundation, the Rolls Royce of psychiatric hospitals.

Except mental patients weren't exactly termed patients; The Foundation insisted they be called *guests*.

As a new nurse graduate, Lauren worked the Flight Deck: the locked unit that housed the sickest of the sick. In the early days, as if birds attempting flight, psychotic patients flew out Flight Deck windows in droves; hence the name. Nowadays, though unsightly, barred windows prevented such mishaps.

Temporary home to the famous, wealthy and powerful—both real and imagined—a rock star, two foreign dignitaries, and the son of a Central American dictator, voices overlapping, played bridge in the lounge. Months on end, such guests stayed on at outrageous expense, awaiting sufficient recovery to resume their swath to power and riches.

A blond Jimmi Hendrix shrieked, horribly, strumming an air guitar.

A barefoot Gandhi strode about garbed in bedsheets. "Blessings." Hand raised in benediction, a longhaired Christ greeted as he stumped past.

This particular Christ—the unit housed several—stepped off a freeway overpass, falling, earth-bound, shattering both ankles, jamming femurs into tibias and fibulas. Companion guest, a weepy Mary Magdalene, scooted along, using her hair to scour Christ's feet.

All humans, Lauren figured, long to be important, or to be famous, or to do good; the Flight Deck abounded with them. Such longing bore a particular acrid scent. As she walked the halls, it leached from patients, staff too, who urgently sought to convey superior mental hygiene—herself included.

This being the nuthouse—mental hospital, if you will—wherein creative distortions of the human spirit boggled, aberrant behaviors got resolved with help from stupefying drugs. Guests ingested Thorazine, then twitched, shuffling along, stiffly robotic. Some got wrapped in freezing sheets to shock sense back into them. Lock-up involved application of medieval leather straps: yet another measure that set Lauren's teeth on edge.

Less frequently, holes got bored into gray matter, permitting disturbed, unacceptable thoughts egress. Sadly, critical chunks of memory and function departed as well, leaving muddled souls who blithered senselessly and curled into fetal boulder-like shapes.

Alas, when the rare mind *did* snap back in line, to Lauren's view, the individual's essence seemed to have departed. Yet staff tended to heave self-congratulatory sighs of relief.

See—when The Foundation—the world in general—confronted behaviors that did not conform to social propriety, they deemed them to be defects in need of amputation. Anger, aggression, for instance, got lobotomized into placidity.

In Lauren's view, states seen as abnormal were actually manifestations of the soul trying to free itself. And so, attempts to enforce conformity merely squelched the soul's rightful journey. Patients did not get cured when forced to adhere to the norm but when fully accepted, cracked psyche and all.

Glaring philosophical differences aside, although she made a fine nurse, it was not her calling.

"You look nice!" Lauren waved at a petite woman.

Tastefully garbed in twinset and slacks, the guest waved back. Yet no one could possibly intuit that jabbering voices had recently dethroned this adorably groomed woman of reason, instructing her to chuck her newborn in the trash.

Further down the hall a courtly gentleman, bent over leaves of a rubber plant, paused to watch Lauren pass. "Hey, Mr. Grant, how about breakfast?"

Mr. Grant shook his head. "Thanks, deary, but no."

Dapper Mr. Grant, who foxtrotted ever so nicely at all hospital socials, hadn't voluntarily ingested a bite in twenty-three years. Thoroughly, he chewed food, then spit it back out, depositing masticated wads in planter boxes, beneath sofa cushions, and on windowsills. If not forcibly fed, he'd have starved.

Arrived at the day room, Lauren halted to gape.

One arm delicately held aloft, other arm curved in front, as if a ballerina about to execute a spin, there stood Miss Spivey, a cinnamon colored woman. Likely, she'd posed thus, hours on end.

Rarely, did Miss Spivey move on her own. Staff cleaned, dressed, and left her propped about; they even ironed her Afro to make it more manageable. As with Mr. Grant, unless food got scooped into her mouth, she sat, fork fully loaded, hours on end.

Years prior, Miss Spivey arrived at The Foundation, courtesy of an anonymous patron. Entire historical portion of her chart a blank, staff clucked over her as a most hopeless case.

Sorrow now festering in the air, it droozled, lazily, out from the woman. Lauren's throat twanged with ache at sight of it.

Quick point about the mentally ill: the insane are not given to delightful fits of whimsy, nor do they perform absurdly far-out acts to amuse. Most are wretchedly miserable and suffer mightily.

Lauren's super-sensitive, lively antennas attuned her to each guest's nuanced gesture, facial expression, or twitch. Give her ten minutes, she'd tease out an individual's entire life story, know names of every pet, their most cherished Christmas gift, and their most sordid, deepest secret.

As if sprung from the Woody Allen movie, *Zelig*, when she sat overly long with Madame Dalsant, she acquired a genuine French accent. Terrific whoop, she rejoiced when Christ of the Shattered Femurs announced diminished horrific visions, and she railed against the God who caused Damien Donofrio to wince as if struck whenever spoken to.

Rounds complete, Lauren swung back to the nursing station to prepare and then dispense medications. Pill cart wheeled back to Miss Spivey, she announced, "Here are your meds."

Still locked, mid-pivot, the woman stammered, uncontrollably, "Yyyooou is only passin' through soss's to relieve your mind that you aaaain't cccc-razy." Lauren froze, flabbergasted.

Oblivious as Miss Spivey seemed, she certainly had her pegged!

"Dddd...diff, difference between you 'n me is only a bitty sliver."

Eyes devoid of light, body stiffly contorted into its impossible pose, the woman stared off again.

In Oswell Nothnagel stepped where Miss Spivey left off. "St. Theresa seemed a supreme loon until the pope gave her a thumbs-up. And most guests here, same as the saints, aren't just freaks." Paused, hands jumbling as if rinsing, he then resumed, "Some of us are mere garden-variety kooks, but others suffer the cursed ability to *see* and can enter many levels at once."

"See—other levels?"

Hands lifted again, Oswell spiraled them round and round. "Imagine,"—his voice went soft—"trying to sort out what's happening in the here and now, while seeing spirits—dead persons and such—without let-up."

"Sounds terrifying."

"Its proper filters that we lack. Thanks to my...ah, gift, I can drop into a parallel universe—places beyond ordinary human senses. At times I get stuck, half in this world, half in another, and have a devil of a time sorting myself out."

Long ago adventure with the healer come to mind, Lauren wondered if she'd dipped into another world at that time and then, luckily, returned.

Further, and tangentially, mind drifted off, she imagined how it would be to be the healer's student.

Couple nights a week, she'd sit at his feet, gaze adoringly, basting in his words as they would fall from his mouth to her ears. He'd explain why she saw and felt the oddities that she did. Naturally, they'd discuss God's overarching place in all of it. The healer would assign techniques to practice. They'd hug goodbye. She'd glow, terribly happy.

Except, sadly, she'd been unable to find him.

Daily after work, she systematically skimmed library phone books in search of *Walker Judson*. Thus far, she'd checked all Oregon, Washington State and Idaho directories: a boggling, tedious task. She'd even tried name variations, some as silly as *Stroller* and *Ambulator Judson*.

The quality of that experience years ago had been strongly etched. Yet at times she feared she'd merely imagined the man, conjured him in a time of great need.

Although her body kept twisting and grew more strange, grace touched her in that storefront church. She had not set that path, had no sense of worthiness, and was not at all clear where her responsibility lay. But that moment, when the healer told her to set hands on that ailing man, she knew she'd been tapped.

But now, as her life's dream steadily ebbed, she fought panic.

Mornings, she awoke to a sense of impending failure. Intervals throughout the day, grief clobbered her. Yesterday, she hid in the janitor's closet, waiting for a spasm to pass, then came back out red-eyed.

"So"—Lauren gulped, bringing her attention back—"how can one tell if a person is chemically imbalanced or if they've slipped through this so-called cosmic crack?"

Sagely, Oswell lifted his chin. "Check the eyes; you'll see sanity or madness. When some folks travel to other realms they get lost, twisted, and evil takes hold. Others see so much senseless cruelty, their spirit vacates. Given the look of her, Miss Spivey is such a soul.

"Most Foundation staff," he continued, shaking his head, "are scared spitless of us crazy folk."

"Why work here if afraid?"

"Same as you: they're working things out." Steadily, he held Lauren's gaze. "I see you hold Damien's hand when he dips into demon-infested places, and know that you fret over all of us. Deep down, though, you fear Damien's self-mutilation...and his grief. You think you don't know how to access your heart's longing, but truly...you do."

"Tell me...how do I get there?"

Pained curious looks, Oswell regarded her as if she already knew.

Two hours later, unable to locate Miss Spivey, Lauren alerted staff to help search.

Nurses, aides, even the janitor called out, checking guest room, closets, and beneath beds.

No Miss Spivey.

Flash of insight, Lauren raced to the tub room, found the woman splayed in the bathtub, wrists slit at perfect angles, water inked red as her lifeforce leached out.

All gone pointy, shrill, Lauren shouted out, "Help!"

Hands beneath Miss Spivey's armpits, she scooped her onto tile, shredded her own shirttails, applied tourniquets to bloody arms, cradling the woman, imploring, "Hang in there. Please don't die!"

I can't fail you like I failed my dad! came her keenest thought.

Yet Miss Spivey seemed only dimly alive.

A fellow nurse showed up, yelped, left to call the medics, then returned.

"Even if you can't love yourself, Miss Spivey, God does!—I do!" Lauren crooned; all gawkers heard. "I love you, Miss Spivey. Allow yourself to feel God's love."

Paramedics arrived, took over, and then carted the woman out.

Sloshed back to the nurses station, Lauren leaned, shook, and shook.

Gentle touch to her shoulder, a voice comforted, "At least Miss Spivey had the good fortune to be cradled in your arms." Head lifted, she glazed into the pools of Oswell's kind eyes.

Chapter Eleven: Young Lauren

Snaggle-toothed Dr. Flowers took a rubber mallet, tapped Lauren's knees, wrists, and ankles. Each tap, her limbs shot out, unbidden. Next, he twisted her torso, side-to-side; her eyes watered up.

Measurements taken, notes charted, he paused to regard her, then spoke, somberly, "You, young lady, have a mild case of polio; that's why your spine is crooked." He addressed Lauren's mom. "I recommend a brace to correct the curvature."

Lauren felt the deepest sinking. Mom wrung her hands. "How did this happen?"

Glasses removed, Dr. Flowers pinched the bridge of his nose. "Possibly your girl here got a bum lump of sugar. Sorry to say, in rare cases the Salk vaccine causes the very illness we seek to eradicate." Glasses re-situated, he swiveled back to Lauren. "You're lucky, child, your case is rather mild."

Lower lip quivering, crazily, Lauren nodded glumly.

God hated her; at least she thought so. He'd relegated her to live in a cage, which, given that she was already large, ugly, and not exactly pleased to be herself, seemed terribly inconsiderate; it took years to overcome her resentment.

Anyways...As if God had reached down, spun her facing wrong, backside never quite catching up, her spine seemed a boney, twisted pretzel. Sprouted at the oddest angle, it torqued below her rib cage to kink her trunk, causing the right side of her chest to cave in, and the shoulder opposite to thicken and hump. Not quite Quasimodo of the lolling eye and loping gait, she *did* seem a close cousin.

Weeks later, Lauren donned the brace, asking, "How long?"
"Only two years," Mom mollified.

But two years is a lifetime at age fifteen!

Sure, it promised to pull out the kinks to make her upright. But it didn't feel right.

Saddled with a ton of discomfort, and frustration, and rage, the brace provoked endless taunts. "Lauren Finch's a pregnant, titless wonder," a kid yelled as she walked this day's gauntlet.

"Hey robot-girl." A zit-faced boy shoved his face into hers. "Sit on this!" Hand cupped beneath underarm, he pumped to make squishy farting sounds.

"Haw, haw, haw," his friends guffawed, their faces kaleidoscoping before her.

Spun on heel, Lauren fled.

Shouts, hollers, schoolmates chased after.

Splat!—Spitballs collided with her hair and backside as she scurried past lockers, into the schoolyard.

Then she turned back and saw it.

Gooey slime dripped from her tormentors' mouths; sparks flew from their eyes.

Well, OK, she exaggerated!

But billowy, nonsensical streams *did* leach from their mouths.

Across the parking lot, into the neighborhood she ran. Heart thrashing, stride slowed, she rounded the corner, headed up the quiet suburban street, cut across a yard, went up the drive, and let herself inside.

"You're certainly early," Mom called.

Kitchen walls papered with every goofy bulb-headed stick figure Lauren had ever drawn—Mom gushed over them as if they were Matisse originals—in her mother rushed to plant a kiss. "No one clomps like you!" As ever, she smelt of talc and seemed freshly scrubbed.

Fate plopped Lauren into a family of gorgeous specimens. Dad was movie-star handsome, and Mom was lovely, near to perfect. Men turned to stare at them. Women did as well.

Mostly, Mom's clear, un-freckled skin griped Lauren to no end. Jillions of freckles dotting her own skin, freckles existed where freckles had no business. They graced her eyelids and inner arms; one even splashed her lower lip. When younger, she prayed, madly, that they'd fall off like chocolate sprinkles. She even tried sandpaper to scuff them away.

"Let me look, sweetie." Hair bushed from her daughter's forehead, Mom searched Lauren's face. "Not so good?"

"I can't do this, Mom. People make fun. I have no friends. I hate that I'm always suffocating. Really, I don't care if my spine stays crooked or if I turn into more of a freak show, 'cause I'm already one."

"You *do* have friends. Patrice Morgan, for one." Actually, Lauren faked a social life.

Last Saturday, she'd hollered goodbye, headed out, circled the block, snuck back into the garage to climb up to the loft. Flashlight illuminating the book, *To Kill a Mockingbird*, which played at the theater, she read enough to grasp the plot.

Come dusk, she breezed in and said through laughs, "That Patrice is such a jokester!" Patrice, a dweebie mouth-breather who also sat alone at lunch, would've been dumbfounded at the adventures they'd shared.

"Don't you get sick of this—of me?"

"Never!" Mom insisted. "Someday the brace will come off, and the memory will fade. Besides, it's who you are inside that matters most."

"I know who I am—I'm a toad."

The brace!

A mix of metal and flesh-colored leather, the chinrest curved beneath her jaw to form a midget-size serving tray. Three bars, one in front, two in back, traveled her torso to embed in a leather saddle-like contraption that contoured her hips. Velcro strips attached to two back bars, each strip stitched to a palm-sized leather pad cinched up to apply spine-straightening pressure.

Weighed down by thirty extra pounds, she hefted about as if on a perpetual backpack trip. A glance side-to-side meant rotating her entire body, robot-like. And only maternity clothes fit.

The emotional pain morphed her into a liar; she cut school, looped report card C's into a A's, and made up stories. Retreated into the world of whimsy, birds developed kindly human faces; their twitters spoke comfort. Her secret friend, a lipstick-wearing dachshund, clomped about in high heels, and halted every so often to jitterbug.

When she described these oddities, Mom recoiled.

Lonely, awkward, wholly unattractive, she skirted along walls, avoided eye contact, and kept as quiet as possible.

But still, kids shouted vulgarities.

So she feigned deafness.

They razzed anyway. The Hulk, Robot-Girl, Animated Appliance they called her, and worse.

She tried not to care, and kept on lying to cover her grief.

Then the itch began. Itches got so bad that she used teeth to chew, gnaw, rip, and tear at herself. Blood flowed; droplets ran down wrists to elbows. When caught munching, she regarded the starer, wiped lips, and announced, "Mmm, deeelicious!"

"Eczema," the dermatologist diagnosed when Mom took her in. "It may be psychosomatic, possibly stress induced. She seems high strung, so it's best not to make a big deal, and likely, she'll grow out of it. I'll prescribe something for the itch."

Back home, she'd checked the definition of *psychosomatic: a physical disorder*, the dictionary said, *aggravated by emotional trauma, stress, or imbalance.*

Solitariness as her signature stance, her caged self defined her. Suffering formed her identity; she had no self without it. In her more enlightened future, she would thank this pain for the many teachings it would bestow.

Just now, though, as the absolute worst thing, Lauren headed for the stairs. "Think I'll go to bed."

Slid between sheets, bedspread eased over her head, she studied the fabric; the weave, crosshatched green and blue threads, she decided, looked best from the underside.

Mom came to check. "What are you doing? It's ten a.m."

Lauren formed a most miserable whisper. "I can't stand this, Mom. I want to stop."

Gently, Mom peeled covers back, twining fingers in her daughter's hair. "I saw this notice in the church flier." Crumpled paper extracted from an apron pocket, she read, "'Come to be healed by Walker Judson. He can fix infirmities—all kinds. He repairs dimming eyesight, removes kidney stones, and even deletes cancerous growths.'"

"Yeah, imagine me with a straight spine!" Lauren took and reread the missive; smells, tobacco and mint, drifted from its creases.

"Even if it's just wishful thinking, it might be interesting. So how about I take you to see him?"

Scalp a-tingle, Lauren felt the slightest lift as she chewed at a ravaged cuticle. "Sorry, Mom, but I'm pretty sure I have to go alone."

Chapter Twelve: Walker

The Sullivan Hotel, with its crumbling facade and boarded-up windows, had seen years of neglect. Worn floors wobbled with weight of footfall; floors so threadbare, one glimpsed through gaps to peer at the level below. Out back, stairs and doors missed each other so that some hasty, poor soul might step into thin air.

Long ago, the building adjacent had slid downhill. Now it teetered in a crumpled heap at ravine's edge. The Sullivan seemed about to join it.

Built in the late 1800's, touted as Buena Vista's most progressive whorehouse, The Sullivan boasted an alley that afforded dallying husbands quick exit from wrathful wives and, secondarily, escape from the common hazard of fire. Protection taken yet further, the brothel offered clientele the option to partake of iodine soaks: a thoughtful, if fanciful, protection against syphilitic outbreak.

These days, volunteers helping, Walker worked sun up to sundown to stabilize the crumbling facade, replace rotting floorboards, and then painted, till the place dazzled.

One day Rosalee dropped by. "I would enjoy a tour."

Paint and sawdust spackling clothes and hair, Walker obliged. "The lobby will serve as reception and waiting area." Front door opening onto a majestic foyer, where stairs swooped onto a landing, The Angel dangled above. "From here," he explained, "she can oversee our comings and goings."

Rosalee waved and chirped. "Hellooo up there."

The Angel's presence meant much to Walker. Angels, he presumed, did not love in the same diffident manner as humans. They did not marry, have families, or form ties that humans term love. Humans bemused them. And although they did not fully understand their ways, they never judged. Angels found humans ridiculously limited, hapless, bumbling, and sentimental. Still, they loved them, albeit impartially.

Angelic love being generic, impersonal, democratic, they exhibited compassion but were not demanding or clingy. Walker's angel, however, differed somewhat. Times, its love bathed him so fiercely it set his heart thumping such irregular beats that he feared collapse.

Adjacent to the foyer hunkered a cozy shelf-lined room. Walker indicated the split door with its countertop ledge. "Here you can dispense herbs. Chinese medicine is a fine adjunct to my work."

Rosalee drew him close. "It is too perfect!"

A hall bisected the building's middle; a series of doors ran along both sides. "These are treatment rooms," Walker indicated. Second floor similarly configured, there female students would reside. Up to the third floor, hammering echoes receding, Walker stepped over heaped donations—piles of them—offering Rosalee a hand to maneuver. "Eventually, this space will accommodate male students and teachers."

Rosalee glanced about, eyes a-sparkle. "You have made vast improvements, I no longer recognize this place!"

"Couldn't have done it without you," Walker fumbled, "my—my friend."

Rosalee squeezed his hand, then kissed it.

Awash with feeling, he made an odd noise. Many would swarm round Walker in adoration, but Rosalee would anchor him.

Stage set, great things coiled within. The town, this building, Rosalee Soo—all of it—comprised the home he so longed for.

Projected into the future, a purple-garbed woman bowed deeply, asking to hug him, and Walker allowed it. The woman sprung up. Walker bent down. She embraced him, kept holding on. Walker saw himself shake violently, step back, grip the woman's hands, speak with such intimacy, as if son to mother. Returned to present, heady with feeling, eyes watery, he wiped them, fiercely.

Rosalee informed, "You must call this place The Living Light Healing Center."

Walker shot her a grin. "The Living Light Healing Center it is!"

Chapter Thirteen: Young Walker

The boy lay in the upper field watching clouds skirt overhead, caught movement, and pushed up to see Ma striding purposefully toward him. Briefly, she halted to fiddle with a string, wound it into a ball, then dropped it into a pocket.—That twine would join her burgeoning stash pile.

"Hey," the boy called as he moved to stand.

"Stay as you are," Ma insisted. Quick glance at the house, she scanned the surrounds, then sat, dress carefully tucked at her ankles.

"We must speak of the Sacrament of Confession." Again Ma peered about, then, gulp of air, hurtled into it. "Die with a blemish on your soul, son, and you won't be permitted into the Kingdom of Heaven. Pray as I might, I've blundered so bad, your own Ma may not be allowed." The boy listened attentive.

Eyes a-gleam, as if beset by a precious inner secret, Ma vacated. Oh, her physical body—the one he knew as Ma, remained—but the rest of her emptied out to become a human shell.

The boy sighed, retied shoelaces, waiting, impatient, for her return.

"Ah..." Ma drew herself back and flicked fingers through grass blades. "Confessing each and every sin prevents you from accumulating them." To the boy's mind, *sin* meant decay, pestilence: something disease-ridden. "But...This is important son. When you *do* go to confession, Pa mustn't know—that's the deal." Spittle frothed as Ma spoke. "I promised I'd never set foot in a church again. Although my promise didn't specifically apply to you, Pa would forbid it if he knew."

The boy shifted, uneasy. "Why's Pa like that? You know—the way he gets mad and whams you."

"Pa—well—he wants us for himself. Anyhoo..." She scanned his face, checking. "You mustn't tell. Understand?"

"Mm-kay." *Hush, Ma,* he wanted to blurt, *don't make me know this!*

Time and again, he hoped she'd explain the disquiet between her and Pa. Only now, as if awakened from deep slumber, she suddenly seemed to realize she had a son to educate and thrust this stuff upon him. "A blemish is a taint upon your soul," Ma persisted. "If sin isn't removed...When you die, your soul goes to hell."

"Will Pa go to hell, then?"

"We're talking about your soul, not Pa's. You must remove all blemishes, and the only way to do so is to confess your sins."

"How's that happen?"

"You go to church and tell the priest..." Off Ma spun, as if such matters were commonly discussed. "And when you take communion, you mustn't chew the host; it's the body of Christ."

Chew and swallow the body of Christ? The boy narrowed his eyes.

Recently, he'd rescued torn Bible pages from the burn pile. Chock-full of details, he figured Christ to be one swell guy.

But why would Christ, a man of such talent and know-how, willingly shrink to wafer-size? Why not transform into a magnificent heavenly creature? And why, for pity sake, transform into toast and get slathered in saliva, chewed, and digested?

Making a froth of whorls, swoops, splashes, dabbing air for emphasis, Ma chattered away, "Prayer serves four purposes. Adoration. Contrition. Thanksgiving. And Supplication. Yet most merely pray to be saved."

So that's why she risks all to pray as she does!

Ma described transgression, atonement, sacrifice, salvation, and enumerated The Seven Sacraments, the holy days, and the rules of the Church—of which there were many.

The boy's mind, tottering, traipsing after her, broke loose from its moorings and spun like a dervish. Little did he care for imparted details; Ma's singular ferocious attention mattered most.

"Gracious me!" Ma fanned herself. "I've been terribly lax to not get at this sooner!"

As sunshine burst forth to warm them, the boy admired the hap-hap-happy person Ma had suddenly become.

"Now you," Ma directed.

Together they reviewed the Ten Commandments: sassing a grown-up was a sin; hosting impure thought was a sin. It was a sin to hate Pa for how he treated Ma. —He got the hang of it; sin meant doing most everything.

Onward, Ma rushed. "Each time you do wrong, ask yourself, 'big sin or little sin?' Little ones, no need to worry, but big ones are tough to erase. You can even sin with your thoughts. Hateful thoughts about Pa aren't good, but you can be rid of them. A big sin would be if you deliberately hurt or killed someone. Even then, if you're truly sorry, God's Grace forgives all."

The more the boy listened, the more confused he felt. "Do evil, say sorry, and all's forgiven?"

"Indeed, God wipes the slate clean. But, see...when you were born..." Head bent, Ma fidgeted. "I baptized you myself. Though not exactly how it's done, you may now go to confession."

"Me, baptized?" A soft smile crept onto his face.

Ma put a finger to her lips. "Mustn't tell." Her voice leaked a passionate throb. "Pa doesn't take kindly to me fraternizing with God."

"Why's that Ma?" Breath held, he felt his whole life depended upon what came next.

Ma ripped weeds; her dry, nicked hands shredded a handful.

She smiled faintly. "That's my cross to bear." Then she took up urgent, graver tones, "I've mucked up my life something terrible, but you...You have a chance to help many."

The day got warm, but not so warm that he should sweat.

He sweated anyhow.

Ma leaned close. "You must purify your mind and heart, and shape yourself to God's will: no easy task. In time, you'll make grievous mistakes and will suffer for them. But this I know...So long as you ask God's forgiveness, you'll do fine. Get cocky—mind me now..." She gripped his shirt front. "You'll be cast out." Abruptly, she released him.

Clouds slid past. Sunlight—hot shimmery—washing the scene, they sat silent.

Help many. Impossible to picture, the boy mused on this, cleared his throat, but could not find words.

"Just so you know...That bird is just the start."

Head jerked up, the boy stared. "Bird. How?"

"You were chosen, born for a purpose past my understanding."

Belly doing a grand swoop, always, he suspected himself to be different.—That she understood amazed, yet pained him.

The two of them being of similar ilk, someday, he grasped, his gifts would surpass hers.

Ma cast her son an appraising look. "One question, I need to know."

"What's that, Ma?"

"Have you the courage to live life full-on?"

"Courage?" The boy blinked, saucer-eyed. "I…I don't know…"

"You'll need great courage." Ma glanced about. "In time, you'll understand. Some of it…I can't rightly explain. Besides, it's not my place to do so."

"Ma, please…" He reached out.

Pulled back, Ma shut her eyes, silently moved lips.

Praying, he surmised—*likely for me!* It thrilled to know.

Lightly, Ma touched fingertips to her forehead, then above her heart, next her left shoulder, and then her right. Eyes blinked open to her son's stare, she clarified, "Sign of the cross."

Mouth a-tremble, she bit back excitement. "Goodness me, there's much you need to know!"

Pa drove into the yard and honked.

Hopped to her feet, Ma marched off to grab supplies from the truck bed. Up the porch steps she went, glanced back, then went in, screen door slapped shut.

The boy stood, was slow to follow. This being the longest flow of words Ma had ever assembled, he tried to figure.

It's a sin to hate Pa. It's also a sin to let Pa keep hurting Ma. I've sinned by not rescuing Ma; yet Ma refuses to let me save her. And it's a sin to disobey my parents—all that seemed clear.

But, if it's also a sin to see a wrong, yet do nothing about it, my biggest sin is that I don't stand up to Pa.

Either way, he had to sin, and had to do something.

Despite Ma's many words, she offered no roadmap.

Near as he could tell, she hoped he and God would work it out directly and leave her clear of it.

Tight band forming, his head throbbed so bad; each solitary hair follicle thrummed with a tiny headache all its own.

As to Ma's remark about his future, a hot rush flooded him. He would not wither and die without purpose. Ma as much said so!

And...surge of gladness, *Ma cared enough to share secrets.* That meant a whole lot!

Nothing changed. Life remained dry and desiccated. Yet something tiny, tremulous had sparked.

Chapter Fourteen: Young Lauren

"You know that man, the healer I saw?" Lauren addressed her mom. "I'm pretty sure he—"

Mom picked up, "You no longer mope, but you never said what happened. Before, you and I shared most everything. Now, it's like you have this big secret."

How to explain what had occurred?

When Lauren left the healer, she felt elated: a long-lasting high. Funny thing: although she hadn't been treated, she no longer felt depressed.

Days later, she'd returned to that storefront. A drunk lolled in the doorway. She'd checked the address. Letter six, flipped upside down; the place all right.

For Rent sign overhead, she'd stepped over the huddled form to try the door; it refused to budge.

"So where's he now?" asked Mom.

"Ah, that's the trouble. He's gone, and I haven't the slightest idea where to find him."

Between ages sixteen, seventeen, and eighteen, figuring Walker Judson might travel in such circles, Lauren read national and local news, checked bulletins about faith healers and miracles, and asked around about him.

No luck—Walker Judson seemed to have vanished.

Sick with longing, hoping to stumble onto him, she dabbled in the fringe world of the crunchy granola types: wore Birkenstocks and tie-dyed clothes and grew her hair long. She learned to douse, trained in aroma and color therapies, got Rolfed and Re-birthed, went to Esalen, took EST training, dabbled in Scientology, and attended yoga workshops. Some practices made sense; much of it seemed terribly silly.

Once, she dropped psilocybin. As a sickish roar pressed down, the boundaries circumscribing her body dissolved to mingle with air molecules. Brain bruised by sound, movement, and light, she envisioned its cavity, soggy gray, crackling sparking as it synapsed. Hair gone smelly, like fried rubber, her body trembled uncontrollably as thoughts—tons of them—hurtled past.

Fantastic shadowy figures, flat, thin as tapirs, nodded as they slithered past. Some paused to wave tentacle-like arms, ogle, cackle and then dissipate. Stranger still, blessed with sudden X-ray vision her eyes worked superbly. Cars and people, visible through solid walls, swum past like fishes.

Imagined or real, the healer came. Glowing cigarette making passes to and from his mouth, face as remembered—bleak, terribly pained — he inhaled a voluptuous suck of smoke. Smoke shot deep into his lungs to scorch cilia, then jettisoned from his nostrils to caress her, lovingly.

Wildly alert, elation bathed her.

The healer came close.

Must've been raining; his suit smelt damp and woolly: each and every thread.

Tongue extended, Lauren gave him a lick. His skin tasted of grit, aftershave, and sweat.

"You are *not* to let yourself go this route! Hear? Not!" Mr. Judson scolded.

Cigarette ash tapped into palm, he sat back and grinned the exact grin as *Alice in Wonderland's* Cheshire Cat but then he shrank into nonexistence.

That escapade failed to produce the healer, but she *did* get so far out there, she scared herself. So much so, she retreated to the safe structure offered by nursing, where she could help and fix to her heart's content.

Chapter Fifteen: Young Walker

Head wet beneath schoolyard faucet, hair slicked back, the boy took off in the direction opposite home and went past the cemetery until he arrived at St. Andrew's Catholic Church. Up the steps he marched, ran hands down his front to smooth shirt rumples, then entered the vestibule.

Eyes adjusting to the gloom, a veiled woman slid past, dipped fingers in a basin, crossed herself, and entered the nave. The boy did likewise, then stepped forth to survey the scene.

Silence shouted down upon the cool, shadowy space that seemed bigger than three barns. Stained glass windows—souls begging for Divine Mercy—ran down both sides, and flickering light from those windows scattered across walls and floors. In the loft behind, splendid cylinders reached the ceiling, where cherubs peeked down from rafters. Each painting, every statue and tassel, even the altar-top box, glittered, golden. And...At room's far vaulted wall, a near-naked man—also gold encrusted—hung from a cross.

God, the boy realized, *has a thing for riches!*

Mindful not to smack shoes, glancing into alcoves, the boy went down the center aisle. Artfully draped statues, accessorized in jewel-laden tiaras, lurked within each nook. Votive candles, dozens, flickered at their feet.

One niche, a woman lit a candle, chirped softly, extracted a photo, gazed at it, longingly. Up to her lips, she gave it a kiss, then added it to heaped articles at the statue's feet.

Ka-chink—coin dropped into a padlocked box, she genuflected, crossed herself, then departed.

Near the front, as the boy peered into the final alcove, quiet joy overtook him.

Outstretched arms offering to embrace him, wide-spanning wings sprouting from shoulders, there an angel stood. Its loving mouth, everything about the statue, addressed him, *I know you. Everything!*

This angel, he surmised, knew what a puny weakling he was with regard to Ma and understood his hatred of Pa—how such matters tore at him.

Despite full grasp of his shortcomings, steadily the angel emanated loving kindness.

It seemed so lively. More alive than Ma. More real than solid, thick Pa. Seemed so real that he marched up, pressed his face to its cool, draped fabric to check.

Light shafted through a window to drench the space. Got so bright, he shielded his eyes.

Whump, whump—flapping sounds—feathery wings unfurled to span wide. And then...and then...They softly flapped—till gradually the wings joined to fold at its back.

Steadily, the angel radiated what he came to know as The Essence of Love.

"Who are you?" he whispered.

I am your friend—it spoke into his head.

"I—well," he groped. "This means so much!"

Never until then had he possessed a real friend. "What do I call you?"

The Angel—it whispered.

Reaching up, he took her hand.

Flesh yielding, it felt solid, warm.

Would that I might stay like this forever!

A distant cough called him back. So he forced himself up the aisle to join a hushed, purposeful crowd, slid into a pew, knelt, inclined his head, pressed palms to face, and grinned into them. *My angel—mine!*

"Bless me Father. I have impure thoughts," a disembodied voice disclosed.

Anxiety overtook him, for Ma had warned: "It's a sin to listen."

Twice, he coughed to drown the noise.

Onward, the voice droned, "I imagine my wife's sister naked."

The boy clapped hands to his ears; the voice kept on, "I can't resist, she's sexy as hell."

Softly, the boy hummed to block sounds, galled that he'd be penalized for hearing against his will.

Meanwhile, people entered, then exited a side door booth, knelt, prayed, rose up again, donned coats, and left. When it seemed his turn, the boy pushed up and entered the booth as well.

Pitch-black closet, inward pressing walls bore down as he groped blindly to steady himself.

Ma said to kneel. He went to his knees.

Uncertain what came next, arms crossed on his chest—this seemed incorrect—so he set them on the narrow shelf.

Rustling, a click, a miniature face-level door slid back. Squinting, the boy made out what seemed a priest's profile. "Let us pray," enjoined a grave voice.

"Bless me, sir," the boy began, "my pa has sinned, he's never been to confession or to church, so I'm here in his stead. Uh—this is my first time too." Deep gulp, he went on, "See—Ma defies Pa. And Pa isn't exactly what you'd call a good man. He—"

Muffled cascade of words collided with his own, "Son...," the priest interjected. "You must listen."

Unable to obey, the boy mustered on. "At first I was scared to come, but so far it's pretty nice."

Swiveled to glare full-on, the priest growled, "You must stop!"

Onward, the boy blundered, "Near as I can tell, Pa's not sorry for being mean." Thoroughly, he enumerated many blemishes: Pa's mostly. Concerns kept under wraps so long—the release—the sloughing of sin enthralled.

Face creased in a frown, the priest looked on incredulous as each word marched smartly out from the boy's mouth. "Pa beats Ma. I don't know how to save her."

He pressed with questions—not one, but several: "Does God care if Pa beats Ma? If He does care, why doesn't He stop it? Do you suppose God hates Ma? Ma calls herself a monster, so maybe He agrees. Does God hate me too? If He does, I can understand, 'cause I don't much like Him either. So..." Nose pressed to screen, the boy slowed, checking. "What do you say, sir?" The priest gaped at him. "Big thing...what I most want to know—does God forgive me for not making Pa stop hurting Ma? Also...How do I make Pa stop?" At last, he ceased jabbering.

The priest appeared to rinse his cheeks, then asked, "Have you ever been to Mass, young man?"

"Nope, never."

"Well then, you must come!"

"Sir?" the boy tried to steer the conversation back. "I need to know...Is Pa saved by my coming? Am I saved as well?"

The priest heaved a sigh. "To be saved, son, you must attend Mass on a regular basis."

"Pa never lets Ma or me do anything, so church is out. He'd hurt Ma if we tried...sir."

"You're here because God willed it, so you mustn't thwart Him."

Awkwardly, the boy shifted. "Actually, I'm here because of Ma. And, much as I appreciate the invitation, I only came to get rid of sins."

Ignited into a series of tweets and murmurs, the priest did the sign of the cross, topped off with a kiss to his very own fingertips. "Regardless of intent, young man, to be truly saved, you must attend Mass and make your confession weekly."

"But I—"

"You must say—" A faraway bell interrupted. The priest tried again, "For penance, you must say the Apostles' Creed twelve times and ten Hail Marys. God be with, and bless you."

"Sir?"

"Father," the priest corrected.

"Sorry, Father. The Apostles' Creed...I've had no instruction for that."

Proper words imparted, the priest asked the boy's name and where he lived, whispered several more incantations, whirled fingers in the air, and slid the screen shut.

Relieved, exhilarated: *Surely,* the boy reasoned, *God will fix everything!*

Chapter Sixteen: Lauren

Within an hour of Miss Spivey's suicide attempt, the call came; Lauren's co-worker held out the phone, so she took it. "Hello?"

"The director," chirped the secretary, "would like you to pay her a visit."

"When?"

"Now would be best."

Waiting room walls quilted with plaques and commendations, a prominent photo featured the director, mid-handshake, with President Nixon. And, since research had proven that color impacts anxiety and aggression, the room—walls, carpet, and upholstery—were serenest robin's-egg blue. Last year's serenity color, all was decorated placid pink.

Waaa!—buzzed the intercom.

Receiver hitched to ear, the secretary whispered into it, then announced, "The director will see you." Ushered into an adjoining office, Lauren beheld a woman who bore the squat look of a fireplug.

"Do sit." The director took a leisurely draw on a cigarette, cocked her mouth and blew smoke fiercely upward.

Several exhalations later, cigarette mashed into an ashtray—one overflowed with hundreds of other butts—the woman leveled cold eyes at Lauren. "It has come to my attention that you fail to exhibit sensible boundaries with regard to our guest, Ms. Spivey. And, as you know, this is strictly forbidden. Hmmm, let's see…"

Glasses plunked atop her nose, she regarded a folder's contents. "How long have you worked here?

"One year."

"According to this, a year and two months." Folder set aside, the director tamped down another cigarette and then lit up.

Hand sharply slicing from mouth to ashtray, she flicked ash, hard.

"Miss Finch, we have an employee behavior code that clearly spells out proper relations with our guests." Pawing through a paper stack, face squinched, she scrawled a note, set both hands on the desk, and twiddled her thumbs. "Oddly, our code fails to regulate staff's spiritual expression, and so bylaws must be amended to include it. But"—she scanned Lauren's face—"that's no excuse as to your lack of sensibility regarding your ravings. Telling Ms. Spivey that God loves her, imposes your personal view. Mention God, you act like the worst of them.—Whatever were you thinking?"

"I said what I felt might comfort her."

"That doesn't justify your verbiage." Face all frowns, the director caressed her Marlboro pack.

These days, Lauren often prayed aloud, petitioning God for specific outcomes regarding any and everything. She asked for courage to face tasks, big or mundane. She prayed for guests, that they might find peace, and prayed for Mom's ongoing health and happiness. Also, with growing impatience she begged for help to find Walker Judson so that she might assume her rightful place in God's Divine Plan.

"Sadly"—thinnest pity conveyed, the director paused to consider her next words—"I must send you home immediately, without pay. You will initiate counseling with regard to your emotional state. Return to work when you have a therapist's note to verify attendance." Cigarette lit from an old one, she dismissed Lauren with a flick of the wrist. "You may go."

What now? Lauren wondered.

Noting the director's facial mole, resplendent with long, dark hairs, that her pantsuit was several sizes too tight, and the woman's cigarette addiction, emboldenment overtook her.

Pulled up to full height, she opened her mouth, careful to modulate her voice, "I understand you have standards and that I may have overstepped propriety with Miss Spivey, but with all due respect, you have no right to insist that I seek counseling because I spoke of God." Steadily, she held the director's drop-jawed glare. "Invoking God doesn't interfere with my work. Matter of fact, it may actually help."

"See here—"

Lauren cut in, "The Foundation encourages honest self-expression for all, so I expressed myself. Sadly, when guests or staff truly speak up, if it's not perfectly sanitized into blandness, you can't handle it. As for my acting like a mental patient, your own regard for them is patently clear."

Chair shoved back, the director spluttered, "This institution—"

"Discipline me all you want, but I refuse to see a therapist."

Sharply, the director clapped hands. The secretary appeared. "Show Miss Finch out!"

Lauren's next words tumbled out, "I'm giving notice."

"Wha…?"

"Excuse me, I have a job to do." Lauren departed, shutting the door harder than intended.

Patients' hall phone ringing as Lauren stormed past, she paused to answer it. "Hello. Third floor."

"Come to Buena Vista," a male voice enjoined.

"'Scuse me, who are you calling?"

"For you, Lauren Finch."

"Who is this?"

"Walker Judson. Come to Buena Vista, Arizona."

"Is this a joke?"

"God promises."

Click—the receiver went dead. Lauren stared into the earpiece, put her head back, and crowed.

Miss Spivey did not die, but she did not exactly thrive either. On return from intensive care, she never left her bed, spoke only in tentative fragments, but mostly, she mumbled.

When one saves a life, one becomes responsible for it. Therefore, as if their conversations were two-way, Lauren sat with the woman, blathering on about anything that sprang to mind: their shared loneliness, how great it was that Miss Spivey had survived; she even mentioned her deepest secret—her affinity for rocks.

Days off, she came back to sit alongside. Administration frowned on this; she came anyway.

Worried how Miss Spivey would fare when she departed, Lauren did not speak of it. Yet, during their time together on Lauren's last work day, Miss Spivey lifted her head, their eyes met, the older woman's mouth opened, and an immense maw of grief drizzled out. Hand scrabbling, she reached to grip Lauren's arm, and whimpered, "You... aaaare leavin' me."

Singed by the haunt, Lauren gently extracted her hand. "Yes, I am." As if administering a Band-Aid to halt a hemorrhage, she brought her hand back to give a pat.

Face enshrouded, darkness dragged Miss Spivey down again.

Throat crimped, Lauren thought to apologize, but could only stare at the ravaged soul before her.

Part II: The Bliss-Ninny

Chapter Seventeen: Lauren

Welcome to Historic Buena Vista, invited the road sign. "So this must be it!" Mom put false bounce to her voice.

Glances side to side, mother and daughter puzzled their way up the rutted Main Street.

A throwback to another era, the town's Five-and-Dime offered fifteen cent banana splits. Boasting the finest in ladies' apparel, Leticia Opplinger Clothiers haughty window dummies wore 1950's fashions.

Further down, half-dozen spruced-up artisan cooperatives lined the street. A bank, a corrugated-roofed movie house, several saloons, two cafes—The Flatiron and Bea's Koffee Kup—comprised the rest of it. No shop looked busy; several sported *For Sale* signs.

"Something seems odd." Lauren slowed the car.

Most brick structures with false fronts, tilted, lopsided; some slumped back into the hillside, near to collapse. "What do you suppose makes them do that?" pondered Mom.

"Dunno, but this place would make an excellent locale for a cowboy movie."

At roadway's bend, Lauren parked among a group of cars. Honky-tonk tunes wafting from a saloon, a man bolted out its doors. Heels smacking the walkway, he lurched to the curb, pressed a finger to nostril, bent over, blew snot, and then tottered off.

Mom's eyes bugged, appalled. "Is this it?"

"No, but I'll get directions." Lauren hopped out, entered the building, and returned momentarily. "That way."

Car restarted, they drove a short distance and parked again. Mom gaped and peered. "It's certainly hard to miss!" *The Living Light Healing Center*—the sign heralded—with its impressive risqué red and plum colors—canted as well, albeit it only slightly.

Warily, Mom eyed the place. "You expect me to be OK with this?"

"You insisted on coming."

Sigh heaved, Mom pulled down the visor to apply lipstick. "Daddy and I used to fight over you. Modeling school was his idea; he wanted you to be more ladylike. I said to leave you alone, that you were just fine, and so we argued.

"Probably you don't recall, but I left him once, put a note in his briefcase and took off. He had to cope with chores, laundry, meals, and take care of you alone. When I got back, he was terribly grim. We never fought about anything but you." Mom gave a weak smile. "Honey... You were so different; I figured nobody had the right to squelch it." Lauren stared, oddly thrilled.

"I had no idea!"

"So once again"—reaching out, she gave her daughter a pat—"I'm trying not to interfere."

Actually, Mom tried to thwart the trip, termed it "foolhardy," said Lauren "chased a mere fantasy." She offered to speak with Uncle Nate, an internist with connections that might lead to employment, and even encouraged her to get rehired at The Foundation. In the end, Mom had called back, voice a-tremble, and said, "At very least, I insist on coming along."

Car exited, the two women entered The Living Light. The receptionist glanced up from filing her nails. "Do you have an appointment?"

"I...I didn't know we needed one," Lauren stammered.

Quick shrug, the receptionist resumed nail filing.

Given such unprofessional staff; the waiting hordes who populated chairs and rested on mats, filling every space imaginable; the hubbub of fretful children as well—none of it as hoped for or imagined—Lauren's heart sank. "This can't be right." Tug to Mom's arm, they headed for the door.

A pencil-thin brunette coughed violently; Lauren absorbed the deep purple of the woman's lips then closely surveyed the scene.

Some folks hunched in wheelchairs. Several bore vacant staring looks. Cheeks quivering and drenched, one woman convulsed into a tissue. Several lay on cots along the wall, a couple were strapped to oxygen tanks, and one had an intravenous drip.

This room, she realized, *overflowed with the desperately ill!*

Gentle swaying above caught her eye.

That beatific face—the exact same angel she'd seen years prior—regarded her warmly!

Gripping Mom's sleeve, she dragged her back. "Name's Finch. We called two days ago to say we'd be here."

The receptionist jabbed a finger at the schedule. "Don't see you.—We're full-up."

Mom took over. "We'll make an appointment now."

"You're too late." The woman resumed nail filing.

"We've come a long way," Mom persisted. "Can we at least be seen tomorrow?"

"I can't do anything today."

Lauren shrunk to wafer-size. Mom warmed into rage. "You're certainly inflexible; the way you treat people is an absolute disgrace!"

"See this room;"—the woman waved, blasé—"it's full of sob stories…every last one."

"I can't believe—" Mom readied to give the woman a shake.

"Thank you, Lucy," the serenest voice intercepted. "I'll see them now."

Smoke clogged the air as a man emerged from the hall. Gaze skimmed over Mom, coming to rest upon Lauren, the fellow stubbed a cigarette into a desktop ashtray and stared intently. "You've come," he said and kept on staring.

Briefly, something flared in his eyes. His intensity wasn't uncomfortable, just odd. "Sorry about that," he indicated the receptionist who glared at him now. "And welcome. I'm Walker Judson."

Heart pounding triple-time, forcefully Lauren exhaled. *Have you any idea,* she wanted to blurt, *how hard, how long, I've worked to find you?*

Within arm's reach of the very person she oftentimes suspected she'd merely conjured into being, struck by pure happiness, she squeezed herself. "I'm Lauren; this is my mother, Catherine. I need your help."

"So I gather." Tension around his eyes eased up a bit; his gaze continued to hold.

Resplendent with human decency, just as remembered, she felt she knew this man quite well. Except, lush wavy hair aside, this Mr. Judson seemed ordinary. She remembered him as tall. This guy was nearly her height. She remembered him as older, but the man before her appeared wearily aged.

She wished him more relaxed, casual, free-flowing, open, but everything about this man—the suit, his crisply pressed shirt, his careful expression—seemed tightly held. Yet this tight cautious aspect also relieved her immensely.

The longer she stared, the more complex he became. His face, brimmed with suffering, crimped her heart so badly, she nearly wailed. She saw anger too, though plainly, he tried to surmount it.

Given his aura of overall goodness, the anger surprised her. It was his anger, she sensed, that would spur him to fight for her. She liked this; it made him more human and also made him seem slightly dangerous.

Curiosity flickered his face as he scanned her up and down. He seemed to absorb her full height; if her spine were straight. And...He saw all of her—that she was hot-headed, often unbearably silly, and not exactly pleased to be herself.

Glamor-puss she was not. Good old Mom insisted she had an interesting collarbone and kind eyes: charitable words, since little else merited mention. Oh, the healer saw a crooked young woman all right, unlovely of face, prodigious splash of freckles, folded body that listed precariously. But also, she desperately hoped, he saw promise.

No longer feeling plain or dull, she thrust out her hand. "Glad to meet you."

He took it in both of his.

She braced for a power surge, an affirming jolt.

None came.

Hand retracted, Mr. Judson gestured. "Let us begin."

Never mind that what happened between them made a giant hole that they both fell into, face, hurting from a full-force smile, hugely glad, Lauren followed.

Chapter Eighteen: Walker

A rare spare moment, adult Walker floated, mildly dizzy, and then, fast as a blink, bi-located, departing home and surrounds to check on Ma. As he arrived, he saw her jump, dangle, swing from a tree branch, hoist onto a limb, wrap legs round the trunk, climb upward, and then pause, getting a glimpse overhead. With ten more feet to go, steadily, she inched skyward.

Atop the tree, she sucked breath. It was night; the moon, at its biggest, illumined the sky. Perched in the cottonwood, tilted over cliff's edge, she studied her surroundings.

Barn and farmhouse visible in the distance, her view of the gully, where scrub sought purchase on steep ledges and the dry creek bed, meandering at the bottom of a hundred-foot drop, held greatest sway.

With one arm round the trunk, Ma unfastened her sweater, shed, then gripped it. Zipper slid down, dress shimmied overhead, she let those garments drop. Socks yanked off, she released them as well. Each one bounced, striking branches as they fell. Undergarments peeled from flesh, she gave them a toss. Whitish blur hitting a branch, it snagged and flapped.

Eyes shut, Ma, leaned into tree's trunk to emit a prayer: "Forgive me, Lord, for I have sinned mightily." Still gripping, she did the sign of the cross, then, arms bunched—Walker watching—flung herself aloft.

Briefly freed from context she arose to float among meshed tree branches. Then, she paused. Seconds she hung there, gravity not yet attuned to its task.

Yet, rather than fly as hoped, she plummeted and tumbled, all legs, knees, arms, elbows.

Smack! She struck a branch and spun, head over heels.

Filmy mist oozed out—her soul, possibly; wafted into the dark.

Thwack! Reconnected to earth, bounced off cliff and rock, her arm snapped; the world blinked out.

Walker watched, helpless.

Must not interact; Divine Rules insisted. Violate this, and permission to observe got revoked.

Shortly, Ma came to, cast deep into a heap of leaves.

Dragged onto a ledge, breezes rustling, there she lay, panting. "Think I'll ever fly?" she queried the night air.

Starry swath brimming overhead, bats careened and screeched. Winds whispered, clattering, yet night itself stayed silent.

She called out again, perfectly cogent, "Son, I feel you near, and, for the record...I still believe in God, because it's intolerable not to. It's just my fault that He's so remote."

Walker squeezed his fists. *Always, she blamed herself!*

Arm clutched to chest, she checked for lacerations, of which there were many. Rocks skittering, she groped for purchase, slid, grabbed an up-thrust root, righted herself, and then made her way up the slope.

Up-top, bare of foot and divested of garb, Ma plodded through brush, located a path, snaked her way home, taking the porch steps into the house.

Walker espied mountains of mail: stacks covered counters; dirty dishes towered above. No place to rest his gaze, although he'd long known of her penchant, the visual accretion of clutter astounded.

Ma waded through the heaps, went past the man who dozed on the couch, puffing cheeks and flubbering lips as he expelled air. "'Night, Hollis," she muttered as she slowly climbed stairs.

Arm ballooned, clearly in pain, she shoved papers from the mattress, clambered into bed, pulled up covers and lay there. "'Night, son," she called out. "Appreciate having you near."

What sort of Father ignores His most loyal daughter? railed Walker. *And what sort of Father ignores prayerful pleas, allows her to be beaten, overlooks her suffering and heaps still more agony upon her?*

No loving Father, certainly!

Ma sensed his thoughts. "God isn't always terribly nice, son."

Sorry for his mother, for her sickness of spirit, dearly Walker longed to give comfort! But the rules forbade it.

Next day, Walker reached back out to extend time and place, checking as to how Ma fared.

Gingerly, Ma probed her arm. Aches blooming everywhere, she winced as she touched."I know secrets of the universe," she announced. "I've heard stars roar, swirling, alive. I've seen planets spin spirals. I've met God. He called me by name. And yet, I'm a complete ignoramus."

Sensing yet something more amiss, she pushed up, fumbled to the mirror and peered into it.

"Oh, my!" Hands flying to her face, she quaked and trembled. Walker saw too; his heart sunk.

"Who—what—is this creature?" she peeked between fingers to inquire of her visage.

Overnight, appearance much changed, her right eyeball protruded, about to tumble from its socket. "A test," she muttered, "or tiny crisis of spirit, perhaps?"

To Walker's mind, he stood abruptly, crossing the room to console her.

For real, he could not. Anyway, she'd refuse him.

Pawing, using both hands, Ma mashed her eyeball into place.

Improperly aligned, it flopped from its socket again.

Unable to let up lest it slip, if she prayed just right, it stayed properly affixed.

Subsequent days, without food or respite, Ma would paw and pray, unceasingly.

Hopeless as it was, never did it occur to her to simply give up.

Returned from his altered state, sickened, enraged, varied thoughts transited Walker's brain. *Was Ma mental?* He wasn't sure. *Was she suicidal?* He did not know. *Was she being tested?*

If this were God's plan, her knowing this to be so might make her anguish bearable.

Chapter Nineteen: Young Walker

Never, subsequent to that enlightening day, did Ma speak to the boy of Catholicism again. Always, he hoped she might, yet when he broached the topic, she shushed him, sent him on chores, or scurried off.

Ma *did* know that he prayed. Times she caught his lips moving silently, she suppressed a grin and twinkled fingers at him. Ripple effects of the cheery change that overtook him actually made her stand straighter and seem less tense.

Mornings, after milking the cows, as boy ambled about in the fields, he sensed Ma's inquisitiveness radiating out as if a giant, watchful eye. Chest puffed, he'd strut smartly, immensely pleased.

Certain that his church foray had piqued Ma's—and God's—interest, the boy turned downright spiritual. He believed in God with all his might: that God's perfection resided within all beasts, within all things, and thus, that every object, every being, seemed a prayerful thing. Nature's wondrous intricacies raised perpetual cause for prayer; humans, plants, animals—even inanimate objects such as rocks—all warranted invocation. Therein budded his lifelong beliefs.

Days he wandered alone, praying, thanking, every spare moment. Steam puffing from his favorite Holstein's fist-size nostrils, heat emanating from its flanks, the boy curled up alongside and sniffed it. Nothing else smelt so swell; he gave thanks.

A hawk's feather dropped from the sky to drift, gently, into his hands; he thanked God that the feather gave the bird flight, that the bird donated it, and that he now enjoyed it.

One night, bedroom curtains rustling, he sensed a presence.

Gradually, The Angel materialized and spoke, "I am here to guide you."—Words, not conveyed by lips or sound, but transmitted directly into his head.

"Who are you?"

"I am your heart."

"Same as the angel in the church?"

"Yes and no."

Thereafter, The Angel stayed by his side to advise, to direct, and to console.

Uncertain as to its needs, he snuck table scraps for it and shared his bed. Come morning, he'd find himself squeezed onto the edge of an empty mattress.

With The Angel's help, he saw varied light emanate from others. Colors perfectly matched to Ma and Pa's inner beings frothed from them. Pa's light, treacle, dense—scarcely light at all—was a smeary sort. Ma's light, a golden glow, followed in her wake as she went about her business. Radiance such as hers signaled holy goodness, so, no way was she the monster she professed to be.

Light did not always come unbidden; he had to keep pure of thought to see it. If he looked too far off or entertained crabby thoughts, it eluded. Times he focused too intently or studied the mere surface of things, he missed it. If anxious or fearful, light faded out altogether. Squint and concentrate just right, varied luminescence haloed all.

Soul shadows, the boy termed them, radiated extra bright around young ones. Light enshrouding infants and small children, close in sharpness and beauty to Ma's, shone a deep purple: a sure sign of purity.

Light surrounding adults diminished noticeably as they aged. There was a single memorable exception: a wizened man going past in a truck swiveled to make eye contact. As a vast smile not only engaged the gent's whole face, but his entire body, the boy halted, dumbstruck. The old fellow's face about split open as more radiance spilled out.

Rushed home to share, Ma beat him to the punch. "Ask your fine friend to pitch in with the chores." She directed words to include something perched on his shoulder.

Mouth open, the boy gaped; being he had no friends, surely Ma knew of The Angel!

Chapter Twenty: Lauren

Footsteps clicking on floorboards, Mr. Judson took Lauren and Mom down the hall, selected a door, and ushered them inside. "Put on this gown," he directed. "I'll return shortly."

Gown donned, Lauren scooted onto the examining table. "What next?" she inquired as Mr. Judson re-entered.

"I check your energy field." Highly focused, gently he probed her neck.

"I know you can't do much, but my spine constantly hurts. My heart hurts. Everything—my life—er, pains me," she muttered, voice small, fading. Mom scraped her chair to table's edge.

"My daughter thinks you're the key to fixing her. She's thought so for years." Mr. Judson kept probing. Lauren tensed.

Did this guy really help that ailing man in the storefront church, or did I imagine it?

Protective hand placed on her daughter's arm, Mom implored, "Tell us, please, what you're doing?"

"We haven't started." Mr. Judson was quiet; his peaceful demeanor calmed the women somewhat. "Situations such as this, I use a specific pattern of touch. Unlike other procedures, though, sorry to say, this one may make you worse for a time.—You willing to risk it?" He pulled back to check.

Avoiding his look, Lauren hunched, terribly discouraged, mad even. Never had she imagined this would be a snap, yet she hadn't given thought to more pain.

"What happens is simple," he explained as he probed. "You don't do a thing. I just touch you in various places, and healing energy awakens."

Gradually, the exact same lulled state she'd felt years prior overtook her. Each press, she slumped further, until she leaned heavily into the healer's chest.

Voice hypnotic, Mr. Judson continued, "You may notice heat or tingling; it's part of the healing. Sensitive folks feel much more. It's fine if you fall asleep. You may get angry or cry—that's healing, as well." As if a spaniel shaking off water, he stepped back, shook his whole body, and flicked fingers. "We're ready now. You all right?"

"Uh...I guess." Lauren thought to ask how he'd managed to find her and if his visit during her hallucinogenic trip had been real.

"I reached through the ethers to find you," he confided, reading her thoughts.

Lauren spasmed, glancing up at him, bewildered.

"Lie down and we'll begin." Mr. Judson settled her on the table. Mom jumped up to help. "Sit please," he said firmly. Mom retreated to fidget. Lauren lay on her side, knees tucked. Sleeves rolled up to reveal well-muscled forearms, hands clasped, breath going slowly in and out, Mr. Judson surrendered his gaze skyward. Mom shot Lauren a fierce look. Lauren shrugged, apologetic, trying to hide her own freak-out.

Fear clawed anyhow. Surged with disillusionment, angel aside, no tangible sign informed as to the rightness of coming.

I am so dumb, so disappointed! Such a cock-a-mamy idea to come so far, to be so certain all these years that this odd man would fix me.

Get up, she chided inwardly, *tell Mr. Judson you've made a mistake, then go.*

Mind a-scramble, she conjured that long ago healing scene—how the shirtless patient breathed with ease and the amazing high she'd felt after.

Languor enveloped as air shuttled in and out her lungs. *We'll stay*, she resolved. *What other choice is there?*

Mr. Judson swept fingers across her skin, touched her eyelids, pressed her liver, kidneys, spleen—other places. Despite a modicum of calm achieved, thus far all seemed unspectacular. Yet his long fingers and neat, blunt nails *did* reassure her somewhat.

And no...His hands did not glow; they merely touched.

"Now, you must sit." Helped upright, Mr. Judson executed percussive claps to her back. Mom leaned in at his elbow, tensely watchful.

Sharp percuss to Lauren's tailbone, a powerful current raced up her spine. All body's cells humming, her head sought to unscrew from her neck. Possessed of a will all its own, twisting impossibly, her nob swiveled till she gazed behind herself.

Energy—a riotous, jagged trajectory—poured through; she sat terrorized. Mom bit back horror.

"Kundalini shakti," Mr. Judson explained. "Presently, these energies are surging up your spine. My job is to release blockages, to help its flow." Face close to Lauren's chest, he emitted a startling throaty growl.

Air gone wobbly, her head untwisted.

Mr. Judson's physical being—all defining boundaries—those separating Lauren from everything else—ceased. Then, an intangible force surged from the healer to enter her. Mom gasped and jumped.

Past and present existed all at once. Eons flew past in a blink. Lauren visited other worlds—many of them—and then, jettisoned back into her own skin, she returned.

Experience so strange, so terribly wondrous, so completely insane, her hands shot out to seek purchase.

Grabbing vacant air she fumbled. Mom too reached out. Mr. Judson waved her off. Lauren felt her mother's fear; her own terror skyrocketed as well.

This isn't the first time you've experienced this, she chided herself.

Mr. Judson cupped Lauren's heart and tenderly rocked her as a lover might. Sorrow, grief, an avalanche released. Wracked by mammoth, wrenching sobs, she convulsed and wept.

Again, Mom reached out. Again, Mr. Judson motioned her off. "It's all right," he coaxed Lauren, "let it come."

Harder, Lauren wailed. Tears coursed Mom's cheeks as well.

Gently, Mr. Judson stroked Lauren's hair and face. "Stay with it. Let it out. Keep it coming."

Lauren's whimpers ebbed; Mr. Judson eased her back down. "We're done for now. You both did fine." Face aglow with unbearable softness, he seemed perfectly refreshed. Lauren on the other hand, lay there stunned.

No ready fix, subtle or overt, she felt far worse.

Hand rested atop Lauren's heart, Mr. Judson elucidated, "Kundalini energies remain dormant throughout most people's lives. Unlike most, though, you're waking up. When these energies activate, impurities from this lifetime and other lives, areas of weakness, illness, pain, suffering, unfinished business, come to the fore. Our work here is to teach you to channel these energies.

"Although these forces don't adhere to a specific schedule, I'm told that we can facilitate their release by treating you every four hours, round the clock, until the currents stabilize. I'll come at required times, but it would be easiest if you stay here so that I can monitor your progress."

Protective hand laid on her daughter, Mom said, "I'm scared this is a mistake."

"This is about faith." Mr. Judson soothed; he shot Lauren a speculative look. "In time, you'll understand."

As he eased Lauren upright, her body shifted, felt fluid and actually seemed to melt and dissolve. Terribly afraid, deeper she tumbled.

Thankfully, Mr. Judson held onto her.

Mom and Mr. Judson helping, Lauren tottered onto her feet to stagger about, and then they moved to a room where she would live for subsequent weeks.

Many years, Lauren's raggedy faith had guided her to seek this man. Faith, in her case meant belief, despite fear and questioning that cried out for succor. So, at long last, the agonizing process of her restructuring had begun.

Chapter Twenty-One: Young Walker

Six weeks subsequent to the boy's church visit, a black sedan rattled up the drive. Peeking from an upstairs window, the boy spotted the priest unfurl from the car, mustered his voice, and leaned out. "Sir, Mr. Priest. Up here."

The priest glanced up, shaded his eyes, and waved. "Say, young fellow!"

"Wait there, please. I'll come down."

Onto the porch came Ma. "Lordy!" she whimpered, then quickly covered, "Afternoon, Father. What a surprise!"

"May I come in?" Finger jabbed at his neck, the priest loosened his collar.

"Ah. Well." The boy envisioned Mom frantically checking Pa's whereabouts. "I guess so."

The priest disappeared onto the porch.

"Whatever happened,"—Ma said in a push—"is my fault."

"Recently," the priest soothed, "I met your fine son. Today, I was in the neighborhood, so I thought I'd pay a visit."

"I'll take whatever I deserve," offered Ma.

"It's not like that, ma'am."

"Please God," the boy implored walls of his room. "Don't hurt Ma!"

God's fiendish reply, heavy vibrations, came along below. Whap of screen door, floorboards groaned as Pa crossed over, disappeared into the kitchen, and then returned.

Muffled voices, chairs scraped. "Ohhhh!" moaned the boy, casting about, frantic. Unable to move, he envisioned the scene. Ma, Pa, and the priest sitting awkwardly. Pa, kicked back on the sofa. Ma, rigidly attentive. The priest in the only comfy chair. Ma offering tea, comporting her rare smiley face. Pa casual-like, but seething beneath. The bewildered priest taking in the rubble.

They'd plunge into niceties.

Fine day, but too hot for spring. Think it'll rain? Weatherman says probably not.

Awkward silence, then the priest would launch into the purpose for his visit—saving their souls. He'd blurt a heap of words, shape them into something sensible, graciously informing Ma and Pa that they'd been remiss, and then offer to cleanse and save them.

Ma would cringe but paste up a sickly smile. Muscles bunched, Pa would menace.

"Come down, son," Ma called up the stairs, using her overly cheery voice.

Frozen in place, shirtsleeves cuffed up to elbows, the boy's feet disowned him.

Rise and fall of yakking drifting up through the floor. Ma's voice fluttery. Priest's voice pressing, amiable, yet adamant. Pa emitting a mishmash of utterances: no exasperated articulations, no sharp raised pronouncements.

So far so good!

Except Pa, being a quick to boil sort, one moment reasonable, relaxed, the next moment he'd erupt.

Palms sweaty, the boy heard his own ragged breath and the thump-thump of his hammering heart.

Ma, at the banister, called again, "Join us, son."

Unable to oblige, the boy stayed rooted.

Floorboards vibrated. Screen banged, Pa's heavy footfall crossed the porch. Truck door slammed, engine revved, off he sped.

"Oh me!" moaned the boy.

Footfall again, a lighter twosome went down the steps. "Nice of you to stop by," twittered Ma. "I'll consider your suggestions." Car door slammed, an engine coughed to life.

The boy sprang to the window, tried to call out, but his throat bunched. Dust eddying its wake, the sedan went up the drive. Dread—relief too—drew down upon the boy.

Hasty footsteps reentered. Cupboards banged. Foot trod through the kitchen, the living room, and hall, Ma clumped about.

Squeak, squeak—footsteps on stairs, in she barged, rucksack in hand, white-faced, saucer-eyed.

"What?" he inquired.

"Why didn't you come?" She thrust the sack at him.

"Ss...Sorry, Ma."

"Didn't expect this." Her dentures clacked, hard.

"I'll…," the boy groped. "I'll make it right. I promise. I'll…"

Ma stopped him cold. "You must go." Figuring she had a chore in mind, he sat to don shoes. "Go," she insisted, "before Pa returns!" She yanked him up. "Hurry!"

"Ma!"

Eyes wild, she screeched, "Go on—go!" Cuffed into the hall, she shoved him downstairs onto the porch to the bottommost step. "Here."—She thrust cash at him—"It's all I have."

"I'll sleep in the barn."

"That priest is exactly what Pa can't stand."

"I don't see why—"

"Leave, else Pa'll kill you." She pummeled him. "Go!"

Protecting from blows, the boy stood his ground. "I did what you asked. Thought it would help!"

"Can't you understand?" She grabbed and marched him to the drive. "I don't want you!"

Breathless and stupid, he stumbled, stubbing a toe. Ma kept shoving, slapped his face, his head. Down the road they went. Hoping to change her mind, he groped for her. "Hurry! Go!" she shrieked.

Hard to make his feet move, he told himself, *These are my legs and they should obey me.*

Again, Ma shoved.

Finally, cordially, feet obliging, rucksack slung onto shoulder, each step ragged, legs, ankles, feet, toes propelling him, at hill's crest, he looked back. Ma, now dot size, waved him onward. He hated her then—hated with all his might, and then descended into the dark alone.

Chapter Twenty-Two: Walker

Sunlight streamed in as Walker and Rosalee slurped tea in companionable silence, steeling themselves for the day's coming demands. "You have great sadness, my son," noted Rosalee. "I do not know where it comes from, or why it exists, but you must set it down."

"Easier said than done."

Rosalee met his gaze. "Yes, but you must try."

In truth, Walker had never felt better. Whereas before he'd always observed from the outside, he now actively participated in the great flow of life. To inhabit an existence, one he'd so longed for, dread had changed to joy for him. Briefly, from time to time, however, that familiar companion, grief, *did* creep up and claim him.

Walker stood, shed his coat, and rolled up sleeves. "Almost time."

"Always, you like to change the subject!"

Good old indispensable Rosalee! The Living Light sprang to life from her motherly efforts. She worked her herbal practice, answered phones, greeted patients, and sought to make their long wait tolerable. Moreover, she meant the world to him.

Given his abysmal relations with Delia—Walker calling to see how she fared—her slamming the receiver down—he gave thanks for Rosalee. Without her generosity, none of his present life would be possible.

Room air clogged with haze, smells of newly mown hay invading, the tiniest fellow, accompanied by a leashed cat, congealed before them.

Eyes glided over Rosalee and Walker, the man smartly saluted The Angel above, "Greetings."

"Can we help you?" Walker inquired.

"We have met."

"Oh?" Walker puzzled, then thrust out a hand. "I'm Walker Judson."

"During your travels." Neglecting to take Walker's hand, the fellow, produced, unwrapped a candy bar, and chomped it down, steadily.

Brows raised, Rosalee and Walker stared.

"Voden Fucols has been asked to help. This is Silly," he indicated the cat.

"So it is." Walker bent to scratch Silly.

The cat, fat and orange, stepped out of reach to glare, balefully, so Walker turned back to size up their newcomer.

A sight to behold, melancholy air about the man, hat now shed, hair cupped his head like a bowl. Dashiki shirt hung well past his knees, paisley patches quilted his bell-bottom jeans, and slogan-bearing campaign buttons festooned his pork-pie hat. *Nixon's the One! Get a Life! I like IKE!:* the buttons rabble-roused. White gloves graced his hands; he would never go without.

Similar to Walker, but far more lax, Voden wore eccentric attire. Socks went unmated, not due to inability to match a pair but because he preferred the look.

What do you think, have I done OK? This nonsensical thought skidded into Walker's brain; yet still, he longed to ask.

"Mr. Fucols must inform you that it is time to begin a school."

Bemused, Walker sat back. "What am I to teach, then?"

"You are to lead others on a spiritual path, imparting knowledge as it is given to you." Walker checked for jest. "So...," this Voden Fucols fellow concluded, "you shall start immediately."

"Let me think on it." Truth be told, Walker dreaded the idea. Heading up a school would further pinch his time. Yet spread of his work as part of The Plan was inevitable.

A lighted sphere formed to ascend the stairs and hover near The Angel.

Walker's heart accelerated. Something definitive clicked into place as the threesome's heartbeats linked up. Walker stood, somber, watchful. Rosalee leaned, hip canted, bursting with smiles. Voden Fucols looked on, also somber, yet proudly comical.

Steady rhythmic pulsings, and immense feeling shaped as the triumvirate birthed.

Walker stole Rosalee a peek.

Cheeks pinked up, she met his eye.

Grin swallowed, Walker inquired, "So you'll be staying?"

"Hee-hee-hee," Rosalee burst into giggles. "Certainly, he is!"

"'Tis the plan," Voden Fucols chimed. As if they shared a significant secret, Rosalee grinned broadly at the fellow.

"You know him?" Walker inquired.

Rosalee burst forth anew, tee-he-heeing. "I just guessed someone important would come."

"'Twas foreordained," Voden added, never cracking a smile.

A rush, elation, arched out from Walker's chest. As one who grasped matters of subtle content, it seemed inexplicable that Voden Fucols's arrival could mean so much.

Chapter Twenty-Three: Lauren

Over the next two months, daily, at precise four-hour intervals, Mr. Judson returned. Each session, Lauren came unglued and wept piteously. "You're so brave," Mr. Judson encouraged. "Don't fight it. That's right...Let it come." Hair rucked up, snot dripping, sweating one moment, shivering the next, Lauren bawled big-time.

As Mr. Judson ran fingers along her spine, she thought, huffily, *How can this flesh-on-flesh contact possibly fix me?*

"Most ill bodies are like batteries that can't hold a charge," Mr. Judson's voice seemed so hypnotic, she thought she might like a nap. "—That's where I come in; I supply the juice for a recharge." Powerfully, gently, she sensed his eyes sliding about inside her, having a look around.

He seemed to move about in there, tickling, itching, bumping into gray matter in search of something. Exceedingly strange...Actually, she kinda liked it. "Do you...Are you inside me?"

Hands paused at her upper spine, he veered off. "Your assemblage point is blocked. It's causing your extreme symptoms, so I'm unclogging it. Soon as it opens, your pain will reduce, and you'll move easily between different levels of reality." He tapped her neck; slight churning, a tiny whirling vortex reared up.

Her torso felt breezy, which was odd, since she wore clothes. Skin at her back began to vibrate and slough off, grappling with her bones. Entire spine now sucked into that vortex, it flung hot, tight pain out and away.

Tilting, off-kilter, she grabbed Mr. Judson's arm. Mom lurched and gasped. As if to prevent her brains from flying out, Mr. Judson tightly pressed her brow. "That's it...Let your cells rearrange themselves." Heat gushed out his fingertips; warmth spread into her chest, then filled her belly. Steadily, her body inflated and rose to the ceiling where it gently bounced about.

And then...Bit by bit, spinal pain eased up, she felt nearly normal. "Thank you for fixing me!" she blurted. Then as usual, she wept.

Between sessions, she slept hours on end. When briefly awake, too scared to ask Mom's opinion of the goings-on, she blocked all thought.

Room clabbered with unwashed body odors, between tears and sweat—the flooding, endless—busily, Mom changed bed sheets as swiftly as Lauren drenched them. Mostly, Lauren felt as if hurricane-force winds swept through to churn and spin her. Body rippling, snapping, a tendril often broke loose, and she felt herself fragment into billions of particles.

Does this, she wondered, *mean I'm dying?*

Telepathic rapport overtook her as water swirled down the drain. *You're a freak! You're ugly!* Blah, blah, blah and so forth, it chortled, repeating the exact same taunts she'd always heard, only amplified.

Those were good days.

Bad days, outer dermal layer peeled back, all nerve fibers exposed, movement, noise, lights, colors overwhelmed. When she pushed too hard, moved too fast, or exaggerated even slightly, loathsome creatures blurted up from dark recesses to scurry about and infest her brain.

Remainder of her life, spine serving as her personal barometer, each time she'd exaggerate, veer from truth, or willfully push too hard, her spine gave a twang, steering her back on track.

A tiny Asian woman appeared one day to place a smelly herbal packet into Lauren's palm. "For you to ingest," the woman garbled as if her mouth held marbles; she had buckteeth and appeared to be chewing. Lauren stared at her hand, then back at the woman. "It will smooth excitable nerves," the woman chirped, then she turned to Mom to hand over a similar packet. "Energy for your pooped adrenals."

Eyes traveling to and from the packets, Lauren and Mom regarded this person, curious.

"Excuse me, please! I, Rosalee Soo, am very pleased to meet you." Twittering, very friendly, as if morphed into *Alice in Wonderland's*

White Rabbit, the woman glanced at her watch, did a nudge, a wink, gave Lauren a pat, and then scurried off.

Subsequent weeks, Rosalee Soo arrived daily to dispense more packets. Each time, as if inducting Lauren and her mother into a secret society, she performed her exact same nudge, wink, pat, and then departed.

Arms linked, Mom and Lauren set off one day for The Overlook, a glorious hillside precipice. Liberal with rest stops, they went down Main Street until arrived at cliff's edge.

Sun rays beating down, they unlatched and gazed out. Easily, the valley and surrounding mountain range spanned a hundred miles across. Likely, prehistoric man stood at this exact spot, gulped in the magnificent scenery, and yowled.

"Being here," Mom began, "has given me loads of time to think. And until now, I've been and done exactly what everyone else expected of me; been the perfect wife and mother, terrific cook, and loyal friend. But, I tell you what..." Eagerly, she clasped her daughter's hand. "Just once...Rather than worry about everyone else, I'd like to find something I really love and do it.—I just have no idea what..." Mom's pale face, a-throb with longing; Lauren flushed with love for her.

"Also, this business here has me wondering. Mr. Judson speaks of healing energies; you gobble it up as if you're onto something spectacular. Lately, I haven't the slightest idea who you are, and it scares me." She paused, waiting.

Lauren reached for a smooth red stone, put it to her cheek. Sun's warmth within, she gave it a sniff—it smelt of heat—then she pocketed it.

"You still do that?" Mom asked mildly concerned.

"I just want to be normal, Mom—but also, I want to be special."

Terrible smile formed; plainly, Mom hated this. "I'm trying to put aside my fear for you." Brief pause, then decisive, she leaned to brush hair from her daughter's brow. "Do whatever your heart desires, love, without compromise."

Flushed with feeling, Lauren saw how staunchly this woman rose to support her and that she'd asked her to accept matters she scarcely grasped herself. "I want to heal people, Mom," she muttered, wistful."I want to do good, to be filled with God.—To...to be a holy person."

Mom's arms tight around her, Lauren envisioned energy lick her own innards as waves might. Bubbly froth coursing her belly, it flowed into her breasts, arms, head, filling them. Then busy molecules set to work, rearranging, fixing all deformed cells—every last one.

At least, she wished it.

Twosome settled onto the bench, Mom swiveled to gaze at her. "You, sweetheart, act like you've stumbled onto a big secret."

"Maybe," Lauren said coyly.

"Are you staying?"

Weeks on end, Mom had cared for her. Now, given Mr. Judson's vigilant ministrations—Lauren sensed he'd make certain her body kept on healing, even if he had to crawl in there to push, pump, and repair it by hand—so Mom was free to go home.

"Mr. Judson—ah, he insists I call him Walker—welcomes me to stay. Eventually, I can work with him." As if a female Rip Van Winkle, awoken from long slumber, Lauren chafed, eager for her life to start.

Light speared the clouds. God glinted everywhere as joy dumped into her.

Hands megaphoned to mouth, Lauren hollered, "Yoo-hoo—I'm home!" Voice echoing into the valley, doves—thousands—swarmed up and soared off.

Chapter Twenty-Four: Young Walker

Wretched with indecision, unsure where to go or what to do, scarcely able to set one foot in front of the other, the boy walked on for days. He hunched in culverts, stole pies off porches, slept in barns, and felt utterly lost.

Why did Ma cast me out? Am I so insignificant that she could just let me go?

Never mind that Pa would've killed him...or so she claimed—she could have figured a way to keep him if she'd wanted to.

Gone two months, he came to a footbridge that spanned a powerful, wide river. Air roiling with fury, twelve or so Negroes, each face a void, stood on the embankment. Whites, all men, took up the side opposite. As if assembled for a Sunday picnic, the whites mingled and strolled about, shirtsleeves rolled-up, collars unbuttoned. Most carried a club or a stick; several toted rifles. Every so often, the puss-bellied sheriff, leaned over the bridge rail and spat. "Don't let that rope slip," he cautioned his men.

A young Negro male stood on the rail, wrists trussed at his back. A noose draped at his neck to wrap the girder above. Shirt and pants shredded, face and flanks a bloody pulp, he quaked, teetered, and tottered, trying to steady himself.

Despite rushing waters creating quite a racket, the boy heard the distinct wild thumpings of the young man's heart, which set his own heart banging in accord.

Eyes wild, the Negro met his gaze. Despair—the young Colored's—flared. Despair so bad, that the boy wanted to yell—to beg.

Yet no words came.

Gaze dropped in shame, he knew the Negro willed that they reengage, yet the boy could not bear it.

"Ready set!" came the call to commence.

Whites and Coloreds surged the riverbank to eye each other, warily.

Taking his own sweet time, the sheriff blotted sweat from his brow, then sharply sliced, signaling, "Ay-yup!"

Two whites stepped forth, shoved the Negro, then hove on slack rope.

The rope slapped back to hit steel uprights.

No twitch, nor shudder, the Colored man crashed back.

Seconds prior to the thrash—*whump*—the hollow clangor, and that great and final outrush of air, the boy had reached in to snatch up the young Negro's soul. So now, countenance placidly at peace, body lengthened, hands oddly outstretched, only an empty shell remained.

Coloreds stood there, tightly muzzled. Whites looked on, bewildered, wondering, not feeling much like letting out a great satisfied shout. Several folks of both races removed hats and held them.

A young Negro woman yipped small screams. Her people restrained her. She broke free, flailed and slapped, was caught again, then emitted a deafening, croaking wail.

In a year's time, hoping matters might've improved, the boy stole back home and stood outside the kitchen window to lurk beneath the eaves.

He saw Pa bunch fists, bring them down to strike Ma.

Again, again, he pounded. Ma knelt, hands up to pray...or to fend blows.

Breath fast, shallow, perfect chance to make his presence known, the boy thought to bust in and save her.

Off Pa stormed. Ma stood, wiped her face, tidied her hair, moved a pot from the stove, set dinner on the table, paused, cocked her head and sniffed. "Who's there?" she called, stared straight at her son, flogged air, and yelled, "Get away from here!"

Ducked from sight, the boy scampered down the drive and kept running.

What surprised him was not Ma's rejection this time but how much it still pained him.

Quick glance back, though, he'd have seen Ma press back sobs to silence a scream. Had he looked, all would've changed. Everything!

Chest singed with pain, onward he forced himself. He tramped through brush—went on for days. Months. Years, ultimately.

With a sense of inner disfigurement as his most loathsome companion, he felt hideously severed, rather than whole. Figuring his suffering to be richly deserved, crazily, he lashed himself, howled loudly, but never permitted tears.

Arrived upon grim, meager lands, a dry parched place where folks clung together and loved one another, he happened upon a farmer who invited, "Stay with us."

Amazed by inclusion, the boy stayed on as a farmhand, lived among the farmer's family, toiled, and partook of their communal bowl. And, seeking to absorb their connectedness, he studied their ways.

Steadily, the stoic farmer wove a watchful, protective web round his boisterous, commingled kin. Profound respect, tenderness, adoration and joy arose between young and old. Wearily, lovingly, the ma gathered up her infant to suckle it. Kids rassled, squealing, limbs intertwined, tumbling in dust, then kissed each other's bruised shins. Such casual, raucous interplay astounded him.

When Grandma died, radiant light streamed out from her skull's top; all received strength from it.

What would it be like to love as they did?

For that, he'd give all.

The farmer's barn burnt down; neighbors assembled to rebuild.

A week later, pestilence ravaged the crops, so folks left food anonymously.

When their infant died, the boy hollered at the sky, "God, don't you care about your creations?"

Silence roared back, so he railed again, "Why, Lord, do you ignore these good people?"

Silence again. He flailed and taunted, infuriated, "You're a cruel, stupid, uncaring God!" This seemed unwise; he felt unconcerned. "Stop hurting your people!" Insane gleam in his eye, he kept on insulting, denouncing.

Eyes darting, the farmer, checking skies for a punishing thunderclap, took him aside. "You must leave us now."

No friendly leave-taking, ties fully severed, bag packed, off the boy slunk.

On the tramp again, the boy, deeming God to be inattentive, ceased to pray. Pray or not, humans suffered anyway, so what was the point?

The Angel, his sole source of guidance and comfort, he now chalked its existence up to childish invention, and pushed it away.

His other gift, his ability to see what others could not—once a source of such wonder—seemed to serve little everyday purpose, so he clamped down to ignore it, till it gradually faded away.

An interval of tuning drew down upon him; he began to resonate with worldly harshness. His own personal darkness, once unearthed, he found to be deeper than imagined. So, seeking to bury this shadow self, to keep his rage at bay, he deliberately numbed his heart and chest.

After years of disconnect, thinness, loneliness, eventually a hole would appear in the region of his heart. This hole, the perfect match to the hole in his psyche—he hated to be touched there—as a mother-hungry son, the hole in his heart was where his mother-hunger festered.

Chapter Twenty-Five: Walker

Screen door slammed, Walker stepped into The Stop just as a woman, wearing the baggiest chin-to-ankle dress, transacted business at the cash register. "Morning, Miss Wilkins." Walker touched his brow.

The woman dipped her head, muttering; Walker thought she said, "We don't like what you're doing to our town." Miss Wilkins, some sort of therapist, well-known about town, didn't much like him. Each time he ran into her and attempted a nicety, she snarled.

Voice disturbingly shrill, she addressed Clayton Lynch, store proprietor, "Thanks for your help. I really must be off." Refusing to meet Walker's eye, she went out. The men watched her depart; Clayton clucked once.

"Say, Clayton," joshed Walker, "sold any worms?"

Night Crawlers: Fish Bait, heralded the overhead sign. No lake, nor stream within miles, Clayton, who claimed to appreciate slime, sold worms anyhow.

"You got me!" Papers deftly scooped from countertop onto a shelf below, Clayton grinned broadly. "So...What brings you in?"

"Smokes." Walker slapped money down. "I'll take a carton of Camels. That...and a favor."

Grin narrowed, Clayton's face shut down. "Favor?"

"Yup." Walker paused, very still. Clayton's face shimmered, curious. "Given so many disabled are coming to The Living Light, curbed sidewalks would greatly improve handicapped access."

Clayton worked his jaw. "What about the town, the effect you're having?"

"Those coming *do* increase traffic," Walker agreed, deliberately dense.

Clayton, developing the keenest interest in a sliver embedded in his palm, dug away at it, muttering, "Traffic's not the half of it."

"As mayor do you suppose you might help?"

Clayton glanced up; anger surfaced, then dispersed. "Gee…" He fussed with, then bit into his hand. "City Council just voted in the first-ever stoplight. I'd like to pave over the vacant lot next to The Five and Dime for sorely needed parking and hire new police officers—four would 'bout do it. Where we'll find money, I haven't the foggiest."

Courtesy of newfound affluence generated by The Living Light, several businesses now underwent renovation. Leticia Opplinger's hung daring new beige awnings, and artisans jacked up prices, fetching unseemly sums for homely clay pots and timid ink scratchings.

As both men knew, increased revenue from parking tickets alone would easily fund the stoplight and pave that lot. "Much obliged if you'd see to that upgrade." Walker latched on, steadily regarding the shopkeep. Clayton stared back, mesmerized.

Abruptly snapped out of it, uncertain what hit him, Clayton cast about. "Uh...Let me think on it."

Grin suppressed, Walker scooped up the cigarettes and departed.

Earlier that morning at The Living Light, Walker sat in his third floor room.

Chomp, chomp—he munched away, tight, precise—on a cheese and radish sandwich.

Door bumped open, hair fanned out, there stood the girl, awkward, inquisitive.

"Yes?" He arched a brow.

"I've been too much of a mess to clarify before this, but do you, for sure, remember me from years ago? I was fifteen, wore a brace; we met in that church." As her words spilled out, tiny sunlit particles jiggled, dancing the airspace between them.

Easily Walker recalled those indelible moments. No paradigm of femininity, not pretty in the slightest, that contraption—the brace—stiffened her body to hold it in place. Briefly, confusion as to the goings-on had damped down her inner light, but quickly, its brilliance reasserted itself as an energetic cloud had spit off from her: the biggest he'd ever seen. His heart, at the time, hurt at sight of her. Hurt in a good way, that is. "'Course I do," he said more gruffly than intended.

"Well, ah, I'm so glad that I've found you." Arms flailing, words failed her.

"That's fine, then."

"Er." She gathered herself with urgency. "My mom leaves next week. I'd like to stay on to help—to become a healer...if you'll teach me." Oddly moved, he rejoiced.

Yes, I'll teach you. You'll be mine to shape.

Noting the ragged energy that coursed through her body, he still saw much work to be done. "You're not ready yet, but will be soon enough."

"Well, sheesh!" Hands wrung, surrounding air particles fracturing, she stood, dismayed. "I'd *really* like to help out as soon as possible."

"First, your energies must stabilize. For now, you may observe while I work."

Appeased, she beamed at him. "At first I wasn't sure how to make sense of this place, but now I'm *so* incredibly glad to be here!" Pleasure overtook him: that of a worn, cast-off shoe reunited with its mate.

Sandwich crumbs brushed into his palm, legs unfolded, he opened the window to sprinkle the bits onto the ledge. "—For the birds," he explained as unaccustomed lightheartedness overtook him.

Working to contain himself, he went to the dresser, slid open a drawer, arranged the socks in precise rows, aligned the brush and comb up top, adjusted their placement, once, then twice. Years effort to contain feelings, he'd developed elaborate rituals such as these to stifle them.

Tension eased, he sat back, steepled his fingers, and saw fit to elucidate, "I detest wrinkled garments, buff my shoes daily, and although I never quite manage to tame my hair, I enjoy a precise haircut." *Why the urge to blurt such intimacies*—he had no idea.

"So..." She cast about. "This is where you live?" His monkish cave wasted no triviality on gewgaws or color, for Walker, unlike his Ma, was a determined anti-collector, and disposed of possessions as swiftly as he acquired them.

Graying curtains graced a single narrow window above his cot. A leaky sink dominated one corner, and he used the toilet down the hall.

Though a hotplate rested atop a rickety crate, he rarely used it. Thickly clogged atmosphere reminiscent of his youth, this place was for sleep, but not for living. "I figured you'd live in a magnificent healing space," continued Lauren.

"Haven't time for it."

"My taste isn't so great, but I'm superb bargain hunter and could spruce up this room." Eagerly, she grinned; her shiny face jolted him.

How would it be to live inside her skin? Saw himself forthright, boisterous, knew he'd enjoy it.

Despite tender feelings, he covered, gruffly, "Room's fine as it is."

"Such a lifeless space can't possibly restore you," she persisted. "So if you ever change your mind, I'll be glad to fix it up. Excuse me now,"—she turned to depart—"I need to tell my mom that I'm staying."

"I'm glad you've come," he addressed her wake. Hand to brow, eyes misted up, he about wept.

Chapter Twenty-Six: Lauren

"Lean to the right, will you," Walker directed Lauren. "Little more… Good! Sit straight. I'll be pounding your shoulder to loosen stuck energy.—Should only take a minute; hum if you like…That'll help."

Lauren hummed away. Walker's sleek fingers pranced and skipped, tracing her vertebrae. Each touch her bones groaned and stretched. Fingers trickled her neck to trail down her arm; abrupt pain twisted and yanked, but then went all jagged and pushed in so deep, she winced and bit her lip.

Idling cigarette taken up, Walker inhaled, set it down, then used both hands to squeeze her brow.

Twang!—went her spine.

"Yikes, I felt that!" She rubbed at her back. "It feels different, but do you see any change?"

"'Bout the same. Soon as you stop seeing yourself as a hideous cripple, your spine will heal. Lean to the left," he directed, resuming.

Slightly disheartened after six months of sessions, she leaned into his grip. "Funny, I thought it was improving!" Pulled back, Walker studied her with the dispassionate interest of studying an ant colony.

"Forceful exhale," he commanded, then tapped her neck.

Lauren clenched his arm. "Ooo, that's bad!"

"Want to stop?"

Cheeks swiped, she blustered, "Naa…Keep going."

"You must also refrain from using your *will* to heal others. As a nurse you take on your patient's suffering, which impedes your ability to help. In part, its why your spine is so bent; you try to carry people on your back."

This seemed unfair. "What's my spine got to do with helping?"

"Establish better boundaries, and your spine will straighten. See...

Boundaries define where we leave off and where someone else begins. Work I do on you helps for a time, but any improvement won't hold unless you change this crucial aspect."

"Ho! I see you with patients; you get downright sorrowful." *What pains you so, Walker?* she longed to ask.

"I have compassion. Pity is different. You have yet to distinguish between the two. Sometimes, I *do* find it appropriate to take on the illness or suffering of another so that their soul can find relief."

"Like Christ dying for our sins?"

"Perhaps." Lauren noted his hollow, weary tone.

Be a person good or evil, Walker poured himself into the needy, without reservation, without end. Beneath his soft-spoken demeanor, Lauren sensed that desperation, impatience, simmered. And, strangely, that her own vitality fed him. He seemed to need her so as to compensate for that which he lacked.

Sigh heaved, she scruffed her brow. "I wish I could figure you out, Walker; it's terribly frustrating."

"Focus on me misses the point. Just figure yourself out." He spoke so grumpily.

Perhaps he resents the time I take!

In the end, after she learned his entire story, it seemed good and bad that she failed to glean his totality in a single, giant gulp. Eventually, once Walker's life story became known, she was forced to revamp her view of him.

Just now, though, Walker touched her so tenderly that she pushed her face into his neck. He stiffened; she pulled back. "Oh jeeze! Sorry, I'm such a dope!"

Stepped behind to percuss her back, Walker spoke, "Pay attention to that area…" He tapped her lower spine. "When it crimps, breathe into it to help it relax, and what's stuck will flow." Coming back round in front, shirtsleeves rolled down, he buttoned the cuffs. "That's all for now."

Gingerly, Lauren slid from the table. Pain, frighteningly worse, zinged and zapped. But then the gentlest humming began emanating from all parts; ankles, wrists and knees, mostly from her spine—as if her bones had taken up singing.

Tears surged. A moan spilled out, as hot-coiled pleasure rose up her vertebral column to spread and flood her with bliss.

Lauren found Rosalee at work in her herb room. "Can you measure me? My usual height is six feet."

"A minute." Rosalee counted stinky pellets into a tin, climbed down from her barstool, then, making much pomp, shed her smock, and brought out measuring tape. "Stand here." She indicated the doorframe and climbed back onto the stool to mark Lauren's topmost height against the threshold.

Lauren stepped away; Rosalee stretched out the tape to take her measure. "Congratulations, you have grown!"

"How much?"

"An inch!"

Lauren rubbed her scalp. "Amazing!" Walker, she knew, would change her; that hope was what had carried her through her lost years. But never, quite honestly, had she believed that he could possibly straighten her spine.

Overcome, she wanted to run hollering: *Walker's fixed me!*

Instead, as she stood, benumbed, a great thing occurred: first time ever, she felt truly complete.

Flushed with pride, as if she'd straightened Lauren's spine herself, Rosalee gave her a hug. "We must celebrate." Hand-carved tea set produced, she put a pot of water to boil.

Steam misting their faces, they sipped the Soo Family's Thousand-Year-Old Tea, enjoying its complex multi-layered scents. "Soo Family tea promises eternal life," Rosalee proclaimed, "but for you, it gives promise of eternal height."

The week following, Rosalee took Lauren's measure, erupted into sweet giggles, exclaiming, "You have added another eighth of an inch!"

Measuring as their weekly ritual—unbelievable as it seemed—eventually, three more inches gained, Lauren topped out at six-foot-four. And, wonder of wonders, gradually, inexorably, her sensational hump—ever the cause of gawking and comment—gracefully subsided!

Everyone knows that crooked spines don't straighten; but Lauren's did.

"Say, Walker, notice anything different?" Lauren asked a month into the change.

"You don't ask so many questions these days," he said wryly.

"Actually, I'm taller," she gloated and grinned. "It's from your healing work."

"No...It's due to work you've done on yourself. Good that you're changing, but don't get attached to the results. Your body isn't what matters." Reaching over, he tapped her noggin. "It's what's inside that counts." Lauren beamed back, forever bound to him.

The more he touched her, the more firmly she bonded. Actually, as if a groupie, she started up a scrapbook of news articles about Walker, even salvaged a napkin from Bea's Koffee Kup he'd used to wipe his lips. In truth, she revered him!

Chapter Twenty-Seven: Young Walker

Severed from the throb of human existence, the boy departed river and cypress to trudge into the highlands. Sky yowling one day, dropping rain, he spotted a hut and checked inside. Briefly, he wondered whose home it was, why it was vacant, then ministered to the hearth.

Fire roared to life, warmth seeped into his bones, so he lay down and slept.

A chill breeze carrying damp earthy scents sent him bolt upright. Long disorienting seconds, Ma glided into sight, paused, tantalized, executed an elegant fluttering wave, and then slid out the door.

Jittery, breathless, striving for calm, the boy followed.

Bobbed in close, Ma forced his gaze to rest upon her. "You committed no crime, son. Your only crime is that you carry guilt with you, always...So let it go."

"I cannot! I jeopardized you."

"You simply obeyed."

"I did it wrong. Besides, you ousted me, not once, but twice. Let it go, and nothing defines me."

"You bring pain upon yourself, then."

"You think I don't know this!" the boy bellowed, huffing crisp morning air.

Hillside bright, mists warming with sunshine, pink wildflowers blotted dirt, as a hushed flock of geese winged past. "Choose to suffer," Ma persisted, "and you're on you own."

"Do you forgive me?" he cried. Any reply—yes, no—would satisfy.

Ma lifted, floating skyward to drift about.

Unable to speak or cry out, awash in loneliness—and longing—the boy watched.

Electric blue flicks snapping, there she dangled.

And then, fast as a blink, she left him.

Melancholy overwhelmed. Scraped out, empty, as if an animal pelt—familiar heartache aside—no insight arose from her appearance.

Oddly reassured anyhow—emptiness felt about right—and so he reposed upon soft, spongy soil, traded mother longing for connection with mother earth, and sank into its welcoming depths. Unaware of his body, without concern, all ties and desires fallen away, peculiar lucidity settled within, till all that remained formed a single smoldering speck named hope.

The boy found hope to be a terrific tease. Hope caused him to tramp on forever. Hope drove him to live in an imaginary future—one he could never quite locate—one that could never possibly exist. Yet that hope kept him alive.

Days on end, as he wallowed, whispers, not rushing wind, called out, beckoning. "You're an abomination!" a disembodied voice roared with displeasure. The boy shuddered, welcoming this familiar sense of wrongness.

Thoughts about Gaia arose, how it floated free in the cosmic abyss. He thought about stars, how, come world's end, all would blink out. Entertained the notion that, even if he arose, his soul would remain, embedded in earth, absorbing, decaying.

Suspended within that grassy calm, his precious gift of old—his visions—rejoined him. As dawn spread over the land, feathery wisps pinking the horizon, terrible, necessary occurrences came to him; he bore witness to them beforehand.

Shortly, he saw himself hurtle through the solar system, wherein magnificent winged beings spun webs in tremendous haste. "What are you doing?" he inquired of them.

We stitch the universe together to increase earth's frequencies, thereby forcing humans to evolve.

Scooped into their immense web with its luminous, connecting filaments, strands threaded throughout his own nervous system to extend past his physical boundaries and merge with the terrestrial nervous system. Time scrambling about in his mind—witness to all things primal, ancient, terrifyingly magnificent—fast, then faster, he spiraled.

Rudely slammed back into his body, fighting for breath, the boy struggled upright to ask, "Why the rejecting shift?"

Do not berate yourself, the winged creatures called, *for you cannot perpetually exist in a state of bliss.* Off and away they flapped, and surprisingly, he no longer felt deeply bereft.

Passing months, thoughts ever shifting, his consciousness undertook a jarring leap.

Sucked into infinity, mid-freefall, prepared for impact, the earth opened to swallow him whole. Embraced within, he sensed its magnificent beating heart and the rhythm of its currents. Linked with nature and the terrain of his own soul, a passion for all things, alive and inanimate, burgeoned.

In full grasp of the manner and shape of The Sacred All, rushing winds sang into his hair, soft melodies sprang from boulders, and his body breathed, resonating with hillocks and trees. Air no longer flat, distant, it caressed and enveloped him.

A chattering chipmunk sat on a boulder, lamenting the dearth of nuts. Deer munched grasses, came close, unafraid to lick his cheeks with soft, plush tongues. Arms flung wide, he embraced an immense gum tree, dipped into its centuries of history dating back to the Crusades, and received its imprint of knowledge.

Mostly he adored the silence: how if he listened just right, the pulse of the universe informed him. Ascended beyond self-limiting beliefs, his anger peeled away, and he thought himself saved.

Two years spent in that haven at world's edge, now age seventeen, in need of no one, he wanted for nothing. Tropical lilt to the air, he lay beneath stars chanting. Voices poured in from otherworldly dimensions; he prayed and communed with them. Steady power pulsed his hands, and on clear days, he saw all with his heart.

Although The Angel kept quiescent, he considered this time as his Great Awakening. Nothing felt separate—even his dark, ugliest aspects—he felt full, but yet the far reaches of his most estranged self stayed empty.

Then, came time to depart.

Chapter Twenty-Eight: Lauren

That first summer Lauren took an apartment at the lower edge of town. Sunlight shone through its windows to dapple walls adorned in Mom's recent artwork to give the place a quirky, snug feel. Best of all, the moon illuminated her bed at night, making her feel like a chrysalis forming within a cocoon.

Romantic imagery aside, the apartment, with its cracked, bubbly linoleum floors and peeled wallpaper, was no palace. Summertime, it heated up like a sauna. Winters, thanks to a finicky furnace, she wore long johns. Most evenings, she looked to her beloved rocks for companionship.

So OK, Lauren had a thing for rocks! A big thing, actually.

Hard objects, formed from intense heat and pressure spit up from earth—psychological significance eluding—she simply had to posses them. Often, she returned from a walk, pockets heavily laden.

No ordinary stone would suffice. Texture, heft, color, complexity, had to speak to her, and heat emission was requisite.

One day, while readying to head down to The Living Light, the phone rang. "The Foundation called looking for you, dear," Mom announced. "That woman you saved has disappeared, so they wondered if you had any idea as to her whereabouts."

Lauren gripped the receiver, hard. "Miss Spivey?"

"They didn't give a name."

Heart squeaking, an image burst forth: Miss Spivey stuck in an eternal pirouette—then, poof—disappeared. "You don't suppose she's killed herself?"

"I have no idea, honey. I just thought you should know. So...," Mom said, switching topics, "how are you doing?"

"Actually, pretty great." Stashing her sorrow, Lauren perked back up. "Recently, Walker waved his hand over a water glass and gave it to a teenage boy with a badly smashed leg, then told him to drink. Next day, I swear, new patches of skin and tissue reestablished, filling gaping holes where bone and flesh had been missing the day prior.

"Near as I can tell, Walker, uses prayer and vibration. Sometimes it works; sometimes it doesn't. And though his work lacks proper science, weird as it seems, its really *big stuff!*"

"Fine dear," Mom replied. "Just don't get too ga-ga about it."

"Too late, Mom. I already am."

Lauren trailed along watching Mr. Judson work. He didn't say much; seems he hadn't quite got the hang of what to do with her. "The aura," he attempted, as they exited a treatment room, "similar to a saint's halo, surrounds and encompasses every living thing. Our last patient's auric shell, weakened from a difficult birth, is further damaged from drug abuse."

"You see that?"

"I do."

"Why can't I see it?"

"Eventually you will."

"When?"

No reply, Walker called the next patient and got her situated.

Silence descended; Walker centered himself and began to touch the young woman, Sheila Pence. Silence overlaid all as he worked. Silence sourced his steadiness and his healing strength.

It was late. Sheila was about the fiftieth person he'd seen this day. For a mere mortal, this would've been grueling. Only rather than depleted, Walker seemed invigorated.

Leaned in to watch, Lauren felt so comfy, so happy. Likely Walker had no idea as to her contentment.

Comfy or not, some healings disturbed her sense of what was possible. Just now, Walker's hands actually seemed to penetrate Sheila's belly; his fingers appeared to melt, then absorb into her.

Shelia, beset with muscular dystrophy, security strap across her chest to hold her torso upright, had first arrived in a wheelchair. Given pervasive muscle wasting and weakness, it seemed impossible that

Walker could help. Yet, five sessions from now, with no difficulty walking, she would sit at the front desk, answer phones, and assist other ailing folks. Lauren viewed this as miraculous, yet threatening—that the world she'd entered still might prove an elaborate hoax.

Miracles, she would learn, could be ordinary or profane. At the core perched the Divine: the spark of perfection that resides within all things. "Human potential is infinite," Walker now informed, attuned to her skepticism. "And love is the conduit. With that...all's possible."

Next day's first healing session, Walker gave Delsie Cringe an hour of undivided attention. Really, he knew how to listen and to touch; it actually hurt to watch.

"I have no money," Delsie lamented after.

"Never mind," said Walker. "Just pass a gift of some sort on to another."

His generosity impressed Lauren very much, but Rosalee took him to task for it. "You promised you would require that something be given."

"I did not break my promise." Walker suppressed a sly grin. "She gave me her gratitude, and I consider that sufficient."

"You"—Rosalee smacked his arm, playful—"are too slippery!"

Lauren too clapped Walker's back as they tromped down the hall to collect their next patient. "Did you get how pain-free Delsie was?" Walker halted to regard her.

"I insist that you grasp your place here. Moreover...," he said, slowly, "avoid prideful thinking. None of this is my doing. Get overly inflated, a swelled head, energies don't like it, and they disappear.—It's happened to me a time or two."

"No kidding—healing energies possess sentient consciousness!" Mind a-twitter, Lauren skimmed over his admonishment. "I'm really enjoying myself, but still, there's a lot that I don't get."

Walker studied her. Hastily, she combed fingers through her hair. "It's so strange, Walker. You mumble odd things, wave your hands over a patient; they get up and leave. Mostly, on the surface nothing's changed, yet something intangible has." Walker continued to look her over, as if no crowd waited, as if he had all the time in the world.

"Come...," he finally beckoned.

Studying his back, wondering if or how she'd offended, she followed.

Same as the man, Walker's office was spare. No requisite photo of the wife; she'd heard they'd separated. At the window stood a dented tin desk heaped high with mail. With letter stacks so perfectly spaced, two tidy inches apart, it appeared that someone had taken a ruler to precisely measure.

A vase of gold roses offset the stark space; Lauren bent to admire them. "A grateful patient brings them daily. Take a seat." Walker pointed to a rickety chair, several back slats missing, lit a cigarette, then pulled up directly across and sat; their knees knocked together, touching.

Fanatic cigarette hater that she was, Lauren enjoyed the tobacco-mint-mingled smell of him. "As your teacher, I frown upon certain activities," Walker began, "and believe they impede one's path to perfection. Therefore, I insist that you not use alcohol, drugs, ingest meat, or have unsanctioned relationships with the opposite sex."

"Uh..." Bolted upright, she stammered, "No...No problem there. I can stop eating meat; the rest are non-issues anyway."

"Twice weekly, you will join a select group of students for meditation. I give teachings and answer questions. Attendance is mandatory; specific reading is required." Pleased to be included, Lauren beamed at him.

"Also...I am re-naming you."

"Er, thanks, but my name's fine as it is."

"From now on, you are to be called Son."

"Huh...you mean Sun, as in sunshine? That's tolerable."

"No. Son—as in my son or daughter." Lauren throbbed, stricken.

"But Son, is...is like in reference to a guy." Walker, she noticed, had yet to address her by name.

Times he tried, the word, *Lauren,* clung to his throat, refusing to budge. Sometimes, he referred to her as *my sidekick, my student, my helper*, or just called her, *You*. She got so attuned that she knew when her attention was required, so mostly he needn't call her anything.

She enjoyed this inability of his; it marked her as special. Being renamed, though, without her consent seemed terribly rude. "The name calls to question your struggle with your femininity." Walker ignored her chagrin. "That's a good thing. It should strengthen you. So now...," he said, switching focus, "what's on your mind."

Taken aback, Lauren adjusted her chair, moving off several inches. "First...I'd like to know exactly how you do what you do. Mentally, I try to replicate it, but nothing, whatsoever, happens." Since arriving she'd wanted to know this, but there'd never been a proper moment.

"I simply set my intent, align with Spirit...," Walker quipped, suppressing a grin, "then let 'er rip."

A joke! She nearly dropped from her chair.

Walker, she'd found, was serious to a fault. "No really!"

"Set your intention into a sharp focus," he said, all seriousness. "Then direct your mind to shape a precise image so as to clear the way for fulfillment."

"That's it?" Healing practices she'd previously investigated seemed so secret, so esoteric—this explanation seemed far too simple.

"Meditate daily. It'll establish a proper foundation for your awakening and will help troublesome kundalini energies to move through."

"How soon will I be done with them?"

"It can take months, even years to subside. So now...Let's hear about you."

"Oh, gee..." Flustered, flattered to be his focus, her mind flitted through topics. "Let's see...I'm an ugly duckling. It's my height, I guess—or the brace—which I tend to blame for my every flaw." Working to correct her tone, she extracted the sniveling. "Sure you want to hear?"

"And so...?" he encouraged

"Do you know if Mrs. Wolcott will live?" Judith Wolcott had metastatic cancer and, despite Walker's attentive ministrations, seemed to be failing.

Sadly, Walker gazed at her, then touched her arm. "That's not for me to tell."

His warm fingers as they rested there made her woozy; she was no swooner, though. "I'm praying hard for her healing. If she dies, it'll be like—such a failure. When that happens, do you feel bad?"

Words racing together, not awaiting an answer, changing focus, she jabbered away, "When I was little, I was pretty sure I could fly."

"Fly hey?" Walker's face flickered, curious.

"You know"—she flapped hands—"with wings and all. In dreams I used to soar high above buildings, clouds, and trees." She shrugged, sheepish. "Should I stop?"

"I'm with you." Walker perched at the corner of his desk. "It's interesting."

"Couple times, I actually commanded wings to unfurl and flutter as I raced about. Once, I climbed the fence, jumped, and belly flopped into a shrub. It's supremely unfair that birds fly, since they have no apparent appreciation of how fantastic it is."

"How do you know they don't?"

"Good point!" Lauren cackled, not at all relaxed. "Flying was once my greatest longing. Often I dreamt of it, only to awaken to find that I hadn't. I was so bummed that I'd sob, uncontrollably. Then finally, I stopped believing—the end of innocence—I suppose." Even now the loss pierced her.

Steadily, Walker regarded her. "You still can, you know. At birth our souls fly free, but as we age, we forget how. In truth, it's only a matter of remembering."

"So you say!" She checked his face. He wasn't kidding. "You mean literally fly?"

"That's for you to discover. Trust me, at some point you'll know."

"Taking bets?"

"My treat, breakfast at Bea's Koffee Kup."

"You're on!" Reached over, they slapped palms.

Lauren sat quiet a moment, then took up again, "Always, I felt different. Never thought I belonged. Don't get me wrong, my parents are great…" Onward, she rattled, conveying every boring detail regarding her wretched, lonely youth. Occasionally, Walker interrupted to probe. The more she spoke, the more she wanted to tell.

Please stop—she envisioned Walker imploring, hands flung up—*I am full to the brim and have no more room for your suffering, or woe!*

Sad stories aching to be told, Walker, she suspected, had heard all of them.

Yet Walker, a generous listener, sat attentive, as if her story held immense import. So onward she gabbled, "I was good with mental patients, understood them perfectly. Maybe that's because I'm unstable myself. What do you think?"

"You're not crazy, if that's what you mean." His grin put her at ease.

"Whew!" Leaning back, she fanned her cheeks. "It helps to know! Also, I need to mention...Forever, I've had this feeling that I was meant to come to you. Like it's my destiny or something." Phlegmy noise, Walker dropped his head, fussed with something in his eye.

"Hay fever," he explained.

Awkwardness stirred between them. Again. Lauren shifted gears, "Can you see my future? I'd like to know what's going to happen: if I become a great healer." Walker regarded her, considering.

"In due time."

"I have this unshakable feeling there's something specific that I'm supposed to do. I just don't—you know—want to miss the boat."

"Don't push."

Fizz departed their conversation; she stood. "I should go. Thanks for listening."

"Don't worry about the future." Walker got to his feet. "Your job is to stay in the present. Otherwise, you'll miss everything."

"I'm impatient." Serenity bathed her—the effect of speaking so long, so uninterrupted. Really, she felt terrific! "But I'd feel much better if you called me something like Lauren-Son."

"Lauren-Son it is, then." As Walker went off to collect the next patient, it hit.

Her questions—what this work was about, or whether Walker meant flying as metaphor or flying for real—did not get answered.

Deftly, he'd steered clear. Perhaps he didn't know either. Or perhaps he found her wanting. His reticence troubled her.

Plus this new name, though she'd had partial say—of all possible options—so totally stunk!

Chapter Twenty-Nine: Young Adult Walker

"Your life is your prayer," the yogi hollered down at the young man as he strode through the vaudeville tent. "Therefore, your every act must harmonize with your higher purpose."

The young man came close to ask, "What exactly *is* my higher purpose, sir?"

The yogi beamed down his stupendous, jutting snout at him. "It's the reason you exist upon this earthly plane...You already know what it consists of." Vaudeville all but faded from the scene, with the yogi as the troupe's big attraction, a tinny accordion belched out tunes as visitors strolled about watching acts.

Taken aback at being singled out, the young man hung there, as the yogi swayed on haunches. "Through discipline and practice, someday you'll easily do this..." Eyes shut, the yogi breathed slow and deep, then opened hands to curve around empty airspace.

Gradually, a teacup and saucer materialized.

Cups and saucers whizzed about before the young man's eyes. One flew close; he reached to touch it. The cup was real, not imagined, not sleight of hand or magic, but created from nothing. "That's a sample of conscious manifesting," the yogi claimed. "Thoughts create reality, so I make objects from thin air merely by thinking about them. I can teach you to do likewise."

"Th...thank you," stammered the young man. "I might enjoy that very much."

"Want a new car? I fly into the fourth dimension, meet up with that precise 'thought form,' tweak it through mental focus and intent, and bring back a spanking new Studebaker for my public to admire.

"I ask, young fella"—abruptly, the yogi switched focus—"what do you want?" Tugging at downy chin hairs, the young man pondered this.

Everything! Nothing! He longed to cease traveling, wanted a steady place to lay his head. Desired the scent of a woman, to eat meals she prepared, to caress the delicate curve of her neck. Most of all...He longed for his life, for his true purpose, to begin.

Unwilling to self-reveal, he gave a pat answer, "To be good, to do good, I guess."

"Bah!" barked the yogi. "God drew you here today so that I might tell you...yours is a life of service—that this is your bodhisattva life!"

"My what life?" The young man had never heard this word, bodhisattva.

"A bodhisattva freely opts to forgo heaven and incarnates into human form, volunteering to take on humanities' suffering with the overarching goal to help awaken the stupid masses. A bodhisattva—life in service—that is your task; it's why you were born." Certainly, this seemed a stretch.

Barely able to place one foot in front of the other, the young man could not imagine more. So the yogi, he presumed, buttered him up to soak money from him.

"Not to worry," the yogi informed. "In time, you'll grow into the role. Presently, your task is to amass power and it's my job to prepare you." He had no clue about bodhisattvas, but power, the young man hungered for.

Power meant making others do his bidding, to get them to squirm and sweat and stammer on command—and also, to make someone adore him. Power, to him, wasn't a means, it posed an end. That this yogi person offered to help him attain it set him a-throb, immensely curious.

Spiking like a percolator, the yogi downed a pitcher of coffee. "Coffee snaps my energy centers awake." Abruptly, he veered off, "What's your view of God, son?"

"I'm not too sure about God these days, but nature I trust."

"Surely, you must believe in God! Life is too sad without Him."

"On the contrary;"—daring, defying, the young man jutted his chin—"life's too sad because of Him!" Yogi about to speak, the boy stared him down. The yogi ran his palm over his scalp.

"Fine then," the yogi finally said. "You'll work for me, assist with my act and do as I say."

∞

Black holes are so heavy, so immense, that they absorb everything. Likewise with the yogi, not at all a quiet, restful sort, the young man found himself sucked into his orbit.

An odd mix of agitation and wisdom, nerves ever a-jangle, the yogi rarely slept. He *did* shout and cuff his assistant unnecessarily.

The young man found the yogi rude, thought to say so, but being that he craved knowledge and being a polite sort, he did not complain. Many of the yogi's insights seemed pure poppy-cock, yet his connection with the cosmic realms sufficed as reason to remain.

Up at dawn, sitting cross-legged on mats, under the yogi's peculiar tutelage, hours on end, as the boy practiced breathing techniques, closets tossed out garments that whooshed and flapped about, books scrolled through pages, and apples, bananas, then melons, lifted from their bowl and juggled, fast, then faster. Such happenstance became terribly ho-hum.

Off the young man spun, to visit fantastical landscapes. Material reality drab, grubby by comparison, he loathed return from these out-of-body states.

"Most humans merely perceive gross phenomenon," barked the yogi, "yet reality is far more than what one detects through the five senses. An invisible subtle level, in which everyone and everything that has ever existed, abides. Breathe with me now..." Breathe, the young man did.

Time yawned, folded in upon itself. Waves crashed and flung themselves out to sea. Gulls flapped, flying tail first, backward. As he observed the earth, the young man's mind and body swirled round it, as his immutable forever-self sprang into awareness.

Mind further divided, he saw that he resided above linear time, existed everywhere, within everything. *Humans are linked as mind, energy, and matter to all that is. From there, consciousness underpins all.* "Who and what I am is limitless," he whispered, amazed, breathless. "It's only my fear that limits my existence, so thank you for this!"

Crystalline light then poured into him; every possible sensation flooding in, the ethereal command came, "Love yourself."

As if he grasped what the *self* was or knew in the slightest *how to love!*

"Next," the yogi cut in, "you must learn to control your physiology at will. Here...Cut yourself, and keep breathing." Knife handed over, then threaded through pink flesh, blood vessels nicked, the young man incised himself.

"Breathe continuous circular breaths!" yipped the yogi.

No drop of blood spilled—deep, rhythmic breaths controlling pain—abiding calm, supreme focus overtook the young man.

"You're gaining mastery of your physiology," explained the yogi.

Freed from physical cares, the young man enjoyed himself immensely.

"Now soften your resistance and do this...," said the yogi.

Emitting nasal tones, lying comfortably on a bed of sharp nails, the apprentice leaned into those sharp points, felt no pain, and thought the yogi—himself too, by association—as pretty darn special.

The yogi never ate. He only drank coffee: not water, or juice, nor milk. "I have no need for food or most liquids. Air and breath are all I need to sustain life. You must do likewise."

Refrained from food and fluid intake for such long intervals, the young man's brain swooned and his ankles loosened. Spirits soaring, emotions overflowing, he got so high, underwent such bliss, he kept at it until he wasted to a wisp. Try as he might, breathe as he did, hunger pangs never fully abating, he'd have died, but for this: one day, as he happened past an A&W Root Beer stand, he cast a longing glance.

There, beneath the orange-and-brown awning, hands steadily feeding his face, sat the yogi, munching down a burger, fries, and shake.

Nauseated by his own trusting naiveté, off the young man slunk.

Carefully, he tucked away learned skills and established clear rules for himself. Never would he put faith in another or let on as to his own gifts. He would not share techniques to alter metabolism, help others control their pain, or display healing skills. As if he never possessed them, he vowed not to permit his gifts to resurface until a certain sure sign showed its face again.

Chapter Thirty: Lauren

"Mind if my student puts hands on you as I work?" Walker asked the elderly Mrs. Thrip. "I'll explain what I'm doing so she can learn as we go along."

"The more the merrier." Garbed in purple pantsuit, hair froth the color of eggplant, Mrs. Thrip winked at Lauren-Son. Shiny with self-importance, now nine months into her stay, Lauren-Son grinned back.

"What can we do for you?" Walker asked the woman as he scrubbed hands in the sink. "You do likewise," he instructed Lauren-Son; she washed thoroughly.

"Well...," Mrs. Thrip began,"Hank's my hubby—been married fifty years; we met at a church picnic. Twenty years back Hank hurt hisself. Maybe it's twenty-one..." Briefly, she paused to ponder.

"Anyhoo, Hank was a milkman. Loading up his truck one day, another milk truck backed up and ran, smack-dab, over him." As she shaved one hand over the flat of the other, Walker observed her closely, not just her body, but the surrounding swath.

"Poor dear, legs like pancakes, he's unable to walk and can't work. I have no talents whatsoever, but we had to get by, so I babysit young'uns. Babysitting doesn't pay much, about fifty cents an hour—sixty if you're experienced." Wriggling adorably, she beamed at them. "Thing of it is, after paying the bills, I manage to save up pretty good, but then I got myself a bleeding ulcer in the process. Doc says I need surgery, except I don't want it."

"Ever hear of the human energy field, Mrs. Thrip?" Walker pitched his voice to include both women.

"Can't say as I have."

"You have an energy field, also called an aura or an electromagnetic field. Presently, your field is disrupted, so work I do realigns, recharges, and repairs it."

"Goodness me!" Rooting through her handbag, Mrs. Thrip extracted a pack of gum, helped herself to a stick, and offered them some. "Where, son, is this energy situated?"

"It's inside and all around you." Brows lifted, plainly Mrs. Thrip didn't believe this, but enjoyed the fuss, nonetheless.

"Never mind that, how do you plan to fix me?"

"You have clockwise spinning vortices called chakras. Energy gets sucked through them, into your body, then flows along to feed your organs. When there's disruption, poor diet, a trauma—in your case prolonged stress—your organs don't receive sufficient fuel to function, so your body weakens, which permits infection or disease to take hold."

"My ulcer tells you that my energy lines are weak?"

"Basically, that's correct." Walker caught Lauren-Son's eye, making sure she followed. "Habitual stress disrupts healthy energy flow and can cause it to leak; presently you've drawn unhealthy energies in, there and there." Walker pointed to her midriff and below to her belly.

"I leak?" Mildly concerned, Mrs. Thrip clasped her bosom.

"Bring your awareness to your stomach, please."

Mrs. Tripp shut her eyes. "Feels fluttery as usual."

"During our session, you may feel a subtle difference and more calm after. From a healer's perspective, all is connected. Your ulcer, caused by hyper-acidity, caused by the stress of caretaking your husband, impacts digestion and your nutritional state, to say nothing of how well you've allowed yourself to be nurtured in this life." Coyly, Mrs. Thrip winked at Walker.

"I eat plenty thanks, but get the gist." She settled onto the table.

Eyes shut, Walker focused inward. "Just now, I'm anchoring myself, connecting with earth's infinite energy sources by way of my feet. Shortly, vibrations will flow up to flood my body. Follow me now...," he directed Lauren-Son.

Hands held prayerfully, Lauren-Son concentrated as Walker continued, "Imagine roots growing out the bottoms of your feet, wending their way into the earth's core; that's called grounding." Feet rooted into earth, tentacles spread beneath subterranean surfaces—she savored the image.

"Once you've grounded, let that infinite energy flow back up. Knees slightly bent—that's right. Locked knees inhibit energy flow.

Relax your pelvis. Breathe. Let it move up. Feel the surge?" Walker watched closely; Lauren-Son shook her head, feeling like a failure.

Walker kept on, "Now we scan, checking internal structure, organ function, and such, to find areas of damage or difficulty within Mrs. Thrip's energy system." Flat of his hand held inches off from the patient's recumbent form he sculpted her contours. Palm circling her abdomen, he moved away, came close, then caught Lauren-Son's eye, pointed, and mouthed, "Here and there.—You try."

Mrs. Thrip cracked an eye, watching Lauren-Son run hands along her torso.

Abrupt churning sensation rising; Lauren-Son gripped at her own belly. Walker looked at her, questioning. "I'm fine," she spoke in haste.

Achy throbbing, similar to sensations experienced at the Flight Deck—an empathic affliction much akin to Mrs. Thrip's had flared.

Later, Walker explained that she possessed a finely attuned kinesthetic sense. For some, their visual sense is their primary healing asset. For others, its their hearing. More rare, its taste or smell.

Kinesthetic recall arose now like a felt sense of knowing. Eventually, as she worked she knew she'd properly dialed in when she took a breath, released it, held very still, felt an opening reach up, grab her, and then excruciating clarity arose.

At table's end, Walker gripped Mrs. Thrip's feet. "I'm sending energy throughout her body. No need to control or direct it, healing energies know precisely where they're needed." He seemed to actually watch Mrs. Thrip fill up; to Lauren-Son's mind it looked pretend.

Slowly he moved about, placing hands on the woman's body. Sometimes he swished and swirled, lifted, then snapped his hands as if releasing static electricity. Then he abruptly gripped Mrs. Thrip's flesh and pinched. More of a squeeze than a pinch, Mrs. Thrip looked up at him, startled.

Confused by such roughness, Lauren-Son too checked Walker for intent.

Serene, full of tender concern, Walker clarified, "I'm reconnecting Mrs. Thrip's energy field. As mentioned, it has several rips." Relieved, Lauren-Son grinned. Mrs. Thrip settled back, all-trusting.

"Follow me," Walker directed. "Put you hands where mine have just been—what do you notice?"

Lauren-Son went to Mrs. Thrip's feet. "I only sense her growly stomach."

"Exactly!" Walker enthused. Proudly, Lauren-Son beamed.

Hands continuing to follow his moves, abruptly, she began to sweat. Rivulets, a gusher, flooded off from her. Walker interjected, "Your metabolic rate's increased; a common experience for healers."

Briefly, she basked: *he called me a healer!*

Walker pointed to Mrs. Thrip's abdomen. "I'll warm that area; its chilled." Head bent, his lips grazed Mrs. Thrip's navel region; Lauren-Son feared he might kiss it. Cheeks puffed, he emitted a nasal rasp, then, much like applying a straw to lips, slurped, turned his head to one side and hawked spit. Lauren-Son gaped, appalled. "Removing sludge," he clarified.

She nearly laughed outright.

Walker stepped back to scan further. "I'm checking for more leaks or areas of imbalance."

Mrs. Thrip breathed rhythmically, deeply relaxed. "Acid foods," Walker informed her, "such as red meat, sugar, would be good to avoid. Our herbalist, Rosalee Soo, can help with your diet and strengthen your digestion." Head cocked as if listening, he paused, moved lips, as if to address an unseen being, then whispered, "Ah, yes, thank you."

Did he just commune with a spirit? wondered Lauren-Son.

Walker addressed Mrs. Thrip. "I'm told you need to get out more and have fun. Worries eat away, gnawing at you." Mrs. Thrip's sweet face crumpled.

Then she reached to grip Walker's chin. "I've got just one itty hankering."

"What's that?"

"Gambling...always wanted to try my luck. So, given your encouraging, I'll do just that."

Walker returned to Mrs. Thrip's feet to hold them. "Take her head," he instructed; Lauren-Son cupped the woman's temples.

Shortly, arms slowly raised, then opening to extend them, he stepped back. "Like applying a bandage, I'm sealing her field.—Lay here as long as you like," he offered Mrs. Thrip. Rest after a session can help stabilize your field."

Mrs. Thrip prepared to depart. Walker gripped her hand in his and bowed deeply. "Thank you *so* much for coming!" Up on tiptoe, she kissed his chin.

Full-up with her loving, his face opened, relaxed. Lauren-Son too basked in the glow.

With each client, she would witness Walker's grave humility. He made no fuss, but always seemed grateful, in the extreme, to each person for coming.

Whenever Lauren-Son went to Rosalee's herb closet, typically, she received tiny tablets—Derma Wind Release, to treat diminished bouts of eczema—and then they gabbed. As pain receded from her spine, she felt better than ever, and Rosalee's wisdom helped her understand Walker and how to make sense of ways that she was changing.

Shiny with beatific smiles, this night Sherman joined them. Lauren-Son, ogling his tattoo—a flicking tiger's tail that disappeared at his neckline—declared, "That's my favorite."

Sherman looked down at himself. "My body maps significant life events. Each encounter, I print onto my flesh, so's not to forget. Met a grizzly once; nearly tore my face off. See here"—he exposed a shoulder—"he's sneaked up." Inches from the bear, a turquoise expanse splashed his flesh. "That's Cuba after the worst hurricane I've ever seen." Shirt yanked further; Lauren-Son stooped to examine two hands, fingertips reached, barely touching, to span Sherman's pot-bellied midriff. "The Sistine Chapel," he elucidated, "where God first commanded me to sing. And this spot"—he indicated an inkless section over his heart—"is reserved for a certain special gal."

"Any prospects?"

He leaned in to chirp, "I've had my eye on the perfect one quite some time."

Lauren-Son wagged a finger. "Don't wait too long."

Voden slid in to join them. More than small, not a big-headed dwarf or a perfectly proportioned midget, but an excruciatingly diminutive man, mostly, he stayed somber, silent, and never spoke of himself. Lauren-Son had no idea what to make of him.

Steam misting nostrils, the group sorted through herbs and prepared remedies.

"I'm having a wonderful time," Lauren-Son enthused. She did not want to recall life before Walker, didn't want to remember the miserable nothing she'd once been. "I'm completely different in my soul, in every cell and fiber of my being. I looked for Walker forever; the search was so frustrating."

Rosalee gave her a pat. "Always, it was Walker's task to find you. In Buddhist tradition, the guru draws the disciple to him, rather than the other way around. Because you, the disciple, are ignorant and have no knowledge, your only duty was and is to open fully.—That is all."

"He's like...my guru?"

"Walker helps you to awaken. Some say it's not possible to achieve enlightenment without a teacher. But transfers of grace can occur in even the most fleeting encounters." Lauren-Son thought back to her first contact with Walker. An awakening it had been, alright!

That she officially had a guru, though, seemed silly. "I'd like to become enlightened on my own, without a...a teacher."

"Ah, but the teacher knows all," said Rosalee, "whereas the student does not." Lauren-Son's first impression of Rosalee Soo had been incorrect. Not awkward in the slightest, the older woman merely seemed so.

Kind acts imparted with Rosalee's every breath; recently, Lauren-Son had witnessed the older woman give her best, favorite coat to a homeless man. Never did she seem to judge or push. She did not appear to want much and seemed, as a result, very content. Lauren-Son found the woman so restful, so understanding; she'd come to treasure her.

Given their new friendship, Lauren-Son feared she betrayed her mother. Twice weekly, they spoke by phone. Life, she reported, was dandy, yet she failed to mention the peculiar sensory quirks that plagued her, and—heaven forbid—her name change. Even still, she sensed that Mom worried.

"The writing called the *Guru Gita*," Rosalee continued, "speaks of ways in which the guru works. Most gurus, like God, can be all compassion but, when necessary, can be harsh task-masters. The guru-student relationship is eternal, unceasing. Your relationship with Walker is like that."

"You know Jocelyn?" blurted Lauren-Son. "That talkative student... She seems to have vanished."

"Ah. Well." Rosalee fumbled, distressed. Sherman took her hand.

Voden intervened, "She criticized The Boss, claimed he was a charlatan, so she was asked to leave." Lauren-Son sat, immobile.

Rumors were correct, then! Criticism of Walker or of The Living Light, deemed evidence of spiritual corruption, was to be avoided at all costs.

Terrified at the prospect of losing her place in the community, Lauren-Son had never imagined it possible to get tossed out for sewing discord. "Walker was, like, her forever guru too, but then he cut her off?"

"Their karma was, ah...," Rosalee groped, "short-lived."

"So...," Lauren-Son inquired, squelching anxiety, "what's the actual goal of my relationship with Walker?"

"Salvation of your eternal soul. Your life is not an end unto itself; it is merely part of your immortal soul's journey to perfection." All Walker's students sought to awaken; Lauren-Son did as well. Several, claiming to see the radiance that surrounded him, surged to elevate their status.

Salvation notwithstanding, she too wanted to get as close to Walker as possible.

Voden roused himself to interject, "Mr. Fucols regrets to inform, The Boss is a mere mortal. Additionally, gurus do not have equals, so if The Boss is your guru or master, that makes you his slave. Further, many gurus are not enlightened, but are expert at manipulation. Thus, the bliss one feels in their presence, which can feel like an awakening, is the misdirected sensation of blind adoration."

"Walker would never manipulate," huffed Lauren-Son. "So what are you saying?"

Voden hugged his coffee mug, gurgled, clearing his throat, but kept silent.

"Well?" Lauren-Son pressed.

All awaited more.

No hurry to explain, Voden's eyes slid along the wall as if tracking someone who moved about, invisible.

Lauren-Son piped up, decisive. "I prefer Rosalee's take. And, perhaps it's my role to protect Walker from criticism."

In the end, hunger to be loved, coupled with the need to feel valuable, drove her to invent Walker to be someone he was not. It's easy to do this: to create a version of another that is ripe either for adoration or for hatred. Except, Lauren-Son would find that she never truly knew Walker at all.

Chapter Thirty-One: Young Adult Walker

Walker Judson took in The Overlook, positively enchanted. Percolating haze oddly alive, morning light illumined lush forests and farmlands to span before him as far as the eye could see. Radiance surrounded each object to extend out about a foot; trees, distant mountains, a bird flitting past—even his hand, seemed softly shrouded.

Wildflowers blazed over cliff's edge to carpet the slope, vivid colors giving way to undulating grasses below. Hillside before him, moist with shrubs and trees, the land at his back appeared dry and barren. There, manmade dirt drifts and rubble had been heaped about: likely, detritus from abandoned mining operations.

Trudging along, he spotted a sign: *Welcome to Buena Vista.* Then, first store he came to, he stepped inside. The place was a hodgepodge, mostly junk; a cola box dominated one corner. Snacks and penny candies were strewn among buttons and glass doorknobs that covered all countertops. "What's this place?" he inquired, handing over cash for smokes.

Majestic sweep of the hand, the clerk informed, "This is The Stop. My sign's down for repairs."

"I mean this town, Buena Vista."

Hair like a possum pelt, face creased into a grin, the gent displayed very crooked teeth. "Usta to be a boom town. You passing through?"

"Thought I might stay. Any work hereabouts?"

Grin faded, the clerk jerked back. "Case you hadn't noticed, you're too late to work the mines. So if it's a job you want, nearby Clarksdale's looking for fellas to dismantle smelters."

"Smelters?"

"Smelters separate and purify metal from raw ore. See"— the clerk licked his lips and leaned in— "when fires spontaneously ignited in mineshafts, townsfolk here usta have a devil of a time putting them out; some burned on for months. Nighttime operations, I recall as a boy, when fires flared, intense heat made trucks and shovel dippers glow cherry red. Quite a sight, it was! Any rate...With so many fires getting out of hand, someone had the smarts to move the smelters a safer distance to Clarksdale. You oughta find work there." Busily, the man rubbed away at a countertop spot.

"Ahem," Walker cleared his throat. "Any idea where I might find a room?"

The fella shot him a stern look. "If you don't mind my askin', why do you want to live here?"

"A feeling mostly." The gent scanned Walker up and down; Walker fought the urge to run fingers through his wild, wavy hair.

"Aren't here to rabble-rouse are you? 'Cause we don't take kindly to none-such. If that's what you're after, Sedona's full of flim-flam arteests. Folk there claim to see flying saucers, say extra-terrestrials talk to 'em through their dental fillings, and—Scout's-honor—claim space aliens kidnap, then set controlling implants inside 'em. Buena Vista...We like our folk normal.

"Last crackpot who tried to pull a fast one sold pyramid gadgets— you might'a seen 'em; they set atop your head. Claimed the gizmo told the wearer anything he wanted to know. Yes siree, we ran him out right quick."

"Appreciate the warning." Walker shot the clerk his special piercing look, then held his gaze, hard.

His eyes, he'd been told, were unsettling. People looked into them, then struggled, mightily, to tear themselves away. Walker wasn't vain about this, but *did* use his eyes to draw people in. Mostly, their disturbing effect helped distract from his numerous shortcomings.

Deeply disturbing darkness emanated from him. No one said as much, but he read faces.

His stare aside, he used his odd nature as a buffer to keep himself separate. Part of this design, regardless of occasion, while laboring in the fields or working beneath a car's hood, he still faithfully wore business suits: cheap, unflattering, ungenerously cut ones. Garbed thusly, he sought to conceal what he meant to keep hidden. Rather than hide, though, his tight demeanor, coupled with his odd manner of person and of dress, made him stand out as a freakish outcast.

Walker dropped his eyes. The clerk shook his head, bewildered. "My aunt has a place. Not too nice, but it's a roof over your head. She's a bit of a crab, but keep up with rent, act courteous, and you'll do fine." Address scribbled, he passed it to Walker, then thrust out his hand. "Name's Clayton Lynch." Smoke slithered across Clayton's flesh; fluidity so subtle, sight of it so long dormant, Walker about missed it.

"Walker Judson." He squeezed Clayton's hand.

"My great granddaddy usta be sheriff here." As if a rooster, Clayton puffed his chest. "Nowadays, I'm the mayor and this is my shop."

"Good to know." Rucksack hefted, Walker went for the door. "See you around."

"Stay in line and you'll be right welcome."

"Thanks, I will." Walker waved as he departed.

Stay in line.

Ha! How to explain the mission he'd been put on earth to perform? Staying in line would prove impossible. His future—one that promised to rile and perturb many—was inevitable. Nothing, not even his own wishes, could thwart it.

Onward Walker tromped, taking in the town. As if an epic catastrophe ghosted its past, many buildings, fallen into disrepair, slouched into the hillside. Main Street was a rutted corridor; switchback roads ran off it. Offshoot roads being so savagely potholed, likely a mild rain rendered them impassable.

Cumulative effects of hillside mining evident: slag piles heaped high, long boarded-over mineshafts with wire and rust-chewed sheet metal, pocked earth. A soil plug gave way underfoot; gingerly, uncertain if it meant gopher action or a crumbling mineshaft, Walker skirted round it.

In time, he learned that miles of unsupported shafts honeycombed beneath Buena Vista streets to destabilize its surfaces. Years of movement, the entire business district had scooted downhill, blurring property lines. Nowadays, the jail resided one hundred yards down the slope, abutting a different street from its site of origin.

Sunshine bathing his cheeks, Walker envisioned long-ago subterranean doings beneath his feet. Coalminers...blackened faces, matted, filthy hair, spitting, coughing up dust from lungs as they worked, submerged within earth's bowels. Cave-ins were common, lives easily lost, posing further reminder as to life's impermanence. Yet none of this pained him in the slightest.

Light now glinted into darkest recesses of his being. Even as he tried, he could not blink it off.

Five years constant travel since he departed the yogi, after years of silence, of solitude, of stark nothingness, slow smile spreading across his face, here he was, abutting sky and forever—it felt so right! And this town, Buena Vista, precariously perched upon the hip of Mancos Mountain, was where all would commence.

Moreover, here's where *she* would come!

That too was fated.

Stride perked up, filled with knowing...His would be no ordinary life.

About this, he was of two minds; one part dreaded it. Just now, though, mouth open, then shut, unable to make a sound, joy dribbling in, arms flung up in a sudden surge, he pumped two triumphant fists.

Chapter Thirty-Two: Walker

Paused, pen in hand, Walker sat pondering a wealthy couple's offer to build him a clinic. Invite mistakenly sent to Delia, she'd come to deliver it. "Go for it!" she'd urged. "This is the break you need."

"I'm not cut out for that fancy scene," he'd replied.

"Oooh, this is exactly what I hate!" she'd grumped. "You need a real vision—not your silly haphazard trust that all will abide—for your future." Out she'd slammed, blighting all the good.

Twice during three years apart, Delia had taken up with other men, yet she and Walker never quite got around to divorce. Recently single again, her life intersected his to increased extent.

Overall, he did not much like his wife but guessed he still loved her. Weaker moments, he wished she were with him. Times she *was* actually present, he wished she were not. When they *did* come together, she turned crazed and they fought.

Oh, he missed her wild body heat merged with his but did not relish the distraction. And since Lauren-Son arrival, his heart's desire had significantly blurred.

And another matter nagged of late: *What to do about those pesky women?*

Earlier, a volunteer came up to brush lint from his lapel. "I twisted my ankle," she announced, batting lashes. "Can you check it?"

Ankle examined, Walker forced a wan smile. "Looks perfect." *Perfect* taken to mean more than her ankle, the woman clung to him. Gently, he'd peeled her off.

As if a flock of hens, women—all shapes, sizes, and ages— peck, peck, pecked, nibbling away at him. Faces dipped in eyeliner, fake lashes, and reeking of perfume, emitting cries of longing, they described mysterious, unheard of maladies, demanding that he fix them, when generally, nothing ailed. When he pointed this out, they kept at it, undeterred, inventing excuses to be touched, to display skin, to be close as Walker watched, repulsed.

Oh, he needed to be needed. Given that healing acts served to justify his existence, he happily gave of himself. Being eaten alive, though, he abhorred. First hint of a whine or of sulky, draining connivance, his innards crawled.

Love he reserved for those who *truly* suffered. Even then, he kept all those he served at a well-controlled distance.

Tilted back in his chair, hands behind his head, he slid into reverie. This was a rare slow day—the sort he enjoyed—the phone, which usually rang off the hook, stayed silent. Students and volunteers had the afternoon off. Voden went to walk his cat, and Lauren-Son had gone home for lunch.

Soft knock, Rosalee entered, tray in hand, moist scents—mango, clove—wafted along with her. Onto the desktop, she dropped the mail. "I brought tea, too."

Tea poured from a dung-colored pot, cups clinking, she passed him one. "It is important to use teacups, not mugs. Heavy mugs interfere with relaxation ritual."

"Thanks, Rosie. This is excellent!" Walker savored his drink.

Daily, Rosalee made herbal remedies, but not the same brew for all. First she took pulses, then formulated a beverage to suit each individual's need. For Lauren, now known as Lauren-Son, she often made a calming tonic. Today, Walker drank a blend of schisandra, ginger, licorice root, and nettles to cleanse his liver. For Sherman, she mixed osha root and turmeric to ease arthritic knee joints. Voden merely received tepid water, chocolate sprinkles on top. "Relaxed Wanderer would be a most excellent tonic for Mrs. Thrip," she informed. "It harmonizes depressed liver chi and nourishes blood." Vial extracted from a pocket, she handed it over.

"How about a tonic to boost student intellect?" Students, mostly female, arrived in growing numbers, begged to learn healing techniques.

In the same bothersome manner as the volunteers, they followed Walker about, chattering, giggling. Rather than contribute, as if circling gnats in need of a slap, they pestered and annoyed him. Petty fights broke out as they vied for attention, pressed him to reveal important secrets, sought to arrange trysts, and then sulked when he declined to succumb.

Rosalee wagged a finger. "You avoid them, hoping they will disappear, assign them the worst jobs—cleaning the lavatory and wiping up vomit—is not a fair trade-off. So...How about we have Voden take charge of them? That should keep them out of your hair."

"Excellent idea! And you could teach them to use herbs as well."

Suitably pleased, Rosalee demurred.

Walker reached to tidy the letter pile. "As usual, I'm behind with correspondence."

Unopened mail stacks heaped his desk; most were pleas for help, gooey thank-you notes interspersed among them. "I offer to assist, but always, you say no." Rosalee imitated Walker's deep voice, "'I must personally respond to each one.'"

Spare moments, he'd read of a sender's desire and broadcast healing vibrations back out.

"OK if I sit?" Not awaiting a reply, Rosalee wriggled into a chair to nurse her teacup.

Pockets patted for smokes, Walker lit up. "This is nice. Rarely, do we have time to sit."

Ankles crossed, Rosalee beamed back. "You push too hard." He liked that Rosalee bossed as a mother might. Last week, after a sixteen-hour day, she'd pulled rank and ordered him home.

Obliquely, she reminded him of Ma...How he wished it could be. As his fortunes rose, thoughts increasingly turned to his mother; he longed for her to know him, missed her much, and hoped she'd be proud.

Face pressed into a desktop bouquet, Rosalee gave it a sniff. Head up again, she shot him the broadest, happiest smile; Walker basked in it. "We have a problem with mice," she announced, "so I will ask Sherman to banish them."

"The mice stay. We must give safe refuge to all beings, human or animal."

Face squinched, preparing to object, noting the set of Walker's jaw, she acquiesced, "Okiedokie, they stay. But what do we do about Sherman? Much of his work makes big problems."

What about Sherman? By rights, building maintenance should be left to him, but he was such a hapless handyman, mishaps were daily happenstance. Chimney fires backed up, clogging the waiting room with smoke. Ask Sherman to repair a leaky sink, he scratched his head, perplexed. Last week, he went to adjust the thermostat, then managed to burst a water pipe and flood the basement.

"I got it!" Rosalee slapped her thigh. "He can sing to calm fretful infants— he is very good at that. When he sings, suffering gets smaller." She looked to Walker, hopeful.

"Singing puts him to good use, but that's not exactly work."

"Let us try him anyway."

"All right then."

Voden glided in. "A word?"

"What's up?"

"Don't do it."

"Do what?" Obtuseness of any sort, annoyed Walker.

"You'll regret taking up with your estranged wife again." Despite his calm, Voden's words held urgency. "Shortly, you shall grasp this."

Often, Voden made useful suggestions, yet this prod—come from nowhere —bore an unusual flair.

More on his mind, Voden stood rooted. "'Tis called 'high sense perception' when you expand your senses beyond the norm. Mr. Fucols thought he'd add this, as you've been seeking how best to term it."

"Ah…thanks!" Gaze fast upon Voden, try as Walker might, he was unable to detect emanations; all he could decipher was a whispered outline.

Overall, Voden mystified. Unlike the relentless, busy vibrations common to most, the man possessed eternal stillness. Curiously, this vibration, or lack thereof, reminded him of Ma.

At the outset, Walker envisioned Voden as a fine teacher and healer, which he was, and a father figure, which he most certainly was not. Installed in a third floor room next to Sherman's, he *did* relieve Walker's growing burden by taking on his share of healings. As Walker's mentor regarding esoteric healing, he filled in knowledge gaps regarding Asian and Christian mysticism. Overall a godsend, little about the man fit the norm.

Not warm in the slightest, rarely did he express sentiment, nor did he bother to behave in socially acceptable ways. During meditation gatherings and classes, mostly he sat quiet, head cocked, as if listening to the stillness beneath the noise. "Feeling the vibrations," he explained when queried.

Rare times, when he did speak, students sat, breathless, at seat's edge. Spare words spoken, succinct, erudite, all then clamored, full of inquiry. Many a time, Voden actually upstaged Walker.

"You willing to take charge of student training?" Walker now asked him.

"Certainly, Boss." Walker flinched. Repeatedly, he asked Voden to call him by his name.

Voden expounded, "The students lack discipline. Mr. Fucols shall shape them into a structured organization, with rules, mandated activities, and expectations." Meditation group aside, student education had been a random, haphazard, disorganized affair.

"Grand idea!" Walker chimed, wholehearted. Voden unwrapped a Mars candy bar, munched it down, and plucked yet another from his full-to-overflowing pocket.

Steadily, more candy bars disappeared down his gullet. "You smoke to achieve ballast; Mr. Fucols eats these," Voden fended, gliding further into the room. "So it is settled...Mr. Fucols keeps students out of your hair and, for that, you shall be eternally grateful?"

"That's right!"

"And your protégé, Lauren?"

"Lauren-Son," Walker corrected.

"Does she join the students?"

"She stays with me."

"Quite so." Onward, they brainstormed. Eyes disappeared into crinkles, proudly, Rosalee beamed, adding suggestions here and there. Feet firmly planted, arms straight at his sides, face without affect, Voden outlined plans: The Living Light school for healers would devote itself to spiritual instruction, meditation, and train students to perform healing techniques.

Conversation drifting, Walker offered up, "A biographer's been pressing to write my story, so I thanked him for thinking of me, then gave him the brush-off." Past weeks, calls from journalists, even a movie agent, had come. "What do you think...Should I do interviews?"

"You have nothing to hide," Voden said, blithely.

"How about you run our business affairs altogether?" To date, Walker and Rosalee had cobbled together management that was less than ideal, but The Living Light had dire need of a person to handle day-to-day operations.

Voden worked well behind the scenes but was no administrator. Rosalee, busy with her own practice, did not relish the hassle. Lauren-Son, though good at triage, was far too green. "Thanks kindly," Voden demurred, "but front man 'tis not Mr. Fucols' thing—oh, a moment." He exited.

Walker and Rosalee exchanged questioning looks.

Sheaf of papers in hand, Voden returned. "What shall we do about these?" Pile slid across, he elucidated, "'Tis a petition, five hundred signatures in all. Buena Vista's citizens demand that we tone it down or depart." Gaze swung between his friends, Walker thumbed through the sheets.

Here's the challenge. "How do they abide those kooky artisans and not tolerate us?"

How dare they! He riled. Conflict, he'd known from the outset, would come, but outright rejection without dialogue angered.

"Most unfortunate," supplied Voden, "but the maelstrom of gossip swarms and builds."

Pleasure erased from Rosalee's face, she wriggled, fretful. Voden clacked his tongue.

"I say"—fist mashed into palm, Walker formulated—"we hold an open house and invite folks to discuss this. Then we explain what we're up to and request input...that should eradicate mystery. Also, we can employ several locals." Rosalee's dear face spasmed in panic.

"That is a good start." Faster, her foot wagged. "But it is not enough."

"People here," Voden asserted, "are accustomed to mediocrity and sameness, so you, Boss, make them nervous."

"I know their minds," peeped Rosalee. "An open house, cookies and juice will not make them change. They need time to grow to trust you."

"God brought me here for a purpose," Walker gritted. "We will not be run out!"

Chapter Thirty-Three: Lauren

"The trick of healing is to become one with your patient," Walker informed Lauren-Son, as they settled Mrs. Thrip in for her weekly appointment.

Become one? Lauren-Son pondered this, along with his previous instruction: *Create better boundaries?* And then she gave him a questioning look.

Contradiction acknowledged, Walker grinned back.

"See what I saved up." Mrs. Thrip opened her handbag; thousands of folded bills, mostly tens and twenties, brimming, Lauren-Son gaped.

"Take care who you show that to, ma'am," Walker cautioned. "Someone might try to make off with it." Mrs. Thrip pinched his cheek.

"Soon as I leave here, I'm Reno-bound by Greyhound to gamble. Just gave my Hank a sponge bath, put new jammies on 'im—the warm flannel kind, which he doesn't much care for. The sitter was running late, so I turned up the radio and left him reposed on the sofa, right comfy. Come now," she jostled. "I have a bus to catch."

"How've you been feeling?" Lauren-Son inquired.

"Fine. Not gassy. No upset. I'm still holding off on surgery."

"You scan and start," Walker suggested of Lauren-Son. "I'll join in shortly."

Centered and focused inward, warmth and electric zaps—astonishing, otherworldly—sprang into Lauren-Son's hands. Concentration intensified, calm certitude supplanted self-consciousness. So much so that she startled when Walker spoke softly, "You have a gift. Someday, it'll surpass any skill of mine." She gazed at him in fond wonder.

Walker went to cradle Mrs. Thrip's head, and cocked his ear as if listening. "Feel her aches and pains? Those are hers, not yours or mine. As you probe her body, feel it all—her soreness, her burdens, her heartache. It's OK to feel, just don't take them on."

Lauren-Son cuddled Mrs. Thrip's foot, and then took up the other. Walker hummed breaths into the woman's chest to vibrate her ribcage.

Energy flowed, emanating from a place Lauren-Son had only begun to grasp. Luminosity in her, in Walker, and in Mrs. Thrip shafted, then lit all of them. They didn't literally become lightbulbs, but definitely basked in light, as fluttery radiance synchronizing their heartbeats to bind them, intimately. Lauren-Son looked to Walker. He grinned broadly.

Quiet with joyful competence, she felt terribly close to him.

"Let's see how you do on this next one," said Walker as they brought in their next patient.

"I'm not ready," quibbled Lauren-Son.

"Might as well start now; it's been a year."

"I'm possessed," announced Peaches, a great wad of a woman.

Walker waved Lauren-Son forth with a whisper, "Trust yourself."

Underarms dangling, jiggling, Peaches hefted onto the table to shimmy about until prone. "So...What brings you here?" inquired Lauren-Son, as casually as possible.

"Months ago, Satan or an alien presence took hold of me. Anyway"—Peaches smacked her own chest, hard—"get it out!" Air clotted up, odors of rot wafted.

Stomach roiling, hand to nose, Lauren-Son sought the source.

The stench, she realized, pushed out from the patient's pores.

"He's punishing me!" Swift slaps to her own cheeks, Peaches abruptly settled.

Lauren-Son shot Walker a pleading look. He smiled, encouraging.

Peaches resumed, "He tried to keep me from coming, made me lose my car keys, caused my gas gauge to go empty, and forced me off the road."

"Sounds awful." Lauren-Son set a commiserating hand on the patient.

"No touch!" Peaches hissed. "For all I know, you're one of them. Satan works through cripples and the damaged."

Lauren-Son glanced at Walker: *How do I heal without touch?* They had yet to cover it.

Merest nod, he insisted she go ahead.

"I need a moment to prepare." Hands mangled together, working for composure, mind flitting through options, she wet her lips, popped knuckles, and slicked her hair back.

What next?

She peered at Walker. "Rid your mind of chatter," he coached, "then stabilize your energies."

"First," she informed the patient, "I check for imbalance by moving my hands about, then I run energy into your body." Several breaths, heartbeat slowed, mind emptied, flats of hands hovering, careful not to touch, she scanned down, and cast Walker a sidelong glance.

Again, he nodded.

Hands back in motion, she noted cool spots—sucking voids—in Peaches's energy field, but could not actually see them.

Suddenly, she felt far away, expansive, yet somewhat remote from herself, and guidance took hold.

Slicing air, flicking wrists, she made assorted, seemingly crucial, yet incomprehensible movements. "Yoooo...," she hooted, into Peaches's kneecaps.

Tiny as a speck now, sucked into the body before her, encompassed, embrace by it, she felt herself break into molecules. Her microscopic self divided, kept dividing, falling, tumbling into her patient's flesh. Able to feel Peaches's capillaries, mitochondria, and lymphocytes, she flooded them with pulsed light.

Jetting back into her body, session perking along nicely, she shook a rattle at Peaches' feet, clanged a bell, waved fist-sized crystals, circled the recumbent form clockwise once, and then counterclockwise twice. Gradually, she rounded and raised her arms over her head, then stepped back, winded, amazed.

Walker regarded her, quizzical. "You done?"

"I...I thought I was." *Jeeze!* She feared she'd failed.

"That's a fair start." Walker went to the table. "Excuse us a minute," he addressed Peaches, who seemed to snooze. "But this matter is more complex than banging cymbals, waving hands, and hoping for the best. By setting your intent as to what you hope to accomplish here, you help Peaches release her emotions."

"Intent?"

"We spoke of this early on. Seeing Peaches as healthy and whole sends a healing message throughout her body to good effect."

"Sorry, I'm way anxious." *Intent* sounded akin to prayer, and lately Lauren-Son's prayers included assorted, specific requests. She prayed that Miss Spivey was alive. She prayed for pleasant conversation with Mom. Prayed that all patients be healed, and she actually apologized to God, and to those whom she'd failed when they were not. She prayed to become a great healer, asked that her happiness last forever, and prayed to never forget how miserable she'd been. Also, she prayed that Walker esteem her.

Just now she exhaled a prayer—begged, actually—for guidance to help this woman.

"Invite Peaches to say how she feels."

"Please," Lauren-Son addressed Peaches, "feel free to express yourself."

Peaches bunched up, paused, then shrieked, "I want to pound someone!"

Lauren-Son stumbled back, then feebly asked, "Who?"

"My ppp-parents."

"Go on, tell them how you feel."

"I hate youuuuu!" Peaches kicked out to dent the wall. Screaming, thrashing, escalating rather than culminating, on she went.

Help! Lauren-Son mouthed to Walker, losing control of the session.

Sleeves rolled up, he stepped in, put hands on Peaches's belly. Lauren-Son expected her to flinch and throw him off, but she actually settled.

Head bowed, Walker concentrated, unhurried.

Hurt, annoyed, Lauren-Son watched, fuming. *Seriously, he misjudged my readiness!*

Shortly, Walker lifted his head. "There's an unfriendly entity lodged here." He traced Peaches' lower belly; she shuddered and groaned. "I command that you depart."

Flurry of trembling, Peaches propped up to retch. Eyes wide, whites showing clear around, she announced, "He's very large, very evil, and refuses to leave."

"We drive him out, then!" Walker griped her feet. Mouth expanded, stretched, he intoned, "Yeoww-humm-yeoww-humm..." Peaches joined in, releasing a deafening, hair-raising howl. "The entity must reduce the volume," Walker shouted.

Decibels lowered to a mild whine, something sinister took hold. "Make him stop; he's doing terrible, immoral things!" Peaches begged, squirming.

Air chilly, gone putrid, face impressively purpled, warped into a rage-filled sneer, body arched, Peaches's stupendous girth levitated.

Lauren-Son went clammy all over; Walker, too, lost focus. Lauren-Son sensed the dark void that blatted from Peaches' mouth and scurried off, but did not see it.

Room warming by degrees, Walker resumed, "So now tell us about your life."

Peaches's cheeks quivered. "Sizzling burning flesh—mine. No, Mama, please no!" Her hands flew up, fending imagined blows.

Features coarsened, a deep, malicious voice inhabited her, "I hit, 'cause you don't mind me."

Voice gone plaintive, she begged, "No Mama, don't!"

"Teach you to behave!" blared the other voice. Peaches recoiled.

Gently, Walker placed a hand on the woman's brow and rested the other upon her heart. "What'd I do that was so terrible?" Peaches implored, reverting to her usual voice.

"Explore this further," Walker encouraged.

A blizzard of words came. "My life's a giant nightmare. My first husband left me. Should've been glad, 'cause he beat me, regular. Rather than glad though, I tried to kill myself. Matter of fact, I stayed in all my marriages, far past staying. I just...just couldn't help it. Oh my God!" Anguish roared out as she detailed a life story of abuse, beatings, deprivation, and the soul crushing death of her infant. "That's the gist," she announced, cutting it short.

Grimly focused, Walker encouraged, "Keep going...There's more."

"You have to help."

"Take my hand, then." Exquisitely kind, Walker escorted Peaches through the most minute, trivial of life details, coaxing recall of seemingly insignificant incidents.

Voice slowed to monotone, gradually Peaches's words came out so impersonal, so matter of fact, as if she described a fictional nightmarish character. Truly, Walker listened. He absorbed every word, nuance and gesture, seeming to treasure each sorry, sordid detail.

"You matter," he spoke fiercely. "Trouble is, darkness implanted in your soul because you thought you did not." Hands gently extracted from her grasp, he stepped back, emitted a single, long nasal drone, let it taper, and then finished.

"Feels like my innards got scrubbed clean." Peaches trembled, but lay calm. "Do you suppose"—she looked to Walker—"I'll ever forgive myself for being such a pathetic mess?"

Walker smiled the tiniest bit. "I certainly hope so."

"But..." Peaches clenched fists. "I cannot, will not, forgive everyone else!"

"Good. Your anger saved you!"

Helped from the table, Peaches probed and prodded herself. "Just making sure I still exist." Continued stroking each body part as if touch affirmed her, she gazed at Walker in wonder all the while.

When arrived, she'd seemed dull, ordinary. Face now radiating loveliness, Peaches pumped Walker's hand, then she gave Lauren-Son a vigorous handshake as well. "Now I can have a life."

"Go easy," Walker advised. "You're having what's known as a healing high. When it wears off, and I guarantee it will, your real work—piecing yourself back together—will begin. Probably, you'd benefit from counseling."

"Don't burst my bubble," Peaches chuckled. "Let me enjoy!" She waved, then departed.

Chapter Thirty-Four: Walker

No more to say, Rosalee and Voden excused themselves.

Walker attended to mail. Rosalee came back, asking if he knew where they might store a truckload of hay: a gift from a grateful rancher whose palsy Walker had alleviated.

Again, Rosalee returned. "What do you make of this?" Magazine deposited, she went back out.

Walker Judson: Medical Intuitive, read the headline; his stony face graced the cover. *Modern mystic Walker Judson possesses extraordinary healing powers. His capabilities handily exceed the success rate of conventional medicine.* Walker cringed.

The piece went on to speculate about his past but mostly drew a blank. Whenever asked as to his origins, he rigorously charmed inquirers off topic.

Delia gone, his folks never quite kin, Rosalee, Voden, Lauren-Son, Sherman, The Living Light, and The Angel were all the family he needed.

In closing, the article referred to The Angel as his trusty mascot. Although more quiescent of late, it served as far more than that. He paused to savor their connection.

Yet never had it revealed its origins, which surprised him. He *did* know: at behest of the Catholic Church, an Italian named d'Angelo had sculpted it. In Vatican II's spasm to modernize, saintly statues got deconsecrated, then removed from parish decor. Some of his icons were sold for private use but most got unceremoniously dumped, so an incensed d'Angelo went church to church, sledgehammering his remaining creations to bits. Miraculously, despite his rampage, The Angel managed to survive.

Low rumble coming up the street, he went to the window.

Chug-a-chug—a red Camaro halted out front.

Day's pleasure fading as Delia exited, Walker smudged his cigarette.

Clickety-click—heels on the walk, in she swooped to grouse, "Again, your bills have come to me." Plopped into Walker's chair, she tossed him a stern look. "All this time, and still, I pick up the pieces."

"You certainly look good."

"Aw!" Delia softened. "Sweet of you." Recently, she'd plumped up yet wasn't dumpy in the slightest. Immense hooped earrings wobbling, adorned in pedal pushers and scoop-neck top, indeed she looked exotic, edible, and somewhat dangerous.

Stack of letters lifted, she let them drop. "See what I mean? You procrastinate!"

"You got that right!" Walker sat back to watch.

Drawer slid open, she rifled through. "Someone needs to whip you into shape. And...I bet you don't make that ugly girl pay. Lessons you give her are the talk of the valley." She stood, hip cocked, and met his gaze. "What do you see in her, anyway?" On cue, Lauren-Son appeared.

Sensing a presence, smirky smile in place, Delia turned to coo, "Ahhh, so you're the one!"

"You must be Delia." Hand thrust out, Lauren-Son grinned. "I'm Lauren—er, Lauren-Son."

Hand ignored, Delia gripped Walker's bicep. "What do you charge for healings, darling husband?"

"Whatever they can pay." Arm extracted, Walker stepped from reach. "Often, nothing."

"Ha—as I thought!" Hand still extended, Lauren-Son stared at Delia, spellbound.

Impossible not to, all got mesmerized. Men fluffed their chests; women did too.

Lauren-Son retrieved her hand.

Walker fretted at Delia's disdain for the girl.

Delia riffled the petition and glanced up, incredulous, "They want you out?"

Lauren-Son turned to him, stricken and questioning. "I plan to fight it," Walker soothed.

Delia launched in, "This town is so backward! Snobby too. If you haven't lived here all your life, you're second-rate. Second rate...What a joke! Given all those kooky, forward-thinking artists, you'd think folks would be more broad-minded, but everyone here, including your pal, Rosie, acts like they own a slice of heaven that you're conniving to steal."

"People hate change," Walker agreed. "That's what we represent: our unconventional activities make us stick out like undies flapping in the breeze."

"I could help defend against this. We'd make a good team." Topic switched, she let slip, "I'm seeing a banker who wants to marry me."

"Ah...," Lauren-Son interjected, "I'll be leaving." She half turned."Nice to meet you," Delia ignored her; she scurried off.

Disdain chapping her cheeks, Delia looked after the girl, then pressed, "Want me or not?" Walker shrugged, non-committal. Delia pouted. Shifting uncertain, he longed for love, but Delia's version of love brought him up short.

"I don't quite know," he hemmed and hawed. "You've been unhappy with me; I'm not likely to change." How pleased, surprised, he'd been to marry her in the first place.

Foolish, giddy back then, he'd reached for her, terribly hopeful, possibly happy. Yet when she left, he'd felt only relief.

Predatory essence shifted into high gear, Delia sniffed and exited.

Returning shortly, face enormous from grinning—apparently liking the place's potential—she cooed, "Let's give it a try." Curious ringing in his ears, Walker felt all wrong.

You'll regret hooking up with your wife again, Voden had warned.

Yet, arms aching, he wanted her, badly.

Should she join him, The Living Light's healing contagion might free up her baser cravings. And perhaps she'd pull this place together. He made a smile. "We could use your help. So yes, but let's take it slow."

"Oooh," Delia squeaked, rolling onto tiptoe to plant a kiss. "This place could be so terrific! You just need little 'ole moi to whip it into shape." All turned fair game for critical comment, she pressed, "Is that pipsqueak Voden Fucols actually your partner, and what kind of a name is that?"

Off she spun onto assorted topics. "For this place to run like a real business, rather than a half-hearted drop-in center, you must schedule volunteers for regular shifts. And"—rosy cheeked with glee, she sashayed a bit—"ditch that awful girl."

"How's about I appoint you office manager?"

"How about director?"

"We'll see how it goes."

Delia's hands flung up, annoyed. "Fine," her mouth said. "We arrange a public meeting to let folks know what we're up to." She argued further over her title. Walker stood firm. She conceded, "OK... But we bring in my pal, Ardis, and train her as back up so she can step right in as soon as I get promoted."

Within a week long-legged, high-haunched Ardis, one-time Vegas showgirl, now wife to paunchy Verde Valley rancher and mother to half-dozen squalling offspring, would be firmly ensconced.

Delia squabbled away.

Weariness overtook him: *Why did I agree?* He knew he shouldn't have.

Granted, his view of Delia already held many holes, but Voden's intrusion into his personal life riled.

Chapter Thirty-Five: Lauren

Lauren-Son followed Walker back to the treatment room. "Why did you think I was ready?"

Walker ticked a finger. "Your ego interfered. You pushed too hard, trying to impress, and expended more energy toward Peaches than you took in. Doing so can deplete and make you ill, and then you're of no use to your patient. I've said before: stop using your will to heal. It's a chronic problem. Divine Will is in charge, not you."

Lauren-Son scoffed. "Clearly, in Peaches's case, God hasn't been terribly attentive, so I tried to make up for the lack."

"You have no idea what you're saying!" Walker's words sliced air.

Lauren-Son shot him a sickly smile. "Guess not." A door slammed. Voices chattered in the hall. "Well…," she fumbled. "I think I messed up."

"No…," he said slowly, "you learned a great deal, which was the point."

"My lack of readiness put Peaches at risk."

"Even your missteps were perfect."

"You hum; what's with that?"

"Sounds rearrange cells, move stuck energy, and open a person up." Hands washed, he toweled them dry, then leaned at the sink. "Sounds, all kinds—vocalization, instrumental, listening to music, the rain, moaning wind, even street traffic—influence health and consciousness."

"When Sherman sings, everyone perks up. Is that the same?"

"Definitely!"

Earlier, as if a rainbow bloomed from his mouth, Sherman belted out a spectacular harmonic; all within earshot cheered for joy or wept, begging for more. Incapable of distinguishing wrench from nail file, whenever that man crooned a silly ballad or swung into vibrato operatic performance, burdens assuaged to benefit all.

Sheet removed from the treatment table, Lauren-Son replaced it with a clean one. Walker hitched himself onto its edge and continued, "As you know, when the body vibrates at a low frequency, disease invades. So certain sounds increase vibration to mobilize healing forces. Mostly though, physical or emotional illness is a matter of spiritual consequence. Peaches vacated her soul because of her horrific life, which permitted that entity to gain hold. What you started, what we did, kicked out that entity, solidified her energy field and anchored her back into her body. Let's just hope it sticks."

"How'd you get so smart?"

Walker scratched his chin. "Knowledge just came because I wanted it. Same for you; it awaits...You just need to ask."

Lauren-Son rubbed hands together. "So... When do I get as good as you?

"Keep meditating." Emitting a long monotone, "Auuuum," Walker continued to make assorted guttural utterances. Gently sucked into his orbit, all her questions and fears eased up.

Bliss-filled mystics also make such noises. Therefore, she speculated, *Walker must be a mystic—Except, he never exactly seemed bliss filled.*

Mostly, he seemed isolated, sad, somewhat lost. She'd noted his immobility, the way he faltered with others...and his loneliness. No one on earth seemed as alone as he.

Once upon a time, she thought only truly happy people possessed such kindness, but Walker seemed a soul who'd endured huge suffering. More than anyone she'd known, he seemed heavily burdened, wounded even.

What terrible things happened to make you like this? She wanted to bang on his brow, clamoring to be let in.

Instead, she asked, "So, Walker, who heals you?"

"Don't worry about me." Thoughtfully, he regarded her. "You fear your gifts. To get like me, you must simply open up." Hand lifted, fingers blooming open, he let the moment drift.

"Me afraid?"

"Most need the illusion of control. A small life is a safe life, and you, my friend, could tilt either way. Just now, you fear accepting more than you figure your limited brain can grasp."

"Not so!" She glared huffily. In truth, he was correct.

Walker stood to smooth the sheet. "Get close to the Divine and you stand at the brink of madness. So, rather than risk it, many keep their lives superficial. Say you'd actually seen the satanic being that exited Peaches. Everyone else insists such creatures are imaginary, so you might also deny they exist or take a risk and declare your belief in them, knowing that in doing so that you'll be tagged a lunatic. Denial is expedient, but it kills off something, because deep down you know that such dark forces abide.

"For most, acknowledging the entity's presence isn't worth ostracism. Yet some herald that they've seen it in order to be deemed special. That too misses the point. The gift, seeing the entity, means embracing it all: seeing the dark force—or the devil—the terror, the longing, the impossibility of it, risking ostracism, instead of picking and choosing what you like and don't like about it." Words falling from his mouth to her ears, she stared at him, dumbly.

"I get it, I think."

"Should you fully embrace this life, now that it's chosen you, at times you'll wonder if your experiences are real or imaginary or if you have, indeed, lost your mind." He went to shut the window.

Lose my mind! She strove for calm.

Abruptly, Walker inquired, "You *see* sometimes don't you?"

"Ah...," she fumbled. "I can't actually *see* inside a body. But lately, I *do* notice dead air space surrounding the sick." Walker nodded, fished a pack of smokes from his pocket, teased one out, lit up and inhaled.

"Eventually, you will."

Realization came to her. Actually, she *had* seen energies that first time, when Walker's whole being surged into that ailing man, when the room's entire contents blurred into one.

Always, she'd possessed the ability to *see*. Only her acceptance had lain dormant!

Separated, going room-to-room to turn off lights, they reconvened in the foyer. Walker resumed, "Today, we entered Peaches's nightmare and helped her find her way back. I move between other worlds, shifting in and out of various dimensions, and can enter the past or move ahead to the future at will. Psychotics do this as well, but they can also tumble uncontrolled and have trouble returning to the here and now." Lauren-Son chuckled awkwardly.

Heaven, mid-earth, and dimensions in between are places Walker actually visits!

He could dip into an alternative universe to delve into a road not taken, examine a choice made that veered an individual from perfection, or retrieve some long forgotten aspect—usually their wholeness—and then return to hand that lost part back. *Soul Retrieval,* he termed it.

Such strangeness made Walker so special; she itched to master such marvels!

Overhead light switched off, fingers to brow, Walker saluted The Angel. "G'night."

The duo stepped outside. Walker locked the door. A dry breeze kicked up. Passing clouds occluded the slivered moon. "One more question," Lauren-Son called out; Walker turned back. "Who hurt you so bad?"

Spun on heel, Walker called over his shoulder, "G'night."

"Sorry!" Lauren-Son called after. Not *truly* sorry, she merely wanted to understand him.

Chapter Thirty-Six: Walker

During meditation group, a dozen students waiting, Walker strode in forty-five minutes late to take his place in the fan-backed wicker chair upfront. Students at his feet, Lauren-Son included, smiling up at him, no words spoken, he slid into a meditative state.

An hour passed. No one dared disturb him during this un-twitching interval. Although he appeared to nap, thoughts about Lauren-Son frolicked in his brain.

Earlier, she'd burst into his office to lean, sloppily, across his desk. "Excuse me, but who is that fellow you speak to during Mrs. Thrip's sessions? You repeat the same name other times too."

"Ah, Mr. Chien! When we have time, I'll speak of him at length." Lick to a forefinger, she'd de-smudged his chin. Fondness surged; he adored such intimacy.

Not all was smooth sailing; he'd sat back to await her usual barrage. Thirsty for knowledge, with each bit of information disseminated, ten more questions itched. "Why? How come?" she'd pester. Truly, however, he relished it.

So the inevitable question came: "Who says there are seven layers to the energy field, and how can you prove they exist?"

Patiently, Walker had explained, "The human energy field supplies the body with life force. I know because I can see the matrix that holds human physicality intact. Most healers see seven levels; each successive level vibrates at a higher frequency. Enlightened beings see many more. Surrounding you, I see a multidimensional egg like shape. Within that, a colorful gridwork vibrates. Alter your mood or become ill, the colors and gridwork shift and change."

"Sounds like hallucinating."

Hands raised in surrender, mildly exasperated, he'd said, "You take many liberties."

"Sorry," she'd spasmed, then lit off. "Gotta go."

Warmed by a delicious sense of his own newfound ease attributed to her presence, Walker had to marvel at the strides she'd made. At first, painfully unsure, every bit of her straight these days, she'd become, if not lovely, quite handsome. He saw energy pour into her and then pour out from her hands to heal others. Emboldened by growing skill, she had an air of competent authority and would eventually make an excellent healer. Moreover, when shaped to best advantage, she'd make the perfect working partner.

Eyes open, Walker stirred. Students, free to move, stirred as well. "From time to time," he illumined the group, "I'm called to alternate worlds, vivid planes of consciousness, where I help resolve individual and worldwide conflicts and downturns. As you know, this region has undergone a severe drought. As a result of work done tonight on the astral to mitigate this deficit, rain will come shortly.

"At some point, a select few of you will easily perform similar services." What came next surprised even Walker, yet he would enjoy its aftereffects. "But your disbelief"—he turned to rebuke, Gwen, a mousy student—"which deeply pains me, interferes with my ability to transit these realms. Therefore, you must adjust your mindset or I cannot abide your presence." Chill invading the room, tears welled in the woman's eyes; for never would he look her way again.

Trembling in the air, all students fearing further admonishment, bid Walker a hushed goodnight. Lauren-Son too pulled back, gathered herself, then spoke, "Life's fullness for Gwen has just been revoked."

"Understand or not, skepticism impedes the overarching good. I expect you to accept this."

Full-up with knowing, he foresaw that, on the morrow, thunder and lightning would clap, clouds would open, and a deluge would drop from skies to enrich parched earth. Moreover, eager to atone for her fellow student's shortcomings, Lauren-Son would show up, front and center, and work extra hard to please him.

Chapter Thirty-Seven: Young Adult Walker

"One ticket for *Treasure of the Sierra Madre.*" Walker slid a dollar through the oval cutout.

The elderly Chinese woman gave back change, inquiring,"Are you religiously inclined?"

"'Scuse me?" Umbrella let down, he strained to hear over pattering rain.

"Each day you come, as if to worship, to see this same movie." Walker blinked, bewildered, as the woman explained, "Movies are big religion in the United States. Actors are like holy people; they are revered as if gods. We admire their clothes and their rich lifestyles—it is very odd."

"Yes ma'am, I suppose." Walker eyed the statue in the booth behind her.

"You like the *Eunuch Christ*?"

"Christ—a eunuch?" *How'd I miss this crucial scriptural detail?*

The tiny woman bounced to attention. "Christ a eunuch...That is too funny!" Off, she spun into gales of giggles.

Later, his confusion would be clarified as he toured her home: "Lookee here," she'd indicated, "this eunuch table is one of a kind."

Fully composed, hand thrust through the miniature window, she announced, "I am Rosalee Soo."

Bones so fragile, fearing he might crush them, he gripped her fingertips. "I'm Walker Judson."

"Very good to meet you, Mr. Walker!" Again the woman cackled, flailing stick-like arms. Then she turned serious. "Always, you sit in back alone. Next time, I will give you a free ticket so you may bring a friend."

"Thanks kindly, ma'am, but I don't know anyone."

"Ah!" Eyebrows shot up, she leaned in confidential. "Care for a buddy, then?"

"A buddy?" It took a moment to realize whom she meant.

"Yes, me!" She pointed at herself.

He blushed so hard, his earlobes ached. Insides all awry, guard slipping, the urge to clamber into the booth to hug her reared up. Hands crammed into pockets, tongue unglued, he admitted, "Yes, ma'am. I could use a buddy, I...I guess." Always, he'd been on his own; wholly, deeply alone.

Following the seasons, he'd traversed the continent, grabbing work wherever fate carried him. He'd picked strawberries in California, laid rail in Chicago train yards, and harvested Florida oranges.

Ten years' travel, now age twenty-three, longing for a home, he arrived at each new town, peered about, wondering if this was it. Bus stations, he saw families greet, cry, laugh, and mash together, all lavish with hugs and kisses. Stories clattering from folks' mouths, unable to speak fast enough as they kissed and teared up, eyes absorbing beloved faces meant the end of missing. Ever removed, familiar ache pinging his chest, he stood in the shadows, watched and hoped.

This recent journey westward, each passing mile, his longing had intensified. Just now, however, being in this town, meeting this woman, liking her quite a bit, abrupt giddiness overtook him.

As a rule, Walker divided humans into two camps: those he felt superior to and those he felt less than. Mostly he felt inferior, grew flustered and dumbstruck in the company of others. Unable to abide those he felt superior to, he tended to avoid them. In summation, he steered clear of most everyone.

Oh, he loved folks, but rather than love them up close, personal-like, he preferred love from afar. So, first time ever, sensing Rosalee Soo to be his equal, he grasped that he would not be able to avoid her. "Care to join me in a cup of tea?" Rosalee then answered herself, "Don't know if we will fit, but we can certainly try."

Doubled over, "Te-hee-hee-hee!" she tittered at her own joke.

"Yessu'm," Walker replied, "tea suits me fine." According to Rosalee Soo's world view, he soon discovered, most everything posed a knee-slapper.

"Let us visit before the movie." Rosalee exited the booth, then steered him inside. "Do not worry. No one else is here, so we may start the show any time."

The lobby overflowed with a mishmash of sofas and recliners. Previous visits Walker noted patrons lounging so comfy that, despite vigorous flashing lights and announcements heralding the show's start, many forgot why they'd come. "Sit," Rosalee Soo commanded; Walker obliged.

Towel thrown over his damp head, she tousled his hair dry. "Too much heat departs the body when hair is wet." He deeply enjoyed the friendly scrub.

"Show me your tongue." Tongue thrust out, she thoroughly examined it. Wrist gripped, she took his pulses and then tsked, "You have liver stagnation; we must strengthen your chi." Dropped behind the snack counter, she hefted an immense vial—a syrupy concoction of dessicated eyeball-size berries and leathery leaves—measured a fistful onto a scale, scooped them into the drink, set a timer to boil the mix three precise minutes.

Liquid let steep, she then poured it into a cup and handed it over. "You drink. And, not to worry, it only looks like bat wings."

First gulp, taste buds flung open, Walker pressed hands to temples. "Ach, it tastes like soapy licorice and mud!"

Immediately clearheaded, warmth seeped in to replenish every flagging cell. "Wow, what is this?"

"None of your business." Rosalee grinned. "But you must sip, not gulp."

Walker sat back, relaxed, expansive, embraced within the fattest, comfiest chair as they discussed their mutual all-time favorite, *Rebel Without a Cause*.

Still curious about the drink, he lifted the cup. "Seriously, what's in this?"

Pat, pat, went Rosalee. As if she'd glimpsed his well-guarded vulnerability and promised to protect it, her competent touch soothed. "It is a special beverage meant to heal body, mind, and spirit, because Rosalee Soo wants you fixed." Teeth covered with one hand, shyly, she gazed at him, then curved the focus.

"In Buena Vista's heyday, my father, Wong Soo, was cook for the Little Daisy Mine. When the mine closed, my father partnered up with Charlie Hughes to open a Chinese restaurant. You know Clayton Lynch who owns The Stop? Charlie Hughes, his grandfather, was a big drinker; Clayton's father had problems with drink too. So Clayton Lynch changed his name to get away from family's bad reputation." Brightness reared up surrounding her to affirm Walker's long-slumbering gift.

Yet swiftly, he suppressed it.

"Because father was a Chinaman," Rosalee elucidated, "he could not own land outright, so he and Charlie Hughes bought up all buildings on Main Street's downhill side. Charlie Hughes drank himself silly, but father saved enough money to send to China for his wife and daughter, me, Rosalee Soo. When I suggested father buy The Nick, he obliged." Proudly, she beamed at her surroundings.

Too out of the way for new releases, The Nickelodeon Theater, showed mostly outdated, sub-titled foreign films that played for months. On the upside, prices were a bargain: double features cost a dime—a fee decades behind the times.

Nowadays, Rosalee owned and ran the theater, transformed her father's Chinese restaurant into a greasy spoon she'd re-dubbed The Flatiron, and rented out half-dozen other downtown shops.

Unmarried at sixty-one, she doted on each building, lavishing attention upon them, same as she might a child if she'd had one. "I work hard like my father, but am not the success he was." Hankie extracted, Rosalee dabbed both eyes.

Uncertain if comfort was required, Walker examined his shoe tops till her sniffs subsided.

Initially, he mistook Rosalee Soo's bobbing stammer and eye dabs for weakness. Beneath her milquetoast demeanor, however, she proved razor sharp. "I returned to China to attend medical school," she continued, "and now practice Chinese Medicine on the quiet. People here do not accept anything that deviates from the traditional, but they *do* enjoy small gifts."

Several times, Walker had seen Rosalee place a bottle or herbal packet—likely a cold or flu remedy—into a movie patron's palm. "No charge. For flee." Meaning *free,* she'd impatiently dismiss those trying to pay. "Just buy a ticket."

"Should I call you Dr. Soo then?" Walker inquired

"You should not!" Rosalee Soo laughed so hard, swiftly, he rescinded that thought.

"Ready to watch?" Squeaking the chair, Rosalee nimbly arose, then reached to give him a pat.

"I am."

"Give me a moment to set the reel." Returned shortly, Rosalee ushered Walker into the theater where they took seats in front.

Credits got rolling, but rain pinged the corrugated tin roof to obliterate speaker sounds, so Rosalee popped up and headed for the exit. "Sorry, I must increase the volume."

Seat resumed, movie running, Rosalee shook a fist at the cocky young actor. "It is not nice to sass your elders!" Unable to contain herself, she booed, flailing, cautioning the hero of a lurking villain, "Look out behind you!"

A man came and sat. He hadn't paid; Rosalee didn't mind. "Control yourself," she admonished the hyperventilating heroine.

Scary parts, she covered her eyes.

Never mind that she gave away the finale or shouted out lines before actors spoke, Walker was thoroughly smitten.

Movie's end, Rosalee reached over to squeeze Walker's hand. "Ah, so satisfying!"

Heart a-flutter with the promise of friendship, he squeezed back.

Given Rosalee Soo's brand of caring, certainly, he would come to love the woman very much.

Chapter Thirty-Eight: Lauren

Mrs. Thrip rooted through her purse, extracted a stick of gum, shed the wrapper, gripped it in both hands, and sat back, stunned.

Always, Mrs. Thrip wore purple. Previously, Walker noted that the sixth layer of Mrs. Thrip's auric field bloomed the exact same shade. This color, he'd said, enhanced her connection to the spiritual realm.

Lauren-Son now stared, flabbergasted, as that layer appeared before her, wafer-thin; a stew of sludge bounded it. She gripped Mrs. Thrip's hand. "I suggest you wear more yellow. It heightens mental clarity and can strengthen against stomach ulcers."

"No, no, no...," the woman muttered, then stood, and crumpled. Lauren-Son reached out to wrap arms round as Mrs. Thrip bleated and trembled.

"Got back from Reno, won two hundred dollars on the slots, and found that my Hank had passed."

"Passed as in dead?" Lauren-Son pulled back; Mrs. Thrip gave a bleak nod.

"He was on the sofa, exact same as I left him. No dang sitter! Hope he didn't hurt none. Hank was my..." She cast about, dazed. "My...my everything!"

"I am *so* sorry!" Lauren-Son tightened her grip.

"Believe you me, the man was not a pretty sight. Head thrown back, mouth agape, he'd stiffened up and smelt a tad rotten. So silly me, unable to deal with it, I came here."

"We should call an ambulance or maybe the coroner."

Tears trailing cheeks, glasses removed, Mrs. Thrip wiped, then reapplied them, yanking earpieces behind both ears. "Think my ulcer's gone, though." Lauren-Son gave her a squeeze.

"How about we have Rosalee get you some tea?"

"Its not tea I need; I want my hubby." Softly, she sobbed. "By the way...Call me Gracie."

"I'll go sort it out."

"First, I'd like you to pray with me."

"Well OK, then..." On bended knee in the waiting area, The Angel overseeing, Lauren-Son led Mrs. Thrip, along with several others, in prayer.

"Ah...Lord, regarding Hank Thrip, I hope he's walking, talking, smiling, free from pain and suffering. But please help his wife, Gracie, to know that she's surrounded by folks who'd do anything to help her." Certainly prayer, these days, helped to shape her intention, but still Lauren-Son wondered: *Why the need to ask if God orchestrates all?*

She asked anyhow, because the ritual meant solace for Gracie.

"Your wife hates me," blurted Lauren-Son. "She acts like I'm a turd she's trying to scrape off her shoe."

"Best stay out of her way, then," Walker replied, blasé.

"I can't; she's, like...taken over. It's impossible to avoid her."

Admittedly, during Delia's brief tenure, she'd redecorated the reception area with cheery colors and replaced those insufferable chairs with comfy ones. To accommodate overflow, she'd also installed benches outside and urged volunteers to keep a constant generous supply of coffee and doughnuts. "Cuddle those fussy babies!" she commanded. "Find cots for those too ill to sit!"

Behind her back Sherman referred to her as She Who Must Be Obeyed.

And obey all did.

"So...," Lauren-Son said, altering focus, "how about your parents? You never mention them."

"Well now...," Walker pondered.

Eagerly, she tilted into him.

He regarded his fisted hands, perplexed, and then released them. "My family was rather peculiar. Pa"—his words came out halting, as if he just might retrieve them—"was a rotten sort. Ma was strange. Pa...see, was hard on her, because she didn't fit any typical wifely mold. Ma"—he got the saddest, faraway look—"Ma was rather…ah, otherworldly."

"How so?

Abruptly, he bristled. "That's all I care to say." Rasp emitted, he grumped down the hall, angry shoulders, angry head tilt, and angry thwacking steps.

Stricken, wondering, she called out, "Didn't mean to pry."

"No problem," Walker said airily, yet prickliness wafted off from him.

Despite scant details, she felt from the outset she'd always known him. Plus, she had this eerie feeling he knew all about her.

In search of clues as to how this could be so, she greedily followed his every action. How he coddled cigarette ashes as if precious gems and then deftly flicked them into an ashtray. How, regardless as to a receptacle's distance, he managed to land those cinders as aimed. How his grand sweeping gestures held meaning, and how he sought to hide his shy reserved smile.

All seemed significant.

Groping to make amends, she caught up with him in the foyer and fumbled further, "Why refuse to wear leather?"

"Out of deference for living creatures, I only wear belts and shoes made from synthetics: canvas, rubber, and Velcro."

"If you're so concerned about the living, then what's with the smokes?"

Mouth twitching, Walker lit up a cigarette and stared, appreciative, at its trailing vapors.

He smoked one cigarette after another, casually blowing smoke rings while attending the sickest folk. Frankly this inconsistency pleased her, making a slight chink in his so-called perfection.

Butt stubbed into an ashtray, he spoke, "Smoking keeps me from floating away."

"How's that make it OK?"

"Come…," he bade her.

Retreated to his office, he settled in his chair. Lauren-Son took the one across. Walker continued, "While I can't condone it, some eat red meat for the same reason that I smoke. Given that I spend so much time out my body, smoking helps anchor me back. And, I'm told it makes no difference to my health."

"What, what!" Lauren-Son threw her hands up. "How about forcing your patients to breathe goopy air?"

"I'm promised they're protected as well."

"Says who?"

"Dr. Chien tells me this. I accept it as fact."

"You mention him at times."

Pointing with his chin, Walker indicated the wall portrait: the Chinese gentleman she'd first seen years prior. "Dr. Lao Chien, seventeenth-century healer and mystic, is one of my guides." He braced for more questions.

"Guides assist you?"

"Everyone has guardians or spirit guides. You have several; they help fulfill your life's purpose."

"Can I see them?"

"Presently, yours congregate behind you. Perhaps you sense them from time to time."

Lauren-Son glanced side to side. "Feels like a buzzing beehive surrounds my head...so maybe. But you actually see yours?"

"I don't necessarily see them with eyeballs. Mostly they speak in my brain, offering support and direction. Some guides have actually lived previous lifetimes. Others have never lived in the sense of animation and breath, but are spirit entities which eternally reformulate and abide. Dr. Chein, long departed the mortal plane, guides much of my work."

"Let's see…" He examined the air space surrounding Lauren-Son, then nodded twice. "One of yours is a six-foot-tall Native American, White Buffalo; he assists as you perform healings. Another, a Russian peasant, wears a babushka and calls herself Raisa. She connects you with earth's abundance."

"Really, Walker, I'm loving this! Except you've just described a delusional state common to the mentally ill. Often, they're convinced that helpers speak to them and that they too are guided."

"President Jimmy Carter," Walker said slyly, "professes to daily chats with God, even claims that He speaks back, yet few call him a lunatic."

"If you care what this town thinks, best not mention this stuff in public."

"You telling me how to act?"

"Ah...no," she backpedaled. Walker frowned. "Really, I'm not. It's just...If word got out that you speak to unseen beings and can also see them, the case against you, against us, might mount."

"Let me be the judge of that. As your teacher, you must have respect!" Lauren-Son's cheeks stung as if slapped. "This is my center," he snapped. *It's ours*, she rebelled inwardly. More of his sharp words sluiced in, "I do and say as I see fit."

Lauren-Son didn't much like him then.

Walker kept silent.

Sheesh, he's so angry, furious, in fact!

Recalling the harsh manner with which he'd cut off the student, Gwen, and had so easily cast out students who'd sewn discord, heart banging in her ribcage, she scrambled to reconcile, "Back to Dr. Chien... is he always present?"

Finally, Walker spoke, "I must invite their presence, then they assess the nature of a given problem, determine what's to be done, and instruct me how to intervene. Helping spirits make it possible for me to do good work. If I fail to properly acknowledge them, or credit only myself, healing energy barely sparks. Keep up with such pomposity, guidance shuts down until I correct myself. Stay humble, and spirit helpers gladly assist. Without them, I'd be lost."

Lauren-Son blew hair off her forehead. "Sometimes I *do* get a sense that unseen hands guide me, but how do we actually get power from them?"

"Again, you're merely a conduit for the free flow of energy and don't actually perform the healings. But when you ask, the Divine—God or Spirit—works through you"— Walker took on a faraway look—"and gives its all. So never abuse it, or it gets snatched back.

"As you know, The Angel helps me as well." He passed an upturned hand to the ceiling.

Eagerly, Lauren-Son leaned in. "As if a living being, many get peace filled in its presence, so I get that it helps us all." Others assumed likewise; offerings, flowers, and gifts, deposited beneath it, spilled down the banister to crowd the waiting area.

"It belongs to all of us, yet also serves as my personal guide. Dr. Chien and The Angel as two of mine, The Angel speaks more to my heart, and Dr. Chien speaks to my intellect."

"Actually, some say The Angel's your mother, giving guidance from afar."

By all appearances, Walker's heart seemed to shift and resettle into deep, protective recess of his chest. "Certain matters regarding The Angel," he rasped, bitter bite to his voice, "I cannot explain."

I'll just die if you stay mad, she thought to blurt.

Awkward, confused, she addressed the floor, "I'm sorry that I annoy you so."

Smoke lingering long after he'd departed, there she sat lost in thought.

No longer fair judge as to what was real and what was not, she *did* know: Walker's thinking, at the far edge of far-out, matched her longing to believe. So... right or not, today she'd seen something spectacularly odd surrounding Mrs. Thrip...more than that...She chose to believe.

Chapter Thirty-Nine: Walker

Rambunctious crowd jeering, waving placards—*Get Out You Phonies!*—the meeting, held in the jailhouse basement, presently used as a makeshift city hall, was jammed. Every seat taken, jostling attendees stood at the rear and along sidewalls. The hubbub, such clamor, set Walker's teeth on edge.

Up front on a raised dais sat Mayor Clayton Lynch, surrounded by members of Buena Vista's City Council. "Alrighty, then! Ladies— gents...," he preened, "this meeting will commence."

Chairs scraped into place. Doors at the back slammed, sucking air. "Tonight we address a petition, against The Living Light Healing Center. First...I'll introduce its manager, Delia Judson. Then, Walker Judson, its founder, will take questions. After that, the council will vote; the issue being, do we continue to allow The Living Light's presence among us?"

A voice cut in, "Cut to the chase and make them loonies leave!"

"Yeah!" chimed another.

"Mind me, no interruptions. If you can't control yourselves, you hafta shove off. So then..." Brief pause, Mayor Clayton adjusted his shirt-cuffs. "Let's welcome Delia Judson."

Airspace succumbing to her perfume, Delia, no longer blonde, sporting a tasteful, frosted feminine hair bob, took a leisurely stroll to the front. Gripping the microphone, she cast a languid smile about. "Howdy all!"

Enthusiasts hulloed back, then Delia began, "The Living Light's mission is to alleviate suffering. Who among you objects to that?" Slowly, she scanned. No one dared fidget. "Good! Now...Who among you has been helped by our work? By help, I mean, whose lives have improved after coming to us?" Hands, quite a few, shot up. "Well then, I'd like to explain our work and talk of our future plans..."

All listened, captivated as Delia beamed her radiance upon them, detailing The Living Light's inception, its brand of healing, and its business structure.

Walker too felt captive—stunned, really—to find himself so thoroughly re-smitten.

Delia wielded such a firm, eager hand, and had slid nicely into her role as office manager. Volunteers showed up punctually for shifts, and phones got answered; many remarked on the improvement. As if The Living Light were a child they'd spawned, she and Walker discussed it, endlessly.

Last night, door to his room at The Living Light creaked open, trench coat shed, into his bed, she'd slid. At recall of slick muscle, sinew, and bone—the pulsing, the pumping—he underwent such a power surge—the residual afterglow shot through him.

Dawn had crept up and Delia arose. Sighting two neat scars that traversed her forearms, pain overtook him as he'd reached for her wrists. "What's this?"

"Mind your business!" Writhed free, coat donned, out she'd flounced.

Circular breaths taken, steadily he'd worked to transit Delia's grief into himself.

Calculating grin now pasted upon Delia's visage, mistrust overtook him. Dull aches began to throb each eye socket. For Walker feared she might toss out an insult or worse, that she'd bare cleavage. "I'll introduce our staff," Delia announced, perfectly behaved. "Voden... How about you describe our healer training program?"

Arms stiff at his sides, Voden stood, slowly shut his eyes, and kept them thus.

The crowd took up muttering; someone belched, several laughed.

Minutes later, eyes blinked open, Voden glanced about as if awakened from a satisfying snooze. "Those up front," he muffled in his odd, sleep-encrusted voice, "all in white—are acolytes that are training to do hands-on-healing. Should you be puzzled, the gentlemen sporting green armbands are here to protect The Boss, Walker Judson. That 'tis the summation." Bland as toast, he sat back down.

Despite his mild exterior, Voden was as riled as he ever got. In light of recent death threats, he'd conscripted male volunteers to protect Walker.

Walker thought it idiotic but agreed...just this once.

Vodun, however, would persist. Ever-after, bodyguards would escort Walker to and from all public events. "Next, you all know our benefactor and resident herbalist, Rosalee Soo." Delia waved a vague hand.

Torso rotated, Rosalee, smiling sweetly, twiddled fingers at the crowd.

"Then there's Lauren Fink.—Where are you Lauren...?"

Lauren-Son about tripped as she stood; hands shot out to right her. A chair toppled anyhow. "Actually, my name's Finch. Walker calls me Lauren-Son, and I have something to say..."

Furious pause, she gazed about. "Look guys...Our presence enhances this town—your lives too. So put up with us, and enjoy the ride. We ask nothing from you but tolerance." Blushing, fidgeting, she dropped back down.

Generously Delia grinned at the girl, yet her cold eyes stayed exempt.

Hair at Walker's nape crawled; didn't take a genius to grasp her distaste.

"Recently," Delia resumed, yanking her gaze away, "we brought in Ardis Westerbom as my assistant. Many of you already know Ardis— if you please..." As if to bestow a delicious peach, delicately Delia extended a hand.

Ardis strutted to the front to encircle Delia's waist. Both bowed. The women—one darkly curvaceous, the other tall, shiny—tantalized. The audience whistled, clapping loudly.

Walker's heart pounded, vigorously. Curiously, limelight shared with one so lovely as Ardis left Delia untroubled. And certainly, Ardis dazzled.

Thus far, Ardis had proven quite the asset. "Why learn hands-on healing...," she'd drawled, sloughing off Walker's invite to join his school, "when I'm a healer-extraordinaire as it is. I come to get a break from my rugrats and because I crave the healing atmosphere."

"Next," Delia announced, "we'll hear from our founder, Walker Judson. And, thanks for being so patient." Vigorous applause followed her off-stage.

Bodyguards surrounding Walker, he clapped proudly for his wife but sped up the aisle, ditching the escort. The volume intensified, laced with cat-calls, as Delia met up to rub his flanks. "More!" "Get a room!" folks hooted. Bounded to the podium, Walker waited as the crowd muttered into silence.

Up front sat Miss Wilkins, surrounded by a gaggle of furrow-browed women. Previously slouched ranchers and townies, now on alert, crossed arms on chest fronts.

How Walker longed to fly at all of them. Really, he wanted to yell, *Can't you see? We're here for your own good!*

Impulse smothered, voice gently sorrowed, he began, "Every night this month, vandals have egged our building. Last week, they tore down our sign. Clearly, The Living Light makes folks nervous. So much, that many"—he patted for smokes, caught Miss. Wilkins's glare, then reconsidered—"have signed a petition to force us to leave.

"About this, I hope to change your minds, for we at The Living Light do not want trouble. Far from it...We just wish to share this great locale and to do good works. And, it's my firm belief, that we can peacefully co-exist. Moreover...If we work together, Buena Vista will thrive and prosper."

Miss. Wilkins shot up a hand. "Yes?" he invited.

"What you're doing here interferes."

"I'd like to know how we do that?"

"You harm my practice, because people come to you instead of to me." Crowd growling agreement, Walker raked his jaw.

"Sorry, Miss," he said slowly. "I assumed Buena Vista had enough business to go around. It seems I got it wrong. We're happy to refer clients to you."

"I hold you to your word." Miss Wilkins sat back, mollified.

"I envision...," Walker continued, "Buena Vista becoming as majestic as its views, and we at The Living Light vow to do our part to make this happen."

Murmurs rippling, pug-face Evan Trout cut in, "What about filling our town with weirdos and riffraff; how do you plan to clear them out?" Walker caught Clayton's agreeing nod, hopped off the stage, and strode to the rear.

"Please, friend, take a deep breath...What do you notice?"

Microphone stuck in Evan's face, the man recoiled. "Ah... Dunno."

"Everyone, take a deep inhale. What do you smell? Anyone?"

Whispers, no response, mike taken back, Walker resumed, "The air here is clear, sharp, crystalline clean. Everywhere you look are pristine, abundant views, enough for all to enjoy. Indeed, Buena Vista is a remarkable place, not just because of the precarious way it clings to this hillside, but its amazing, thanks to all you good, remarkable folk who live here.

"Never did I expect to be so blessed as to live in such a paradise, and believe me, I've been many places. How do you feel about living here?" Again, he stuck the mike in Evan's face.

"I – I...," stammered Evan.

"I make you as nervous as hell, don't I? That's because I, The Living Light as well, represent change. Change"—Walker swiveled to regard Mayor Clayton, who blanched—"upsets you. See...Many Buena Vista residents fear that we entertain evil designs, that we plan to force you under our sway. Our mission here, however, is simple. We merely want to help. And I promise, I'm not the sort of fly-by-night huckster some assume that I am.

"Back to living here, though, what makes Buena Vista special is this: recently, Tookie Tatum's boy, Shem, took sick. As many know, Shem's a bleeder. Tookie lost his job a while back, so the hospital refused his boy admission until Tookie could guarantee payment." Crowd huffing dismay, Walker pressed, "An acute bleed can't wait. Thankfully, this time the boy had a slow one. Well then...Some anonymous person saved the day and paid the bill." He caught Delia's eye; she nodded sagely.

Actually, this wasn't quite accurate. "It's possible," Delia had asserted beforehand, "to tell a lie with honorable intent and still do good." The lie had been Delia's; Walker agreed to it. So, at Delia's generous initiative, he wrote a check to cover Shem's hospital bill.

That they'd conspired together for good helped ameliorate Voden's caution. *Therefore*, Walker resolved as he now scanned the crowd, *I'll appoint Delia director of The Living Light.*

Pitcher lifted, he filled a water glass, gulped the drink, then took up again, "I apologize for any mystery surrounding our work here. Additionally, Miss Wilkins has helped me to grasp the impact of our center on this town."

Gears shifted, he inquired, "How many of you hunger to belong to a close-knit, caring community?" Most hands shot up. "All of us want to belong. And that's precisely what The Living Light can offer if you give us a chance. Believe me folks...We aren't out to steal your hearts and minds."

"How do we know that?" a voice cut in. The crowd stirred. "Yeah, why take your word?" Voices raised, a nasty guttural noise blurted; several chucked. Walker waited, head bowed.

A rancher burst down the aisle, heading straight for him. "You're so full of bull, you sick mother-f—!"the gent bellowed, livid, quaking with rancor.

Fricative tones in the air, an avalanche ensued as bodyguards surrounded and grabbed the fellow, then bunched up, headed for the door. "Search your own selves for the truth!" the intruder screeched.

"Shut up!" "Get out," came shouts.

The fellow shook free to wave a fist. "Question all he says" Guards cut him off and dragged him out.

Mysterious malaise overtook Walker. Had he permitted the man's rage to penetrate and embed, he'd have become physically ill. As it was, stealthy, unseen spirals of darkness roiled; faster, faster they spun and tore at him. So, taking deep, deep breaths, he worked to cleanse and transmute the venomous daggers that sought to tear him asunder.

Outrage throbbing, the clamor settled.

As if nothing were amiss, Walker looked back up to examine faces. "I apologize if I may have caused this gentleman's distress.

"However...back to the topic at hand...like Mayor Clayton, many tell horror stories of scalawags trying to ruin this place. And many have felt the impact of Sedona's New Age overflow. Rest assured though, we have no plans to harm Buena Vista. Fact is—we love it." Walker coughed into his hand. Several in the audience coughed as well. "Buena Vista has such potential. I wish you could envision it." Walker leaned in to the audience. En masse, the crowd leaned too, hanging onto his every word, doing the very thing he cautioned against: allowing him sway over them. "What we're trying to accomplish is simple. Our mission, as stated, is to ease pain and suffering. I know you want this too.

"For those who don't know me, I'm serious—scrutinize our work. Keep us on our toes. Speak up. Feel free to question. Pester us at every turn. If you don't like what we're doing, we want to hear from you. But please, give us a chance to show what we can do." Hands clasped, Walker stood silent.

"We now go to Dalrymple Gooch," he said shortly. "She's written a letter she'd like to share."

Hair sprayed and carefully coiffed, Dalrymple stepped to the podium. "Hi. Ya'll know me." Delia had asked her to speak. Walker had objected.

"She's popular with townsfolk," Delia had asserted, "so let's use her to advantage." Dalrymple being ga-ga over Walker, sent him frequent, adamant missives. More like love letters, they made him squirm.

"This"—Dalrymple waved a paper—"explains how The Living Light, Walker Judson, in particular, changed my life." Voice lilting, she read a sappy poem; Walker put his head down.

Smattering applause followed Dalrymple off the stage. Delia resumed, "Thank you, dear Dalrymple. Thank you all for being here tonight, for giving us the opportunity to share. Now, I'd like to announce…" She waited for silence.

"The Living Light will help pay for repairs to Buena Vista's streets. We'll also donate to the sidewalk improvement fund." Appreciative murmurs simmered.

"And recently"—she did a modest pirouette—"a donor gave us a prime piece of land, which in turn we give to Buena Vista to build a new city hall." Hesitant at first, folks clapped.

Momentum gathered, crowd erupting, all thundered thanks. Mayor Clayton called for order. Loud cheers overrode; he smacked the gavel. "Council must still vote regarding this petition!"

The audience surged to clap Walker's back, then to kiss and hug Delia till her lipstick smudged.

Incredulous, spluttering, Mayor Clayton succumbed to a petulant foot stamp and stormed out.

Gathering, so circus-like, yet so necessary to fulfill God's plan, nothing could interfere.

The moment should have been triumphant, yet Walker shook off a sense of foreboding to reassure himself: *Certainly I can protect Lauren-Son from Delia's dislike.*

Chapter Forty: Lauren

"When did you realize you could fly?" Walker inquired as they took a booth at Bea's Koffee Kup. Lauren-Son scooted in across from him. The waitress swept up, took their orders, and returned momentarily, plates nimbly stacked up her arm.

Noisy kitchen calls, toast smells wafting, sleepily, Lauren-Son poured cream in her coffee and sat back to watch the dark liquid merge, blend, and overwhelm the creamy whiteness. "Do you suppose,"she inquired, "that good and evil can comfortably co-exist? Or does bad usually win out to overcome goodness in the end?"

Walker sat back bemused. "To quote Dylan Thomas, 'I hold a beast, an angel, and a madman in me.' Every human struggles with good and evil. Some ultimately surmount their dark aspect and live lives of great goodness. Some do not."

Petition hoopla having fizzled, tensions still simmered. Many way-too-smiley town residents still wanted them gone.

"Say, Walker." A burly fellow thundered to a halt at their table. "Hello young lady."

"Hello yourself, Elmo." Walker stuck out his hand; Elmo took it. "How's the rash?"

"Nearly gone, thanks. Just thought I'd say hey." He cast Lauren-Son a speculative eyeball, then rushed off.

"What was that?" Lauren-Son bit into her toast.

A waitress raised her voice to all within earshot, "Suppose they talk cosmic stuff in bed?"

Lauren-Son checked; the waitress and patron exchanged droll glances, all other eyes studiously avoided hers. "Anybody who cares," she called out in an angry flare, "Walker's only my teacher."

Diners a-titter, the waitress blanched, then quickly recovered, "Sorry, doll, didn't mean you."

174

Questions wafting anyhow, calm as you please, Walker scraped away at his plate and chewed.

The very idea—she and Walker together—sent a shiver.

According to Rosalee, word went round that Walker paid Lauren-Son too much attention. "Be careful. Many think you are out of line. They say you are—ah, snooty, full of yourself."

In a town rife with busybodies, given that the duo spent loads of time together, tongues wagged, madly, about them. Gossip flew from mouth to mouth; nothing could stop it, not even truth.

Delia laid full claim to Walker, though. Just yesterday, three gabbing women averted their faces as Lauren-Son greeted them. Many thought Delia wronged by Lauren-Son's closeness to Walker. And certainly, Delia, took full advantage, making frequent mention of Walker's neglect.

Napkin pressed to lips, Walker held Lauren-Son's gaze.

Granted, she wasn't much to swoon over. Not particularly ugly, nor attractive either, suddenly, she felt gorgeous, smart, amazing. And jeeze, she ached to touch him!

Hands fidgeting from effort of restraint, she pushed her plate away.

"Back to our reason for celebrating…" He tapped for attention. "When did you start to think you might fly again?"

Quick glances about, head tilted close, Lauren-Son whispered, "Sounds crazy, but the other night I awoke, feeling as if thumb-size nubs had sprouted from my shoulder blades." Walker nodded solemnly. "Gradually those nubs transformed into rippling, flapping wings. It felt so familiar—like it had happened before. I didn't have a sense of actually flying, though. I just thought I might. Mostly, it was about unlimited possibility. Know what I mean?"

"Yup."

"Well…That's it." She sat back, expectant. "After, I was glad—am still glad."

"Let's see if you can truly fly at some point."

"Like my life taking off in the metaphorical sense?"

"Fly, not just in your dreams or by imagining, but actually fly."

"Right!" Reaching over, she gave him a friendly poke.

"I'm serious. Someday, you will." His voice, as if a caress, left her tremulous.

175

Walker formed the center of her universe. All at The Living Light orbited round him; he induced a dizzying sort of awe.

Mostly, he tried to moisten brains—to pry open earth-bound minds to grasp the inexplicable. "A true master doesn't let on that he actually is one," he'd recently declared.

Not that he didn't enjoy being adored; he did. He just wanted tidy discrete adoration, not a noisy, messy fuss.

"What did you do to me?" wailed Bernice Trabing later that morning.

Before their eyes, the woman's already ruddy skin bubbled to form a single giant welt.

Hand clapped to mouth, Lauren-Son looked to Walker. "Sometimes," he reassured, "these things get worse before they improve. Give it time; it's merely a healing crisis."

As if conducting a musical score, he danced and slid fingers across Bernice's flesh. Patient and healer merged to fill the universe—there seemed nothing more.

Minutes later, Bernice sat up to check; the welts remained. "I'm worse!" she whimpered.

"I guarantee you won't look like this for long," Walker promised.

"You lousy trickster!" she blurted, scrambling from the table. "I trusted you, and you've messed me up." Chubby arms crammed into jacket, torso sloshing independent from footfall, she plowed through the throng to the waiting area.

All eyes glommed onto her, she sputtered, "He put his hands there and there!" She pointed to her breasts.

Walker, trailing after, listened, attentive—not mollifying, not sorry, but respectful as she ranted, "You're a bad man! I'm telling the police..."

No bother to defend, he just took it, so Lauren-Son inserted herself. "I was there the whole time; no such thing happened."

Out Bernice slammed with a shout, "This isn't the last you'll hear from me!"

"Whew!" Lauren-Son watched the woman's backside as she thundered down the walk. "How do you stay so nice?"

"It's not a problem."

She searched his face; his mildness troubled her. "She'll probably make a stink."

"Trust me, tomorrow her skin will be fresh as a baby's bum, and she'll sing our praises."

"How can you know?"

"I just do."

How confident he seems, so self-assured! Yet huge secrets bumped about inside him, lackadaisical, no need to be revealed.

Only, someday, she determined, *I'll win you over and learn them!*

"You make predictions...," she said, taking up a fresh tact, "but often, you're wrong."

"Indeed, I'm quite fallible. Yet certain information comes to me. That man by the door..." Chin lifted to point, he spoke softly, "He's destined to choke, pass out, and drown in his soup bowl."

Lauren-Son stared, incredulous; Walker ushered her to a more private locale. "If you know, why not save him?"

"Beats me why or how I know. I'm never certain where my responsibility lies. For the most part, I'm merely instructed to notice, not to interfere. There are gaps in what I foresee. I can't predict the stock market or the next president, for instance. So why see certain things and not others? Why perceive things at all if I can't change them?" A grumble arose in his throat. "It troubles me too."

"I'd tell anyway. Otherwise, what's the point?"

"It's my challenge to keep quiet." As if transformed into a near-extinct creature, Lauren-Son stared at him outright.

Gifts or not, Walker's burden, knowing, being unable to change things—surely, this ate at him. Yet he *did* try to ingest other's pain; that anguish turned him ghostly with solitude.

They parted; Lauren-Son brought back the next patient and retrieved Walker. Paused outside the treatment room, he resumed, "I see the crushed-down energies of a cancer patient and the ticking time bomb of an impending coronary, but believe me, it never goes over well to inform some gent, 'Excuse me, but you're about to be hit by a passing truck.'" Sadly, he shook his head. "Telling interferes with the soul's rightful journey, so I seek to impact a life without disrupting its preordained trek."

"That's my worry too! I thought I was helping my dad die more comfortably. Instead, I interfered horribly to hasten his death."

"We're responsible for our every act. Yet, you did nothing wrong with your father."

Wildness—relief burbling, she emitted a sucking sob.

Doorknob turned to enter, Walker drew to a halt. "Another thing…"

"What's that?"

"How about you take this next patient? You're past ready."

"Fine by me." Grinning so hard her cheeks hurt, thrilled to be acknowledged for a year of hard work, hours of mediation, and heaps of prayer, at last he believed in her! Possibly, he even felt more.

Forcibly she reigned in her fantasies.

Her first solo patient checked her over with a frown. "I prefer Mr. Judson. He's why I've come."

"Sorry but I'm fully trained, so you work with me."

Despite the man's grumpiness, the session went beautifully.

Given growing demands on Walker's time, increasing numbers got assigned to second-string Lauren-Son. Some crabbed to her face. Others left in a huff. She felt bad. Walker set her straight: "Don't apologize; don't compare yourself to me or try to imitate. Work you do is unique: perfect unto itself. Besides, you have attributes that I lack."

"What do I have that you don't?"

"Yourself," he said succinctly.

Yup, she saw auras—human subtle anatomy—which was not physical and could not be perceived by ordinary senses—with increased ease, and immense heat flowed from her hands into her patients. Although these wonders came easy, none of it ever seemed ho-hum.

The Croft Foundation, Lauren-Son's former employer, requested Walker's help to test the effects of hands-on-healing on the medication needs of their mentally ill guests. Regrettably too busy, he declined. Had he done so, credibility achieved might've boosted his public persona to help mitigate the mess to come.

Chapter Forty-One: Young Adult Lauren

God takes what belongs to him, which means utterly everything, and so He claimed Lauren's dad. During her third month at The Croft Foundation, Mom rang up to report her father to be near death. And so off to her hometown hospital she sped.

When arrived at five p.m. Dad wasn't dead. He was merely dying—a whole lot different than dead—and he knew who she was.

"Hi, Dad, it's me."

"Hi, honey," Dad burbled through a hissing oxygen mask.

Not crying but wanting to, she stroked and nuzzled him.

Pumped full of fluids, forty pounds soggier, Dad smelt of ammonia, of cancer, and of death. "Hey Mom." Lauren gave her a kiss.

Eyes red rimmed, barely acknowledging, Mom cranked the bed up and then cranked it back down again. Lauren wiped her own eyes, fiercely.

Eczema, her personal stigmata, bloomed, abruptly. Hands intolerably itchy, she scratched. Blisters erupting, she popped away. Pink oozed out, bumps crusted over and wept. Fingers refusing to bend; she thought to apply bandages, but it seemed unwise to leave her dad's bedside.

Working to refocus, hands rested on Dad's chest, she tried to envision how that long-ago healer might make him well again.

Human flesh exudes liveliness and holds a particular sort of yield. Yet Dad's tissue had turned inelastic, lacked heat, and siphoned off all warmth.

Trying to sense his pulses, she willed herself to merge and meld with him. No tingles, no heat, nothing came.

But at six p.m., Dad still knew her. And she thought she had a chance to save him.

"I need a breather." Mom announced, then stepped out.

Dapper, luminous Dad, a Cary Grant look-alike, always perfectly groomed, used to comb his hair into precise formation before retiring to bed. And as a child, she bragged, shamelessly, as to his prowess. "My daddy throws me in the air a hundred miles and drinks a whole Hamm's beer in a single giant gulp."

Splendor now sucked out of him, sweet vulnerable bow of his lower lip as his solitary familiar feature, skin gone watery, transparent, each breath taken, his face contorted horribly as if drawing air into his lungs were a job only his cheeks could perform.

Six thirty-five, desperate to do something—anything to help— Lauren, losing all good sense, pressed the call button.

Given what happened shortly, she was terribly sorry she had.

"Yes?" the nurse asked.

"Morphine please, for his pain."

Shoes squeaking, the nurse came back and shot medication into the intravenous tube that dumped into dad's arm.

Eyes blurted opened Dad mustered breath. "Why did you do that?" He sounded angry, hurt, perplexed.

Gradually, tension raveled as his body, shrill with pain, flattened. His gaze grew cool, impersonal, taking in the enormity of the vast and growing cleft between them.

Heart flipped, Lauren clambered onto the bed to hold a man impossible to recognize by look or smell.

Dad's breath slowed, making increasingly long stoppages, till life pulled out to become nothing.

Morphine, even a new nursing student knows, hastens death.

Six forty, five minutes later, Dad was dead.

Grief bulging her throat, there she lay next to a dead man whom she failed to recognize, who based on look and smell bore no semblance to the man she so adored.

"Is anyone out there as stupid as I am?" she whispered, apologizing into her father's neck.

Gently, she rocked that vacated body. *I've interfered with the most important journey of my dad's life; a journey rightfully all his.*

What is Divine Will and what constitutes meddling? Years to come, she'd hash this over.

Six forty Dad lay dead.

But at six thirty-five p.m. he was merely dying and...He knew who she was.

Chapter Forty-Two: Young Adult Walker

As Walker sat at The Overlook soaking up the view, Rosalee Soo, who smelt of green tea, arrived to scoot in alongside. Convivially silent, they watched luminous clouds pass overhead, then hunker over far-away ridge tops. Gradually those clouds turned darker, assembling and disassembling.

"Storm's coming," Walker announced.

"Ahem." Rosalee cleared her throat, setting the tidy bun atop her head a-bobble. "Please speak of your first time."

Walker pivoted to blink at her. "First time what?"

"First time you fix someone."

"Ahhh...Well, I'm no good at this."

"Ssst!" Rosalee made a shooing gesture.

"What to say..." Walker searched his mind: wondered how she knew and what he could tell without sounding a nut job. "I—I grew up on a farm..."

"Not that—You know what..."

A minute taken to examine his hands, he then murmured, "Long ago, I tried to resuscitate a dead bird but failed." Recall of that long-ago afternoon swarmed up; the dust-choked air, the swishing grass—the surrounding countryside radiantly transformed—and exactly how it changed him.

"There is more, so please say." There *was* more, yet he merely nodded.

Rosalee shot him an odd look. "Why do you not speak of family?"

"Ahh..." Walker leaned to rest forearms atop thighs. "I never really knew them."

Rosalee pondered this, then started in, "Maybe this does not interest you, but one day my father brought home a cello. He did not ask if I wanted to play; I just obeyed. See...Father played violin. Whole male side of Soo family had much musical talent, so father wanted his daughter to play instrument as well.

"But in China, a girl who plays music causes big scandal. Old way believes striving is only for boys, not for girls. Chinese have idea that males have much bigger brains, so it is easy for them to do these things, and that creative endeavors use up too much of small female brain." Rosalee wrinkled her nose with a shrug. "Such wrong thinking!"

"Father's Chinese friends cautioned against such forward behavior, and honorable mother feared my brain might explode." Walker sat straighter and stared, wondering where she might be headed. She gave him a jab. "Please, bear with me...

"My father believed it very important for female to know as much as a man. In China, when just a boy, he survived deaths of parents, lost all twelve siblings to war and famine, and was quite familiar with the gnawing ache of an empty belly. Though father started life with no prospects, he believe all things to be possible. 'Mark my words,' he say to me, 'you can do and be anything.' So when father brought home a cello—taller than I was—I did not argue. Lucky for me, after much tears and very much practice, I come to enjoy the instrument very much."

"So you're glad he pushed you?"

"Chinese parents are harsh disciplinarians because they hope to give children a better life. Father criticized much, so always I feared failure. Nevertheless, one day, he listened to me play, put his hand on my shoulder, and said, 'Daughter, you are not the best but are good enough.' This make me very happy, for being best is not what mattered. That day forward I knew, no matter what: Rosalee Soo is good enough." Broad face tilted, she grinned at him.

"You *are* good." Still, he knew her message had been meant for him.

"Always, I wanted a family." Rosalee regarded him coyly. "So now...I have you."

"Ah...that's..." Walker shifted, uneasy. "Good to know." Weekly, he met with Rosalee to learn of herbal remedies; sessions he thoroughly enjoyed.

For Daisy Heinz, who underwent monthly rages, Rosalee gave Women's Precious Pills. "To calm tension and to nourish the blood," she explained. For Mrs. Baker, of the perpetual dry eye, she prescribed Rheumannia. Holy basil calmed the Adams boy; yet the child still attested to psychedelic visions. Chinese medicine made perfect, intuitive sense, but mostly Walker enjoyed their time together.

"It is important to let people care for you; that is what family does. So from now on…" Solemnly she pressed his heart with the flat of her hand. "Mr. Walker Judson is member of Rosalee Soo's family. Though not big in number, my family is *very* big in love."

Elation settled upon Walker's shoulders, fluttering as if wings. "Thank…," he stammered, blushing madly, "thank you kindly."

Is happiness a commodity to be rationed? he wondered. *Do we receive a finite quantity at birth, and can it be replenished if used up?*

Concerned that he might deplete his rightful allotment, he thought to avoid her for a time—to undergo a dry spell—until worthy again to be replenished.

Thus far, he'd known three great pockets of joy: the time he saw Pa on fire, plus his boyhood attempt to heal the bird, and now, finding Buena Vista, with Rosalee Soo as a large part of that.

Hand still rested atop his heart, Rosalee continued to study him.

Her eyes, sincerest pools, held only kindness. "Walker, you must let people love you. For even hard love is better than no love at all."

A great, unaccustomed bloom of warmth sprang up to envelop him. Always, he'd kept separate, yet Rosalee made it seem safe, so easy, to join the human race.

She released him.

Clouds crept forth, quilting the valley below.

Perfect tartness tanging Walker's throat, heart drifted back to normal, he accepted, "Well OK, I guess."

Single delighted clap, Rosalee swung her legs. "You make me so very happy!"

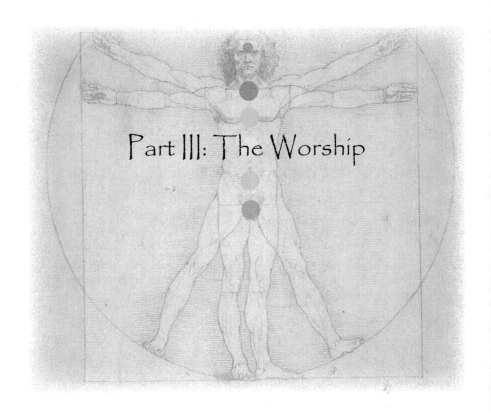

Part III: The Worship

Chapter Forty-Three: Lauren

As three years flew by, magic happened; no other word fit. When Lauren-Son relaxed just so, didn't try too hard, and fuzzed her eyes, she saw flesh turn incandescent, lit from inside to make asymmetric furrows and juts that underscored the distorted energy fields of the sick visible. Smooth, steadily pulsed emanations of the robust danced before her eyes, as well.

Gerold, town drunk, floundered about in gray, sticky mucous. That goo, it seemed, mired him in an onslaught of lousy luck and frequent mishaps. One day, being so impaired by it, he tossed himself off an embankment onto his skull, which didn't kill him, but it certainly didn't improve his lot, either.

Intricately connected streamers drifted out from the solar plexuses' of the Talmadge twins, who always wore look-alike outfits and exact same poofy hairdos. Walker termed such streamers, *akashic threads*. Rosalee's energy streamed out in the tenderest cotton candy-like puffs. Pink, related to the heart, signified love. And Walker's steady, gentle energy bathed one and all.

Sauntering home at night, Lauren-Son liked to flick her wrists, sending lighted tendrils shooting out, arcing into darkness. After a rain, she tossed those beams into puddles, sizzling them into vapor.

Actually, that didn't happen, but it was splendid to imagine.

Times Lauren-Son worked with Walker, intense harmony sprang between them. Merged into each other's hands, brains, and arms, together they created an invisible network of strings to reweave body, mind, and spirit together again. And always, Walker knew precisely how to give aid and comfort.

No longer fumbling, Lauren-Son performed admirably. Mostly, of late, she worked solo. Danielle, a quadriplegic who suffered painful spasms, was a favorite.

Danielle lived with her stout, solemn mom, Vera, in a dilapidated rental outside Buena Vista. Daily, Vera hefted Danielle to and from her wheelchair, bathed and fed her, wiped drool from her daughter's chin, and repositioned her every few minutes, all day, round the clock, to prevent pressure sores.

One spring morning, as Lauren-Son lifted Danielle, Danielle's face creased in agony, so Lauren-Son clambered onto the table, wrapped arms and legs round the young woman from behind to assume the Lamaze midwifery position. Danielle slumped at her chest, Lauren-Son, breathing rhythmically, set her intent: *Guides—Raisa, White Buffalo, and The Angel—please free Danielle from suffering.*

Room air abruptly shifting, punctuated by distinct sucking sounds, she sensed, but did not actually see her guides arrive. Thinking brain halted, intuition sharply honed, her body began to vibrate, then morph into a healing conduit. Her own chakras spinning clockwise, she linked them through to Danielle's, gently rocked them both, then began toning, "Aummm..." And Danielle, with all her warbly might, chirped back.

Holding, rocking, cacophony eddying, overlapping, and colliding, building to create a latticework of sound, an hour later, a gush tumbled through, and they were done.

Lauren-Son settled Danielle back into the wheelchair, then crouched, checking. "Let's see..."

Danielle's usual facial creases had reduced, somewhat. And something else lingered.

Blink, blink—Lauren-Son cleared her vision, then checked again.

Sharp bluish flicks jetted beneath Danielle's flesh.

Eyes squeezed shut, Lauren-Son glanced again.

Blue lit licks remained.

That light—Danielle's energy field—extended out an inch to bath her in a delicate, watery grid work.

Sight of this energetic grown increasingly common, still, Lauren-Son had to marvel.

Students bragged about such matters: loudly proclaimed they saw lights, experienced visions, felt such bliss during healing sessions. They all seemed so embarrassingly egotistical, so clueless, so irreverent, so worshipful; only just now, she felt that exact thrill.

"I can bear my suffering," rasped Danielle, "so long as I feel love.

And love's what I get coming here." Careful squeeze, Lauren-Son gave a hug and then wheeled her down to the foyer.

"Oh..." Danielle strained to catch her eye. "My doctor doesn't approve. He insists Walker's a quack and plans to investigate you both—your credentials and all. I begged him not to." Danielle tried a hapless shrug.

Unable to form words, Lauren-Son gave the barest nod.

"Danielle may never be physically well," Lauren-Son noted as she and Walker reviewed the day, "but she's better just the same."

"Correct!" Walker shot her a prodigious grin. "While there may be no physical improvement, often true healing occurs at more subtle levels."

"I see this with Danielle." Sometimes a healing took. Most times it did not—at least not overtly. When a patient improved, Gracie Thrip for instance, who no longer needed surgery, all rejoiced.

When nothing changed, Lauren-Son sternly reminded herself, *God's will dictates this soul's rightful journey, not your puny desire!*

"Your work with Lester Jefson," added Walker, "is an example of a more subtle shift."

"Ah, Lester! I worry about him." General consensus holds illness to be purely physical in its basis, yet, as with Lester, much illness derives from a sickening of spirit.

Sad eyes of a manatee, Lester came twice weekly, claiming a fervent desire to be rid of warts. Given she'd not actually seen said warts and given that Lester stood too close, talked too fast, non-stop, scarcely taking a breath, making an overall pest of himself, the warts, she surmised, to be fiction.

Lester lived alone, had no family or friends, and seemed starved for human contact. Months of sessions, Lester jabbering away, each time she tried to speak, his voice overrode hers; rarely, did she get a word in edgewise. "Likely," Walker noted, "Lester's mere presence at The Living Light—the attention he garners—is healing."

"Makes sense!" Deep inhale, Lauren-Son took up another track.

"By the way, Danielle's doctor plans to investigate us—The Living

Light. You—me—all of us." She chewed a cuticle. *An uneasy truce,* she figured, *simmered with the town; one that wouldn't take much to pulverize.*

Yet Walker winked any concern away. "We're perfectly safe.

"I *do* need to say something..." He went to the window. Closely, Lauren-Son watched him. "Given your progress of late, how about you help us teach?"

"Yeesh!" Extravagant swipe to brow, Lauren-Son came to stand alongside. "I feared something bad."

"Would you?" Palms flipped up, he turned, toggling hands to underscore the question.

"At first, Walker, it seemed way absurd that frozen psychic time conglomerates could actually exist, that each chakra could vibrate a specific color, that skilled healers see seven major levels of the energy field but that you actually see nine. Now that I experience such things myself, I've wondered when you'd notice my competence. So yes, definitely, I'd love to!"

Cheeks aflame, she sought a hug. Walker stepped back. She gripped his sleeve. Walker stared at her hand. She released him.

"So, er...," she fumbled, "does this change things?" Walker brushed off his shirtfront.

Keep to your place, you dope! she admonished, inwardly.

"We'll pay you a small stipend to cover living expenses. In return, you'll teach and work long hours, six, sometimes seven days a week."

"It'll be great to get paid. My money's run low. The rest is no problem."

The original homey group of seekers, essentially humble, lacking in trappings, the exact community Lauren-Son had so longed to join, consisted these days of a bunch of bored rich glitzy know-it-alls who sought a comfy, fast-track to enlightenment. Not really her kind of people. Teaching, however, would allow her to keep tabs on anyone surging to supplant her in Walker's favor. "I like your faith in me, but what about Delia, won't she be mad?"

"I'll have more time for her. That part should please her."

Voden's cat, Silly, slunk in, tensed, braced himself, and sprang onto the desktop, scattering papers.

Papers gathered up, Lauren-Son went to pet him. Walker did too. She willed that their hands touch; it did not happen.

"What if I need more money, say...if my car acts up?"

Silly cocked his head toward Walker, inquisitive.

"You ask. I take care of you."

Something of a sob arose; she gulped it down. It bloomed into her chest anyhow.

She liked that he'd see to her welfare, might protect her even.

Walker located a cigarette, lit up, and stood there, overwhelmingly separate.

All this time, despite failing to glean the tiniest drop of his inner workings, she felt worshipful.

And...What exactly is worship?

Worship comes from the awesome experience of love: God's love or love granted by another person or deity. Then, amazed at being bestowed such compassion or mercy, one responds with reverence, devotion, adoration, or intense love.

That's how Lauren-Son felt about Walker Judson: *worshipful*.

Chapter Forty-Four: Young Adult Walker

Although not his true calling, Walker Judson got a trucker's license and proceeded to haul rye to the West Coast, then backtrack with a load of oranges, being on the road weeks at a time. Work, a fine match, afforded loads of alone time. Wherever he went, however, return to Buena Vista felt like homecoming.

As he prepared to depart an Amarillo truck stop one day, a red Capri spluttered to a halt. Quick rule of the road: truckers look out for each other. And so, although not a truck, Walker, hung around out of courteous impulse.

Five, then ten minutes passed. Rigs idled, raucous. Vehicles whizzed past, kicking up dust. As he basted away in midday sun, eyes shielded, Walker attempted a peek inside the vehicle, yet the glare bounced off the windshield to obscure any view inside.

Twenty minutes gone by, he lit up a smoke.

Car door flung wide, red high heels exited, followed by generous, round hips. Tightest mechanic's suit imaginable, chest unzipped to display bosoms, a woman slammed out.

"Damn car ran out of gas!" Swaying side-to-side, more of a roll than a walk, more of a shimmy than a roll, the creature propelled herself at him.

Pulse pounding, strong, fast, endless curves grabbing Walker's breath, can't say how he knew, but this action-packed body would rearrange his life.

The woman extended a hand. "Odelia Garcia. Delia to my pals." Sunglasses off, nostrils flaring, standing too close, she looked him over.

A curious odor, not perfume but the scent of a female in rut flamed out from her.

"Name's Walker Judson." Tugging sensations flooding his groin—pained to meet her eye—he fought the urge to lick and nuzzle her.

Likely a brunette at some stage, now blonde, given her buttery-bronze skin, he pondered as to the shade of her thighs.

Guessing his thoughts, she fluttered her lashes. "Most fellas wanta look-see if this skin's courtesy of Coppertone. But truly"—she leaned, hush-hush—"it's all mine." Perfect pearly teeth, top and bottom, glinted at him.

"Yes, ma'am." Flesh at her neck swooped into cleavage making him go giddy, realizing he still gripped her hand, he released it, then jammed fists into pockets.

"Aren't you the funniest, sweetest thing!"

"Thanks kindly." Truck stop lot-lizards often made eye contact, aggressively thrust bosoms forth, then flopped down alongside him. Sad eyes being the initial attractant, his silent, mysterious nature, odd manner, and tight politeness quickly drove them away.

As if overtaken by a vast, silent undertow, the two stood in that parched lot, tilting back and forth as steamy currents swam between them. Never mind the shimmering heat, never mind the horn blast—its sound fading in the distance—never mind the short-lived breezes kicked up by passing vehicles; immense weight lifting, the hollow, stark places of youth peeling away, he left that self behind.

Slowly, Delia scanned. "Your eyes," she purred, "are odd, but gorgeous."

Madly, he blushed. "Surely, I cannot claim credit, ma'am."

"Why do I have the urge to know you? Usually, fellas clamor to know me."

"Don't rightly know."

Coyly, torso twisting, she leaned to bump his left hip bone. "Ready for me?"

"Uh..." He pulled back, embarrassed, excited. "That I am."

"From the look, you're a fella who's going places. It'd be a hoot to be with you when you do." She caught herself, blushed, and got awkward. "Lordy! You must hate me for being so forward."

Walker really liked her then. She seemed an inspired mix—sweet, sad, coarse, and nasty. Also, he glimpsed deep solitariness much akin to his own.

All of her posed such a powerful attractant. So much so, a fragment dislodged in his chest to swiftly manifest, awkward, ungraceful, upon his tongue. "Would you…Would you care to dine with me?"

"Love to! But"—disdain chafing, she scanned the truck stop—"let's go elsewhere."

Off they sped to the Tickled Pink, where everything, waitresses' mini-dresses included, were hot pink.

Every table filled, famished crowd waiting, restless children ran screaming down the aisles. "I like that you're well built," Miss Delia Garcia announced over steak and potatoes. "And so far, you've none of the slavish tendencies I find repugnant in most men. Know what I mean?"

"No, ma'am, I do not."

"Please…Call me Delia."

"So OK, Delia, tell me about yourself."

"Well…I live in Clarksdale. Don't much like it, but it'll do for now."

"We're neighbors then. I live in Buena Vista."

"It's a sign!" She grinned, all shiny.

Indeed, it was a sign! But not the sure sign he'd long awaited and searched for. "So what else should I know?"

"Anyone involved with me has to put up with my family and my birdies. More than anything, I love my finches." Her face softened, suffused with love. "I'm the only girl, got oodles of brothers. My mama—I take good care of her—send money, call twice a week, and drive her to her sister's in Arlen each month. Thing of it is…" Her face crumpled. "Mama gushes over my brothers, bails 'em out of jail when they get DUI's, claps hands and squeals when they visit—which is rare—hugs them tight, but never bothers to fuss over me.

"My baby birds, though…" Longing gaze cast at a passing family, she sighed. "Don't get me started."

Abruptly, she flipped focus, "I work as a secretary, but am an atrocious typist. Bad as I am though, bosses slobber over me, trying to get into my pants. Really…It's such a drag!" Reaching across, she touched Walker's hand. "Know what I mean?"

Staring down at their hands' intertwining, politely Walker extricated himself.

"I refuse to take orders and come to work when I please. Called my last boss a pathetic pig to his face." Meat skewered, fork held aloft, she raised a brow. "Incompetent and rude…That's me. But if you're gonna be a snot, it helps to be good looking. One poor slob refused to dump me, 'cause keeping me around mattered more than his dignity. Got so bad, I demanded to be fired."

"Good for you then!" Beans squeaked his teeth; Walker concentrated, hard, on chewing.

Meal's onset, they'd taken opposite sides of the booth.

Gradually, Delia scooted round till their thighs touched.

Slurp, slurp—she swizzled the straw, lips and tongue teasing, sucking, pulling.

Walker imagined himself as her straw: would give all to be sucked and swirled like that!

Despite air-conditioning, of their own accord, his pores snapped open. As if caught in a torrential downpour, he paused to dab his brow.

"Wanna know my favorite thing?" Delia beamed.

"Certainly would."

"I have this naughty habit of liberating guy's wallets. See...I lift 'em when they feel me up. Funny thing, the horniest guys carry oodles of photos of the wife and kids. Older men carry cards with emergency information, in case they croak. After we finish up, I pretend to primp in the john, but really, I'm flushing the guy's life down the toilet." Chin rested on palm, she took up the dreamiest look. "Lordy, the rush— watching photos and credit cards drain away! I dump cash, too, but probably should keep the bigger bills." Walker stirred, ill at ease.

"Half the fun is telling them after," Delia chortled. "You oughta see their faces! I sent my photo to one fella's wife. Woo-wee, he'd have liked to die. Curious though, he begged me to go at it again, which says a lot about men, doesn't it?" Her face clouded up, wistful. "Just once, I wish some guy would put me in my place."

Cocky grin clamped back on, she slid his wallet across the table. "Got yours by the side of the road without even a kiss. No photos, no cards, and no cash—saddest, emptiest thing I've ever seen."

"How…?" Confused, then angered, he fought an urge to slap her.

"We bumped shoulders, remember?"

"Pe…," he stammered, paused, taking a moment to recover. "People reveal their true nature if given half a chance, but you've spared me the trouble, so I thank you for that. My guess, you're not half as bad as you like to seem."

Knife slammed down, methodically she licked each fingertip, drying them on her napkin.

Fearing she'd leave, Walker reached to restrain her. Eluding grasp, she slithered to booth's far side and crossed arms, scowling.

He thought her unbearably lovely, felt breathtakingly dumb, and wondered if he owed an apology.

Apologize or not...Given what he'd seen, she wouldn't speak again until mood struck.

Forking though salad, chomping steadily as the jukebox crooned a mournful cowboy tune about disappointed love and redemption, he noted two things. First, this Delia person would be quite the handful, so life with her would not be easy. Second, none of that mattered; he wanted her bad.

Moreover, she wanted him...Or so it seemed.

"Afternoon, Walker." A fellow trucker loomed. "Who's your gal?"

"Red..." Walker gulped. "This is Miss Delia Garcia."

Hand draped, Delia beguiled.

Courtly bow, Red took her wrist, flipped it over, kissed her palm. "How do, ma'am." Unable to tear eyes away, Red inquired of Walker, "Wonderin' if you'd be interested hauling alfalfa?"

"Might," Walker said, uneasy.

Delia, he soon found, ever on the strut, invited attention. Men, old or young, blubbery or scrawny, flexed muscles, bragged, and swaggered, turning downright idiotic in her presence.

What Delia had, see—what made her stand out—she gave constant promise that she just might up and fall for any fella.

Stocking foot settled into Walker's crotch, toes wiggled, she smiled sweetly at him.

Eyes pinched shut, he gripped the table's edge.

Red, still hovering, sensed something. "You OK?"

"Yeah, fine," Walker insisted, gravelly of voice. "Can't say if I'm up for a trip, though."

Every nerve a-tingle, no longer aware of the room, of the clamor around him, nor of the man who hovered alongside, fleshy patch between his legs thrumming, he feared a groan might escape his lips.

"Let me know, huh? Nice to meecha, miss." Whap to Walker's shoulder, Red moved on.

Foot extracted, Delia shot him a wicked grin, delicately dabbed lips, and then reapplied lipstick.

Walker bestirred himself, glanced about, *blink, blink*, then stared at her, marveling.

Gentle rain began pattering inside his brain. It fell, continued to fall, throughout their years together, only ceasing during times she left him.

Scooted back alongside, she produced a Salem pack, handing over matches. "Light me."

Light her Walker did. He lit one for himself, then slung an arm round Delia's shoulder.

Simultaneously, both inhaled.

Eyes dreamily at half mast, Delia leaned back, presenting her golden neck as if offering it up for vampiring.

Chapter Forty-Five: Lauren

Lauren-Son overheard raised voices and peeked into Delia's office.

Weird tension in the air, Walker and Voden faced off across the desk; actually, they seemed to quarrel. Voden stood, fists clenched. Walker glared down at him. Delia sat back, ticking, tapping her pen atop the desk.

"Mildred Sharp has taken a turn for the worse," Voden curtly stated, "so straightaway, she must be told to access traditional medical care." Anger from Voden seemed odd, for typically, he emoted little.

"I don't feel good about it," Delia jumped in, "but that article's coming out, and she's touted to be a medically documented success story for The Living Light—she's been cancer-free for years, thanks to us."

"Tests may say she's clear, but one look at her, energetically, Boss, and you know she's ill."

"I see that!"

"The story is a sham, though."

"I've worked hard to win over this stupid town and we're finally receiving major press," huffed Delia.

"Have you spoken with Mildred yet?" Voden addressed Walker.

"Mildred still believes she's well and wants to persist with our treatment."

"Did you *actually* inform her as to her condition?"

"She recants...and we look bad," Delia interjected.

Voden pressed, "Mildred Sharp will do precisely as you instruct, Boss."

Delia jumped in, "Say nothing, then."

"Hush!" barked Walker, not bothering to glance at her.

"You choose the center's reputation over a humane act?" growled

Voden. "This does not please Mr. Fucols. That woman shall die because we are selfishly remiss, then all bets will be off."

Delia bunched, then shrugged. "I say, we go forward as is."

"It's my decision!"

Room pin-drop quiet, there Walker's words dangled.

"Delia—Boss," Voden sighed, "you both disappoint."

Lauren-Son entered further. Walker turned to address her. "As you can see, we're at odds."

Delia spotted the girl, bolted upright, and seemed to yell before words exited, "Shoo—get outta here!"

Stupefied that the matter should be up for question, as Lauren-Son glanced between the threesome, she longed to locate a snug, warm pocket to climb into. *Sadly, Walker,* she thought to blurt, *I mistook you for an enlightened being!*

Abruptly it dawned: *to be enlightened does not necessarily mean one always exhibits perfect judgment or clarity of thought.* Enlightenment, just now, meant that Lauren-Son needed to cast aside her stupendous ignorance to repair the moment.

Wracking shudder—neither faint, nor fuzzy—she pulled up into a powerful presence and locked eyes with Walker. Entire body a-tremble, she wagged a finger. "You must do the right thing, Walker. And I trust that you two will support whatever he decides is best."

Chapter Forty-Six: Walker

Walker arrived home that evening to find Delia at her desk counting out tens, twenties, fifties, hundred-dollar bills, and then cramming them into a fat satchel. "Let's see...," she muttered. Ledger opened, she applied whiteout, allowed it to dry, inserted new numbers, then blew on the page.

Peering over her shoulder, weariness overtook him as he gripped her hands. "What are you doing?"

"Sorting the day's take." Hands peeled from his, ledger snapped shut, Delia gathered up the satchel, carried both to the wall safe, dialed it open, shoved the items inside, and met her husband's gaze. "Counting it gives me such a rush." Surged into his face, she pushed him back a step.

"I detest Buena Vista. If you care to notice...It's unbearably slummy. And quaint? My ass is quaint...That's what I tell anyone who admires this place. Never mind the new construction; those buildings are drab and cheaply made." Walker opened his mouth. "I know," she cut in, "you'll remind me of the enriching views. Frankly, love, so much sky annoys."

Acquiring money as Delia's fondest pastime, she refused to open a bank account and squirreled away all cash. Studiously, she tracked gold and silver prices and bought bullion. At each change of season, she got fitted for a new wardrobe: designer garments so skillfully sewn, she seemed poured into them. "As director," she'd argued, "it's essential I look the part." The rest she spent on a derelict mansion perched high above town.

"Ahem." Walker cleared his throat.

Thunder erupted, rattling windowpanes.

"Are you taking money?"

"Course not!"

Thunder rolled again, then lightning flashed.

Overhead lights flickering, Walker spoke, succinct, "If you are... It's a bad idea."

"You, dearest husband"—face full of fury, Delia spat—"had best get your own house in order!" Last of the cash scooped up, she headed back to the safe. Walker reached to restrain her; she shook him off.

"I can't let you do this."

"This"—she indicated the money—"is the best thing I've got."

"You have me."

Anger spasmed her face; anguish followed. Sadly she shook her head. "No, I don't. You're like a library book that I borrow, then hafta take back. I share you with everyone."

Having assumed that Delia liked their arrangement, Walker stepped back, stunned. "What do you want of me, then?"

"Your attention and your time."

"Ah...I can't promise, but I'll certainly try."

Delia rewarded him with a heartbreaking smile. "Oh, honey!" Eyes moist, as if the benevolent queen of the May, forgiveness oozed from her every pore.

Abruptly, she wound back up again, "I hate that you go looking for that awful girl first thing. When I find you, heads together, you both come up grinning. What's the big secret?"

"There's none."

Delia lit up a cigarette, took a toke, and then swiveled to regard him, exhaling an expressive clot of smoke. "The two of you...It's strange, you both get so animated, so damned jolly. Plus..." Reaching out, she gave him a poke. "When you catch me watching, you try to hide how happy you are. What's with that?" Face etched with grief, she met Walker's gaze. "Anyways...It hurts."

"I—ah." Walker floundered, "She's a big help. We have much to discuss."

"What about her holds your interest?"

"Dunno." Walker raked his jaw. "I care about them all."

"Don't give me that! She's your favorite. Yet she's big as a lumberjack, ugly as a mutt, and she follows you about like a drooling slave. It's the talk of the town—like you're an item."

"It's strictly platonic." Chill air blasted in from the window as an owl swept past and shot earthward, hunting its prey.

Walker's thoughts went to the girl. She *was* queer, more masculine than feminine.

Greatly changed of late, however, as if the bearer of secrets, she radiated certain allure as well as the slick sheen of self-esteem. High-spirited, she moved with new-found rippling grace; heads pivoted to gape. *How had I missed it!*

"More important," Delia continued, "—about Mildred Sharp... Though Voden doesn't agree, he'll never speak against you. That girl, though, has heard too much, and is full to the brim with a giant conscience—"

Walker cut in, "I spoke with Mildred. She knows her situation."

Delia's jaw dropped. "That kills the article, then. I fought so hard for it!"

"I never intended to leave Mildred in the dark."

"Fine! Don't bother to come to bed tonight or any other night. Ever! Again!"

First off, she liked to bluff. But secondly, despite his intellect warning him otherwise, the sound of her curvaceous voice caused him to tilt into her.

Musk of her scent making him squirm, crawl, and debase his highest, best self, like it or not, the healings he performed underwent heightened potency that fed on the wild tumult she caused. He hardened at thought of it.

"See to it," Delia continued, "that the girl keeps her mouth shut about our little conflict, or I go after her. I'm serious. She blabs about problems—any sort—she hasta leave. I'll do all in my power to make that happen. Do you agree?"

"Don't tell me what to do!"

"Well then,"—Delia gathered herself—"you've been ever so kind, taking valuable time to have this lovely chat!"

Rain slicker applied, Walker, instead of Delia, headed for the door. Delia came fast at his heels. "Where are you going?"

"I have something to attend to."

"Take care of her, or I make a stink."

Jolt of anger, he stood very still. "You harm her...We're done."

Slowly, Delia circled. "Set her straight, or whatever it takes, I smash her like a bug."

A clear, nasty scenario traipsed through his brain—one that involved his wife hurting Lauren-Son. Yet he who possessed a knack for hiding feelings then smiled benignly.

Years back, the yogi had him pegged; "The more soft-spoken the man, the angrier. And you, sonny-boy, are one angry fellow!"

Walker *was* angry: furious in fact.

Recently, while treating a sniveling, complaint-filled lady, rage had consumed him. So, he slid both hands up her neck to tighten at her throat. Eyes smarting, the woman looked at him, questioning. "Unclogging your fifth chakra," he'd explained.

The woman wagged a finger. "Oh-ho, you're a strange one!"

Yes, he invaded and sucked energy, memories, and intimacy from patients. A terrible thing, really.

Try as he might to contain it, urge overwhelming, he thought himself a *soul sneak.*

Rain sheeting, Walker got in his car and drove off.

What's wrong with me? Why can't I love her? And...*What does a normal relationship feel like?*

Awash with conflicting wants—wanting Delia, yet not—his parents' marriage sprang to mind.

Clearly, they never had anything together, yet together they stayed.

What sort of love involved over thirty years suffering? What caused Ma's failings, Pa's rage, and my ongoing shame and self-censure?

Never had he been adored by his parents—that he'd gleaned. Never had he breached the wall surrounding Ma to find intimacy. Yet, during years of wilderness walking, he'd dared hope that Ma might have possibly loved him all along.

Realization slapped him now: what passed for love only existed between Ma and God.

Never, had it included him.

Furthermore, life forged between him and Delia, unable to achieve a foothold on true intimacy, spanned a chasm. For he, who offered solutions and comfort for many, had no answers.

Answers or not...He resolved to manage his wife.

Chapter Forty-Seven: Lauren

Lauren-Son ate a light supper, bathed, donned pajamas, scooted an armchair to the open window, and sat. Evening fine and warm, gradually, the night sky clouded up, and raindrops fell, pitter-patter, as she pondered recent events.

How could Walker possibly hesitate to tell Mildred?

That thought circled round to complete itself.

What seems so pure and straightforward about him may not be so goodness-filled after all.

Knock at the door; she went to answer.

"Hello there!" Walker bounced, falsely jolly.

She stepped aside to let him enter. "What's up?"

"Thought I'd drop by."

"Well...Uh, it's a surprise." Despite closeness, they weren't so informally chummy that he'd visit on a whim.

Walker moseyed about. Proudly, she swept an arm. "You haven't seen since I decorated."

"This place has good energy." He stroked an immense, indolent spider plant splayed atop a table.

"Actually, I'm behind on rent, so the landlord's given me notice."

Walker supplied her with rent money. Too busy to attend to such trivia, as usual, he was late. It annoyed her to ask, to be dependent on his over-taxed memory, but naturally she forgave him. "Have your landlady call me," he directed.

"OK, I guess."

Awkwardly, they shifted. Lauren-Son's pits got sweaty. "Take the tour...," she invited. "This, I got at a yard sale..." An Oriental rug, as if a magic carpet about to lift off, assorted pillows heaped upon it, spanned the space. Walker admired it, then went to heft a rock from a humongous corner pile.

"You collect rocks?" Face lit with concern, he studied her.

"It's my secret vice. Don't know why; I just seem to need them. Possession, acquisition, having...lifting them...soothes me. An addiction, I suppose."

"Best keep it under control."

"Not to worry!" She shrugged extravagantly.

Walker halted before a watercolor—red poppies splashed onto a grassy field—ticked eyes to her, then squinted back at the picture. "I didn't know you painted."

"That's my mom's."

"She's got talent." He moved to the window, then shot her a questioning look.

"I know." Come alongside, they gazed out at the streetlight illumined, scarred hillside. "Given Buena Vista's infinite panoramas, I could've done better, but this crummy view's all mine."

Abrupt awareness hit—*Walker and I are completely, privately, alone!*

Ill at ease, uncertain what to do or say, she flipped the radio on.

Yet the beat—too bouncy, frazzled.

Dial adjusted to Vivaldi's *Four Seasons*, she exhaled. "Check out the rest..."

Down the hall to the bedroom, she went. Walker followed and surveyed the space.

Dried leaves, artfully strewn, graced the dresser top. A carved gourd and pair of boji stones resided there as well. Chief Seattle's death mask—a replica—hung over the bed. "This is certainly the home of a creative spirit!" Walker beamed broadly.

Lauren-Son chuckled. "Most consider collecting feathers, rocks, and leaves an infantile pastime. To me such things are treasures." There they stood; she, ripe for the taking, Walker more uncertain than she'd ever seen him.

What of the skin at his belly? she wondered. *I suppose it's warm—taut, but soft, where his abdomen merges to meet his groin.*

He cut in to her reverie. "How many years has it been?"

"I was twenty-three." Quickly, she calculated, "It's been nearly four years."

"You're much changed."

"Hope so!"

"That part of your life has nothing to do with me...It's a bit of a surprise."

"Actually, you're my full time occupation."

Walker deflected, putting his nose to a framed photo. "When was this taken?" In it the two stood, shoulder to shoulder, postures identical, only he appeared somber, watchful, while Lauren-Son grinned, big time.

"Ardis took it last summer. Notice our matching poses? I think that happens from spending so much time together...It's like we've merged or something." Walker stiffened.

In she swooped to correct the moment, "Want tea? I was having some."

Walker followed to the kitchen and leaned at the counter as Lauren-Son extracted a pitcher from the refrigerator, slopped tea into a glass, thwacked his knuckle handing it over, and then pulled out a chair. "Do sit."

"I'll stand." Drink downed in a single gulp, he gazed back at her, polite, stiff, as if about to quarrel.

Tension wafting, she heard herself blurt, "Please hug me."

"Best not."

Ridiculous person that she was, still wanting his touch, working to banish all feeling from her face, impatient at the tension—or by his meandering—she broke in, "So why are you here?"

Grimace leaking from Walker's mouth, silence bore down.

Shadows lengthened, merging, and darkness deepened.

The room, all stillness, held its breath.

Finally, he spoke, "You must not speak out about any conflict that arises, now or in the future."

Don't ask me to do this! she wanted to shout. Instead, she said, "Mildred Sharp will die if she continues without traditional medical care."

"I took care of it—planned to all along."

Koof—Lauren-Son expelled relief.

Walker continued, "However, I cannot interfere with the course certain future matters must take and ask that you do likewise. It is the singular way you can help me." He seemed so uptight, so mournful;

Lauren-Son's heart sunk. Walker pressed, "To stay part of my family, you must agree."

More silence ticked between them.

Miserable, at a loss, she met his look, jammed hands in pockets, extracted, and then let them drop. "You're giving me the willies, Walker. What, exactly, is about to happen, and how can I give an open-ended promise to something so vague?"

Voice tender, sorrow sparked his eyes. "I only have your interest in mind. When time comes, you'll create a world far beyond this place, so now, in preparation, you must grasp your responsibilities. Can you agree to this?" Still as a statue, there she stood.

"I have to say so right now?"

"I am the intermediary you need to achieve enlightenment. You are my disciple, possibly my chosen one. But with guru-disciple relationships there's an inevitable power imbalance. That's just how it is." Gurus in Eastern thought personify all enlightened beings, therefore, for all practical purposes, the guru is to be worshiped and obeyed as if God-like—that's what she'd signed on for.

"Do we agree; you're a divine teacher, but aren't actually Divine?" She cracked the thinnest smile.

Walker pressed, "To fully embrace this work you'll scarcely have time for a boyfriend or family, and when you get good, if you let them, people will eat you alive. If truly committed, those you love must come second. Perhaps hardest of all, though surrounded by admirers, you'll be completely alone."

"What about you, you have Delia?"

"Or...She has me."

"Same as you"—Lauren gave a shrug—"I can't possibly go back to my old life."

"Your next challenge...I want you to take charge of my evening talks—the ones we offer students and all comers. Understand me: you must keep quiet about what will soon come, and I will permit you to oversee our speaking needs." Lauren-Son looked far off, considering. *Here's the exchange; the taking away and then the giving.*

She grasped what he asked: that she side with him, regardless as to what the future held, and that this test of loyalty bound her, inextricably, to him.

Street sounds forced her back. She spoke softly, "I understand."

Her obedience—a near-joyous rush appeared to overtake him. Walker breathed easy, while she flushed, confused, resentful.

What he said next came out deliberate, precise. "If you *do* speak out, much as I don't like to say it...You must leave." She stared, stricken, wondering. "I must have your word on this."

"Ah..." Such strangeness—his late night presence—the request—her heart pounded, hard. And the prospect of banishment meant loss of community, loss of self—the end to all she loved. "I..." She raked hands through hair. "I guess. Yes, definitely."

Walker gave a curt nod. "I hold you to your word. Most important... You must keep safe."

Amazed to be the sudden focus of his concern, she longed to ask: *What exactly do I mean to you?* Instead, she acquiesced, "You know best."

"I'd better go." He went for the door, tested the dead bolt, then, hard rain falling, departed, stiff-shouldered into the darkness.

Puzzled as to what she'd agreed to and what was *really* wrong, she latched the door, briefly pressed her forehead to cold, unyielding wood, and then went to bed.

Back then she had no idea what Walker meant by "keep safe," or why he rejected her hug or that he'd do the things he did. So stupidly, she neglected to question further.

Chapter Forty-Eight: Young Adult Walker

One fine, sultry evening, six months after they'd moved in together, Gene Krupa wailing away on the radio, Delia, sheathed in a slip, slitted to thigh, spaghetti strap slid off her shoulder, began shimmying to the beat. Walker reached to grab her; she slid from reach and posed, saucily. "Bet you're too uptight to dance."

"Me uptight!" Tongs seized, he banged pots and pans, did a tentative, modest hop-step, and crooned in fits along with the hi-fi.

Never before had he danced. Neither parent ever did. Times migrant workers invited him to join their jigs, he'd always demurred.

Just now, however, as he executed a series of clumsy moves, Delia came in close, then, vibrations quickening, building, overtaken by erotic thrusts and thrums, their skins throbbing out sounds via pores, they moved to the beat, circling each other. Turned itchy fingered on account of her body heat, her alluring roundness, he rubbed her all over, kissed her neck, throat, and lips.

"Ooo—" She broke it off and went to coax her finches from their cage. "Dinner, my sweeties."

Gently, she chucked Frankie and Gwennie's beaks, fed them scratch, and then placed one on each shoulder. "Thought Mommy forgot you?" she cooed as Walker watched, wistful.

Figuring her relationship with the birds offered hints as to their own potential happiness, he studied how she was with them and then, again, reached to grab her.

"Not now, honey," she evaded, going off to shower.

The birds, it seemed, would shower as well.

Wherever she went, those two tiny epaulets accompanied her. Beaks pressed to each ear, solemnly she listened to Gwennie's gossip and to Frankie's twittering fears and then planted fervent kisses upon them.

Delia returned, slid into a dress, toweled her hair dry, and they sat to dine. "Ever see your parents?" she queried.

"No, never."

"Do you miss 'em?"

Chair pushed back, arms casually stretched, Walker tried to figure. "My Pa…," he said at last, "is a mean cuss. Ma—she sent me away." Delia examined him.

"Mine aren't so nice either, but they're all I've got." Given the somber way she lifted a hand to cup his cheek, she understood perfectly.

Abruptly perked back up, she demanded, "Marry me!"

"Nice idea." He wanted to leave and wanted to stay. His relationship with this woman was both the best and the worst that had ever happened. Bonded to her in ways beyond the physical, ways that transcended flesh, he also gave thought to Delia's wallet thefts and her incendiary temper.

Then Rosalee's words sprang to mind: *Even hard love is better than no love.*

Delia scooted over, face glossy, anxious, impatient.

Arms wrapped round her, gently, he scoffed, "You're crazy if you want to settle in with me."

"We're both crazy then, mister!" Pulled back, she directed, "Gimme a kiss."

He moved to obey; Delia jumped up, yelped, and ran. Whooping in fits, he chased, caught, and carried her to bed.

Lovemaking done, they embraced, cheek to chest. Delia stroked hair off his forehead—a move more intimate than any he'd known.

Amazed delight filled him. She felt so warm; he wondered how it would be to live inside her—to wear her as if a skin—to bask in her robust energy, and then also wondered if he'd enjoy her need to touch. A lifetime spent being lost, he felt newly found.

Sound of sobs; Walker tilted her face to check. "What's this?"

Wet streaked her cheeks; she regarded him, bewildered. "This has never happened." Sniffing, she slapped tears away. "I'm OK!" She seemed utterly vulnerable, so lacking in artifice, he thought he might actually love her.

Abruptly, she pushed away. "And…There will be no children!"

"Suits me fine." He pulled her to him and squeezed, hard.

A week later Frankie took flight, bonked a window, and tumbled down, dead.

"Noooo!" Delia wailed, cradling the tiny, crumpled corpse.

Sobbing, inconsolable, she raked her cheeks; they came away red. She examined her fingernails, perplexed. "My birds are my life!" Walker led her to the sink to wash her face; she leaned into him, snuffling.

Demeanor sharply shifting, she slapped his hands away. "How dare you touch me!" She caught herself and blinked, bleary eyed. "Sorry, sorry!"

Hours subsequent, her moods swung wildly. She sobbed, shrieked, lashed out, and then apologized.

Ever the careful student of conflict avoidance, Walker clucked and soothed. Anticipating her every need, he sensed how it felt to sweet-talk a hurricane into altering its path.

Hours later, he tucked Delia into bed, held her hand until she slept, then spent what remained of the night sanding away, polishing, carving Frankie's likeness onto a pine box lid. As he worked, he pondered, what it might take to resurrect the bird. *If I try and fail, Delia will freak. Indeed, if I succeed, she'll freak as well.*

A small voice arose: *Your time will come soon enough.*

It suited him to wait as long as possible, for he savored this present near-normal state. When word went out and folks grasped his talents, all semblance of normal would fade.

At dawn came a quiet knock. Walker went to the door; Rosalee handed over a paper sack. "I prepared a calming tonic for your lady. If you like, I will return later to officiate at the service."

Wearily, Walker scratched his temples. "Thanks Rosie, that'd be a big help. I'll call soon as Delia gets up."

When Delia awoke, Roslaee returned, and they went into the yard. Arms tight at her sides, Delia wailed as Walker troweled earth and slid

Frankie into the exquisite, tiny box. Rosalee spoke several kind words, then each participant—Gwennie included—bid Frankie farewell, and they buried him.

An allegory as previously told by the yogi, sprang to Walker's mind: a frog jumps into a pot of scalding water, then immediately jumps back out. However, if the frog jumps into a pot of cool water, and then the water is heated up to a boil, the frog, lacking the smarts to hop back out again, gets boiled.

Point being: slowly turn up the heat, and the frog adjusts, little by little, neglecting to react when the heat turns deadly.

Life at first with Delia being all sweet and comfy, gradually, her simmering temper would achieve boiling point. So, as with the frog, Walker grasped that eventually this exact scenario would apply to him.

Chapter Forty-Nine: Lauren

Seeking to carve a life separate from Walker, Lauren-Son dated Arvin, a young farmer who'd come to The Living Light to alleviate bursitis.

"Why do you call me Mama?" she asked one day while hanging out at his farm.

Arvin pulled her close and smooched her hair. "'Cause you feel kinda homey."

"Nothing's homey about me; I'm a terrible cook, dress sloppy, and hate to keep house."

Arvin scrutinized her. "You exude big energy, have a big heart, heck...You have big everything, and I, for one, love big!" Lauren-Son rifled his corkscrew hair, inhaling his strong earthy scent.

Arvin was kind, self-contained, and his hands were surprisingly gorgeous for one who toiled hard on the land.

Actually, the first time she saw his hands—so capable, so manly—she ached to have them hold her. And...To some extent, they reminded of Walker's.

"Gotta feed the pigs." Boots donned, Arvin clopped out, Lauren-Son following. Pen spanned out front, pigs oinked, squealing, grubbing about, as Arvin spread mash, replenishing their trough, with Lauren-Son helping.

Cornstalks shimmering with breezes, they then entered the field to examine ears of corn for bugs. Lauren-Son gathered up damp, warm soil, sniffed, then sifted the loam through fingers. The world felt about right; at ease with herself, she enjoyed this man, whom she figured she just might come to adore.

Daylight waning, they sat on the porch swing, listening to the food bin clang, then slam back down as the pigs snorted and grunted. Far cry from life's usual hectic pace, Lauren-Son nestled her feet into

Arvin's lap; he gripped and squeezed them. Scent and heat of their proximate bodies, coupled with the serenity of day's end, life richly uncomplicated, she envisioned life as a farmer's wife.

But was it love?

"Hi, Mom. Just called to check in."

"Hello, dear, how are you?"

"Dandy! Healthy as a horse!"

"Terrific, honey. When will you come to visit? It's been quite a while." A yank, then a tug washed over Lauren-Son.

"Uh…I'll come for your birthday." Bad daughter that she was, she knew she'd weasel out.

"I miss you." Distinct lumps edged Mom's voice; suddenly Lauren-Son missed her too.

They spoke less; she felt guilty about this. Once they'd been so close, yet she now felt far closer to Walker and Rosalee. "I can't leave just now, but you could come here."

"Thanks, dear, I might." Mom coughed, then continued, "I don't pretend to grasp what goes on there, but since you're happy, and Walker has helped you, I give my whole-hearted support."

Quite the ruckus had ensued when Walker renamed her. Mom had wondered why it was necessary, was hurt that her daughter had allowed it. Lauren-Son complained that her mom didn't understand the world she inhabited, so their hard feelings never fully resolved.

"Really, Mom, life's great!" Receiver cocked to her ear, heaped clothes kicked from her path, she paced. "I like teaching more that I thought. I enter a room; students get all smiley, expectant, hoping I'll notice them." Often, she overheard them quote her: *Lauren-Son says*…as if she were a mini-guru or something. She found the fawning creepy…yet nice too.

"Walker claims I'm such a pro at public speaking; so I now do our PR too. Likely, he just butters me up because he hates doing those jobs himself.

"So tell me, Mom…What are you up to?"

"Ah, well, the usual boring stuff. Garden Club, Red Cross,

museum docent, Bridge Club, editing the church bulletin; meetings, meetings, meetings about sums it up. Best thing is you convincing me to go back to painting. But say...How's that fellow you're seeing?"

"Arvin? I like him a lot. He likes me too, I think." Bombed onto the sofa, she stretched, luxuriously. "What about you? Are you happy?"

"I'd say so...Yes."

"Yes really, or yes maybe?"

"Yes...Although this isn't at all the life I envisioned."

"What did you envision?

"Definitely not being a mother."

"Oh?" Lauren-Son scooted upright.

"Sorry, sweetie. I always wanted to paint, so now I am!" Pleasure suffused her voice. "To be good, at least by my standards, one can't paint while dangling a baby on one hip. So I never thought I could have both family and career. My last year of college, all my sorority sisters got engaged, then married, as soon as school let out. Too scared to do otherwise, I let go of my dream. Besides..." She perked up. "I met Dad and fell in love. Being a mother, I adored every moment and, well...You know the rest."

"I thought you life was way-perfect."

"It was. It is!" Mom chirped, convincingly. "Painting was the road not taken. Life would've been very different had I gone that route."

Roads not taken, lives unlived: at every turn there's choice. That Mom had to choose love and family over career, though, seemed just plain wrong.

Noting the time, she sprang to her feet. "Gotta go. Love you!" Hasty kisses sent into the earpiece, receiver clattered into its cradle, leave-taking posed an ongoing challenge. Threads, tangles of ectoplasmic-goo, persisted long afterwards to connect mother and daughter.

More on akashic threads—also termed ectoplasmic streamers: according to Lauren-Son's present understanding, when people interact, streams of bioplasmic energy flows between them. As these streamers intersect by way of conversation or when concern—even crabbiness—gets expressed, interacting energy fields flood with color, liveliness, and vibration. The more intimate the relationship, the greater the exchange.

Just now, those streamers informed that Mom missed her daughter, badly. And guilt pierced Lauren-Son as if she'd been run through.

Workday's end, Lauren-Son prepared to depart. "Any chance you might take a new one?" asked Ardis. "This gal's in serious need and insists she'll only see you."

"Can you show her to room five? I'll just be a sec."

Shortly, Lauren-Son entered the room. Heavily scented campfire smoke blasting her, an elderly woman, brown skin stretched taut over cheekbones, glanced up. Queerest blaze ratcheting out, it hung in the air as if a nebulae.

Slipping, sliding, Lauren-Son gripped the door frame. "Miss Spivey?"

The barest whimper of words came, "Pppp—please…Help."

"How did you—? It's been years!"

Slow motion, Miss Spivey reached into a pocket, extracted and handed over a rock—as if that explained all—and then shuffled to the table.

Lauren-Son helped the woman lie prone, then scanned her field. Blocks, leaks, tears, damage rampant throughout, she ran healing energy into the trembling figure. "You can stay here if you like."

Miss Spivey moaned assent.

Silly smile spread across Lauren-Son's face, she rejoiced. Glad to have Miss Spivey here and alive, she figured: *Certainly, Walker will heal her!*

Chapter Fifty: Lauren

Day's end, Rosalee swooped up to grip Lauren-Son's arm. "Let us walk. I have something to say."

Streetlights blinked on as they stepped out the door. Walker's office window casting a buttery glow, they peered inside. Light hit his bent head to create a halo effect.

A quick breeze creaked The Living Light's sign.

Head lifted, he spotted them, face gone crinkly with pleasure.

Lauren-Son waved. Rosalee rapped the window. "Do not stay late!" Walker saluted and grinned.

"What's up?" inquired Lauren-Son of her friend.

Sunflower seeds dropped into her mouth, Rosalee squirreled them inside cheek pouches, then busily spat husks into her palm as they went along.

Finally, she launched in, "Though Mr. Walker is a powerful healer, it is a big mistake if you think he is different from other people. You are powerful too, but what you learn here is just the start. Also, it is important for you to know…You are *one* with him."

Neck craned, Lauren-Son stared. "You mean partners, Siamese twins, same person?"

"You"—Rosalee touched her arm—"are Walker's *twin-flame.*"

"What's that mean?" Image of interlocking hearts congealed in her brain, indeed, Lauren-Son felt she belonged to Walker. After all, he'd renamed her, which meant he owned her in part.

"Mmm." More seeds deposited in her mouth, Rosalee signaled that's all she'd divulge.

Sidewalk ended, the women took to the road, heading uphill. Summer had just opened up to lengthen the balmy dusk. The moon, saffron bright, illumined the hillside.

Rosalee emitted a fretful sigh. "I love Buena Vista and all my friends, but Walker...I worry about."

Pleasantly, she'd mothered him that morning, "You never eat a proper lunch, so again, I fixed you one." Thermos handed over, Walker had unscrewed the lid; a steamy hiss leaked out, accompanying the scent of tomato bisque.

"What's this?" Walker had inspected the string wrapped round the thermos top.

"Untie and pull it up," Rosalee had directed. String eased up and out of the soup, Walker dangled a tofu wiener aloft. "That way it stays hot," she'd proudly enthused.

"Your most inventive meal yet!" Bun retrieved, pre-slathered with mustard and relish, precisely the condiments Walker preferred, he'd plopped the wiener onto it. "Prepared bun saves time," Rosalee explained, handing the identical thermos to Sherman. "Also you get a hot meal."

Apropos to mothering, Arvin called shortly after. "Come over. I'll fix dinner and rub your feet. It's been weeks since I've seen you."

"Can't. I have to work late." Increasingly she made excuses, saying she was too busy, too exhausted, to see him. She often made her priorities clear and Arvin never argued. "I'll make time this weekend," she'd promised. Yet, if Walker asked, she'd put work ahead of Arvin.

Uphill trudge continued, Lauren-Son probed, "I'm all ears."

Pfft—pfft—Rosalee passed shucks into her palm. "It is your job to help Walker remember that he is just a man. That wife..." Hands wiggled, wildly, she cut curves to convey whom she meant. "She is supposed to help, but that has not gone well, so it is now your task. Just don't make her mad."

"Everything I do makes Delia mad." Lauren-Son knew she should like Delia, but the woman bossed, scolded, and yelled unnecessarily— often at her—so all possible affinity had gone sour.

She *did* appreciate Delia's impressive rudeness toward the women who fawned over Walker. And saddened that she poked fun, laughingly describing herself as selfish and pushy. Lauren-Son glimpsed her worry-lined face, saw that she had no real friends.

Mostly, Delia beguiled, manipulated, and then took hostages.

Lauren-Son felt sorry that, despite all her lackeys, Delia was alone, as she, Lauren-Son, had once been...a fact she never forgot.

"Delia," she griped anyhow, "treats Walker like a leashed dog at a canine show—one she trots out to be admired. Last week she had to meet with the mayor about plans to dedicate the new city hall, and insisted that Walker come along. When he declined, she pulled a snit-fit, so he went anyhow. I stayed till ten to cover for him." She twisted to regard Rosalee. "Oooh—he shouldn't take her crap!"

Rosalee squeezed Lauren-Son's arm. "I do not like to gossip, but Walker will never leave her. If he tried, Delia would never let him go, not unless it suited her to release him."

Lauren-Son returned to the matter at hand. "And so...?"

"Ah, yes! Walker is able to penetrate many dimensions, not just this one. Mostly, he would prefer to stay gone and not return. You are the bridge to bring him back, because you share such knowledge."

"Walker also says this to me."

"As a child, you knew this ability too."

"Age five or six"—Lauren-Son mused—"weird things used to happen. It seemed like a dream, but I'd be wide awake, then my surroundings would compress inward, and I'd feel squished—like being inside a waffle iron, splurting out at the edges. My body seemed to elongate; my awareness would expand. During those glitches, I fully understood infinity and timeless matters— matters of grave consequence to the entire universe."

"That is it!" Rosalee administered her special pat.

"First time, I ran hollering to Mom, 'Can you see me? 'Cause my insides have gone elsewhere, leaving my body behind'. Mom looked at me so strangely furious; her anger surprised me. 'Stop this nonsense!' she insisted. 'You must not go crazy!' That odd experience, coupled with Mom's fear, made me feel naughty, so I never mentioned it again. But the shifts happened anyway."

Sadly, Rosalee shook her head. "Her fear kept you in line. That is usually the way."

"Those aberrations were like cosmic hiccups, as if I'd dipped into another dimension and then returned."

"That is correct!" Rosalee slowed her pace; Lauren-Son slowed as well.

"Walker"—Rosalee hushed her voice—"knows the exact date and time he will die. He say he does not understand why he is shown this. 'The purpose is not yet revealed,'" she said, imitating his shuddering voice. "I ask him to tell when my time will come, but he refuses to say."

"You really want to know?"

"Maybe not. But certainly...That is the limit!"

"Seems a curse, not a gift!"

Up the steps to Rosalee's house they went, then sat on the porch swing to rock a bit. "Did you say what you wanted to?" Lauren-Son shifted, uncertain.

"Soon things will change. I do not know exactly how, but Walker makes people angry."

"Given that the community's livelihood is at stake, why attack us?"

"Walker's actions reside outside their frame of reference, beyond the comprehension of most. People think he is evil, because they do not understand. So Walker pretends all is hunky-dory, but many here still want him gone. I try to warn him bad things will come from burying his head. He tells me I worry too much. You...he may listen to. You must warn him. OK?" Face lit with concern, Rosalee peered at her.

"How do you know that problems persist?"

"I know the minds here. Walker's work turns their heads. This makes him glad, but people are not ready. They get angry, scared, confused, then want to hurt him. He acts immune, but he is not."

"I see." Lauren-Son brooded. "Okay. Yes, I'll speak to him."

"You make me glad!" Foreheads pressed together, they bid goodnight.

Lauren-Son took off, working Rosalee's concern round. Vivid before her came an image: She and Walker, impaled to twin crosses, flames licking, atop Mount Mancos.

Chapter Fifty-One: Walker

Walker had sent out that informing spark to draw Miss Spivey forth. So now she lived—if one could call it that—in a room on the second floor of The Living Light.

Air a-quiver with desolation, her misery leached out and crept into all corners to flood the building. Her grief, a constant, utterly lacked expectation or hope. Yet hope, he'd used, to lure her.

"Please see to her, Walker!" begged Lauren-Son, fearing failure if she undertook to heal the woman herself.

"Miss Spivey has been a significant thread for us both," he revealed, "but she's solely yours to heal."

"But..."

Pain overtaking his breath, she had no idea that, all too soon, her skills would surpass his. "This task is yours alone," he tersely informed.

Her face mobilized and began to twitch. Mouth shifting, lips formed protest, then shut. She struggled to absorb this. "Well, sheesh... If you say so!"

Later, when Walker stopped in to observe, Miss Spivey's smoldering eyes met his and moved slow, watchful, upon him, as if she understood.

Between patients, Lauren-Son stayed adjacent to Miss Spivey as much as possible. Most nights, she slept in the woman's room, held her hand, brought water, read books aloud, and ladled soup into her upturned mouth.

Months of daily healing sessions, nothing Lauren-Son did—run energy, pray, chant, meditate for guidance—brought the slightest improvement. He witnessed her edgy annoyance and once, when exiting Miss Spivey's room, she emitted an odd yelp, tugged her hair, then stalked down the hall. Yet all this, the struggle included, served The Plan.

Walker checked; the clock said midnight. Edge of sleep lost, he lay staring at the ceiling, then felt himself abruptly flung, transported through space, and dropped into a tunnel. Not a dream; it felt so real, yet he stayed separate from the scene spanned before him.

Awareness hovering above the ancient farmhouse of his youth, he heard a knock; Ma came to the door and swiftly shot a hand to cover her cheek. Not merely aged, but deeply altered, right side of her face gone missing, a hollow cavity existed where features should've been.

Walker strained to see; her face stayed hidden.

"Yes?" Ma inquired of the Lilliputian-sized man who stood, statue-like, before her.

Slow blinking eyes of a cat, visitor adorned in marmalade-colored shirt, lime-green shorts, and immense fringed hat, Walker searched his memory banks, yet recognition slid from reach. Ma squinted, trying to place her visitor as well.

"You're here!" She then bounced in recognition. "Sorry, my sight's bad. One eye's wrecked." Door swung wide, she stepped aside. "Do come in."

Chocolaty scents—Hershey's Kisses—wafting, her guest entered, careened sharply, narrowly missing a magazine stack.

Newspapers shoved from the sofa, splashed onto the floor. "Do sit," she gestured, palming her cheek all the while.

"What makes you live like this?" the gent tsked.

"I...uh, so enjoy mail order purchases. It's like sending myself a thoughtful gift."

Frown cast upon the ocean of packages, the fellow primly sat. "Yet, you never open them?"

"Content is beside the point."

Abruptly, the man bellowed, "You, madam, once boldest of us all, even gave God a run for His money! You can too see; you merely elect not to. Open the eye, midbrow, and your vision will correct." Steadily, Ma appraised her caller.

"You've changed. Back then, you were terribly timid and looked up to me. Now you seem ever so bold, and I'm the awkward one."

"We have both changed."

"What's it like these days?" Chair pulled close, Ma sat across, hand still at her cheek, eagerly leaning in. "How I'd love to see God's face! He's with you, but plainly"—she grimaced, visage fraught with grief—"has abandoned me."

"You of all people, dearest, recognize *stigmata*; it's a sure sign of God's love. You've been blessed with the facial version: an enviable rarity. I, too, bear the mark. It's my newest asset." Gloves shed, wincing as he did so, his palms gaped with holes clear through.

Blood dripping, splashing the floor, he neglected to staunch the flow.

"Me...*stigmata*?" Exploratory touches to the ruin that had been a cheek, Ma brightened till she positively glowed. "As my face deteriorated, I assumed God's wrath to be upon me. But stigmata... well, I had no idea!"

"Stigmata, as you know, separates truly great saints from the lesser ones."

"Does this mean I'm saved? Because you see...Overall my life's been unspectacular."

"Certainly, you could've done better, but your life has served a fine purpose."

"What purpose is that?"

"To birth superior offspring."

Tears sprung to Ma's eyes. A hankie went to her nose. "I—well... Thank you so much!"

Gusted with grief—Ma's, his own—Walker resisted the urge to give comfort, knowing full well all would fade should he do so.

Reaching across, the guest administered a light thump; Ma cringed as if smacked.

Gloves replaced, each digit squidged into place, the fellow continued, "You seek to fill emptiness with junk, and so you must give something up." Cheek tapped, he glanced about, spotted a particular prospect, and lit up. "It is requested—no, insisted—that you send what you treasure most."

Up Ma reared to clutch at her throat. "Oh no, I couldn't!"

"They will go to one who will glean and hence will abide their wishes."

Catching his drift, Ma's face suffused with panic. "Surely, there's something else! They're my only comfort." Grandly, she gestured at the rubble as a queen with a kingdom might. "Please—anything but my shells!"

"You are far too attached. Besides, you please God with your sacrifice."

"But..."

"Tut...mustn't refuse!"

"Ah well…" Sifting through piles, Ma located a suitable box, then, as if bidding farewell to beloved offspring, she kissed each seashell— the periwinkle, abalone, nautilus, scallop, and all treasured others— shredded newspaper, carefully wrapped each one, then lay it in the carton. "I've never seen the ocean," she sadly mused. "Probably never will." String and tape located, she affixed the box shut.

"And?" Her guest raised a questioning brow.

Ma regarded him, blankly.

Daintily, he lifted the tea towel. Beneath it huddled her favorite: the conch. "This."

"Must I?" Adored shell hefted, she studied its fleshy, pink lip and smooth entryway.

"God wills it." Being eyed with such disdain, Ma positively wilted.

Box undone, tenderly, she set the shell inside.

"A note," came the prompt; hand aloft, the man scribed.

Message scrawled onto a mailer's backside, Ma dropped it inside, then taped the box up again.

"Am I to come with?" Closely, she searched her companion's face—a dear face—she'd known since forever. "Ceasing to exist holds great appeal."

"Not now, but shortly."

Ma traced a fingertip across the package top. "Ah well, then, do as you must."

Box hefted, the man gave her hand a squeeze, then, no need to open the door, simply glided through it.

Ticks and creaks of the house settling, Walker listening with more than mere ears, steady breath upon his arm—Delia making guttural gurglings alongside—then drove back in to use *the sight* again.

Long separating dimensions—miles of them—overcome, he sensed the invisible demarcating line, knew not to cross it, located Ma and watched over her, helpless.

Ruin, emptiness—an infinite expanse, unearthed—his grief lingered. This sorrow, hers, would haunt him, unrelenting, and cling, as a haze, to permeate and embed all cells of his being.

Chapter Fifty-Two: Lauren

"Come." Voden cricked a gloved finger as he and Lauren-Son converged in the foyer. "Mr. Fucols shall help you sort this matter out."

No pitter-patter of feet, no swinging of arms, nor swivel to his neck, off he glided to Rosalee's herb nook. Lauren-Son followed and dropped onto the sofa, while Voden took a straight-backed chair across. Then, with profoundest solemnity, hands folded, he shut his eyes and seemed to purr.

Time passed.

Sometime later, eyes open, he began in slow monotone, "What do you notice with regard to your feelings about Miss Spivey."

"I'm annoyed…actually mad that she's suffering and that I haven't a clue how to help."

A single nerve ran through The Living Light. Folks shared everything: success, failure, laughter, tears, but mostly, solidarity of purpose—to banish suffering. Being stymied as to how to help Miss Spivey, Lauren-Son feared she'd failed everyone.

"You feel deep outrage on Miss Spivey's behalf," Voden said kindly. "So…Follow those threads into the depths of your consciousness. Do not deny or try to repress them. What do you notice?"

Deep breath, she checked her feelings. "That my confusion, my rage, is immense."

"Most excellent!" As if something incredibly fascinating were occurring at ceiling level, gaze firmly affixed there, Voden continued, "Permit your heart to break open. Fall into the core of your anger, your despair, and confusion. Feel your emotions thoroughly. Permit all of it to flow through you. Recognize that this part is about you, about your own suffering. If you neglect to do this, 'twill be impossible to assist Miss Spivey to release hers. Recognize this…Delve deep. Examine how your need to fix her interferes. Can you grasp this?"

"Er, somewhat."

"Process your feelings fully, then set yourself outside the equation, and you shall reach Miss Spivey."

Fixing her with an unblinking gaze, he continued, "Humans, no matter how dire the injury, struggle to live. Many on the cusp between life and death, uncover the purpose of their earthly existence and return to thank God that they survive. Some are disappointed, though. Miss Spivey is such an individual. Her pain is so immense that she does not know if she wants to live or die. Her injury poses a challenge to her soul, so it is your task to help her figure out if she has a reason for being."

"Makes sense, but…Can you give me any specific tips as to my actual work with her?"

Despite his mild overall demeanor, clearly Voden found her dull. "Check your intuition."

"I have but get nowhere."

"Try sound."

"Sound?"

"Music, song." He bobbed a tad. "Miss Spivey hungers, thirsts for it."

"Ahhh!" *How had I missed this?*

Each time Sherman crooned while Miss Spivey was within earshot, an oh-so-subtle, intangible sense memory seemed to stir her.

Radiant, otherworldly light emanating from Voden; profound respect overtook her.

However, if he were to depart just now, she'd have scarcely taken note. Oftentimes, she got the sense that the man wasn't really there, that need merely conjured him.

Times I feel imperfect, she realized, *Voden makes me more kindly, assists me—really all of us—to be more complete, whole beings.*

The next morning, Lauren-Son gripped Miss Spivey's feet, ran energy into them, then moved up to place hands at the woman's heart and throat.

Miss Spivey lay silent, watchful, then spoke, "They mmmm... murdered my husband." Voice flat from disuse, it did not lack feeling.

"Care to say more?"

Faraway look taken up, Miss Spivey seemed to depart.

"Back then," Lauren-Son said carefully, "you may not have had a choice, but please know that I'll try my best to help you face the cause of your suffering and then release it."

As prearranged, Sherman sang out from the hall a glorious, dense succession of powerfully forceful sounds.

Fraction of a second, Miss Spivey dropped her glazed look.

Sherman trailed off.

Face clouded up again Miss Spivey retreated to that numb, frozen place.

Spectacular harmonic keened again, Miss Spivey lifted her head.

Sherman halted.

A-tremble with sorrow, Miss Spivey shut back down.

Uncertain what she'd witnessed, Lauren-Son thrilled anyhow.

Next session, Lauren-Son played a soothing Brahms lullaby on the phonograph. Miss Spivey stared straight ahead, stone-faced throughout. John Phillip Souza's marching band came next; Miss Spivey slammed eyes tight. African drums got forcefully banged; she retreated further. Yet just out of reach, an elusive wisp tickled and tantalized.

It wasn't the humming, the words, or the song. Definitely it wasn't the beat, the pace, or the rhythm. Yet, when music played or a song got sung, some intangible something reached up to grab Miss Spivey's interest.

Chapter Fifty-Three: Lauren

A group, mostly Arvin's neighbors, spent the morning mending his fences. Come noon, the women hurried off to fix lunch and, as the men lolled against pickup trucks, Lauren-Son marched past, lugging an apple crate.

"Isn't she something?" bragged Arvin, stepped up to give her a pat. Several men snorted, ribbed each other; some hitched their pants, adjusting their gonads.

Jumpy all morning, as if a pesky mosquito cloud lurked, ready any minute to dive-bomb her head, Lauren-Son thought about sacrifice. Sacrifice meant pleasing God, taking the best she had up the mountain to slay, and then offer it up. Not that God literally needed Arvin— currently one of Lauren-Son's favorites—but sacrifice meant saying, "God, I give up this relationship and in exchange, You keep my life with Walker intact."

"Uh, can we speak in private," Lauren-Son asked of Arvin.

Room smelling of suds and clover and earth, into his tidy kitchen they went. Arvin cupped her face and kissed it; her thoughts went to Walker. "I've sure missed you!" he blurted.

Giddy splash of his hair, corkscrewed every which way, fingers threaded through, she then released him and stepped back to announce, "We have to end this—us."

"Did I do something?" Arvin scanned her face, hurt, perplexed.

"No. Not at all. You're great. Perfect, in fact. It's just that...well... It's unfair. I can't exactly reciprocate the way you want me to." Not another word or backward glance, into her car she clambered.

As she drove off, last week's conversation with Walker sprang to mind: "Your young farmer friend detracts from your life's purpose. And, much as it pains me to say, although he's a good fellow, he is not your spiritual or intellectual equal. So you must choose: take up an ordinary life with him, or live out the life you are destined to with me."

Stricken and wondering, she'd stared at Walker. "You ask me to choose?"

"It's quite simple."

"No, it really isn't."

"Are you committed to me or not? That is the question. Only you can decide."

"I hope you're satisfied!" she shouted into the rearview mirror, unclear if she addressed Walker, herself, or God as she barreled along.

Nine months, exact interval required to gestate a fetus, sad, bewildered, having murdered a precious gift, already she missed her dear friend or missed the potential of how life might've been.

Sole focus shifted onto Walker, anxious to please, over-reliant upon his good opinion, increasingly she would become compliant, even dumb.

$$\infty$$

A day later, Sherman's voice soared down the hall, and Miss Spivey awoke.

Sherman trailed off. Miss Spivey slumped back into herself.

Morphed into a living human conduit, song forming his very being, Sherman sang out again.

Head lifted, Miss Spivey glanced about.

Song ceased, Miss Spivey's head dropped onto her chest.

Slightly comical, Sherman sang out in brief, rapid bursts. Each time, Miss Spivey perked up, then, at words' end, shut back down again.

Sherman entered the treatment room to croon, "Amazing Grace, how sweet the sound..."

Something opened then: an awakening. Mumbles mostly, but no stammer, Miss Spivey's sorrow found voice and met Sherman's joy. "That saved a wretch like me...,"

Midsong, Sherman halted.

Louder, clearer, Miss Spivey kept on, "I once was lost, but now am found."

"Was blind," Lauren-Son joined in, "but now I see." Voden,

Rosalee, Walker chimed as they moved into the room. "'Twas Grace that taught my heart to fear." Aching words flooding all with love, onward, they sang, "And Grace, my fears relieved. How precious did that Grace appear the hour I first believed." Words rippled, shifting, rearranging to cleanse and heal, all present merged to create a single perfect note.

Sound and vibration—that was it!

"Song, listening to music, Miss Spivey," Lauren-Son proudly informed, "rewires your nervous system!"

Miss Spivey wrung her hand. "I, I, I, I...just knew you...you'd figure it out!"

A-buzz with happiness, victorious glance tossed Walker's way, Lauren-Son laughed and laughed. Huge Technicolor moment, spine now straight, an accomplished healer these days, her life seemed to culminate.

Hope glinted from all of them, but mostly from Miss Spivey.

Subsequent weeks, Spivey—as she insisted all call her—eyes shiny, emanating life and light, flooded the halls of The Living Light with the purest of song.

Music—song—you see, is powerfully healing.

Chapter Fifty-Four: Young Adult Walker

Two months into marriage, after a wedding, presided over by a justice of the peace, Delia marched in, arms laden with shopping bags, to proudly announce, "See what I bought..." Rhinestone belt, tight fitting Levi's, assorted shirts with button-down pockets—piping at their edges—pair of pointy-toed cowboy boots extracted, she gushed, "Perfect, aren't they?" Walker regarded her, quizzical. "For your party, silly! To introduce you around. I know a ton of people."

Full of plans, she chattered merrily, "We'll rent The Grange, invite my family, everyone in Clarksdale, Buena Vista too. We'll barbecue and have music. Oooo—it'll be such fun!"

"Sorry, but I'm no good at social functions." Matter of fact, Walker detested them.

"Try these on." Delia indicated the garments.

Most subdued garment selected, Walker slid arms into armholes, snapped up the shirt, stepped into the Levi's, and cinched the belt. Fancy boots cramping his toes, he gave a hapless shrug. "I can't wear this." Delia rubbed his flanks.

"Do it for me, OK? Everyone's coming—almost forgot!" Off she spun to fish through another bag. "Bought myself a pair of pumps. Naturally, they're red." Delia had a thing for red high heels.

When unable to immediately locate a matched pair, instead of hunt them down, she'd buy yet another set. Last count, she owned three dozen. "Puleeze, baby, do this for me."

"OK." Walker girded himself. "We'll do this."

"God, I love you!" Delia gave him a quick hug, then assumed another tact. "Honey?"

"Mmm?"

"Wouldn't it be great if you ran for mayor?" Envisioning her husband to be destined for greatness, she fleshed out her role as mayor's wife, planned teas, benefits, socials, and heaps of adulation; couldn't wait for the day to arrive.

Oh, she loved her man all right—wouldn't stay if she didn't. Better than good sex, though, what got her hot were happy images of places she'd go soon as her husband blossomed.

Happily, she prattled away; Walker felt a sudden surge of what he assumed to be love.

Party commenced, Delia, dangling off his arm, introduced Walker to a boisterous, beefy passel of brothers. "This is my biggest brother, Danny. Here's Roberto. Rohellio and Buddy are around somewhere, and this is the baby, Miguel." Each brother smacked Delia's backside—a greeting Walker didn't much care for—then pummeled and spun him round.

One brother, possibly Buddy, garbed in a spectacularly awful polyester leisure suit, shot through the crowd to howl, "Oweee, you've landed yourself a wild one!"—meaning his sister.

Fellows within earshot chuckled knowingly.

So much a-buzz, room thrumming, party-goers slapped backs, emitted effusive guffaws, and performed elaborate high fives as Walker stood peripheral, observing. Delia breezed up, put a beer in his hand, gave him a nudge. "Talk loud. Raise your voice over theirs." Off she floated to swan about.

Decent interval endured, he retreated outside. "Come see my bunny." A girl-child led him next door to a rabbit hutch.

Delia located him and snuggled beneath his arm. "I knew you'd be hiding!"

Rohellio stumbled up, booming, "Say, bro, Sissy says you're psychic, 'n promised you'd give us a show." Walker shot Delia a look.

"Uh, not now," he stammered.

Delia unlatched to frown at both men. Rohellio pressed, "Say something I don't know about myself."

"I don't catch your meaning," Walker mumbled dumbly.

Rohellio leaned in, suggestive of planting a slobbery kiss. "Jus' tell my future."

"Sorry." Hutch door rattled open, Walker poured the rabbit inside. "I don't do parlor tricks."

"Sissy promised." Rohellio menaced. Delia stiffened, then smiled weakly.

Pride overwhelmed. "Well all righty, then." Hands smoothed down his front, Walker concentrated. Heard muffled voices: Delia and her brother bickering. Felt a slight tickle as an expanse—knowing—spanned out, further than his ordinary eyes could see.

Stop now! He warred with himself.

A lifetime of discretion flung aside, he bypassed all rules set for himself.

No, he wasn't drunk. Knew later he'd regret it. Yet he acquiesced to keep peace with Delia.

Lips pressed together, he tried to seal them.

"Hmm...Let's see." He slowed his words. "Rohellio...You have the beginnings of liver failure, caused by drink. Also...sorry to say, you have a lung lesion, possibly due to cigarettes."

Rohellio digested this. "Isss that it?"

Arms crossed, Delia suppressed a troubled smirk.

Rosalee rounded the corner, sensed what was up, moaned, and bit her lip.

"No." Walker smiled faintly. *God gave me unique talents*, he reasoned with himself, *so why not use them?*

Should've known better, could've called a halt, but did not care to. "Your wife's having an affair. Her lover treats her far better than you do."

Jaw dropped, Rohellio spat a great wad and lurched off.

Clayton Lynch, The Stop's proprietor, showed up, several chums in tow. "We heard you'd tell our fortunes."

Flushed with shame, fists shoved into pockets, knowledge of future events gently ebbing, a mere dry, achy buzz at the base of his neck remained as Walker addressed Clayton, "Sorry, but no."

Lips pursed, Delia gave a prompt.

Head shaken, Walker mouthed, *No.*

Shoulders squared, Delia inserted herself to announce, "Your partner steals from you."

Clayton stumbled as if struck, then he too stormed off.

"Tell us!" Hungry for details, the crowd clamored round her.

Imperiously, Delia obliged. "Your daughter is pregnant with triplets," she informed her brother, Buddy. "And her husband is not the father." She turned to inform Shelby Nurple, Buena Vista police officer, "You'll be passed over for promotion. The sheriff thinks you're a cheat and liar."

On she went. None of it went over well. All pressed to know anyhow. Impossible not to tell, the release—Delia's delighted joy—deafened.

Something else astir, strident voices raised over the ruckus; the crowd did an about-face, swarming en masse, following the commotion to the parking lot.

There Rohellio gripped Chika, his wife, gave her a shake, hollering, "Sleeping with Paco, eh?" Chika staggered, recovered, and whapped her husband with her handbag.

"You pig—I hate you!"

Koof—Rohellio bent double expelling air.

Chika jumped him.

Rolling, cursing, biting, kicking, slapping, both went down till the crowd wrestled them apart.

Chika broke free, yanked his hair, howling, "I'm *not* having an affair!"

Guests muttering among themselves, cast furtive glances as they gathered up platters and foodstuffs faster than imagined, slammed car doors, and drove off without usual leave-taking.

Tension palpable as they arrived home, Delia started in, "Why'd you refuse?"

"So they'd leave me be. Besides, it's inappropriate to nose into other's lives."

"But they asked!"

"What you did—what I did, was cruel—"

Delia cut him off. "How can I ever face my people? I promised all of them.

Walker tried again, "You had no right—"

Hand up, Delia shushed him. "It's just that...I married a wimp!"

"For your information..." he began. *I'm capable of so much more. If you could grasp the half of it, your head would spin.* Mouth shut, he bit words back.

Jagged recrimination thundered his brain. *How dare I! I'm such a rotten abuser, a mocker, a satanic vessel. My low-life behavior gives perfect proof that I'm wrongfully equipped to assume any power handed to me.* He'd overstepped, applied willfulness when patience and sequential revelation were required.

Ever patient, waiting for his life to begin, grown weary of the wait, he'd slipped, committing indiscretion with Rohellio and permitting his wife to run rampant.

Livid, growing more so, Delia gripped the chair back. "Who do you think you are, Mr. Holier Than Thou?" Walker shrugged, apologetic.

"Look, I'm sorry. I'm just not permitted to act until told to."

Face all frowns, Delia slumped onto the sofa. "I didn't make that stuff up, you know."

"What's that mean?"

Indulgent pause, she met his gaze. "I *see* too." She tapped her temple. "Sort of."

"No," he said, evenly, "You spread hurtful gossip. So did I."

"Huh, you did?"

"Listen, mind me now. When my earthly mission taps me, it will not ever be on my terms or yours. God will tell me how to proceed and when to begin."

Chapter Fifty-Five: Lauren

Should've knocked as she stepped into Walker's office, but Lauren-Son rarely did. A pretty new patient, Melissa Dworkin, who sat opposite Walker, yanked her hand from his. Staring, trying not to, Lauren-Son backed away. "Sorry. Didn't know someone was here."

Hands rubbed together, Walker stood, all business. "I was about to come find you."

Melissa arose, glanced at her, and departed, *scritchslap, scritchslap, scritchslap*—scrape of shoes on floorboards. Given her gait and tight press of lips, each step pained her, for she'd had polio far worse than Lauren-Son.

Originally arrived for a healing, she stayed on to attend the school. Each time Melissa sought Walker out, she cast him a beam of delight. It happened so often, Lauren-Son about hurled.

This would not have been a bother, except Walker too singled Melissa out, inviting her to join him while performing healings. One time, she caught them as both sat humming, eyes shut, gigantic grins plastered on faces. Throat locked, breath held, resisting the urge to break in, Lauren-Son tiptoed from sight. She now got how Delia felt.

A week later, Melissa and Lauren-Son slid into a booth at the Flatiron. As Melissa examined the menu, Lauren-Son sized up her competition.

Facial planes a tad too perfect, mouth overly large, Melissa caught Lauren-Son staring, did this marvelous sweeping move with that super-lovely neck of hers, then inquired, coquettish, "Why does Walker treat you so special?"

Snootily, Lauren-Son replied, "I ask you the same."

Quarrelsome noises burst in from nearby. "You have to run him out," spiked a voice. "That place is *so* unprofessional!" Lauren-Son whipped round.

Two tables off, four women sat with Mayor Clayton Lynch. Words crisply clipped, that persnickety therapist, Miss Wilkins, addressed the mayor, "My practice is failing. I don't see why you can't do something." Mayor Clayton spotted Lauren-Son, muttered, and put his head down. Miss Wilkins glanced over, lowered her voice, but kept talking and gesturing, all animated.

"Looks like we've got a problem," Lauren-Son groused, turning back to Melissa, "So...What's your story?" Spoon clanking, Melissa stirred sugar into her tea and blew to cool it.

"Well...I used to live in an ashram. When my guru underwent a transformative awakening, all of us, myself included, got flooded with bliss just being in his presence. I had profound revelations—at least I thought so at the time." Her voice reverberated with reverence and sorrow.

Lauren-Son pressed, "What brought you here?"

"We followers gave our lives to our guru's every whim. He wanted money; we gave him every cent. He insisted devotees stay celibate— even married ones. All of us obeyed." Eyes misted up, her voice quavered. "I had a husband and a two-year-old son. We, too, avoided behaviors remotely construed as sexual, were careful not to touch or even to gaze at each other." More sugar heaped into her cup, she stirred, then set it aside.

"We credited our teacher with special discernment and unique spiritual insights and assumed that he had only benevolent intent. Consequently, when he violated his own rules, we ignored it. So then, when he demanded sex"—palms pressed into eyes, she muffled her voice—"I complied."

Hands from her face, she sniffled. "Later, he took up with another woman, and I went public. He denied our relationship. I overdosed. My own husband voted I be banished."

"Your husband did that?" Lauren-Son sat back, mystified.

Mayor Clayton's group stirred, then stood. Miss Wilkins thanked the others for coming. Clayton paid the bill, then cast Lauren-Son a sidelong glance as he went past. Pointedly, she grimaced.

"What's that about?" Melissa asked.

"Never you mind!" Lauren-Son snapped, then lightened her tone. "Go on...I'm listening."

Head shaken, Melissa regained her place, "When eight other women came forward with similar allegations of sexual misconduct, my guru again denied them. Finally, in light of so many complaints, the community *did* investigate and found I told the truth. Some apologized, but the damage was done. I'd already lost my husband and my son." Face taut with grief, she looked up.

Gusted with kindness—jealousy too—kind self winning out, Lauren-Son covered Melissa's hand with hers, whispering fiercely, "You poor thing!"

Discomfited, she prompted, "So you came here for Walker to fix you?" Power dynamics, she would learn intimately, are complex. Power is seized, used, abused, and yet, repeatedly, followers permit themselves to be harmed.

"I left the ashram, then heard about Walker. You have no idea how kind he's been. He tells me I'm exceptional, that I have a bright future." Her face got all moony.

Lauren-Son stared, amazed. "Funny, he tells me the same." Itchy spots exploded her flesh.

Torment indescribable, as if she were a wild, woolly animal, Lauren-Son leaned into her chair back to rub and scratch.

Get a grip! she scolded, inwardly.

Palms flat on thighs, she ran energy into herself.

Itch subsided, she relaxed. *OK, so I'm jealous!*

"I overhead the mayor and Miss Wilkins at the Flatiron," Lauren-Son informed Walker the next day. "She's huffy at us; so are several others. Recently, Rosalee asked me to stress concern about this to you. She's worried that trouble is brewing. Actually, I feel it too."

Walker nodded grimly. "Guess we must mind our p's and q's, then."

"But—"

Walker cut in, "I fully accept what is to come. You must too." He turned away.

That was that—no further concern, no strategizing how best to protect themselves.

Fretting on both fronts, Lauren-Son began to pay close attention to the town's disposition and to all manifestations of Walker's favoritism. She took inordinate delight when he expressed displeasure with a student; Melissa, in particular. The more he did so, the more secure she felt.

Chapter Fifty-Six: Walker

A helicopter spluttered to land on Buena Vista's spanking new parking lot—resurfaced courtesy of Delia's efforts. Head tucked to avoid whirring blades, a nurse and an exquisitely coiffed woman brought a man out on a gurney. Walker flagged an arm, ushering the arrivals into a waiting ambulance. Doors slammed, away the group whisked to The Living Light.

Coat handed off, the woman floated over to Walker and Lauren-Son. "Thank you for seeing us on short notice. I'm Sheila Millbanks, David's wife." Folks in the waiting area ogled as she draped her hand, offering it up as royalty might.

Walker shook it warmly, introduced Lauren-Son as his associate, then indicated that they follow.

Gurney clacking, Shelia Millbanks's dress seductively scrunching, Walker, Lauren-Son, and the nurse went down the hall to a treatment room. "Darling," Sheila Millbanks said, rousing the patient, "here's Mr. Judson."

With great difficulty, David Millbanks lifted his head to eye Walker.

Exertion being too much, head flopped back, he quaked and pulsed as they transfered him onto the treatment table.

Sheila Millbanks gave a nod; the nurse departed. "Presently," she began, "David is in the throes of a severe palsy that started three weeks ago. He's unable to walk, can barely swallow, and is confined to bed. We've seen neurologists at the Mayo Clinic, Stanford, and Sloan-Kettering; none know what to make of him.

"David has followed your work with keen interest and was so dreadfully sorry that you turned down his offer to build and run our clinic. David's father, you see, was an evangelical minister, so David witnessed many miracles as a result. And, night before last, he dreamt you healed him; hence his insistence that we come." Delicately, Mrs. Millbanks rolled her eyes. "Who am I to question. I do as he bids. Isn't that so, dear?"

"Are...are you a man of God?" mouthed Millbanks. Tremors overwhelming, his eyes lost focus and rolled up in his head.

"Yes, I'd say so." Walker scanned Millbanks's energy field, assessing the man's true nature.

Past collapsed into present, smooth blue-blooded exterior being so thick, Walker had to slog through to view Millbanks's life, one spent accumulating power, objects, esteem, and knowledge—all to stave off nothingness; fear of the void.

Protective hand on her husband's, the wife cut in, "David fears he is demoniacally possessed."

"I see no evidence of possession, but something definitely holds you in its grip." Walker leaned close to ask, "A crisis of faith perhaps?" Tears whetted Millbanks's lashes.

Rush of tenderness, Walker cupped the man's cheek. "May I look?"

Tremulous finger lifted in assent, Walker shed his coat, rolled sleeves up, peeled covers back, examined the body closely, then placed hands at the man's temples.

At table's end, Lauren-Son blew into her hands to warm them and then gripped the patient's feet.

As is common with powerful individuals, Millbanks's sixth and seventh chakras buzzed away, highly charged. Imbalance of this sort prompts neglect of the lower chakras: the energy centers requisite for everyday function. When this occurs, the world has an Einstein; a brilliant soul incapable of attending to life's mundane details, unable to find his way home. Or worse, a Hitler or a Jim Jones, founder of The People's Temple, perpetrator of the cult's mass suicide. Both visionaries possessed huge energetic holes where hearts should have been.

Skin hard as pebbles, as Walker kneaded Millbanks's flesh, icy stones rattled about within veins where emotive fluidity was requisite. A lifetime of ruthless acts, it seemed, had ossified the man.

"Your body, sir," Walker announced, "has hardened from the inside out. So even if we loosen you up, you must face that which you protect from."

A rolling surge rocked Millbanks. Walker gave a nod. Lauren-Son readied herself. Expansive flutter, a pause within realities, the two linked energies—a quick pop confirmed this—and then, performing duo magic, they began.

Walker wended into and through Millbanks's tissue and met Lauren-Son there as well. They moved in unison along opposite sides of the patient. Whereas he held back, listening, and kept hands steady, as if a butterfly, Lauren-Son flitted to a new fleshy patch every few moments.

Utter joy suffused her face. Fluid, yet highly focused, entire body whipped into liveliness, she danced with the energies, sensing his moves before he made them. She was good, very good; his breath came difficult from watching.

Healing results she achieved surpassed his: not just in terms of depth and success, but owing to the way she treasured her patients; each was a singular, exquisite, awe-inspiring mystery to study and to learn from.

Walker placed hands on Millbanks's ribcage. On the side opposite, Lauren-Son did likewise. Walker emitted a nasal whine. Ear cocked, adjusting for intensity and breadth, more odd assorted noises exited from him. Lauren-Son joined in. Simultaneously they shook the man's torso, vibrating, toning into it.

Minutes along, Walker emitted a high weary cry, then began to hum, "Owmmmm."

"EEEeee," Lauren-Son joined to intone.

Each vocalization into Millbanks's forehead, chest, and abdomen allowed his flesh to soften, loosen, and stretch. Ribcage given a final vigorous shake, Walker stepped away. Lauren-Son did the same.

Face serene, David Millbanks lay quiverless. Walker leaned into him. "Let's pray that you experience relief." Millbanks motioned his wife, who helped him upright.

Hands exhibiting the merest shakes, slowly he brought them together. "Bless you."

Coats gathered, nurse returned, the couple bade goodnight and departed.

Next morning, before the day got rolling, a gentleman staggered in through the door, repeatedly paused, as if a religious penitent, to kiss the ground. "Uh, hello there," Walker said, going to greet him.

"I...," David Millbanks deliberated. "I am well!" Hands shakily raised, he blurted, "It's God's mercy!" Shuffled forth, he pressed Walker's cheeks and kissed him.

Walker blanched and gave him a pat. "Now, now, good fellow, mustn't tire yourself."

Lauren entered. "I heard noises?"

"Praise be!" Loopily Millbanks came at her to plant kisses. "I am restored!"

Sheila Millbanks appeared, wringing her hands. "He insisted we come. Believe me...Such demonstrativeness isn't at all like him." She adjusted his coat, fussing over her husband. "He says you have cured him."

"Imagine that!" Madly, Walker blushed.

"If...." Millbanks rasped, smothering Walker's hands in his. "If you ever need anything—anything at all—do not hesitate to ask!"

More hugs and kisses, the couple departed.

Friendly, chaste, Lauren-Son gave Walker a hug. "Walker, that was *so* great!"

"Yup, it was." Firmly, deliberately, Walker kissed her mouth.

"Oh, wow!" Flustered, Lauren-Son flailed arms and stepped away.

Mouth tightly crimped, eyes affixed, there in the shadows stood Delia.

Chapter Fifty-Seven: Lauren

Air hot, dry, a free afternoon spent in the garden alongside The Living Light, Spivey, now a most gorgeous shade of mahogany, stood, arms cast wide, bursting with song, "If it be Your will that I speak no more, and my voice be still, as it was before, I will speak no more and shall abide until I am spoken for…" a Leonard Cohen song.

Lauren-Son joined in to croak off key, "If it be Your will to let me sing…" Past six months, stammer gone, Spivey had turned fiercely fabulous.

New person, scarcely recognizable, each time she spoke or sang, all leaned into her words—words held back a lifetime—and felt blessed.

She plunked down at the picnic table; Lauren-Son passed her a sandwich.

"Soon as I finish collectin' myself," Spivey announced, "I'm off to find my man's bones."

"Where will you begin?"

"We was just outside Harperville, Mississippi. That's where I plan to start."

Bit of silence and chewing, Spivey stared off, not in that eerie way of old, but somber, thoughtful.

"Care to say more?" Lauren-Son asked, highly attuned.

"Ain't much to tell." Squarely, she set her food down. "Him and me wasn't married by a preacher, but we lived as husband and wife. I was fifteen. Ozzie was sixteen. He worked the next farm over; that's how we met. Lan' sakes, he had right-tolerable eyes, a most luscious mouth, and loved me bunches!" Modestly, Spivey fluttered. "See... Back then, I was a pretty little thing." Eyes misted up, napkin gathered to her face, she wiped.

"And then?"

Spivey sat still; it seemed she hadn't heard.

"What happened?"

"Heard you the first time." Spivey worked her jaw. "They lynched him."

"Lynched...as in hanged?"

"Tipped his hat for a white woman," she practically spat. "'Cept whites claimed it was more than that." Lauren-Son sat back, dumbstruck and thought to apologize—for everything.

Her hand crept out; Spivey ignored it. "How do you live with such sorrow?"

"You stopped me once, as I recall. Mostly I tried not to exist, but the good Lord kept me goin', anyhow. Now, thanks to you, gal, life looks a mite tolerable."

Eagerly, she lurched forward. "I got a lead from kin down south. Neshoba County records makes mention of a young black man who died 'bout the same time as my Ozzie. This one's got no name, but was kilt and buried somewhere near Harperville, so I aim to have a look-see."

"How will you know they're his bones? Dental records can be inaccurate, and despite scientific breakthroughs, it'll be tough to be certain."

Spivey lifted her chin, defiant. "I'll just know."

"What then?"

"I plan to bring him back, place him in the ground, right respectable, so he'll be nearby."

"Sure hope it's him."

"It's all I ever wanted." Resolute as she seemed, Lauren-Son recalled their first contact—Spivey barefoot, shirt lifted over her head, crouched pantless in a puddle of urine, an endless scream raging from her mouth.

Muffled, distant scuffing, then a loud crash, Lauren-Son tracked the commotion upstairs to Voden's door. "Voden, you there?" she called, knocking.

Scratches again, Silly, Voden's cat, meowed. "Voden?" Lauren-Son knocked harder.

Silly gave a pitiful meow. Lauren-Son cracked the door; Silly pushed out to rub her legs. "Cooped up, boy?" Crouched to pet him, Silly, lacking usual aloof disdain, squawked happily, then lolled onto his back: a move only reserved for Voden. Immensely pleased by this, for ages she'd worked to win him over, brought treats and dumb pet toys, which he always ignored.

Fussy and highly expressive, habitually Silly stood at his food bowl, grumbling until fed. When thirsty, he climbed into the sink and glared, sternly, until the faucet dribbled just so. If anyone but Voden dared cuddle him, he swiveled to glare as well. And, heaven help the sorry soul who breathed in his face: the cat punished with the severest hiss.

Not demonstrative in the least, Voden, acting as if Silly were a furry infant, cooed and petted him. Matter of fact, all cats magnetized to Voden.

Voden went out for his morning stroll; felines rushed up to follow in droves. On return, The Living Light transformed into a soup kitchen for homeless cats who lined up to receive Voden's thorough rubdown. After that, he fed them, setting down a city block's worth of food bowls.

Thin hollow-eyed strays plumped up nicely, yet Voden refused to name them—said it wasn't necessary—that they knew who they were without being tagged or labeled. Moreover, he insisted that Silly had named himself.

Another sight, of late, was common: Voden gliding along, Spivey, rapt sheen to her face, loping along after him. Never did they seem to converse, yet Spivey passed days serene, without traces of pain blanching her face. Lauren-Son's take: the wake of Voden's preternatural calm soothed her.

Sick of being petted, Silly scampered off.

Lauren-Son stood to shut the door, peeking as she moved to do so. Voden's room, divested of comfort, contained no furniture—no bed, no chair, no clothes—nothing but a large, elegantly framed photo hung, dead center, at room's far end.

Torn between entering or backing out, curiosity won over. "You here Voden?" she called.

Knowing he wasn't, she tiptoed in to examine the picture.

Nuns! Twelve in all. Frisky, frolicking, downright festive gals rushed forth. Varied height and weight aside, each identically garbed bride of Christ, headgear reminiscent of Gothic flying buttresses, posed jauntily, hamming for the camera. All but one, that is.

In the lower right-hand corner, trying to slink off frame, frowned a thirteenth nun.

Lauren-Son leaned closer to squint.

Same nose, same eyes, somber face and lack of height...

"Mr. Fucols 'twas once of their ilk." Voden stood stiff in the doorway.

"Oh!" Lauren-Son jumped. "Silly wanted out, so I opened the door, then saw this... I had no business coming in." She moved to go.

Voden slid alongside to regard the photo and kept his expression, as ever, bland. "'Tis fine."

"First a woman, now a man? D'oh!" She smacked her brow. *Such an impertinent dangling question!* "Sorry to be so nosy!"

"No harm." Candy bar extracted from a pocket, wrapper peeled back, he crunched away. "First a woman, now a man, indeed. Mr. Fucols began as a Doris, then became Sister Anne Marie."

"Wow!"

"Surprising isn't it? Currently, he's nursemaid to fledgling healers. Some days he doubles as bodyguard. He possesses other talents of which he is not at liberty to divulge. Before this incarnation, he was something else altogether." His voice trailed off, a touch wistful.

"You see the future too?"

"Mmmm." Candy bar consumed, he neatly folded the wrapper in half, then repeatedly folded it into tinier squares. "Better as a woman or as a man?" he asked, eyes so crinkly he nearly smiled.

Lauren-Son appraised him, then checked the photo. "Better as a man."

"Ha!" Voden laughed short, quick: first and only time she ever heard him do so. "Don't tell The Boss, OK?" He dabbed his eyes from the effort of the laugh.

"I'm not a blab!" Given his pursed lips, he assumed she'd tell.

Ordinarily she would have, but Walker would chide her for being a gossip, so there'd be no fun in it.

Candy wrapper folded into oblivion, Lauren-Son stared, half

hoping such intricacies might reveal more of the man. "Sorry," she repeated. "It won't happen again."

Voden winked—sly, conspiratorial—wholly out of character. "Let's just say God works in mysterious ways, and leave it be." Smartly, he spun on his heel and glided off.

Door shut, Lauren-Son hurried to grab the insistent ringing phone.

"Hell…" a voice wafted from the other end.

"May I help?" she inquired.

Kkkkkkkkk—crackles over the line; she jiggled the earpiece.

Abruptly, the line settled, then words came out, clear, low, unmistakable, "Look out, girlie, they're coming."

Line thudded dead, heart pounding ridiculously fast, she stared into the receiver.

Chapter Fifty-Eight: Walker

Stiletto heels clicking, Delia entered the foyer. "You here, Walker?" More clicks, she swept through the house.

Their home, a mishmash of tastes and architecture, overlooked Buena Vista and beyond to Verde Valley. Some termed it an eyesore; the more generous called it overly large. Walker enjoyed its extensive views, but thought the place trashy. It was, however, a prideful thing for Delia.

Curious pervasive odor—aspiration—scenting all rooms, Delia attempted sophistication, but missed the mark by flooding the place with bric-a-brac, chunky, modern furniture, and a smattering of antiques. Her penchant for loud colors went un-squelched; the jumble jarred the senses. "There you are!" Plopped onto the hassock at Walker's feet, Delia drummed her nails.

"Where've you been?" he asked mildly.

"At Mama's." Carefully, Delia smiled. Unwillingly, Walker smiled back. Delia concentrated on twisting her bracelets. "You got my note." Indeed, Walker found her scrawled missive, but facts were bare. *Gone to collect my wits, back...whenever.*

"Your mother hasn't seen you."

A peek, Delia's rage surfaced as she pushed up and scurried off to return shortly with her birdies—two chirpy epaulets—perched atop her shoulders and a serving tray in hand.

Lemonade poured, she held out a glass. "Want some?"

Walker fended, "No thanks."

Birds set on the window ledge, she slid in at his side, wrapped arms round his neck, and planted juicy kisses.

Taste of her filling him with bleakness, Walker leaned back to think: *Are we born fully formed or can we re-shape ourselves?*

Years on end this question nagged. Pretty sure his destiny—and hers—to be preordained, never had he found a suitable answer.

Face buried in Walker's chest, her fleshy warmth exuded her familiar combination—cigarette and pikake scents. "I miss you." she muffled.

Stroke to her hair, he insisted, "She's done nothing."

Delia unbuttoned his shirt to lick his chest. "I saw you with her." Walker stiffened, gripping her head. "Start anything with her," she growled, "I ignite a shitstorm of ostracism that'll tear this place apart."

"Do not harm her!" Harder, he squeezed.

"Ow, you're hurting!"

Walker moved off. "I repeat, not!" Mouth opened several times, Delia raised her chin. "Why do you do this?" he pressed, straightening his shirt cuffs.

Quick glance at him, whirring, ticking brain sorting through, she tried to explain, "You don't seem to want me, which I'm unaccustomed to. You prefer others—mostly that horrid girl—over me. Not being wanted is scary." She grinned, hopeful.

Walker scruffed his jaw. "You overreact. I cannot allow the girl to be harmed and will do whatever it takes to prevent you. Understand?" Delia nodded strenuously.

Depth of his bind hitting hard, Walker regarded his hands.

Way back, Delia reached across the barrier behind which he'd cowered—for that alone, he owed her. Plus, thanks to her efforts, hysterical amounts of money poured into The Living Light. And...He needed a successful marriage to keep the veneer of normalcy at the forefront.

Deferring to her stern rule to cover his own lack of organizational skills, Delia insisted on authoritarian discipline to run the healing school: she implemented controlling bylaws, mandated meetings, required chores, expected adherence to rigorous, strict class and meditation schedules, and he allowed all of it. Criticism of The Living Light, deemed evidence of spiritual corruption, was not to be tolerated, so she acted the heavy and banished students and volunteers who overstepped.

When students attained goals, she handed out badges as if they were Girl Scouts. Hard-won invitations to their home—also her brainchild—were prized and sparked jealousy. And presently, she pushed to retitle The Living Light, The Judson Healing Center. Already, a parking lot and plaza bore his name.

A rush of emotions swept through: anger, frustration, sadness, mostly guilt at the moment. He belonged to Delia; that was a given. His remoteness had transformed her into an unhappy woman: he'd repeatedly left her in the lurch, insulting her sense of self worth.

Recently, acting the lounge singer, she'd gripped an imaginary microphone, stretched herself over the coffee table, then slithered back up to belt out:

How can people be so heartless? How can people be so cruel? Specially people who care about strangers. Specially people who care about evil and social injustice. Do you only care about the bleeding crowd? How about a needing friend?

Those lyrics to the rock opera sensation *Hair* held truth. As one who'd helped many, he'd been incapable of giving comfort to his wife.

Delia came close, stroked his face, abruptly tensed, swung back, and gave him a terrific slap. "You think I'm clueless? I know what I saw!" Second slap readied, Walker gripped her wrists.

"Enough!" Releasing her, he stepped out of reach, massaging his cheek.

Spun on heel, rushing tick of shoes on tile, Delia swept down the cavernous hall to their bedroom suite, Walker following.

Dress so daringly short as to barely cover her rump, she slid out of it to pose before him. Wearing black panties and brassiere, breasts pushed up, nipples peeked over the top—danger building, he absorbed her at her finest.

Back turned to him, Delia spritzed perfume at her neck.

Walker gripped her shoulders and turned her to face him. "Look at me, honey." He tilted her chin; their eyes met. "We need you. I need you. You have a tough job—harder than mine."

"Oh?" Delia wavered, wistful, fussed with his lapels. "Do you love me?"

"You tell me…," he asked, slow on the uptake, "do I love you?"

"Yes, definitely!"

Laughter barreled out of him. "You're quite something!"

Clothes shed, he tumbled into bed, pulled the covers back, inviting her to join him.

Undies dropped in a heap, Delia slid between sheets.

Craned to kiss her, noting her frown, he thought better of it.

"I'm still mad!" Flopped onto her side, she faced away from him.

Wary lest he receive another slap, Walker addressed her from behind, "You've done a tremendous job, Delia. You run a tight ship. We…I couldn't function without you."

She turned to beam at him.

Shame flooded his brain: shame for his spousal failings as well as shame for failure to see this coming. Sorrow and forgiveness for Delia, too, overcame him. He'd demeaned her through neglect, made her feel bad enough to consider doing harm. "I'll do better," he promised.

Face pushed into his palm, she kissed it. "You're so good!"

Nestled close, Walker wrapped arms around her and sighed.

As twilight drew down, cocooned within that embrace, they gazed out upon the town.

True to his word, Walker would come home earlier, would defer to his wife's whims and adoringly hold hands in public.

Inclusion would make Delia kinder, yet her essential self, as known from the outset, would remain forever reckless and hurtful.

Chapter Fifty-Nine: Lauren

"What do you make of this?" Spivey handed over a ledger titled, Living Light Finances. "Someone left the safe open, so I peeked in." Spivey, who took a regular shift at the front desk and did a credible job, stood by nibbling her pen top as Lauren-Son skimmed through.

No entries whatsoever for the past month, she leafed further. The ledger, a simple system of income and outgo, used data entry basics, but month after month, entry after entry, pages replete with whiteouts, erasures, and penciled-in changes had been altered.

"Where's the intake from healings?" Lauren-Son, who rarely gave The Living Light's finances thought, certainly did so now. "And what happens when money's needed to pay bills?"

Spivey waved airily. "That witch's very private 'bout them books. But something sure ain't right, 'cause past weeks, creditors have been comin' by demandin' cash payment."

Lauren-Son regarded her, perplexed. "So where's it all going?"

"This here's also a problem..." Spivey raised a wad of receipts. "These were crammed in the safe. And I found this at the back..." She produced mortgage documents: two loans totaling $950,000. Both bore Delia's signature in the name of The Living Light. "I ain't the best at math, but far more money seems to be goin' out than's comin' in."

"If these are real, we're deep in debt." Lauren-Son flipped back through the ledger.

The Living Light had no overhead. Rosalee's token dollar a month aside, they paid no rent. Donated labor took care of repairs, and office supplies were gifted. "If the IRS knew 'bout such shenanigans"— Spivey waved at the pages—"they'd have a heyday!"

"Seems like...," Lauren-Son formulated, "Delia's ripping us off!"

"Love ya, gal, but this ain't my fight. And...Just so's you know, I'll be leaving shortly." Tongue clicking, Spivey strode off.

Air succumbed to perfumy scents, Delia swept in. "Hello there!"
she chirped, using her newfound singsong voice. "How's it going?"

"Ah..." Lauren-Son pulled up to full height. "I'd like a word."

"Only have a minute, but do come." Delia strode into her office.

Close at her heels, Lauren-Son followed.

Delia enclosed Lauren-Son's hand in hers. "What can I do for
you?"

Lauren-Son pried herself from Delia's grip. "Hate to be a stinker,
but this place is in a fix."

Smile fading, Delia bristled. "Whatever do you mean?"

Any other matter, Lauren-Son would've soothed, acted conciliatory,
but Delia's actions jeopardized everything. "Looks like someone's
cooking the books," she said, holding her tone neutral, indicating that
she'd be understanding—magnanimous even.

Chilly smile crimping Delia's mouth, firmly she pressed knuckles
into the desktop. "What are you talking about?"

"Some call it stealing; probably it's just a mistake. All the same...
That money isn't yours to take." Lauren-Son waved the ledger.

Face hardened, Delia rounded the desk. "You've no business going
through that!"

"Don't need permission. In fact, given the way this place is run,
anyone can see the fix we're in."

"Aren't you the sorriest thing!" Arms crossed, Delia's voice rang
out shrill, mocking. "I'm in charge, and frankly, I don't recall asking
your opinion."

"I'd like us to straighten this out."

Delia sniffed. "Who appointed you Grand Moral Compass? Point
of fact..." She gathered herself. "You're the most pathetic excuse for
a female I've ever seen! And...Since you accuse me of stealing, how
about you stealing my husband?" Her words—fighting words—landed
as a spit wad in Lauren-Son's face.

"This isn't about me," Lauren-Son said evenly. "Or about how we
feel about each other. It's about this place. Word gets out, and you'll
destroy us."

"You dare threaten me!"

Air roiling with escalating fury, the two women seemed evenly matched. Delia, though soft on the outside, was a scrapper. Bigger by far, Lauren-Son, readied to tear Delia's head off.

Yet swiftly, she reined herself in.

Delia regarded her haughtily. "You evil, repulsive thing, you've turned my husband against me!"

"Evil"—Lauren-Son jabbed a finger—"is pretending something isn't happening when it is. And you, lady, are evil!"

Short bark of a laugh, Delia slapped the hand away.

"Don't point, you freak!"

"Return the money; it isn't yours."

"You impertinent shit!" Fists bunched, Delia readied a swing.

Smoothly, Walker stepped in and shut the door. "What have we here?" he inquired, clearly pained.

"This big galoot"—Delia forked a thumb—"accuses me of stealing! I want her gone!"

Firmly, Walker directed his wife, "Go home. I'll meet you there shortly." Delia spluttered, shooting barbs at Lauren-Son as Walker helped his wife into her coat and ushered her out.

Door shut again, he addressed Lauren-Son, "Take the day off. We'll discuss this later."

"But, Walker, we need to talk."

"Another time!" His dry distance infuriated.

"Walker," she pressed, voice raised, "you have to stop her. She's robbing us blind. If you don't deal with this now, you never will. She—"

He cut her off. "How I relate to Delia is not your business!"

"But...," she said, lowering her voice, "I don't see why you refuse to see what she's doing. I—"

Again, he overrode her. "Let it go."

Even if he could take her side, she got why he didn't. Delia was his wife; they had to stick together—she respected that.

But the main point was getting lost: Delia's shady ways and extravagant lifestyle jeopardized their future.

Walker put a hand to her cheek, then let it drop. "You're the only one I trust."

Utterly absorbed in that touch, she stroked her face.

That contact, she chided herself, *is merely conciliatory—nothing more.*

But if he'd lingered, sure as heck I'd tangle myself in his arms, kissing more than just lips!

Spivey knocked, ducked her head in, addressing Lauren-Son, "The missus wants a word; she's out in her car. Think she wants to 'pologize."

"How about it?" cheek still tingling, Lauren-Son queried Walker. "I'd like to clear the air."

"Fine. Go."

Delia in her Mercedes, stared straight ahead, gripping the steering wheel. "Look, Delia…" Lauren-Son ducked to window level. "I've handled this wrong. It's probably just a misunderstanding."

Delia swiveled to glare. Her hand crept down to the door handle; door half open, about to exit, she halted. "Fine! But from now on, respect this…" Hand jerked up to show her wedding band, Lauren-Son leaned in to view it.

Door shoved open fast, hard, as the doorframe hit, no helping hand shot out to break her fall, then Lauren-Son dropped onto concrete.

Head cracked, felt split like a melon, searing tongues screamed.

Last image she recalled was Delia's wide-eyed surprise.

Or was it rage?

Chapter Sixty: Young Adult Walker

Up at dawn, Walker prepared to head out on a trip hauling across The Rockies. "Hon…?" He touched Delia's cheek.

Groggily, she reached out to him. "Get back here, you."

"Much as I'd like to, I'm late."

She stretched out, provocative. "A few minutes can't hurt."

"I'm behind as it is."

Covers tossed back, Delia bolted upright. "What's with you? Everyone says you're strange. You cross your legs like a girl. You're shy as hell, and you avert your eyes when we talk. Why is that?"

"Er, I don't know," Walker fumbled. "I try to—"

She hadn't yet finished. "And, lately you sit for hours just staring at your hands." Reaching over, she grabbed his wrists, flipped the palms up to examine them. "It's so creepy!"

Walker sighed. "You want me ordinary, yet you want me to stand out. You can't have both.

She shot him a pleading look. "There's something you aren't saying."

Walker warred with himself. *Tell her all of it—everything. She'll understand. And then my burden will lift.* "It's like this…"

Abruptly, he reconsidered. *She won't accept me or the situation, and will leave.* "Look…I'm not your average guy. So if it's normal you want, you've made a mistake."

"Oh yeah!" Naked breasts a-bobble, Delia leapt up in all her pouty glory. "I'll show you normal…" Fists flailing, she pummeled him.

Dodging blows, Walker, grabbing wallet and jacket, rushed out to his truck.

"Fine. Go!" she hollered, letting him know nothing was fine in the slightest.

Engine revved, off he drove, detouring to The Overlook.

Day gone sour, bitterly cold, hands crammed into pockets, he pondered: *How do I make Delia happy?* What skimpy knowledge he possessed of happiness came from knowing her.

I can change, he resolved. *I'll be the man she wants, make myself fit into a world of rules, where folks are duty-bound.*

Then what?

I'll wither and die. Not all at once, but gradually, bit by bit.

Sigh heaved, Walker pulled up his collar.

Quietly, Rosalee came alongside.

He forced a smile to greet her. "I'm here for my dose of vastness."

"Me too." Contented sigh fluttering her body, round face, soft eyes, wind gusts frothing her hair, she appeared an earthbound cherub.

"Nice here. It awakens the senses." Walker mumbled.

"Please, Walker, tell me what you *see.*"

"Uh, I see this valley before—"

"No," she cut in. "You can tell me."

"As I dream?"

"What do you *see* on me?" Their eyes met. Eagerly, she nodded.

Walker glanced away.

Rosalee persisted, "No silly tricks like at that party. Do not speak about my garments but tell what you really *see* with this?" Tug to his sleeve, she turned him to face her, rolled onto tiptoe, and tapped his brow. "I know you *see* people lit up. Question is: what you do with it? Also, I understand; if you allow your gifts to flow, it will mark you as different. But if you leave it alone, you will not live out your destiny, as you are supposed." Walker shifted, uneasy.

How could she know? For *seeing* hadn't occurred in years...at least not until recently.

Last trip hauling, deadheaded back from Abilene, something about a passing apple orchard catching his peripheral vision, he'd pulled over to check.

Crosshatched light emanating from tree branches, hand passed over his eyes, he'd stared.

Indistinct buzz blinked on, top of his skull lifted off to leave brains exposed, breezes rushed, chattering as sense memories rushed back... *Seeing,* he'd abruptly recalled, *is best achieved by fuzzing my gaze and not looking directly at the object of interest.*

Gaze softened to absorb the surrounding haze...There it was!

Air tightly woven to surround all trees, kindred vibrations pulsed in unison as if the orchard comprised a single energetic unit.

Swiftly, he dismissed the oddity, made a mental note to get his vision checked, and drove off.

Miles later, a solitary oak loomed alongside the road; a silvery cloudlike radiance bounded it.

"What the...?" Neck craned, he'd sped past.

Further along, a lofty windbreak of poplars sucked light, spitting curlicues at the sky.

Then came the dying cottonwood. Denuded, shrimpier in size, darkly constricted, lacking vitality, his heart crimped painfully at the sight. Neighboring trees, regardless of species, appeared mournfully shrouded in solidarity.

Trees, he'd remembered, *communicate and feel!*

So, Rosalee had named his dilemma. Certain responsibilities came with *seeing:* fully embracing the gift being one of them.

At last, Walker spoke, "Demonstrating my—ah—talents will make me an outcast."

"Perhaps so." Rosalee gave him a knowing pat. "God often gives gifts we don't much like, but that does not make it is OK to ignore them."

"Well then, uh...Sometimes I do *see*, but not so much in recent years."

Rosalee nodded sagely. "But, my friend, it is no longer right to pretend to be what you are not. You are not a trucker; that is not your life purpose. You are a great healer. That is inevitable, so you must permit your gifts to thrive."

"But..." *Soon as the floodgates open, how will I maintain my carefully erected protective shield?* "Although I've awaited this my whole life, it arrives too swiftly."

"Accept your gifts." Rosalee squeezed his bicep. "They have waited, patiently, for you to claim them. You long for them too, yet also avoid them...That makes them confused."

Lightening quivered the sky, illuminating far-off mountaintops.

Raindrops fell, brushing lash and cheek. Walker yanked his jacket over their heads and tucked Rosalee close. Dread, elation too, settled within him.

"Grief trapped in heart makes big anger," Rosalee declared, transmitting great kindness. "And so you must release it."

Feeling terribly cared for, Walker nodded solemnly.

"I go now." Rain sluicing, Roslaee moved off, then called back, "Keep your heart open to what will come."

To accept my gifts will transform me...not in ways that will make me seem sane or normal. Delia won't like it one bit. I've kept my life small to savor stability, but even if I wish to, I can't call a halt.

Heaviness falling away, joyous recklessness overtook him.

Destiny bearing down full force, he spun on his heel, resolute, and trotted back to the truck.

...And so it began.

Chapter Sixty-One: Lauren

Two weeks post head bonk, waiting for the bus to arrive, Spivey placed hands on hips and glared at Lauren-Son. "Your silly head gets stitched together on account of that witchy wife, and your big hero does nothing 'bout it!" Palm licked, she reached out to plaster down an errant spike of her pal's recently shorn locks.

"Please, not again!" groaned Lauren-Son.

Spivey scuffed dirt, persisting, "Thanks to you, Old Spivey ain't gone completely crazy. So I see, right plainly, that you act as if that big shot, Walker's appointed himself God Almighty. And…If you ask me, this place takes advantage."

"That's not how it is. Walker gives all credit to God. I wouldn't stay if he didn't."

"Ho!" Spivey snorted, folded arms across her chest, then dove in again, "Believe me, that man ain't as swell as he seems. And that wife o' his…She's from the devil. Only thing makin' a lick o' sense is that angel. From the look, it smiles at our silly gyrations and puts up with our fuss."

"At least we agree about that!"

"Listen up." Spivey mushed Lauren-Son's cheeks. "That wife's fixin' to run you outta here and your mister ain't standin' up to her like he should."

"Please—let's not…" Heart a-flutter, palms moist, Lauren-Son turned away.

Like it or not, Spivey poked at the exact festering spot she feared to examine. *Quite possibly Delia and Walker both hurt me—Delia carried it out, Walker saw it coming, and, by virtue of his passivity, sanctioned it.*

Notion swiftly booted aside, it seemed an unfair conclusion since Walker had been too busy to discuss what happened.

More unpleasantness inserted itself: that day, when her mouth opened to receive Walker's tongue—a kiss long hoped for—disappointment overwhelmed, as if he'd extracted something sacred.

Thanks to your obsession with the man, she scolded herself, *you so totally deserved that!*

Shirt lifted at the neck, she wiped sweat off her brow, then fended, saying, "We're doing something big here. I'm exactly where I belong."

"Glory sakes!" Spivey fanned her face. "You gots to get a grip. 'Cause you're far too comfortable lettin' that man tell you what to think and how to act. It's like you're fixin' to rest your brain, right permanent."

"Nobody tells me how to act. Besides, present weirdness aside, what I learn from Walker is invaluable." Off her mind slid to yesterday's scene:

"Phone for you," Rosalee had called out.

She picked up; Mom's voice came through the earpiece. "I called your apartment and got a recording saying your phone had been disconnected. So I find you at Rosalee's?"

"I—ah, moved here temporarily."

Totally Walker's oversight, she got evicted for nonpayment of rent. While she recovered from her head injury, Voden and Sherman collected her junk, settling her in at Rosalee's, and deposited her beloved rocks in the flower garden. Blasé as she tried to act, she stayed peeved about the move, though.

"And not tell me about it?" Mom had asked, hurt and huffy.

"Sorry. It was a snap decision."

"You sound strange." Suspicious tremor to Mom's voice, Lauren-Son thought how comforting it would be to topple through the receiver into Mom's arms. "Is something wrong, sweetie?"

"No biggie. I just hit my head." Words coming out overly loud, she lowered the decibels. "I'm OK, though." She hoped she sounded convincing.

"You sure?"

"Everything's—ah—fine." Vigorous nod, brain tumbling, lurching within her skull, she made a hasty retreat. "Gotta get back…Love you." Ashamed, not wanting Mom to know all, out she'd clomped to Rosalee's garden to try to weed.

Head hurting each time she bent over, she called it quits and lay down.

Spivey now resumed. "I'm saying this, gal, 'cause ain't nobody else gonna tell you straight—that healer fella's got you under his spell."

"It isn't how you think!"

"I 'spect if he tole you to balance an apple on your sorry 'ole head, cram carrot sticks up your nose, and run round flappin' your arms, you'd be plenty pleased to oblige. And if he demanded you take spit baths, with no scrubbin' or immersions, you gladly get all smelly and refuse to see it as deprivation, 'cause he'd insist such silliness be necessary for your growth."

"Try to understand—"

Spivey cut in, "Wipe the foolish dew from your eyes, girl! That man's got hold of your mind. And his crazy wife ain't nothin' but trouble. I say…Recognize the truth and get away from here." Daring Lauren-Son to contradict, she glared. "You think that head bump and the wife are the only problems? You ain't seen nothin' compared to what's coming.

"Mind your own self too so's you don't get caught on the wrong side, 'cause stuff goin' on here's prit' near to crazy. So, even if you help fix them townsfolk, if they get a mind, they'd sooner crucify you."

Hands raised in surrender, Lauren-Son sought to reconcile. "OK, OK, I give up!"

Spive overrode her. "I can't abide what you is doing, 'cause you is headin' for a whole heap o' grief, but rightly or not, anybody says things against you, and Spivey'll smack them upside o' their head."

"Thanks my friend."

Swift shift in tone, Spivey gripped her hand. "How can I ever thank you?"

"Just keep me posted, OK?"

"Main thing I got outta bein' here—aside from you givin' me life—is that it don't make sense to look for answers from anybody else. Truth is right here." She thumped her chest. "Seems so plain…Don't know why you don't get it."

"I know the problems, but this place does far more good."

Tote bag repositioned, Spivey rolled her eyes.

Greyhound pulled up, eddying dust, idling raucously. "Mark my words"—Spivey raised her voice—"you is goin' to regret stayin'."

"My life is here."

Doors folded open, the women hugged, and Spivey boarded.

Following the windows down, Lauren-Son watched her friend's jerky moves as she stuffed her bag onto the overhead rack.

Window clacked open, Spivey leaned out to shout, "Don't lose yourself—OK?

"We agree to disagree," hollered Lauren-Son, fingers spread wide to wave. "Love you anyway."

Bus brakes chuffing, Spivey sat down.

Pained sense of wrenching, dust swallowing the receding bus, Lauren-Son watched her go.

What if she's right? What if my tidy, precious world isn't as it seems?

Little things, inconsequential matters, began to go wrong: nothing she could exactly put a finger on. The Living Light ran out of coffee and doughnut money for patients. When the ever-fitful spastic plumbing pipes broke and then the heater went out, promised repairs never happened. Volunteers forgot to cover shifts and didn't seem contrite about their oversight. Then Rosalee took a tumble, tweaking her back; it never really healed.

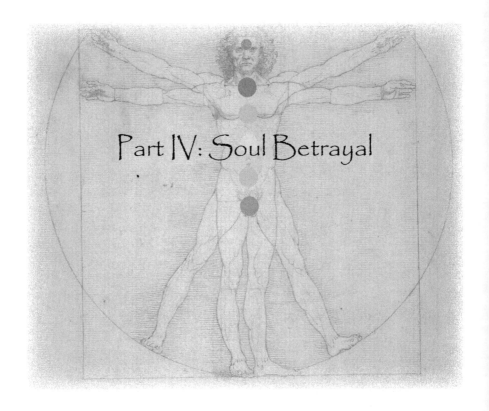

Part IV: Soul Betrayal

Chapter Sixty-Two: Walker

Morning sunny, warm—September 27 to be exact—Rosalee burst in The Living Light's front door, wild-eyed, arms flapping. "Heavy bigness!" she blurted, meaning business.

Two policemen barged in. The older officer, a recent transfer, Mortimer Gobnick, handed over papers. "We have a warrant for Walker Judson's arrest."

Waiting room patients gazed at him in horrified silence, then stirred to raise overlapping voices. One woman fainted dead away. A skinny fellow jumped up and headed for the back.

"Halt!" hollered the younger officer, Stan Powell. Stan, as a teen, according to Rosalee, used to sneak into The Nick, then come back later to apologize.

Hands over his head, the man returned. The officers paid him no mind.

Officer Gobnick *did* cast uneasy glances up at The Angel. "You sure this is right?"

"I'm sure," insisted Officer Stan.

"Morning, fellows. Hello there, Stan," Hands rubbed together, Walker greeted the men as if their presence were of utmost delight. "Wondered when you'd come."

"Are you Walker Judson?" queried Gobnick.

"Yup, he is," chimed Officer Stan.

Brow plunged into a frown, Gobnick turned to address Walker. "Hafta do this by the book. As I said...Are you Walker Judson?"

Successive emotions—anger, frustration, resignation—contorted Walker's face, giving way to a wry smile. "I am."

"You're under arrest, then." Gobnick recited the Miranda Act, finishing with, "You gotta come with us."

Calm on the surface, Walker's voice came out whispery rough. "I'll just be a minute."

"Sorry, sir." Gobnick blocked his retreat. "We can't let you outta our sight."

"I understand," Walker said evenly, taking leave anyway. "I need my coat."

All gone blurry and vague within office confines, Walker bent down, hands clenching knees, to shake.

Hand pressed to brow, he collected himself. Grim resignation is what he felt, for forces conspired—a long sequence of them—that he lacked authority to change.

Jacket donned, returned seconds later, noting the sizable crowd, he instructed Rosalee, "Have Lauren-Son take charge."

Those waiting grumbled; tempers escalated into sharp annoyance.

Officer Stan licked his lips. "Should I call back-up?"

Gobnick eyed the crowd. "Naaa, we can handle this."

Voden appeared to watch from the hall.

As if the diminutive man posed a threat, both officers shot him nervous glances.

"Ready?" Walker asked.

"Sorry, sir," said Officer Stan, "we have to frisk and handcuff you."

Hands at his back, Walker obliged.

"Uhh—sir," apologized Stan, patting him down, "hands in front, otherwise you can't sit."

Stan went to apply the cuffs, let out a yelp, clattering bracelets to the floor. "They're hot!" Palms examined, he blew to cool them.

"My flesh gets that way from time to time." Manacles scooped up, Walker gave them back.

"About that limp...," he addressed Gobnick, "it began when your pa died and is easy to treat."

Yap opened, then shut, the older man ogled him.

"Shall we?" Walker presented his elbows.

Lauren-Son interposed herself to roar displeasure. "What are you doing?"

About to call the officers brainless stooges or offer to go in Walker's stead—worse yet—to pummel them, Rosalee gentled her aside to caution, "Anger will only increase trouble."

Threesome headed for the door, the crowd too turned quarrelsome. "Why are you taking him?" probed several. "Please don't," another interrupted. "We've driven two days to get here," chimed another. "I brought my sick child, and Judson is all the hope we've got."

Jeering boldly, the crush surrounded them, forcing the officers back-to-back, with Walker sandwiched in between. "Send help!" Gobnick shouted into his walkie-talkie.

Minutes later, three squad cars roared up. Officers jumped out; doors slammed.

Sizable mob jostling outside, unable to muscle his way in, Chief Hosley stood curbside, bullhorn to mouth, barking, "Let my officers through!" Yet no one budged.

"Thanks for your support," Walker addressed the crowd, "but step aside."

Bodies peeled back, allowing Walker and the officers to inch along.

"Please," Walker requested, "a detour?"

Officer Stan glanced, questioning, to Rosalee, who eagerly nodded approval; Gobnick, however, vetoed the move. "Not within regulations."

Walker called to the woman who gripped a squalling, fitful child, "My assistant, Lauren-Son, will see to your little one."

"I'm ready now." Head high, acknowledging as many as possible, he allowed himself to be taken; the mob fell back, parting as a wave.

What came next, though, shouldn't have.

Exact second the men reached the door—great whoosh above—wood groaned, hardwood parted, splintering as The Angel dove, head buried shoulder deep into floorboards, landing where Gobnick stood seconds prior.

"Just stating her opinion," noted Voden, pushing through to inspect.

Feet jutting from shattered floor, The Angel brought China's first Emperor Qin to Walker's mind. Rather than take his living army into the afterlife, as was the custom of the time, Qin commissioned the sculpting of thousands of terracotta statues; life-size soldiers, their horses, and chariots. At death, all icons were entombed with him. Centuries later, archaeologists unearthed his vast clay army, with bayonets, hips, legs, thighs and heads thrust up from soil. Yet The Angel, rather than yield from earth, seemed spit down from heaven as if a reprimand.

"Please…," Walker called out, "see that she gets straightened up."

Why that exact moment the statue took a tumble remained a mystery. Nobody could've foretold the time of Walker's arrest so as to rig its fall. And yanking it back up would prove arduous. A month later it remained embedded, immovable. Those forced to step around it grumbled that it seemed an appropriate form of protest.

Out the door, alongside the cruiser, Officer Stan, reluctant to re-apply handcuffs, lest he be sparked again, fumbled and fussed until Voden intervened to deftly click the cuffs onto Walker's wrists. Then he addressed Chief Hosley, "One catch… Mr. Fucols must be permitted to ride along."

Surprisingly, the chief assented.

Voden helped Walker slide into the squad car, then climbed in alongside, tapping the cruiser's roof to signal readiness.

Officers sprang to vehicles and took off, sirens silent.

Somber crowd watching sedans bump downhill, Walker turned back to lock eyes with Lauren-Son. Sudden sense of searing entering his chest, he nodded, attempting to convey apology, love, confidence—hoping those lingering ripples might sustain her.

Chapter Sixty-Three: Lauren

Healer Charged With Rape and Sexual Assault blared the next day's headline.

Hands flung at her throat—not the embezzlement charge Lauren-Son imagined—this boded far worse!

Walker Judson, the article read, *founder of The Living Light Healing Center, was booked on charges of sexual assault. Advised of the allegations at the Preston County Courthouse, he was released on bond in the company of his wife, Delia Judson, and assistant, Voden Fucols.* The photo showed grim-faced Walker, Delia on his arm, and a blurry side-view of Voden.

Breath held; her pulse throbbed.

Walker, a powerful force for good, was a respected healer, an important civic leader, and it seemed way obvious he'd never harm a bug.

Hands together, she knelt to pray.

Quick update regarding her present, evolving view on prayer: controlled studies had proven undirected prayer to be twice as effective as prayers requesting a specific outcome. And so, figuring that God did not require a list of her needs, *For the highest good of all concerned, Thy will be done*, now comprised her formulaic request for everything.

Just now, however, she snuck an extra plug: *Please clear Walker of all charges.*

Attempting to absorb this news, information being all too harsh, she spent the remainder of the afternoon and evening staring at the wall, and slept not at all.

As arranged by Delia, the attorney showed up the next day to ascertain the workings of The Living Light.

"Bert Twain." The fellow pumped every hand in sight, then swaggered about, sampled the coffee and got extravagant with the cream.

Full of zest, teeth so shiny they hurt one's eyes, Twain wore two pinkie rings and possessed a most unsightly head of hair. Hair so carefully frothed, yet rigidly affixed, an entire hairspray can, Lauren-Son guessed, got used to achieve the effect.

"How's about you give me a tour," Twain suggested.

Lauren-Son showed him the first and second floors, third-floor attic included. Treatment rooms of greatest interest, the attorney took notes as he inspected them. "Is Mr. Judson alone when he works with clients?"

"Mostly there's a student or two: occasionally a family member is present. Sometimes, I'm there as well." Tongue passed over lips, Twain eyed her.

"And who might you be?"

"His second in command."

Tour complete, briefcase set at his feet, Twain rubbed hands together. "Well then, thanks kindly. So...Where's my client?"

"He should be along any minute."

Twain smiled benignly.

Not all nicety, Lauren-Son heard that Twain had worked several local sex cases, exonerating a most horrid array of clients. His relaxed, engaging, non-confrontational style lulled his prey into ease, then he trounced, and made mincemeat of many a trusting soul.

Faced creased in seriousness, Walker came forth, Delia by his side. "Sorry to keep you waiting." The men did a sharp, quick handshake.

Relaxed, steamy—as if an exotic hothouse plant—Delia extended her hand. "You know me. Ardis says hello."

Twain gripped longer than called for, then gestured, forcefully. "Shall we?"

Walker seemed affixed to the spot. Curious looks on faces— patients, staff, and volunteers ogling—Twain peeked at his watch as Delia fidgeted. Dumbly naive, Walker sought to press a point, "It seems someone's eager to shut us down. That—"

"Uh," noting all ears attuned, Twain broke in, "let's talk in private."

Walker headed for his office.

"Sweetie....," using her sweetest voice, Delia restrained him, "mine's more comfy."

Headlong angel sidestepped, Twain raised a questioning brow. Walker followed Delia and shut the door. Lauren-Son hovered. Momentarily, Delia stuck her head out. "Water, please."

Two hours later the trio emerged.

Hair rumpled, Walker showed strain. Delia came out as fresh as she'd entered.

Considerably pinked up, Twain counseled, "Here on in, you are not to speak to anyone about anything pertinent to this case. I do the talking—that's what you pay me for."

Pockets riffled to jangle change, he grinned. "Arraignment's our next hurtle; we'll review the process beforehand."

Vigorous handshakes ensued, and then he addressed Lauren-Son, "Good day to you, young lady." Delia frowned mightily.

Vibe ignored, Lauren-Son wanting, needing, to believe in this man, grinned broadly back.

Chapter Sixty-Four: Walker

Arraignment day, Walker sat at the table up front of the jammed courtroom, feeling stiff, slightly stunned—that and a mix of frustrated boredom.

Relaxed, hypercompetent, Twain preened by his side. Delia leaned over the rail to smooch encouragement. Walker's eyes met Lauren-Son's.

Hello—she mouthed, hand held up. She kept on watching, troubled, hurting for him.

Quick nod, he looked away.

Judge Attic, so said his nameplate, scurried in, thumbed through a sheaf of papers, then snapped his gavel, calling court to session. "According to charges filed by five complainants, the defendant, Walker Judson, is charged with felony and misdemeanor sexual assault." Swiftly, the judge read off the names of the aggrieved parties, concluding with Miss Melissa Dworkin's.

Corner of Walker's eye, Lauren-Son's hands flew up to hiss, "How dare she!"

Judge Attic continued, "In sworn statements, victims allege repeated and ongoing nonconsensual sexual assault, including rape."

Voices chorused outrage. Lauren-Son passed Walker a stunned look.

Swiftly, he blocked her from thought.

The judge went on, "During the past six months, the defendant, Walker Judson, has been discretely under investigation. Mr. Hicks...Do you certify the correctness of said charges?"

Prosecutor Hicks stood, adjusted Coke-bottle thick eyeglasses, then replied, "Yes, Your Honor, the charges stand as is."

"So now...How does the defendant wish to plead?"

Twain stood and cleared his throat. "My client enters a plea of not guilty."

"At this juncture," Judge Attic proclaimed, "the court, that is to say, Preston County, finds sufficient"—Keenly attuned, Walker lifted his head as Attic continued—"cause to prosecute the defendant, Mr. Walker Judson, for second and third degree sexual assault. The case goes on calendar for trial next month. Dismissed." He smacked the gavel.

Supremely weird mess of it all, unfulfilled, scorned females being capable of summoning immense wrath; such behavior chilled.

Waning days of autumn drawn down, leaves scattering walkways, Walker and Lauren-Son traversed the downtown.

Rat-tat-tat—construction noises sliced air. Thanks to newfound prosperity caused by The Living Light, many buildings underwent renovation, and Buena Vista bustled, lively.

Sidewalk narrowing, Walker trudged up front, while Lauren-Son, as if the two were an aged Chinese couple, addressed his backside, "Can we talk about what's going on?"

"Not entirely."

"But..."

"What's happening"—Walker slowed to pull ponderously on his lip—"including Delia hurting you, is a test for us both. As part of it, I seek a successor."

Flustered with troubled joy, Lauren-Son demurred, "No way can I take your place, but if it's a partner you want, believe me, I'm it. I *do* have trouble believing that guru mumbo jumbo, though."

Walkway widened, Lauren-Son came abreast; Walker plucked a leaf from her hair, twirled it between his palms, then let it drop.

Across the way, two women ceased gabbing to ogle.

"Woo-hoo," one hailed, then covered her mouth to hack.

"Say there, Belle," Walker called. "Come by. Lauren-Son will work on that cough."

"Sure will," cooed Belle.

Walker dropped his voice. "My successor must not resent or

question me as you do, so I'm not entirely certain that you are my chosen one."

Poor, scarred brow bearing the indent of her sacrifice, gingerly, she touched there and leaned into him. "But I'm so totally devoted to you, Walker, I scare myself."

Meanwhile, Belle and her companion moved curbside to gawk.

Walker gripped her elbow. "Let's move along."

Going up a steep stretch, they halted at The Overlook.

Hands jammed into pockets, Walker spoke in a push, "Defaming me is one way to hurt The Living Light. God willing, though, our work will continue anyhow." He looked her over, head to toe.

Certainly, she'd taken getting used to: her bald honesty, her longing for connection, her constant urge to confess deficiency. Her disarming nature made him feel the urge to protect her from the likes of himself and also caused him to be more open than he'd be otherwise. *Careful there*, he often thought to insist, *you are far too trusting of me!*

Of late, their relationship had undergone a notable shift. Less of a supplicant, more of a treasured right hand servant, he relied heavily upon her. "You've matured considerably. That's good. You can't do this work unless you're strong."

"Thanks...I guess." Ill at ease, she spun on her heel to fake bravado.

"We both have difficult paths."

"*We*—you say!" Immensely pleased, she beamed at him. "*We*—meaning you and I might, somehow, be equals?"

A surprised mix of pride, sorrow, annoyance—jealousy—arose. For slowly, steadily, she'd begun to surpass and leave him.

Question ignored, he kept on, "I must tell you...Healing others isn't your true calling. Helping folks awaken to the fact that they were never unwell in the first place, is."

"Wow! I thought I was meant to do what you do."

"Not exactly." Bent to pry a tack from his shoe, working to conceal his feelings, a rush of tenderness overtook him.

Head back up, he hurtled into it. "The moment your soul projected into your mother's womb, you were a perfect being. Fact is, we're all born complete, but forget our wholeness along the way. Ultimately, it's your job to remind folks of this and set them free so they no longer need the stuff I do."

"I don't get it..." She squinted at him, confused. "You've trained me for work I thought I was destined to do, but now you say this isn't it. Tell me Walker..." She kicked a dirt clod, exploding it into powder. "Why, exactly, am I here?"

Walker met her frown. "For preparation."

"What am I preparing for?"

"In due time," he said sharply.

"Right-o!" she said, sarcastic.

Cigarette extracted from a pocket, Walker lit up, inhaled hard, then absorbed himself with its burning embers.

Lauren-Son floundered. "I'm worried I've wasted a huge chunk of my life following a dead end." Clump of lupine spotted, she yanked up a fistful.

"Don't." Walker restrained her. "Ripping them out is hurtful."

"Sheesh!" She dropped the petals.

"Your destiny doesn't end in Buena Vista. You're meant to do much more."

"Oh?" She eyed him, uncertain.

Walker cleared his throat. "You manifest qualities few others have; you posses a perfect balance between mind, body, and heart. I lack that. Mostly, I work from my mind. See—I have many shortcomings. Yours is an open heart, but you also use your intellect, and have learned to keep your body healthy. I merely serve as the conduit to help you to achieve your full potential."

"Oh...like I'm *so* important...and so *very* perfect!"

Sigh heaved, Walker spoke with great forbearance, "I must mention...I only have a limited time left." Mouth agape, she regarded him, stricken.

"What...Like you're stamped with an expiration date, and, come due, you get tossed out?"

"Enough said."

Back downtown, a pneumatic drill tore up concrete.

Voice raised over the racket, Walker spoke with urgency, "You must prove your unquestioning allegiance."

Yes, Walker foresaw many things. Lauren-Son would outstrip his potency as a healer. Only the slightest hint of it now in evidence, she'd also become a strong leader.

Most of all, as foretold, she'd find another calling altogether.

But that was the future, and, just now, unable to fathom any of it, bewilderment spasmed the face of his dearly beloved.

Chapter Sixty-Five: Lauren

Trial's eve, Lauren-Son stood at Rosalee's sink juicing lemons when Mom called. "Are you OK, dear?"

"I'm fine."

"Look, sweetheart," Mom launched in, "you've put Walker on a pedestal—so has everyone. He's surrounded by needy, dependent people, which has created a recipe for disaster." Brief pause, she then asked, "Truth?" Lauren-Son took a swig of lemon juice.

Bitter, bitter, she scrunched her face. "I'm listening."

"You think Walker is a mythic being, but he's not all good. And... ah...it embarrasses me to ask, but are you...ah...in love with him?"

"Course not!" Receiver cocked to chin, she paced. "Look, Mom, have you ever had the privilege of knowing a person who awakens and enlivens your best self?"

"Not exactly."

"That's how it is with Walker. With him, I say the wildest, deepest things, and he totally accepts me. According to his view, I'm smart, brilliant, and kind...It's pretty great."

"Oh, honey, let's not fight. I just want you to know, you can come home any time."

"Walker needs me. I refuse to abandon him, or these people, and besides...This is my home."

Mom heaved a sigh. "Walker's got this strange hold over you; you just can't see it."

"How can you say that? You know how he's helped me! Besides, I'm close to him—more than most—so if he's done wrong, I'd know."

"I know you're happier than ever, but you revere that man too much."

"When all was well," Lauren-Son huffed, "you claimed to

appreciate and respect Walker. So now, just because you have questions, you expect me to jump ship? Well…nothing doing!"

Here was the rupture.

Although they didn't always agree, she and Mom had enjoyed a lifetime of trust. Just now, though, something had come undone.

Mom pressed, "You mistake Walker's healing skills for saintliness. I'm just trying to point out that apparent goodness does not make for a saint. Because Walker speaks of truth and love, dear, doesn't mean he knows how to love or that he's actually honest. Many seemingly heroic saintly figures turn out to be cruel and selfish."

"Stop it, Mom!" Lauren-Son flung an arm, toppling a vase.

Glass shattered. Water sprayed everywhere. Lilies landed in a heap among glass shards.

Stepped over the mess, she continued, "The finest man I know is being persecuted. And now, when the chips are down, many—you included—turn against him. But I won't. That's all there is to it."

"Speak of turning, I worry they'll turn against you."

"That's just nuts!"

"You think I like saying this?"

"It's just that…Oh, never mind, I can't talk."

"My dear, I love you."

"Yeah well...Just don't love me so much!" Phone plunked down, she didn't bother to sign off.

Last patient of the day departed, Lauren-Son lifted Silly, who'd been rubbing her ankles, and carried him to the foyer.

Hair forming a cabbage-like mass, there Walker sat. Transparent, rinsed look about him, he communed with The Angel still embedded in floorboards.

She chuffed out a sigh. "I thought you'd gone."

Plainly tired…possibly of everything, he looked up. "Care to join me?" Pat to the bench, he produced a cigarette, then lit up.

Cat put down, Lauren-Son sat alongside. Walker inhaled a long draw, then allowed smoke to trickle out. The two stayed silent, watching it drift.

Past weeks she'd scarcely seen him and missed him quite a bit: missed their conversations and arguments, missed all that he meant. He hadn't actually left but might as well have.

Walker huffed a smoky exhale. She moved to leave. He restrained her. She studied his face for traces of nerves, but saw only fatigue… and sorrow.

Ordinarily, if he were anyone else, she'd have flung arms around him.

Instead, she sat on her hands.

They crept up anyway to give him a tap. "You OK?" Walker met her gaze.

At once, she felt close to him: close because he invited her presence. But his eyes, best indicator of his true mental state, discouraged pity.

"How are *you* doing?" he inquired, as usual, turning the tables.

"Fine," she insisted, not truthful in the slightest. Efforts to crucify Walker infuriating her, flooded with feeling, she longed to rip someone's—anyone's—head off.

"Nobody asks if I did it." Walker continued to regard her. "I figure you might want to know."

"Aren't you supposed to keep your mouth shut?" Swoop of fear to the gut, same as when she'd first heard the charges, she considered Walker's possible guilt.

When annoyed, he popped his jaw, then buried his anger. When truly pissed, he spoke softly, struggling to contain himself. The softer he spoke, the more he seethed.

Yup, he was angry! Uncork the anger he sought to squelch, and he might levitate into the stratosphere. When asked, though, he always denied it.

So was he capable of abuse? More to the point: *Had he abused those women?*

"Don't you want to know?" he persisted.

She slid him a look.

Entrenchment in Walker's world meant being dependent on him to a great extent. The longer she stayed, the deeper her roots grew, the more impossible it was to extricate herself. "I have no doubts about you."

Walker induced doubts all right!

Actually, he invited them.

When questions got raised, he skillfully address them yet never bothered to fully dispel them.

Silly stood at their feet and meowed. Walker put out his hand; the cat ignored it.

"For most," Walker said, "real truth is beside the point. People prefer to ignore relevant facts and accept only what suits them. But for me, the truth—every facet—is vital. So I speak truth, and it makes folks uncomfortable." Lauren-Son clicked her tongue, agreeing.

Slid from his seat, Walker reached to scratch the cat.

Silly flattened his ears, hissed, then rolled, belly up. Walker riffled the feline's fur.

Lest her own bald longing to be petted convey itself, Lauren-Son tore her gaze away.

Walker's pale forearms and light hair tufts were those of any ordinary man's. But also, he possessed the kindest hands. Those fingers in particular—long, beautifully sculpted, attached to those competent, gorgeous hands—restored one and all. So whatever mischief he might be guilty of, his hands could not possibly be part of it.

By mischief, she meant transgressions. So any transgression on Walker's part would've stemmed purely from bumbling, inept altruism. And…Given, the relationship of his hands to the rest of him, no way could he be the immoral abuser those women claimed he was.

Ears perked to form two pert triangles, Silly righted himself and sauntered off.

Walker pushed up and went to rummage through desk drawers. He located a pen, scribbled a note, folded it in thirds, then shoved it into an envelope. Postage stamp excavated, he affixed it in place. Lauren-Son looked at him, questioning. He shrugged, sheepish. "A prayer request."

"Pervert!" A passerby shouted from the street.

They looked to the window.

A horn honked. Sudden harsh blast—crazed laughs—burst from a passing car.

"Tell me what you really think. Ask anything." This, as close to pleading as she'd ever heard from him, Walker engrossed himself, arranging desktop papers.

"What's to say?" she addressed the ceiling.

Deliberately, since the start of this, she'd kept too busy to reflect.

Just now, however, she wanted to ask: *Could you, Walker, possibly say one thing and practice the exact opposite?*

Except if he answered affirmative, her tidy world just might crumble, so she refused to delve.

More thoughts pranced through. She admired him for many things yet pitied how separate he kept himself. Studiously solitary air about him, he held people at arm's length, which made him seem haughty, arrogant. If only he confided, permitted closeness, perhaps this mess could have been avoided.

"You give excellent advice, Walker. You just don't apply good sense to yourself. If you were more self-protective, and if you handled matters head-on, rather than ignore them, we might not be in this fix."

"Really?" Walker regarded her, bemused.

"I love your unique understanding of the universe—that every moment, all things, all creatures, regardless of stature— matter. And personally, I adore the life you've given me. I'm incredibly blessed to do work I love. I hope we continue as we have, but at this point, something precious is broken." She swiveled to face him. "Want my opinion?"

Walker threw back his head and laughed, an eerie, inhuman laugh, anything but joyful. "Seems you're giving it." Closely, he watched her.

Squarely, she placed knuckles on his desktop and leaned in. "You talk about protecting others, but you're far too casual about protecting yourself." Despite Walker's grin, his eyes stayed exempt.

She pressed, saying, "In part, physical illness seems due to the absence of love. Many coming to you certainly seem starved for it. You treat them in the kindest way, so they feel your love. When they get better, many identify you as the sole cause of their well-being, get infatuated and carried away, fantasizing about you as more than just their healer."

"I know," Walker said, thoughtful, "but I care about them all."

"That's your exact problem!" Lauren-Son paced. "You treat everyone so special. It sends a confusing message. You were the one who established our protocol. Patients who develop crushes get transferred out of your care and passed to me or to Voden, only you never do this.

"Remember that volunteer...the one Delia called an oversize Kewpie doll—Twinkie? She got carried away, lost all that weight, and envisioned a serious relationship with you. Are you aware she left her husband? She claimed you refused to get involved with her until she did so."

"Twinkie?" Walker puzzled. "I don't recall."

"You sent Delia to befriend her. So your wife, armed with her own list of complaints, raked you over the coals, trying to pulverize Twinkie's infatuation. Except Twinkie, all the more enthralled, pitied you for having such an unloving wife."

"Ah, I *do* remember. But I *did* care, felt sorry for her."

"Exactly!" Lauren-Son threw herself onto the bench, vexed.

Healing others allowed Walker to be loved without risk of loving back. When a patient got too chummy and wanted more, it scared and angered him; time and again, she saw this. Yet, he forcibly smeared his awkward brand of loving kindness around to impact one and all.

"You take a back seat, trusting God—or the rest of us—to sort out the mess. If you gave those crushes more thought, you could refuse to treat them." Walker stroked his chin.

"I see what you mean, but it's too late to change what already is." A look passed between them.

Walker's face shone open, receptive; she refused to let the moment pass, "You can still change, you know." From the start, Walker had prepared her for something, so just maybe that time had come.

She'd grown to like herself quite a bit, apologized less and had become a fine healer in her own right. Walker needed her now as much as she'd needed him, so she hammered home these vital issues. "This thing we've worked so hard to build—The Living Light and all it means—must continue. But without you, Walker, it won't. Even if this blows over, you have to change. All your work, my work, the good we've done, will disappear if you don't."

"Understood." Walker appraised her frankly. "And...What else?"

"The power of your work scares people. That's why you're being persecuted."

"Perhaps so." He nodded cautiously. "What you say is accurate, but regardless as to what I want, the matter must play out to the bitter end. My fate, this trial, and any accompanying torment, cannot be avoided."

"You can't change this?"

"I cannot. My difficulties—yours too—will be revealed as part of a larger wholeness. Someday, it'll all make sense."

"Explain to me now!"

"I'm not permitted." They fell silent beneath the weight of it all.

Walker thought he had no say in what happened to him. Yet every moment is a turning point...roads not taken, choices made or not... Except, always, one has a choice.

That he chose to believe his life's path to be immutable and figured he had full and precise grasp of his part from the start—that his life had been written in stone beforehand—would undo him.

Walker tamped the butt end of a fresh pack of cigarettes in his palm, removed the cellophane, shook the box to release a single smoke, and lit up. As glowing embers made arcs to and from his mouth, Lauren-Son wished the morrow would never come.

"My take"—Cigarette to his lips, Walker inhaled, exhaled, then continued—"the human race is like a bucket of crabs. Crabs mill aimlessly about, but every once in a while a resourceful crab hooks a pincer over the bucket's lip and begins to haul himself out. About to reach freedom, all other crabs rush over, and latch on to drag him down.

"Same with humans...When they see you rise up, they get the jitters, spread falsehoods, and generally interfere. Point being...The world's full of jealous folks who try to pull you down, yet it's up to you to refuse to permit it. On occasion, one tenacious crab *does* escape; all hell breaks loose, and the entire universe shifts as a result." Walker stared, appreciative, at his cigarette.

"I think of this trial in terms of that bucket of crabs. Forces in this town, even my so-called friends, want to silence me because they're intolerant of change. But even if they do stop me, they'll fail in the end. Others will carry on—you, for one." Walker placed his hand atop hers and gently stroked—almost a caress, which surprised her.

"Stay with me on this," he continued, "regardless of consequence, and I'll reward you."

Repeatedly, she'd visualized their perfect future together: a time when she would, for all to see, be his. And so, in that moment, she loved him—loved him mightily. Honestly, she wanted a kiss.

Sensing her thoughts, Walker inched away.

Series of insights cobbled together: the first day at that storefront church, she recalled Walker's parting words, "You'll be back." Years of search for him, she remembered his phone call to come and how strikingly familiar the world of The Living Light seemed at first sight.

Even before that, she'd sensed Walker's guiding hand, particularly in her work with the mentally ill. Likely he'd been with her forever, shaping all she did.

Gratitude is a funny, complex matter. Kindness is done. Obligation gets created. Depending on the size of the kind act, the need to give back can be unceasing. Often, she worried about balance, about give and take.

Am I reciprocating fully? Do I express sufficient appreciation? Is this enough? Am I still obliged?

At times she wished Walker hadn't impacted her so thoroughly. She wanted his guidance, yet she chafed against it. Oftentimes she tried to repay him, yet he refused—even acted as if he owed her back.

Round and round they went, the cycle, endless. "Anything I can do to help?" she now asked, braced for his refusal.

Tenderly, he reached out, running fingertips over The Angel's surfaces. "Get this thing pulled up."

About to leave, he turned back to her. "By the way…Someday that freed crab will be you." Slowly he moved on, bunched hands thrust deep into pockets.

So precious, so vivid before her, he'd as much as promised her a bright shiny future. So to prove her worth, resolved to squelch all doubt, every inch of her believed in him.

Chapter Sixty-Six: Lauren

First morning of the trial, several volunteers gentled The Angel out of the woodwork. Nose gone missing, where its left cheek had sheared off a gaping hole easily fit a fist.

Ignoring Delia's protests, Lauren-Son insisted it stand, mid-lobby, to oversee all from a closer perspective. And the typically undemonstrative Voden climbed a ladder, to tenderly press his brow to what remained of its shattered jowl. There he swayed, hours at a time, grieving, communing.

Preston County Courthouse a-buzz with press and spectators, Rosalee, Sherman, and Lauren-Son fought their way to seats up front. Next row back, Clayton Lynch, surrounded by cronies, met Lauren-Son's glance and smiled smugly. Gracie Thrip hopped up to wave. From her wheelchair, Danielle shot a sheepish shrug. Twain, showboating up the aisle, shook hands with familiars.

Heralded by a gasp, Walker entered through a side door to steal Twain's thunder. Voices swelled as he strode, energetically, to the defendant's table, greeted his lawyer, took his seat, glanced at Rosalee and then at Lauren-Son.

Scrubbed-looking, unruly hair plastered in place, wearing the fanciest business suit, tension gusted out from him, as she scrambled to asses his mental state.

Guard up, he blocked her from examination.

The five so-called victims traipsed in: wide-eyed Dalrymple Gooch peered about; broad-hipped, plainly dressed, Gert VanBeck plunked down and stiffly faced forward; bosoms aggressively up-thrust, Bernice Trabing waved to friends. Beneath a torrent of make-up,

Betty Jean Cowdry's usual dull hair and tired eyes shone as she scooted in alongside them.

Defiantly proud, younger by far, Melissa Dworkin slid into the row behind. Lauren-Son grimaced and reached to squeeze Rosalee's hand.

Murmurs swarming, spectators swiveled. Eye-popping to behold, Delia strummed up the aisle. Promising to slap anyone silly should they make the slightest snide comment, glaring everyone down, she sat directly behind Walker, then leaned over the rail to plant the steamiest kiss upon him.

Twain—even Prosecutor Hicks—paused longer than seemly, watching her settle alongside Ardis.

Delia looked fabulous, knew she did. Frosted hair neatly styled, garbed in cream-colored suit, with shoes and clutch purse to match, seemingly sculpted into that getup—nary a quiver of chubby flesh— just now, she held it nicely in check.

"All rise," called the bailiff.

All rose. Judge Attic climbed into his seat and lazily smacked his gavel. "Call to session as pertains to *The State versus Judson*." Documents shuffled, he read aloud, "The defendant, Walker Judson, is charged with one hundred-fifteen counts of felony sexual assault."

One hundred-fifteen counts! Lauren-Son hands flew to her mouth; the number flabbergasted!

Attic continued, "These charges allege that the defendant, Mr. Walker Judson, engaged in forcible sexual intercourse under the guise of healing treatment and other forms of inappropriate, non-consensual sexual contact, including indecent assault and forced oral copulation."

Twain came next to give his opening statement. "We're trying this good man, Walker Judson, but shouldn't be. I plan to show the court why he is innocent of all wrongdoing and intend to restore his credibility." Forceful exhale, Lauren-Son sat back, grateful for this straightforward start.

Prosecutor Hicks shambled up to stand before the court. "Walker Judson calls himself a healer, yet his deviant acts have wreaked havoc upon the Buena Vista community. I will prove that he violated the trust of these five women and that he forced upon them lewd, unseemly sexual acts, essentially violating the trust of all who seek his help."

"Unbelievable!" Lauren-Son muttered softly.

Next, Judge Attic gave instructions as to courtroom etiquette and then dove into jury selection.

The task posed quite the challenge, for nearly everyone had been treated or knew someone with ties to The Living Light. Prior to arraignment, the original prosecutor disqualified herself; Walker had treated her arthritis.

Five days, thousands of mind-numbing questions later, eight women and four men were selected. Lauren-Son thought them an uptight, stuffy bunch: all men wore business suits and ties; the women, bland as biscuits, wore hats and gloves. Yet, Twain expressed pleasure with the pick.

The trial started up in earnest when Prosecuting Attorney Hicks addressed the court, "I call complainant, Mrs. Dalrymple Gooch, to the stand."

Dalrymple, once one of Walker's biggest fans, recoiled as she waddled past him to be sworn in.

"Mrs. Gooch," Hicks began, "you've been treated at The Living Light. Is that correct?"

"Yes, I have." Dalrymple cast demure glances about.

"What was the purpose of those sessions?"

"Well…" Given Dalrymple's lacquered, super-tight hairdo, her face barely moved as she spoke. "I got treated for skin troubles, and for weight loss, but mostly for a sex problem."

"Why go to The Living Light, rather than see a physician or a therapist?"

"I'd seen dozens of doctors; none helped." Abruptly, Dalrymple fixated on the floor, staring at it with avid interest.

"What was the exact nature of your sexual problem?"

Dalrymple blushed clear down to her sensible shoes. "I…I didn't like it."

"Ahh…" Hicks nodded, sympathetic. "You did not like having sex, then?" All watched, mesmerized, as Dalrymple fretted her handbag handles into a knot.

"Yes," she finally said. Hicks shuffled close, confidential-like.

"Why not see a therapist about this?"

Eyes stitched forward, Dalrymple managed a grimace. "Because my husband told me to see that man... Walker—er—Mr. Judson." Her eyes watered up; Hicks passed her a tissue box. She extracted one and honked her nose.

"How often did you visit The Living Light for treatment?"

"Weekly, over sixteen months. Sixty times in all."

"Please explain what occurred during those sessions?"

"I—I got forced to have sex. I..." Dalrymple bawled in earnest. Hicks reached across, kindly pried the box from her grip, extracted a wad of Kleenex, and handed them over.

Cheeks wiped, Dalrymple looked up, ready to resume.

"You were forced by whom?" Hicks inquired.

"Him. Over there. Mr. Judson." Dalrymple pointed at Walker.

All looked. There Walker sat, inscrutable.

Beforehand, Lauren-Son begged him to show concern.

Way too sure of himself, he'd warned her off, saying, "It's fine. I'll just be myself." His idea of self-defense seemed on par with toting a butter knife to a gunfight.

"Exactly what did Walker Judson do to you?"

"First..." Dalrymple sniffed. "Walker...Judson...," she spoke, eyes affixed floorward, "just caressed me. Then he—he told me to remove my...panties, so he could check my—you know what."

"What, please, is a 'you know what'?"

"My...er—cooch, then."

"What happened next?"

"Ahhh." Swift glance up, Dalrymple's gaze scooted down again. "Well...Mr. Walker Judson...He stuck his fingers in—you know— down there." She pointed below her midriff.

"Did he explain why he did this?"

"Mr. Walker insisted touch was needed to determine changes in my condition. And...after a while—months into it—he stopped touching and just...just sort of...put it in."

Put it in! Lauren-Son's jaw ached from clenching.

She'd attended those sessions. Nothing whatsoever, even slightly fishy, ever happened! "That is so asinine!" she whispered, fiercely. Rosalee gave her a pat.

"Pass the witness," said Hicks with a satisfied smirk.

Twain sidled to the stand. "Please, Mrs. Gooch, tell the court why you permitted such liberties?"

Dalrymple flared. "I trusted Walker, because his weight-loss treatment worked so good. I didn't ask for this to happen. And my husband sent me, so I didn't see it as being unfaithful." Suddenly hunching, brow knitted, she continued, "Walker said we were sweethearts in a past life. He even talked some language I didn't understand."

"Did you object in any manner?"

Dalrymple paused to shift and squirm. "It was *so* terrible, *so* wrong!"

Twain consulted papers. "Did Mr. Judson do anything else to you?"

"Well…" She wrung her hands. "At some point he grabbed my— ah—boobies."

Twain leaned close; he and Dalrymple nearly touched, nose to nose. "Tell me, Mrs. Gooch," he inquired archly, "have you ever had an extra-marital affair?"

"Objection!" Hicks raised a hand. "Mrs. Gooch is not on trial here."

The attorneys argued away. Dalrymple fidgeted.

As annoyed as Lauren-Son felt, able to see what should be invisible, she stared at the woman, fascinated. Shape of Dalrymple's energetic outline evident, jagged clicks and claret-colored vibrations notable in her aura, such details commonly indicate deception.

Neediest of the needy, for all to see, Dalrymple threw herself at Walker. Plainly, she made him uncomfortable, and as the target of her insatiable need, plainly, he failed to reciprocate.

Someone, put her up to this.

Her grump of a husband, involved in half-a-dozen past lawsuits, perhaps?

Two aisles back, Duke Gooch sat, arms crossed, frowning at everyone.

But Dalrymple and he were such simple folk that malicious conniving on their part seemed unlikely.

Not just one individual, but likely, several sought Walker's downfall. That petition and the townies' ongoing negative sentiments suggested this. Walker had enemies all right, and winning this battle, Lauren-Son realized, would be no slam dunk.

"Mr. Twain," Judge Attic saw fit to announce, "you will refrain from inquiry that delves into Mrs. Gooch's possible extramarital activities. It's irrelevant to present circumstance."

"Certainly, Your Honor."

Deliberately shaping circles, he resumed. "Was anyone else present when Mr. Judson fondled your breasts?" Catching his moves, Dalrymple flinched, lowering her head.

Head back up, eyes grazing Lauren-Son's, she fudged, "Nobody else was there."

Lauren-Son reared up with a hiss, saying, "Hogwash!" Rosalee stilled her; slowly, she settled.

"Quite so." Twain veered off. "At this juncture, counsel shares the following…" He produced a card and read aloud, "Dear Walker, I wish I had nerve to say to your face that I love you. Still, I think about you all the time and feel such peace knowing you have special feelings for me. I even fantasize that we're married. Imagine, me as your wife! I love you above all others, Dalrymple." Daintily, Twain dangled the flowery missive between thumb and forefinger. "Mrs. Gooch, you wrote and sent this note to Mr. Judson. Is that correct?"

Head down, Dalrymple bobbed. "For the purposes of this court," Twain prompted, "you must speak aloud."

"Yes," she mumbled, "I sent it."

"Is it true, that you complained to the district attorney when Mr. Judson failed to respond to this?"

"I…" Face contracted, Dalrymple glanced at her husband to beg direction. He grimaced and looked elsewhere. Feet firmly planted, she shifted, then arose, as if wishing to fly up the aisle and make a run for it. She sat back down and spoke, forcefully, "No, I went to the authorities long after."

Lauren-Son craned to check; Walker stared at Dalrymple, utterly amazed.

For sure, he's done nothing, whatsoever, to encourage this woman!

"Did you consent to sexual contact with the defendant?" Twain asked.

"No," Dalrymple squeaked, affronted, "I didn't!"

"Yet you didn't exit the room or the building when said advances occurred. Why was that?"

Mouth puckered, she fought a new wave of tears. "Mr. Judson had total control. I felt helpless, confused—didn't want to think of a man I held in high regard, as taking advantage. That being too terrible to accept, I—I didn't want to believe what was happening."

"Yet, you kept coming back?" Twain prompted.

"I wanted to trust. So, after the first time, I figured he'd explain what happened, that he'd prove it wasn't really—uh, you know—sex." Sadly, she cast her gaze about.

Gently, Twain pressed, "Did you find your answer?"

One hand up, fingers splayed to protect her breasts, she offered up, "I knew I was bad for going back, but my husband—he...," she trailed off.

"You returned voluntarily to have sex," Twain pressed. "Isn't that consensual?"

Hicks smacked the table. "Objection, leading the witness!"

Judge Attic glared. "No theatrics Mr. Hicks. Mr. Twain...Repeat the question."

"Of your own free will, you repeatedly returned to The Living Light for treatment that included sex, did you not?"

Dalrymple wiggled primly. "He made me feel kinda good."

"Despite uncertainty as to the ethics of his behavior, you permitted his actions?"

Dalrymple cogitated. "I was desperate. Walker, ah—Mr. Judson, was the only one who helped. My doctor told me to see a shrink, but my husband, refused to let me go. See...We had such troubles. I felt so hopeless. I got scared Dukie would up and leave me."

Twain leaned over the rail. "Was this act, Mrs. Gooch, I ask again—of sexual congress consensual? And second, did the treatments help?"

"Yes," Dalrymple whispered, "I'd say so."

Unclear precisely which question Dalrymple had answered, Lauren-Son huffed beneath her breath. "And this is the thanks Walker gets!"

"Thank you Mrs. Gooch," said Twain. "You may step down."

Dalrymple paused to dab her eyes. Twain watched her retreat. All watched her go. Pointedly, however, Dalrymple's husband looked elsewhere as she slid in alongside him.

Next up, Hicks announced, "I call Dr. Emory Plath."

Silver of mane, easy of bearing, bigness of frame, Emory, radiating friendliness, took the stand. "Tell me, Dr. Plath," Hicks began, "would touching, as described by Mrs. Gooch—touching in the vicinity of the female genitalia—serve any legitimate medical purpose?"

"Depends upon context, but physical contact as described would serve no legitimate medical purpose, nor would such acts be consistent with reasonable medical practice in treating Mrs. Gooch's specific complaints." Emory, a throwback of sorts, invited all to call him by first name and was the only local physician to still make house calls. Extremely kind, willing to go out of his way, he and Walker vied for title of Buena Vista's Most Beloved.

Hicks cut to the chase. "Would you say that Mr. Judson did anything illegal during these sessions?"

"If he prescribed or diagnosed or recommended specific treatment, then yes, but I fail to hear that this occurred, so no."

"Who is legally permitted to make physical contact with their clients?"

Emory pulled at his lip. "As a physician it's within my legal purview to touch and to probe the human body if confined to appropriate, discrete limits."

"Who else is authorized to touch?"

"Chiropractors, acupuncturists and ministers have a legal right."

"Dr. Plath"—Hicks coiled to pounce—"do you have knowledge as to whether Mr. Judson is licensed to touch his clients?"

"Walker Judson is an ordained nondenominational minister, which gives him the legal right to touch. I believe he took a correspondence course; his certificate looks like it's on the up-and-up."

Hicks turned aside, nonplussed.

"Numerous times over the years," Emory added, "Walker—Mr. Judson, that is—helped with endangered births, saving many lives in the process. Couldn't have done without him."

Approving murmurs rippled through.

"Thank you, Dr. Plath," Hicks said, hurrying Emory off, "you may go."

"One more thing..." Emory paused to address the courtroom. "I've seen my share of shysters, so I certainly know when I see one, but I trust Walker Judson with my life."

Way to go Emory! Lauren-Son grinned ear-to-ear at him as he resumed his seat.

Twain sprang to his feet. "I'd like to recall Mrs. Dalrymple Gooch for further questioning."

Dalrymple shuffled back up and resettled. "Mrs. Gooch," Twain inquired, "did Walker Judson ever perform any sort of surgical procedure on you?"

Again, as if it might offer a reply, Dalrymple affixed the floor with a stare. "Can't say as he did."

"Did he ever diagnose, prescribe drugs, or recommend medical treatment?"

"No, he did not. Well, actually, he *did* tell me to keep contact with my doctor."

"I want it duly noted," Twain appealed to the judge, "Walker Judson did *not* attempt to practice medicine without a license."

"Fine. We'll break for the day," said Judge Attic.

As the crowd eagerly chatted among themselves and shuffled out, Lauren-Son sat brooding.

How could things go so wrong?

Walker was championed by some and tolerated by others. Until now, though, she had no idea how despised he was. And given all the good he'd done, these efforts to crucify him seemed way unfair.

Basically, she understood the complainant's' pain. Her own suffering, once her greatest treasured wound, had so thoroughly defined her. Before coming to know Walker, she felt less alone when others suffered as she had. But never, had she sought to destroy another because of it.

Next morning, big-boned Gert VanBeck took the stand. "As part of my pain-reduction program for an inoperable brain tumor," Gert announced, "Mr. Judson required that I perform oral sex." The courtroom sucked up its collective breath.

Several questions later, after Hicks passed to Twain, Gert got released.

Mouth crimped in distaste, shouting at Walker with her eyes, she resumed her seat.

Tale being similar to Gert's, Bernice Trabing gave testimony. Next up, Betty Jean Cowdry whimpered through her version, disclosing that stress from these events had led to severe depression.

Lauren-Son refused to believe any of it.

Previously, when Walker mentioned conspiracies, she'd thought him paranoid. Given these women's similar testimonies, she no longer felt sure.

Days into the trial, Walker grew thinner, and his fancy suit hung loosely. Despite the ravages, he still sat aloof as if dipping into the trough of drama were beneath him.

Evident to Lauren-Son, though, he was not at peace. She saw exhaustion; and beneath that, immense sorrow sundered him.

"The prosecution now calls Miss Melissa Dworkin," Hicks announced.

Scritchslap, scritchslap—uber-svelt, with coppery hair, Melissa came to the front and settled in to stare, steadily, at Walker.

Sick with jealousy, Lauren-Son watched.

Hicks came to the rail. "Miss Dworkin, please describe your relationship with the accused."

Eyes still glued to Walker, Melissa daintily touched her lips. "Walker demanded we have an affair and swore me to secrecy. At first, I was thrilled. Actually, he told me if we kept at it, I'd become enlightened."

"Why did you cooperate?"

"Refuse, and I'd lose him." Melissa tossed Delia a defiant look.

Nose in the air, spine rigid, Delia, all teeth, grinned back.

Personal scandal hushes most wives. Not so with Delia. The more dirt, along with Walker's flaws, that got trotted out, the more outspoken she became. As a result, many esteemed, even idolized her.

"I thought that sex with Walker would, in some way, make me"— chin tucked, Melissa spoke softly—"holy."

"What made you change your mind?"

"I made my needs known, asking Walker to make our relationship public. He said he'd force me to leave if I did. That's when I realized

I'd been exploited." Eyes briefly shaded, quickly she recovered. "I felt horribly abused."

Lauren-Son stifled a scoff.

Naturally, Walker would want such a lovely, fey woman! And, given the way the two exuded in each other's presence; they seemed a perfect pair.

She, Lauren-Son, being large and ugly, and still not exactly pleased to look as she did, felt self-hatred—doubts of old—swarm and return.

A tight band in her chest squeezed air from her lungs. Mouth open, she gasped a hollow rasp.

Get a grip, she warned herself. *You haven't worked all these years to succumb to this!*

Twain, up next, started in, hotly aggressive, "How can you possibly call what occurred between yourself and the defendant abuse when you kept coming back of your own free will? A glutton for punishment, perhaps. But victim? I say not!"

"Badgering my client," Hicks called out.

"Kindly refrain, Mr. Twain"—Judge Attic ticked a finger—"from such tactics."

Twain hammered anyway. "As a woman whose affections were spurned, did you retaliate to damage Mr. Judson's reputation?" Head down, Melissa muttered something. "Speak up!" Twain barked.

Forcing a pause, Melissa sobbed and shed tears.

Glommed onto the many falsehoods heard thus far, Lauren-Son hoped Melissa's tale merely posed another. Yet, unlike the others, Melissa's involvement with Walker seemed credible.

"I appeal to the court," Twain said, fingering his lapels, "it was not abuse Miss Dworkin suffered, but an infatuation gone-sour. If anything occurred between this complainant and Walker Judson, plainly, she wanted it too."

"I'm *so—so* sorry!" Melissa spluttered, gulping air.

"We're done." Twain gave a nod.

All waited as Melissa composed herself.

Red-eyed, skin blotchy, she stood, then went—*scritch-slapping*— past Walker and caught his gaze.

Air crackling, highly charged, swiftly, she glanced away.

Chapter Sixty-Seven Walker

Jurors looking on, impassive, Walker sensed their condemnation and felt the cold fury of the courtroom crowd. Fully, he grasped the complainants' hatred and deliberately drew their emotions into himself; their rage sundered him.

True, he resented their insatiable need, but also, he loved these women. Full-up with regret and shame, ultimately due to his inability to diminish their suffering...on some level, he'd failed them.

Staunch upright Gert VanBeck glared as if she'd like to tear his heart out.

Trembling inside, Walker looked back.

Never releasing him from sight, Gert drew a pointer finger to incise her neck.

Pain afflicting him as if he'd been run though, he wondered: *Am I truly a monster, a manipulative actor; or a frightened, lost soul; or possibly a heroic figure; how about merely one who wishes to retreat and pretend nothing's awry?*

All selves jostling inside, mind in an uproar, episodically his solid sense of self, along with the certitude as to his life's guiding principles, eluded.

Perhaps I should speak up to alter how folks esteem me.

Yet what matters most —my puny life—or my everlasting soul?

Challenged to fix the world yet unable to blend into it, poised between the mundane and the infinite absolute, it mattered not what acts of self-preservation he might undertake. What mattered most was the heightened consciousness he might contribute to human existence—the light he helped shine upon it—not his guilt or innocence.

And so...Egoic self-defense being of no consequence, as his physical body endured courtroom proceedings, surrounded by judge, jury, and complainants, veils thinning, potent winds gusting within, he departed surrounds and placed his consciousness elsewhere.

Daydreams—visions—engulfed. Earth and sky breathing as one, he synchronized his pulses with planetary forces. Bodies birthed, loved, suffered, lost, and then decayed. Yet immortal souls—an infinity— endured, as Walker hoped his might.

Gregorian chants droning, he communed with saints—Theresa of Avila, Saint Francis, and a cacophony of others. Images of cavorting nuns cropped up, then thoughts of Ma—her imagined life as a nun— flooded his brain.

Soft clicking rosary beads, Mother Superior's arthritic joints rubbed, painfully, as she knelt to pray. Nun's robes rustling; sweet cloying incense; stern, mute, plaster icons; and God's presence flooded into him. Blessed to witness, he glimpsed the promise of cup-overflowing goodness that had been gifted to Ma, but then, somehow, got lost.

Unable to grasp the why as to her loss, he guessed it pertained to himself...and to sacrifice. Onward he spiraled, hours on end, plummeting into a silence so deep he heard blood pulse his ears.

Trial's seventh day, Ma visited. "I know you can't speak to me, son," she chirped, "but I'd like to share about my favorite saint. Padre Pio, an Italian monk, who can appear several places at once. Perhaps he'll offer you comfort as he often has me." She beamed, triumphant, as if the padre's acts, somehow, heightened her.

"American World War II pilots, as the story goes, under the misapprehension that Germans had captured the Italian town, San Giovonna Rotundo, headed off to bomb and to liberate it. And so those pilots, yet to hear that Nazis hadn't actually overtaken the place, spotted the great padre, flying among cloudbanks, entreating them to turn back.

"Later, those airmen gave sworn testimony to seeing a man, enrobed in monk's cowl, skimming through skies. But when grateful townsfolk came to thank the padre for helping spare them, he confessed he'd never left the monastery." Shoulders scooched up, she dropped them in delight. "Imagine that!

"Same as Christ's crucifixion wounds, Padre Pio had stigmata—lesions of the palms, feet, and ribs. They pained him something fierce and bled, constantly."

Where's she headed with this? Walker could not guess.

"Son...," Ma kept on, "I've prayed for the privilege to meet this holy man—that I might touch his wounds and be sanctified. Sadly, that's never come to pass. Yet when I catch the scent of violets, I sense him nearby." The apparition that formed Ma met her son's gaze, then leaned close. "You too have stig..." Voice fading, she disappeared.

Frustrated by yet another near-miss grasp of her, great roar blasting Walker's ears, lines blurring, shapes shifting, courtroom ceiling pried opened, he gazed skyward, stunned.

Heavens a-swirl with stars, each one spun clock-wise, creating luminous comet-like swaths, as jewel-encrusted celestial bodies aligned to shape a most familiar, beloved outline.

Whoosh of wings throbbing, The Angel descended to enfold him.

Serenest warmth flooded his being to fill every crevice. "Regardless as to what comes to pass," The Angel caressed, "your soul shall endure forever."

Abruptly, it released him and soared off, calling out, "Fear not. And forgive all."

Violets scents clinging to air wisps, returned from faraway thoughts, reverie shaken off, a wondrous thing occurred.

First time ever, Walker felt full, not empty.

"Thank you," he whispered, strongly at peace.

The guard shook his shoulder. "Time to go bud. Everyone's left for lunch."

Chapter Sixty-Eight: Lauren

Court convened the next day. A dozen witnesses, specifically those treated but not overtly healed by Walker, trotted up to complain.

Finished with that earful, Hicks announced, "Prosecution calls Mrs. Mildred Sharp to the stand."

Fight between Walker and Voden sprung to mind, as well as the pledge she'd made to keep her mouth shut, Lauren-Son braced herself.

Very thin, pasty pale, Mildred Sharp got sworn in, then began, "I too was a recipient of Mr. Judson's unwanted attention. I didn't want to get involved in this mess but am here anyway under duress."

"To clarify," Hicks elucidated, "the witness is testifying without a subpoena. Is that correct Mrs. Sharp?"

"One of the victims—my dear friend, Betty Jean—said she'd kill herself if I didn't do this."

"Well then, Your Honor..." Twain popped up. "I request this woman be released."

"Her testimony," countered Hicks, "is necessary to establish a pattern. So...may I?"

The judge waved a hand. "Proceed." Twitchy, annoyed, Twain lowered into his seat.

"Please, Mrs. Sharp," Hicks said, getting back to it, "tell the court what happened."

Mildred shut her eyes so long, it seemed she might not reply.

Eyes open, she began with great reluctance, "One day I—I was naked, receiving a healing from Walker Judson whe—when he told me to roll on my stomach. Ne...next thing I knew, he—he climbed on top and sexed me in my—my bottom."

Room pin-drop silent, next words, softly spoken, every ear strained to hear. "When he did this vile thing, I lay there begging God to kill me." Mildred sobbed into a handkerchief, then brought her face out.

"As if a life-threatening illness weren't enough, that man...well...You can't imagine how I've suffered."

Courtroom riveted, hanging onto every nuance, Mildred bellowed out grief. "Whe...when he did what he did, I thought...There are things worse than death, and surely, this is one of them!"

Please don't let this be true! Lauren-Son craned to check Walker's countenance.

Ever so slightly he worked his jaw but overall stayed impassive.

*Oooo...*She wanted to beseech him, *Show your goodness!*

Instead, he sat, stiff necked, coldly remote.

The jury judged him for this; it showed in their faces.

"According to Karmic law," he'd said the night prior, "all is preordained. So everything, even the worst, happens for a higher, immutable, purpose. It's merely my job to fulfill the narrative."

Therefore, according to his mindset, no need to defend or to protect. Trial's outcome already written in stone, he found it pointless to fight its outcome.

"Fight with all your might anyhow," she'd entreated.

Gaze returned to Mildred, something seemed amiss.

Air clotted, motionless, above her—an oddity only noted surrounding the newly deceased—bile arose in Lauren-Son's throat. Yet, swiftly, she shut down awareness of it.

Twain's turn, he came forth, soft of tone. "During this episode, Mrs. Sharp, did you struggle, cry out, or demand that the defendant stop?"

"Nnn—no." Anguished, eyes haunted, Mildred cast about. "Pe... people were nearby, so I didn't want to create a disturbance. I never mentioned this to anyone, except my girlfriend. Not until now, that is." Fighting for composure, fingers on one hand crimped, she pinching them with the other hand.

"Again...Why did you not speak out until now?"

"Walker's wife was an acquaintance...That's partly why. And at first, I thought I was the only one to receive such advances. Mostly though...because he...he healed me."

What, what! Lauren-Son whipped round to stare at Walker.

Hadn't he told Mildred her cancer had spread, insisted she seek traditional medical intervention?

Plainly, Mildred still thought she was well when she was not.

Galloping unease—the possibility that Walker had actually violated her reared its head, and a sharp chink in Lauren-Son's faith in the man started to fester.

Twain softly pled, "Why did you wait so long to divulge this?"

Mildred took a minute to reply.

"When diagnosed, I promised God I'd do anything if He'd make me well. So I thought Walker Judson's behavior might be part of God's plan, planted as a test, and did exactly as he asked—submitted, kept quiet, and endured all of it." Eyes squeezed shut, she whispered, fiercely. "I just wish the cancer had killed me!"

"Are you still well?"

"I've been cancer-free several years, so...Yes." Twain shrugged affably.

Bleary-eyed, excruciatingly slowly, Mildred exited the courtroom.

Chapter Sixty-Nine: Lauren

Forcing herself to act, on merit of his previous offer, Lauren-Son called David Millbanks, who then insisted on testifying, so she put him in touch with Twain.

"I'll not be beholden to anyone," barked Walker when he heard what she'd done.

In the end, Millbanks made a substantial donation to Walker's defense fund and also sent a letter: *Walker Judson healed me of a terrible, wasting debility when he laid hands on me, causing my health to return. More important, he restored my flagging faith. Walker Judson is a heroic individual of integrity and miracles. I stake my reputation on the man.*

Dandy words, except Walker refused to permit their use.

More infuriating, she overheard Twain shout at Walker behind closed doors, "How can you not testify? If I were to prosecute your case, I'd say I had a winner if the defendant refused to stick up for himself." Walker must've replied, for Twain growled, exasperated, "Defend yourself, man! I'm trying my best, but you force me to work with hands tied behind my back. Speak up! Say what you know."

"Sorry, but I can't," murmured Walker. "I'll just take my chances." Lauren-Son thought to burst in and shake him.

Twain laughed, cheerless, horrid. "Chrissake, have your wife testify, then!" Walker argued further, then Twain threatened, "Keep this up, I resign!"

As Walker showed Twain out, Lauren-Son accosted him. "If you're innocent, why not say so?"

He shook his head, disappointed. "You still don't you get it. This entire process is about trust."

Scrabbling to believe in him, increasingly tough to do so, she glommed onto the notion that much of Walker's survival seemed based on manipulating his pain. So perhaps he compartmentalized trauma too overwhelming to confront.

If true, perhaps his rotten family life caused this. "Did your mother ever say she loved you?" She grabbed this fresh tack when their paths crossed next.

Stock still, Walker frowned. Eyes holding hurt from eons ago, clearly, he did not enjoy that she'd invoked his mother. "My sorrow"—his voice held a tone not previously heard—"as compared to the enormity of humanity's sorrow, means nothing whatsoever in the grand scheme of things."

She nodded, not sure she agreed.

Abruptly, he gripped her wrist, then drew back to stare at his own palms as if to disown them—and to disavow their contact. "I am not trying to win this," he informed.

Air punched from lungs, she buckled as if struck, then pulled back up. "I don't get why not. Your attitude's incredibly disheartening." He motioned her to depart, went past down the hall, and she judged him further.

No longer wanting to know the truth, afraid he might lie to her or actually reveal the unthinkable, she thought to completely avoid him.

Defense opening their case, Twain announced, "I call Ms. Malouise Shrampton as a hostile witness."

Forty-ish, heavyset, a private investigator hired by the victims, the woman scooted into the witness box. "Did you, Ms. Shrampton," Twain began, "seek treatment at The Living Light?"

Legs crossed, mannish, ankle of one leg rested atop knee of the other, she gave a sharp nod. "Correct." The top foot started wagging.

"Were those treatments to do with a personal matter or for investigational purposes?"

"I was hired to ascertain the nature of any alleged hanky-panky at The Living Light."

"Did your investigation include receipt of healing treatments performed by Walker Judson?"

"Yup, he treated me." Foot now gripped, she restrained it from jiggling. "Twelve times to be exact."

As Twain consulted papers, Lauren-Son recalled Ms. Shrampton as a fantastic busybody who'd nosed about, barraging patients with questions.

"What reason did you give for being seen?"

"I fabricated a heart condition, claimed I suffered from cardiac failure when, actually, I did not. Or…" her voice trailed off, "didn't think so at the time."

"Ms. Shrampton, where you harmed by Walker Judson in any way?"

"No!" Her voice fluttered sharply. "In fact, he was the perfect gentleman."

"Do you suppose, Ms. Shrampton, the defendant had an inkling who you were?"

"Nope, not at first. That is…until he said something."

"And what did he say?" Twain suppressed a grin.

"Believe he said…'You do me no harm. In fact, what you learn about me will help.' Didn't grasp his meaning at the time, but do now."

"Did you, with Mr. Judson's help, discover you have a cardiac condition, and did he urge you to seek immediate intervention for it?"

"Yup, he certainly did!" Ms. Shrampton nodded vigorously. "He said fixing my bum ticker was beyond the scope of his skill, yet repeatedly, I returned."

"What happened last year, June seventeenth?"

"I had a cardiac arrest at The Living Light and"—pointedly, she swiveled to make eye contact with Judge Attic—"Walker Judson saved my life." Approving murmurs rippled through.

"During your time at The Living Light did you see evidence of sexual misconduct?"

"None in the slightest, sir." The woman's other foot tapped, wildly. "Except for the fact that all the women were so ga-ga over Mr. Judson, all seemed on the up-and-up."

"Would you care to comment regarding Walker Judson's character?"

"The best…I can't say enough good about the man!"

"Thank you. You may step down."

"Next witness," Twain announced, "also hostile, I call Miss D. P. Wilkins."

"Please," Twain prompted after she settled, "describe your involvement with the complainants."

"I'm a psychologist," Miss Wilkins said primly. "I specialize in women's crisis issues and treated each of the five women in therapeutic counseling sessions. For the purposes of disclosure, I also accompanied them to police interviews." Twain plumped fingers together.

"Miss Wilkins, are you familiar with the term, therapist stimulated recall?"

Miss Wilkins sat rigidly erect, hands clasped in her lap. "Indeed, I am."

"Please explain to the court exactly what that term means."

"Therapist stimulated recall occurs when a therapist, either willfully or inadvertently, plants ideas that stimulate false memories, prompting an individual to remember events that never occurred."

"Take for instance," Twain interjected, "sexual violation." He leveled his gaze at her. "Could a therapist suggest such a violation happened when, in fact, it had not?"

"Why yes, it's possible."

"Miss Wilkins…" Twain strode past her, paused before the jury, then returned to ask, "Did you, on July ninth of this year, complain to a client that Walker Judson stole business from you?"

"Ah…" She hesitated. "Er—I did. I'm sorry. It was inappropriate."

"Did you ever express desire to shut down The Living Light Healing Center?"

Miss Wilkins flared.

"I most certainly did not! My only complaint was to criticize their unsightly paint job." Snickers ensued.

"Is it possible, Miss Wilkins," Twain asked, archly, "that you planted ideas of abuse in your clients' minds because of a personal vendetta against The Living Light?"

"I'd never do such a thing!" Giant, welty splotches leapt onto her neck.

"Miss Wilkins…" Twain said, spooling faster, "we have documentation regarding three occasions where you gave written statements against The Living Light to the Buena Vista City Council, blaming the center for your flagging business, demanding that they be closed down. You *did* write said letters, did you not?" Twain waved papers. Miss Wilkins sat very still; up her neck the rash crept to splash her cheeks.

"Well, yes," she finally said. "I guess I must have. But I bear the place no ill-will."

As Twain finished up with Miss Wilkins, her face, hands, neck and arms glistened, tomato-red.

Twain announced, "I now call Ms. Lauren Finch."

Settled into the witness box, Lauren-Son tossed out a silent prayer. *Please God, let my words help!*

"Ms. Finch," Twain queried, "did you overhear a conversation this past July, wherein Miss Wilkins addressed a gathering at the Flatiron?"

"Yes, I heard Miss Wilkins speak with four others, one being Mayor Lynch. She said, and I quote, 'The Living Light offers false hope and causes harm, so I'll do all in my power to shut it down.' Mayor Lynch objected to this, but she insisted, again I quote, 'I'll see that place decimated.'"

"I submit to the jury..." Twain stood squarely before the group. "Miss Wilkins's negative sentiments against The Living Light Healing Center prompted her attempts to sway the complainants." He paused to permit this to sink in, then abruptly veered off.

"How long has Mr. Judson been married?"

"Ten years." Distortion flung from her mouth, it strutted about, daring to be questioned. For ironically, it became her task to convey Walker's fidelity—to stress marital longevity—so she fudged to enfold Delia's several years absence.

"And how long have you worked with the defendant?"

"Five years."

"I understand that you and Walker Judson have a close professional relationship. So...,"—carefully he posed his next words—"have you ever known him to have improper relations with anyone?"

Prior to leveling of charges, one time she'd blundered into a treatment room as Walker cupped a woman's bare buttocks and the woman glanced up, biting her lip. Sensing something inappropriate, electing not to identify it, Lauren-Son had backed out, insisting inwardly that Walker's action had been part of the healing. Yet, she fudged again, "No, never!

"I might add…I was present when many of these alleged incidents occurred. There was touching; that's what Walker—I mean Mr. Judson—does, but none of the touching could be construed as even slightly sexual. And none of the women ever indicated they'd been violated. If such a thing happened, I would have heard. None of them seemed upset. On the contrary, all were happily grateful and usually hung around to socialize after."

Twain nodded, appreciative. "Pass the witness."

Hicks stood before her. She studied him closely. His chin was strange and weak, yet he hadn't proven the wimp she'd hoped. "Perhaps you're mistaken, Miss Finch…that you were not actually present during the sessions in question."

"I'm certain I was."

"Some suggest that you," Hicks offered mildly, "have personal motives to protect the defendant."

Lauren-Son spluttered. "I was smack-dab in the midst of much that happened. And…No, there's nothing between us! Besides, it's not in Walker's nature to have done these things. In fact, it's unthinkable! Walker…Mr. Judson offers tremendous hope and inspiration to all. Plus, he'd never bring disgrace to his wife or to his work."

Delia shifted, smiling thinly.

"Walker's not unstable," Lauren-Son pressed, hunting for a proper tone, "or…or a sex maniac. He'd never, ever, harm a living thing." Fervently wishing her mouth hadn't let loose, she pressed anyhow. "Several Buena Vista residents are doing this. Walker makes them nervous, so they're trying to discredit him—to—to frame an innocent man, to stop his work." Sharply dismissive, Twain flicked his hand.

Lightheaded, giddy, pivoting to glare at the courtroom crowd, she kept on, "Who are any of you to criticize? No one, me included, is awake enough to appreciate Walker Judson's sacrifice."

"Beg your pardon," Hicks steered her back, "but such matters are not the court's concern, so please confine yourself to the issue at hand."

Woozy, mortified, she sought to compose herself.

Hicks reviewed notes, then continued, "Are you trained to assess victims of sexual assault?"

"I'm a registered nurse but have no special skills to spot such victims."

"Thank you. You may go now." She went past Walker, caught his eye, and shrugged, apologetic.

"It's OK," he mouthed.

Had Walker transgressed? she pondered as she settled.

Regarding Mildred Sharp, she was uncertain. But surely, he didn't assault any of the alleged victims and likely had good reason to cup that woman's buttocks as he had.

She *did* loathe her dependence, her willingness to lie and cover up to protect him. To keep her tidy world intact, though, she'd happily sell out for a shot as his beloved.

Twain's assistant burst into the courtroom, strode briskly to the front, and passed a note to the clerk. The clerk handed the paper to the judge, who read it, then announced, "We'll take a five-minute break, but keep your seats. Mr. Twain—your aide wishes a word."

Off to the side the two men spoke in low, urgent tones and perused the complainants. More murmurs, several head nods, Twain clapped the aide's shoulder and turned to the judge. "In light of new information, I request that court adjourn until tomorrow."

Gavel smacked, the courtroom cleared.

Chapter Seventy: Walker

"In here, hon," Delia helloed as Walker arrived home.

Necktie released, he hovered at her office door, she beckoned him in. "How you holding up?" she asked.

"I'll be glad when it's done." Subsequent to the day's session, he'd stayed on to meet with Twain. Jury soon to go out, he suspected, they'd render swift judgment.

Busily, Delia sorted papers, tossing them into boxes. "Sorry as I am for the fix you're in, you've only yourself to blame. I tried to protect you, but—nooo…You had to do it your way, trusting all would be fine. Still…I'm furious with myself. If I'd paid closer attention, come back to you sooner, I might've been able to prevent this. Here—give a hand."

Half-dozen boxes hefted to the living room, Delia opened the lid of one, tossed its contents—invoices, receipts, and ledgers—into the fireplace, then lit a match to it.

Steadily, she emptied the other boxes, chucking papers into eagerly licking flames. As Walker looked on, her machinations—destruction of evidence being so minor to the overarching plan—anger, frustration, grief, sundered him. Anger for what could not be changed, and grief for all that would soon be lost to him.

Whoosh—smoke escaped to clog the air. "You, my love," Delia nattered and coughed, "are so gloriously flawed. I tried, hard, to make you stronger, but you refuse to cooperate."

Neither the dark nor shiny aspects of her husband's persona being places Delia cared to examine, Walker, figuring she had every right to vent, leaned at the hearth, braced for more.

"You're like those Russian dolls—the kind you open, where there's always a smaller doll inside. You have secrets, deep ones. I hate not knowing, and certainly don't like how this mess makes me look. Sometimes"—she turned wistful—"I think you dislike me."

Exposed, uncertain—states he didn't much care for—vulnerability building, he dove fists into pockets, rocked onto balls of his feet, cleared his throat once, and then a second time. Hands extracted, he let them drop.

Desperate to contain fidgets, he reached to squeeze Delia's hand. Becalmed by contact, he stepped back and spoke softly, "Likely, Delia, I'll be going away."

"Away?" She stared at him, blankly.

Tongue run over lips, Walker stared back.

As ever, they made the oddest pair. Walker, stodgy, slump shouldered, preferred invisibility. Delia on the other hand, gorgeous, bright, flitting, fluttering, adored the limelight. She worshiped money, worshiped her body, and inconsequential material objects. Delia, with too many words, too much need, and...depending on interpretation—having too large or too microscopic an ego—overflowed with narcissism and sought to gulp down the entire world from want. Whereas he—on the other hand—scarcely wanted at all.

Correction...What he wanted was to stay true to his gifts.

Aside from a shared business life, they had little in common. If only she'd appreciated him as more than a status-enhancing meal ticket, their life could've altered. Yet, it occurred to him: the glue binding them together was their mutual capacity for self-deception.

Boxes emptied, Delia surveyed her work, and grew somber. "Aw honey, I'll really miss you." She stroked his cheek, then stepped away. "I've tried to help, but you've been too preoccupied to notice."

"I *have* noticed." Walker grabbed her. She let out a squeak. "Actually, you've been a big help." Her fragrance enveloped as he nuzzled her neck.

In her own particular way, Delia *had* saved him. She'd offered refuge, a resting place, taught him plenty about human foibles, and about relationships as well. "Shall we?" he asked, gripping her hand artfully aloft.

"Yes—let's!"

Off to their bedroom suite they went.

Dress peeled off, she gave it a toss, turned to him, cupped both breasts, and then released them. Full to voluptuous, they did not drop.

Age thirty-five, her body bore no unsightly creases or god-awful sags.

Delia reached up, latched onto his lips, unfastened his shirt buttons, slowly unzipped his pants, slid down his slacks, grinding her pelvis into his leg all the while. She led him to the tub, ran water—steaming hot—added soap bubbles, then they both climbed in.

Lazily, they lathered each other up. Each curvaceous inch of her calling out to him, they soaked a bit, rinsed, got out, and dried off. As she sat, bare bottomed at her dressing table, Delia eyed him. "See my little finger...," Walker said as he came up behind to crick a pinkie. "It's making love with every cell of your being." Lips licked, Delia shivered, deliciously.

"Oooo, Walker, when dressed, you're so rigidly uptight. Naked, though, you revert to the brutish primal man you truly are. Frankly, I adore the contrast." Naked, nipples tilted teasingly upward, she pranced about. "You like?"

"Yeah!" Throbbing, fully hardened, Walker scooped her up and flung her onto the bed. Delia squealed, unresisting. Flipped onto her belly, he pinned her down, yanked her hair, then, grunting, panting, took her from behind.

"You are *so* nasty!" Delia laughed and moaned as they gripped each other tight.

Full up with longing, Walker smelt her hair—a mix of perfume and smoke—and wished, fervently, that his arms held another.

Chapter Seventy-One: Lauren

Court convened the next morning; Twain recalled Dalrymple Gooch.

Rosalee, sitting between Sherman and Lauren-Son, reached to grip hands.

"How is it...," Twain inquired of Dalrymple, "though you and your husband are unemployed, you suddenly pay off your entire mortgage?"

Dalrymple paled and looked to the judge. "Do I have to say?"

"Please respond."

"Last week"—Dalrymple blurted a pressured surge—"I found money, all cash, on our doorstep. Figuring it might be stolen, my husband and I checked the banks, but none laid claim to it, so it's ours."

Twain recalled all complainants. Lauren-Son lurched from hope to despair, and back to hope again as each woman, with the exception of Melissa Dworkin—who swore she knew nothing—revealed recent receipt of a large cash windfall. Yet probe and threaten as Twain did, each vehemently denied knowledge as to the money's origins.

They *did* divulge plans to indulge, as never before: Dalrymple slated her jackpot for cosmetic surgery—a jowl lift and tummy tuck; Gert had her eye on a Tioga recreational vehicle, with plans to travel; Bernice gave a sizable donation to her church; Betty Jean would attend cosmetology school. Only the liar Melissa insisted she was as poor as ever.

Lauren-Son fought to suppress a holler: *Who bribed you people?* And—hoped a plot by Walker's enemies might be revealed.

"For my redirect," Hicks announced the next day, "I recall Mrs. Dalrymple Gooch."

Sporting a new-fangled poodle hairdo, Dalrymple marched up and situated herself. "Let's review…," Hicks prompted. "Please clarify exactly what's befallen you as a result of Walker Judson's unwanted attention."

Dalrymple held Walker with a cold stare, addressing him directly, "Thanks to you, I can't disrobe in front of my hubby, and I refused to let any doctor examine me. Also, I blame you completely for my lack of trust." As if in agreement, Walker nodded politely.

Hicks joined in, "To sum up, Walker Judson committed forcible rape upon the person of Mrs. Dalrymple Gooch. Violent acts of this sort shall not be tolerated. Thanks kindly, ma'am"—he nodded, admiringly—"you may go."

Framing his closing argument, Hicks summed up, "How is it that each of these five women suffered similar sordid tales of abuse? I submit…that they did not ban together to cook these horror stories up.

"This man"—he indicated Walker—"though regarded by many as a saint—is a sexual deviant who, transcending laws of human decency, hid beneath the cloak of goodness to pervert the trust of many vulnerable individuals." Hands twisted together, he shambled over to stand before the jury. "Walker Judson used that trust to violate these women, perpetrating unspeakable abuse—abuse that went on, week after week, month after month."

Again, he pointed. "Walker Judson preyed on the trust, ignorance, and hopes of these women, and then betrayed them without the slightest remorse. And for this…He must pay. So please"—Hicks took a long pointed pause to make eye contact with each juror—"find this man guilty…and see that he is fully punished." Walker's stoic countenance gave away nothing.

No one else saw the harm, but given the droop of his shoulders and his glazed-over look, certainly Lauren-Son did.

Why God, she railed, *have You allowed this?*

Not exactly a Christian herself, she *did* consider Christ one terrific guy. But also, she felt pretty sure that belief in the man didn't represent the sole path to God.

For, regardless as to belief, God, she sensed, resided within all people. God was nondenominational, surpassed human opinion and judgment, was boundless and big enough to encompass all paths. Just now, however, she promised to believe forever in the supremacy of

Christ if he'd kindly swoop down to bash in a few heads and right this mess.

Voice projected to the rafters, Twain came next. "Each of these women knew Mr. Judson's treatments did not involve sex. Yet, despite complaints of sexual abuse, of their own free will, they sought healing sessions, even repeatedly returned after alleged incidents of rape and assault. Two of the five complainants, mind you, subsequently went on to be trained in The Living Light's healing methods. I ask, is such behavior consistent with that of an assault or rape victim?

"Each complainant failed to protest or to struggle during alleged incidents. To explain such passivity, they asserted they'd succumbed to Mr. Judson's immense persuasive powers. How is it that each woman"—Twain swept his arm to indicate the complainants—"was controlled by my client, Mr. Judson, and powerless to resist his advances?

"If sexual congress *did* occur"—he paused to make certain the jury was with him—"it was strictly consensual. Walker Judson"—his voice throbbed, impassioned—"is as fine and decent a man who has ever walked the earth. Humble, unassuming, asking little in return for his services, he has, in fact, devoted his life to service.

"Please." Twain faced the courtroom crowd, culminating, "I beg you...Do not silence this good man!" He spun to face the jury box. "Godspeed making the right decision."

Judge Attic gave final instructions before jurors filed out.

Chapter Seventy-Two: Lauren

Time passed slowly.

One hour—four—then six, came and went as Rosalee, Sherman, and Lauren-Son paced the courthouse halls, even tried small talk, but no heart was into it. Slack absence to his flesh, Voden merely sat, ensnared in rumination.

Seven that evening, the jury requested certain of Walker's written records and then broke for the night. So the four pals drove home to The Living Light.

Building cool, musty, Rosalee scurried about tidying up. Sherman swept floors without carrying so much as a nervous tune. Up the ladder Voden went to press his brow to The Angel's, and then he vacated.

Lauren-Son paced. Confused thoughts skittered round: *Is Walker the victim of an infecting vortex of ill will or of predestined fate? And have I outsourced my brain, letting him do my thinking for me?"*

"Say, old chum," she paused to ask of the statue, "what do you think of this mess?"

No reply. Its wretched face, frozen in sorrow, spoke volumes.

Being with Walker, she felt she'd come home to herself, for he'd mended and expanded her. Without him, she had trouble remembering who she was. Without him, she'd have to reinvent a new life. Without him, she felt as if she were nothing. Worst of all, if Walker were *truly* guilty, the best years of her life had been a giant lie.

She dropped onto the stairs; Rosalee scooted alongside.

Anxious as to her next words, Lauren-Son gave her friend a fierce hug. "While questing for clarity, I came across an article in *Psychology Today* about the abuse of power, which got me thinking about the possibility that Walker might actually be controlling all of us. Want me to read?"

"Please proceed," Rosalee said cautiously.

Dog-eared papers slid from a pocket, Lauren-Son began, "'Studies show that incidents of manipulation and malfeasance on the part of numerous healers, spiritual teachers, and other leaders are commonplace. No single institution is left unharmed by the moral failings or scandalous acts of its leaders.'"

"This is fact?" Rosalee ogled her. The water cooler belched, startling them both.

Grim nod, Lauren-Son pressed on, "'Such abuse tends to be far-reaching and nonsectarian. Numerous evangelical ministers, Protestant clergy, and Catholic priests commit inappropriate sex acts. Jewish congregations, Muslim and Buddhist communities, along with Hindu ashrams have their share of scandal as well. Politicians lead the pack among professionals, with physicians and attorneys close behind. Abusers are of varied race, color, creed, and geographic location.' And sadly, all perpetrators are male!"

Rosalee chaffed her brow, frowning. "Certainly, this does not make Walker one of them."

"I know. But get this…Even when found guilty, every man still denied it!"

Rather than achieve clarity, Lauren-Son regretted what she'd learned.

Worse yet, growing awareness pried her eyes open, forcing her to see that she too shared a part in this mess. "Wonder why abuse of power is so common," she mused. "Moreover, why are followers so quick to relinquish control?"

"*Hubris,*" Rosalee said succinctly, "overbearing presumption of infallibility. That is the crux of the biscuit. Only, Walker is not like that; he lacks esteem of self. Most bad men in that article have too much esteem. And usually, no guru or priest takes advantage without our agreement." Hands folded in her lap, she sat back to regard Lauren-Son. "So…Do you blame him?"

"I'm not sure what to think. Walker made such an ambivalent guru. He was particularly rude to the students, treated them like servants, assigning them the worst, most unpleasant chores. And mostly, he avoided them."

"Their adoration pained him," Rosalee, affirmed" He coped badly with that. Yet it is the guru's job—the guru in this case being

Walker—to dispel ignorance any way possible while one is en route to enlightenment, therefore, the teacher may shame a follower, rage at them, or abuse them. But insofar as I know, Walker has done none of this."

Maybe that's where he permitted his anger to leak. Or maybe he did not love every living creature as he claimed to.

Lauren-Son willed her heart to slow and for air to chuff slowly in and out her lungs. "You'd think Walker's years of service would offer proof of his innocence. Besides, "—she groped to support him—"no man as good, as gifted as he, could be evil."

"So sorry," Rosalee countered, "much as I believe in my boy, apparent goodness and special gifts do not necessarily mean one has integrity or is spiritually evolved. Many powerful individuals possess the Divine Spark but then use badness and contempt to control and to abuse."

"Have we looked the other way, Rosie, refusing to see Walker's shortcomings?"

"I hope not. I *do* know, the role of guru is to awaken each of us— not to be perfect." Tenderly nursing her back, Rosalee stood and slowly departed.

Chapter Seventy-Three: Lauren

Door swung open, Rosalee rushed in the next morning to blurt, "Walker has been kidnapped!" Quick pause, she gasped a breath. "Earlier, he showed up at the center to fret and pace. I have never seen him so troubled. I ask what is wrong. He said he is fine, but he seemed so worried. Shortly, he went out to his truck. When he did not return, I went to check. His pickup was there, papers scattered, door open, but he was not to be found." Lauren-Son stared at Rosalee, horror-stricken.

The evening's news sought to fill in gaps: "As of seven o'clock this morning," Chief Hosley grimly announced, "Walker Judson, founder of The Living Light Healing Center, went missing and hasn't been seen or heard from since. Some insist foul play. We haven't ruled this out, but see no signs of struggle or injury at the scene. On trial for sexual assault, Mr. Judson's verdict is to be read tomorrow."

"What about kidnap?" a reporter asked, jabbing the mike in the chief's face. "Any ransom note?" another clamored. "Is there something you aren't saying?" a third voice butted in.

"No, no, and no," Chief Hosley repeated, "nothing whatsoever, suggests abduction. And...," he added, "usually we involve the FBI when there's hard evidence of kidnapping, but so far, there's none." Paused to moisten a fingertip, he smoothed an eyebrow. "If Mr. Judson ran, he faces a stiffer sentence than that originally required." Rosalee gripped Lauren-Son, whose throat went dry.

Kimmie, neighboring pet shop owner, also featured in the segment, gave her take. "Yesterday, I noticed a Jeep Wagoneer full of camping gear parked next to Walker's truck. Last week, I spotted that same vehicle, but didn't get the license plates and have no idea whose it is."

"He's dead," the piece concluded, showing a woman blubbering into the camera. "They've killed him—I just know it!"

No way was Walker dead, for presently his vital throbbing heart, his every breath, engulfed Lauren-Son.

Three others had also gone missing: The Angel had disappeared, Voden and Silly were gone as well.

Some speculated that The Angel had been stolen. Given the bustling activity at The Living Light, sneaking it out seemed improbable. Besides, Walker never liked to be far from it, so if he'd left of his own accord, he'd have taken it with.

Detractors suggested Voden as the mastermind of Walker's getaway. So when authorities sought to track down details regarding a certain Voden Fucols—no records, none of the usual detritus—no fingerprints on record, no birth certificate, no drivers license, or credit cards, or even so much as a library card—existed.

Lauren-Son could have supplied a juicy tidbit, but saw no reason to offer it.

When court convened the next day Walker failed to appear. "It isn't in my client's interest to flee," argued Twain. "Only a fool would run and risk a far tougher sentence."

"Mr. Twain," Judge Attic interjected, "do you have credible evidence to support abduction?"

"I have no idea where my client is or what's going on."

Hugely unmoved, Judge Attic announced, "Mr. Judson's bond is forfeit. I'm issuing a fugitive warrant for his arrest. Also, I want further charges filed against the defendant, regarding his failure to appear." Gavel smacked, he called out, "Dismissed!"

Courtroom emptied, the place smelt of failure, the sheer bitterness of it. Lauren-Son stayed affixed to that hard, unyielding bench the longest interval, scared, angry, searching for clarity.

Chapter Seventy-Four: Walker

Come dusk, highway merging with gravel, dry grasses scraping sides of his rental truck, Walker pulled off to park. Day still hot, no signs of let up, yesterday's telepathic missive—*Death is near*—swelled his brain.

Ma's dying, he sensed in his gut. Unable to secure permission to leave—the court would've refused if asked—the timing could not have been worse.

And so, sensible self-preservation cast aside, curiosity and sense of duty winning out, he and Ma would now reconnect.

Walker reached for a smoke, thumbed the lighter, studied the flame, decided against it, climbed down from the cab, and marched past the hen house, till he came to the barn. Wood planks missing, doors sagging open, he peered inside.

Past and present blurring: stalls empty, feed bin long unused, the scythe, the harrows—all farm equipment missing—the stairs to the hayloft, his favorite boyhood place, had rotted and crumbled.

He backed up to study the fields, the house, and the pens where animals once lived. The farm, he recalled, had been small: eighty acres in all. The upper pasture, once grazed by cows and sheep, the lower pasture for planting—all had fallen into disuse.

Across the way an old woman, enveloped within an immense, droopy sweater, crunched through gravel. Hand cupped to cheek, the woman—Ma—traced, then re-traced steps, muttering softly.

Hugging shadows, Walker crept up.

Ma sniffed air, whirled about, peering into the shadows. "Anybody there?" she called out.

Walker tucked back to elude her.

Loneliness of old overwhelmed. Always, his sense of emptiness blurred with this place. To find *home*—his idealized version—he'd once hoped, might permit him to know a normal state.

Yet, certainly, *home* never existed here. And mistakenly, he'd imposed himself upon Buena Vista, hoping it would prove to be that elusive, safe haven.

Yet *home* had nothing to do with where his body resided. *Home* was where his soul found peace.

But peace had yet to be found.

"Where you at woman?" a husky, stooped man—Pa—called out through the screen. "Come...Git in."

Screen hinges groaning, Ma disappeared inside.

Reached back through time, no longer a grown man, suddenly a boy—memories, longing, crippling helplessness hit full force to jam and engulf him. Straining to recall happy times—Ma's seashells aside—a single memory came to mind.

Pa brought home a card table with four metal folding chairs and set them beneath their shadiest, broadest oak. Chairs being of deepest blue, the precise shade he imagined the ocean prior to setting eyes upon it, offered welcome respite from sweltering heat. So, seeking to cool himself, he pressed his face to the smooth chairseat. Ma caught him at it once, then mushed her own cheeks onto the soothing blue.

Both fell back convulsed, giggling.

Sorrier memory drifting up, picking time done, Ma filled a box with cast-off clothes and took him along to a migrant farmer's shack, where a droop-bellied woman invited them in. Body folded to enter, chicks clucked, clambering within a blackened fry pan that rested atop a makeshift stove; a lone mattress served as the room's only other furnishing. Yet the space glowed, happy, warm, as a crop of runny-nosed children, in various stages of undress, stared shyly.

The woman motioned her biggest, who dragged in a crate and offered it for Ma to sit. The smallest, croupiest, scooted into Ma's lap, then all clambered, vying for attention.

Ma, cooing, tickling, gathered and hugged each of them as Walker stared, stupefied, then leaned into her knee. She pushed him off, distracted.

Desperately he'd sought Ma's touch. Longing so strong, one time he'd wrapped arms round her neck; she'd pulled back, averting her face, claiming her lips to be ticklish.

Rare occasions, when she attempted a kiss, she studiously leaned in, eyes squeezed shut, lips puckered to smooch air. Gone awkward at such demonstrativeness, she'd then fluster and go blotchy.

Physical contact rare, the boy created his own form of caress. Satin binding salvaged from a used-up blanket retrieved from Ma's saving pile, he carried the silken strip about. Then, when craving hit, he'd whip out the ribbon, run it round his neck, behind ears, trail it inside his shirt, and seesaw it between toes.

Urge satisfied, fabric crammed into a pocket, he'd resume his business.

Now, as he lurked in the shadows, irony hit. Delia, an invasive toucher, stabbed with fingers, encircling with tentacle-like limbs, depositing an onslaught of juicy kisses upon his lips, cheeks—any and everywhere. Neglect to reciprocate, she'd pout and punish, pulling away.

Touch, it seemed, confirmed Delia's very existence. Whereas, touch these days for Walker meant subjugation and risk.

And so, much akin to touching those whom he healed, observing Ma from a this distance felt about right, with Ma vulnerable and him in control—wholly different from how he'd felt as a child.

After years of preparation...imagining how their reunion would go—unaccustomed feelings unleashed just now—*Tomorrow*, he resolved, *I'll show myself.*

But not today.

Chapter Seventy-Five: Walker

Walker slept in the truck and awoke as Pa drove past.

No longer gargantuan—yet to cave in to sagging fat—his father's bold, red facial scar leapt out.

How, he wondered, *had that scar—that permanently fixed snarl—shaped Pa's mindset?*

Surely, Pa was once an innocent. Afraid. Sad. Alone—same as Walker had been. Yet the notion of Pa as vulnerable eluded capacity to fathom.

Most who share blood ties are bonded by unconditional acceptance. Yet, despite passage of many years, Walker's lack of feeling for this man—good, bad, indifferent—discomfited.

Scratching a day's beard growth, he gazed about. City sprawl cresting the hill, houses spit onto former orchards to engulf his family's farmlands. Sight of such clutter intruding upon the landscape careening his thoughts the direction of his own inevitable future, firmly, he tamped them down again.

Climbed down from the cab, he hopped the fence. Mud sucking at boots, he went down the drive past the debris-clogged cattle chute.

The farm, as it loomed, never given to spit and polish, appeared far shabbier in daylight. Once a tribute to Ma's green thumb, weeds choked the vegetable garden, and a loosely hung gate permitted animals to plunder freely.

The orchard, a scatter of rotted stumps where trees once proudly stood, had grown the juiciest fruit. Ma tended each tree as if a beloved pet, lavishing them with compliments and treats of extra-rich soil. Behind Pa's back, she'd named each sapling for a martyred saint: Saint Agatha of the amputated breasts; Saint Lucy, whose eyes got plucked; Saint Jude, not martyred, but patron of hopeless causes.

Openly studying the house, Walker crossed the yard. Blurred

beneath peeling paint and years of neglect, the structure seemed a giant soggy stain. Several windows had been broken out; others were boarded up; a blue plastic tarp, tacked up top, gently lofted with breezes. Haphazard junkpiles: newspapers, heaps of furniture, boxes, dishes, and the innards of several refrigerators were strewn about. And machinery parts—all kinds—spilt forth giving the impression of an ongoing yard sale.

Halted at the porch steps, intake of moist morning air, Walker sought to relax. Up the stairs he then went, threading across the porch— newspaper stacks wobbled, spilling, sliding underfoot—to rap on the screen, and then step back. "Did you forget your wallet, Hollis?" Ma called straightaway. Her voice, familiar—yet not—sounded as if her head were underwater, bubbles blown from nostrils.

"Ah…" Walker sought a reply from the clutch of his throat. "No, ma'am."

Fireplace poker aloft, a shadowy figure came to the screen. "If you're selling stuff, I'm not interested."

Achy tenderness flooded him. "It's me, Ma. Your son."

"Wha—? No!" Hands flung up; poker clattering, Ma hid her cheek. "Go now. You're trespassing!"

Terrible pain spread in waves, scalding, cleaving him.

Suddenly curious, Ma peered out. "What is it you want?"

"How are you getting on, Ma?"

Walker came further onto the porch. Daylight yet to reach there, surrounding chaos stunned. Balls of string strewn everywhere, flies buzzed, swarming. Broken dishes had been tossed among food-filled canning jars. Worn-out furniture commingled with new. Kitchen utensils, price tags still dangling, lay in heaps, and smelly buckets of goo, as if guarding the junk, lined the veranda.

Over the years, against his better judgment, Walker sent Ma a steady trickle of donated items: crated mangoes flown in from Hawaii; radio innards, most likely stolen; a wig collection left by a deceased patient. Sight of the jumble, everything askew, he deeply regretted having done done so.

Screen door unlatched, side of her face covered, Ma poked her head out to give him a once over. "You've grown," she announced, as if he'd gone off, overly long, to run an errand and had just returned.

Walker grinned, friendly-like. "Been a while, hasn't it?"

"I suppose you want to come in." Turned away, shoulder blades jutting as if truncated wing stumps, Ma walked off, door whapping shut.

Hinges squealing, Walker stepped inside.

No way had the yard prepared him for the madness within. Supersaturated spectacular mess, a tornado seemed to have swirled all contents. Broken parts attempting to be made whole merged, striving to integrate with those that were intact. Objects clawing, clinging, his breath came with difficulty as he surveyed the scene.

Mountains—cardboard boxes, heaps of newspaper, and stacked buckets—loomed in the dusty haze. Piles of catalogs—Sears, J.C. Penney, and others—clambered roofward to obscure walls. Antiques, treated with equal esteem to junk, were randomly scattered. Unopened mail accumulated atop all surfaces. Likely, Pa's ancient sofa hid there beneath debris. And mildew scented everything.

His own habit—he drew the parallel—stealing bits of people's lives to then hoard power over them—same as Ma's proclivity to hoard objects—suggested both were empty, trying to fill up.

Ma nowhere in sight, figuring she'd taken the narrow path to the kitchen, Walker crab-walked sideways, stepping over magazines that slid underfoot and detoured around five TVs stacked, totem pole fashion. The antenna plunked up top—bent double—hit the ceiling.

Sweet fruity spoilage assailing, trying not to gag, he called into the kitchen, "You here?"

Clutter everywhere, this space, too, debris filled, no surface had been spared. Window ledges studiously slathered with salvaged lard blobs, dirty pots, pans, dishes, and past-ripe fruit covered all, floor included. Grease stained curtains, begging to be washed, dangling limply, there Ma stood in the only cleared space, ironing.

Ironing! Walker snorted to abort a chuckle.

Hand whapped up, Ma hid her cheek.

Walker gripped the doorjamb, tried to speak but could not.

He *did* stare openmouthed.

Poorly hidden behind Ma's joint-swollen hand, resided a misshapen smear of a nose. Her right brow, eye socket, cheek, and jaw bore a deep indent. Easily, a balled fist fit within its curve. No teeth present, dentures or otherwise, her gums sloshed. Her right eye's mucus-orbed socket failed to move or focus. Rag drawn, she wiped fluid as it steadily wept.

Burst of breath, Walker asked, "Did Pa do—?"

She cut him off.

"Dredging up the past won't help. Besides...It's really a gift."

Walker tried again. "Looks like someone poured hot—"

Ma cut in.

"Never mind!" Bad side turned away, she kept ironing. "I'd ask you to sit, but as you see, can't."

Diesel truck roaring past in the distance, Ma froze, looked to the window, then turned her gaze upon him. Past rushed in quivering, pulsing—watching, warily, she studied her son.

Reunion imagined in all possible permutations, having longed for this moment his entire life, nothing, whatsoever, prepared Walker for how it was.

Debris used to insulate—to seal out life—Ma lived among chipped, strewn dishes and an infinity of tightly wound string balls. Her life had been ground down into a groove, a groove so deep, she could not climb back out of it. So, despite the urge to prove his worth, he who'd helped many, saw the futility of rescue.

Sorrow—pity mostly—overwhelming, tempted to hug her, if he tried, she'd scurry off.

Worse, she'd throw him out.

And so he leaned at the doorframe to wait.

"Well now"—Ma made a guttural prompt—"tell me about yourself."

"Let's see...," Walker groped, "I'm a healer, founded a healing center called The Living Light. I'm married. Delia's my wife."

"Any children?" Ma's longing, so naked, incised him.

"Work keeps me too busy."

"Ahhh." Steam hissing from the iron, she made careful passes over fabric.

"I live in Buena Vista. It has amazing views. You'd like it."

"I know." Steadily she stared him down, daring him to question.

Surprise covered, Walker chatted away, describing the leaning, nearly toppled buildings and the out-of-style apparel sold at Leticia

Opplinger's. Wanting her to know him, working to seize her interest, he thought to add, "I have this friend, Rosalee Soo; she's like a mother." Ma looked up, pained.

"A mother?"

Oddly satisfied to have riled her, he switched topics. "There's also this strange man who works with me; he's a powerful healer, probably better at it than I am."

"What's he like?"

"Very short. He's a great help." Fondness surged as Walker spoke. "He gives fine advice and is my...my best man."

"How about his hands?"

"Funny you ask. He always wears gloves, never goes without."

"Quite so!" Lint brushed from fabric, Ma resumed her task. "I enjoy the gifts you've sent. Particularly the piano."

"You knew, then?"

"Naturally." She flapped a hand: a move he dearly loved.

Awkwardness in the air, silence opened to engulf.

The clock ticked away, relentless.

Having steeled himself for Ma's imminent death, this animate person required adjustment.

"And..." Ma urged, "what else?"

Tongue come loose, onward he blathered about his youthful travels, how lost he'd felt, yet how he'd found his way; the conflicts with Delia; his success as a healer, the satisfaction garnered. He even touched on his current tribulations.

Life rendered up for her approval, he talked to fill the great abyss, talked to reclaim his place as her son, talked to fill years of absence, of loss, of longing that spanned a lifetime.

Love me, please, he thought to implore. Desperate, he asked instead, "Do you suppose it's possible to have thought without words?"

"Dunno." Ma shrugged, hung the freshly ironed garment on a hanger, fished through the hamper, pulled our another, placed it on the ironing board, and took up a steady rhythm again.

"I don't know either," Walker allowed, "but words give life to what we think and feel. Words give us a way to see this room, for instance." He paused, unsure what came next.

"Yes?" Ma urged.

"Words help us forget pain and silence. Words uncloak mystery. Speaking enables us to connect, to keep us from feeling alone. Ma...," he plead, "say something." Ma kept on making passes over fabric.

"I'm out of practice," she said at last, "but *do* want you to know one thing. See these eyes..." Head lifted, she dropped the guarding hand.

Catching full view of the ravages, Walker emitted a dry rasp.

Ma continued, "They aren't much to behold, but they've seen wondrous, unimaginable sights. Trouble is... When I look in the mirror, I'm confounded to see the peculiar creature attached to them."

"Yessu'm."

"So now you think you can help, but, truly, what I need, only God can fix." Craned close, she assumed a low tone. "What I need, what I crave is a spiritual atmosphere."

"You mean a convent?"

"As my time draws to a close, my longing to know God expands and grows. Longing forms in my mouth like a pulpy rind, so strong, I taste it. Words, fancy or not, are useless to describe it. You'd never guess..." Drip wiped from chin, she twinkled at him. "God was once easily accessible to me." Good eye sparkling, Ma turned mischievous. "Remember the conch?"

"Sure do."

"Put to my ear, it shared wondrous tales." Ma reprised that familiar ecstatic far-away look.

"You still have it?"

Ma bent her head. "Had to send it off. All of them, in fact." She looked back up.

"That reminds me...," Walker interjected. "As soon as you sent The Angel, my life—"

Ma interrupted.

"I never sent it. Is that why you've come?" Walker regarded her, perplexed.

"I assumed you had. After it arrived, I started doing healings. I always wanted to say how grateful—"

"But I didn't!" She shot a sharp look, then resumed ironing.

Long had he believed she'd catalyzed his life as a healer by sending it, so he retreated into his mind, baffled. *If Ma hadn't sent The Angel, then who?*

Furthermore: *Was this a mistake, risking so much to come, and was Ma truly near death?* No sure signs evident, no fleshy transparency common to the moribund, her energy field, though not potent or lively, vibrated at a decent rate.

"Tell you what you can do for me," Ma spoke in a rush. "I'm partial to bananas. Not the stubby, fat kind, but the long, pointy ones. You can't just grab any old bunch, they have to be individually selected. I'd appreciate if you'd buy me some."

"OK. Sure." Bananas being easily gummed, he moved to go.

"Also…," she called him back. "I need this stuff—I just had it…" Scrabbling through an imposing heap, she produced an empty bottle of denture adhesive.

Bottle in hand, he departed, pondering, *What had I hoped to find here? Forgiveness? Connection? Healing? Cleansing?*

Toting grocery bags, Walker helped store foodstuffs and hung cheery, red curtains, bought on impulse, in the kitchen window.

Face shiny, Ma rolled on tiptoe to finger the fabric. "Really, you shouldn't have!" Pivoted to reach for him, halted mid-air, she let her hand drop.

Making it safer, Walker extended a hand. "Sometime back I changed my name. I'm called Walker Judson. Hope you don't mind."

"I recall, we never called you much except *Boy*." Ma tapped his palm, examined her finger, then shot him a quizzical look. "Is your skin always so hot?"

"Energy summoned from healings causes it."

"I lost a baby, you know." She punctuated the announcement with a tiny cough.

Swiftly, Walker switched topics. "How's the farm?"

Ma kept on.

"Got her out myself, but she died before she took breath. The Lord told me to keep her final whereabouts to myself." Walker's every fiber at attention, here was the terrible secret—one he'd long sought—that she'd withheld from Pa, it had shaped them all. "All of it was God's punishment for trying to have a normal life."

"Did you let Pa know what he'd done?"

Fists clenched, prepared to be struck, Ma braced. "That loss was the hardest thing—that and making you go—about killed me. It's just that..." Faint rumblings—curtain parted, she glanced out.

Loss of this life pivotal to shaping his, hollowness filled him. Ma had one child she hadn't the slightest idea how to raise, birthed a stillborn Pa had beaten out of her, and then blamed herself for all of it. Losing one child, then forced to send her first offspring away—the grief of it swelled.

Sorry images of old returned, he revisited the welts that bloomed into scars at Ma's neckline above her collars and at her leg backs, and heard Pa's hideous laughs as he chucked spare change, knives, and mallets at her.

Years ago, young Walker, in the manner of a bodhisattva, determined that Ma not bear her sorrow alone, seeking to match her grief with his own, applied the strap to his boyhood self to rip and sunder himself. Silence so deep, no screams could possibly fill them, came to him; at last, he understood her.

Starkly aware that his herculean efforts to be good, to heal others, altered nothing whatsoever, unwilling to delve deeper, he seized the moment to interrupt, "Gotta go, Ma."

"Come tomorrow, will you? We have matters to clear up before I go."

"I will."

No longer protecting wounds, Ma accompanied him to the door.

"Come with me?" he asked on impulse.

An impractical offer, for likely he'd be remanded to prison. Then, who would care for her?

No way, could she stay with Delia. If asked, Rosalee would take her in. Best yet, Lauren-Son would do whatever asked.

"It ends here," Ma declared, detaining him atop the porch steps, "I must know... Have you found courage yet?"

"Courage?" He gave the matter a grave moment's thought. Unquestionably, he possessed courage to act rightly in the face of opposition, shame, and scandal. Never mind how discouraged he felt, daily, he scraped himself together, despite precise knowledge as to his future, to adhere, steadfast, anyhow.

"Yes, I believe I have."

"Thanks be to God!" Ma clasped rough, veiny hands together and beamed. "Many celestials of the higher realms said you wouldn't, but they got it so very wrong!"

"See you tomorrow, Ma." Cutting across the yard, Walker hopped the fence.

Chapter Seventy-Six: Lauren

News swirled in all media of the metastasizing crisis at The Living Light. As rumors abounded, gossip and petty divisive arguments broke out among staff, volunteers, and students. So with Walker and Voden absent, and Delia and Ardis busily chumming about, Lauren-Son took charge and called a meeting. "Why not close up?" Sherman asked, gripping Rosalee's hand as the group convened. Several students nodded, fuming. Others fidgeted, refusing eye contact; it wasn't exactly great that Voden had abandoned them.

"I'm as mystified as you are about what's happened," Lauren-Son soothed. "But...No way did Walker disappear voluntarily, and if he did, there's a reasonable explanation."

"Yeah, yeah," a volunteer muttered, "the old white-wash number."

"He's dead," chimed another.

"He's alive!" snapped Lauren-Son.

Last night, she'd sensed him courteously climbing round inside her. Then abruptly, as if suddenly lurching, blindly into walls, she'd felt his pain gush out and release.

No idea what it meant, she elected to assume it boded good. "Walker knew taking off would seriously complicate matters, so if he *did* leave without good cause, he's a total dope and has let us down."

Students and volunteers turning fractious, many questions got asked, and none were answered.

To maintain order, to keep the place running, Lauren-Son assigned senior-most students to work shifts and had the newbies observe and assist them.

"We must pray," Rosalee supplied, "for Walker's safe return."

"I suspect...," Lauren-Son hastened to add, "Walker would also want us to pray for those who might be involved in his disappearance. Wish another ill, the entire world gets harmed." The group stared at her, askance.

Working to sound like Walker, to lull all into a sense of wellbeing, ignoring the looks, hands clapped hands together, she led a brief prayer. "Let's pray that each of us gains as much growth from this, regardless as to the outcome." Longing to strangle Walker, filled with the urge to get as far away from the mess as possible, her present strategy was to erect a firm wall against thinking and feeling.

Whirring clicks of her wheelchair, Danielle came late that morning. "My doctor says I have to stop coming—that the stress is too much. This whole thing has definitely broken my heart." She stared at the floor, stricken.

Squatted before the young woman, Lauren-Son sought eye contact. "Does your mom agree?"

"She refuses to bring me any more," Danielle affirmed, avoiding her gaze.

"Well then." Lauren-Son sighed, pushing up. "It's past time for me to teach you how to control your pain. Are you willing?"

Dull of eye, Danielle looked up. "I'd like that."

Lauren-Son guided the way to a treatment room and gentled Danielle onto the table. "You—everyone—possesses unlimited healing energy; it's always available. You just need to ask it to flow, then it comes." Lauren-Son flipped Danielle's hand, palm-side up, and hovered her own hand inches above. "Imagine you're running healing energies from your hand into my palm." Eyes shut, Danielle concentrated.

First as a gentle trickle, heat flowed from Danielle's hand into Lauren-Son's. And then, as if a faucet turned on, it gushed. "You've warmed my palm!" Lauren-Son enthused.

Danielle frowned at her, skeptical. "If you say so."

"I'm turning your hand over and placing it on your hip. Now, visualize that same healing energy flowing from your hand down your leg. Breathe into the pain; try to relax, soften around its edges—that should make it less intense. Imagine your hands touching all places where it hurts; mentally run healing energy in those areas to reduce discomfort. Any change?"

Tears falling from brimmed eyes, Danielle nodded, staying silent an interval, then spoke softly, "What will I do without you? Coming here gave me hope. It's...It's all I have."

Lauren-Son gave her a quick hug. "I know how strong you are. Keep doing as you just did, and you should be fine."

As Lauren-Son watched her depart, having long resided in a loving, comfy world, an unbridgeable distance opened up. Loneliness, long buried, yet familiar—same as she'd lived and breathed as a child—unearthed, as friends and patients shunned her. As a result, forgotten parts, as if displaced persons granted amnesty—insecure, neglected fragments—traipsed back, to re-implant within her psyche. She worked hard not to believe them.

Featured in a televised interview, the adorably fetching Delia, coming across unsuitably blasé, deftly dashed aside questions that annoyed, freely switched topics, and complained about her marriage. "Believe me, I have no idea where my strange husband got off to, but I assure you, he's fine."

Ardis at her side, gripping her hand, Delia addressed the camera. "Walker fancies himself a holy man, so for all I know, he's off communing with God, doing a forty-days-in-the-desert-trip."

"What a piece of work!" Lauren-Son whooped, shaking a fist at the screen.

"No sense trying to make that man adhere to a schedule," Delia continued. "He'll show back up when good and ready. And"—she leaned, suggestive, toward the interviewer—"let me tell you, honey, living with a man who thinks he's the Second Coming of Christ ain't no delight."

Hands trembling, Lauren-Son clunked her teeth with her coffee mug. Drink spilt onto her chest, into her lap, container set down, she pressed one hand with the other to still them both.

Chapter Seventy-Seven: Walker

Montage spooling before Walker as he drowsed in the truck, snippets of Ma's youth appeared. Beaming smile, high forehead, perfect straight nose, a lanky girl-child stood, mid-alfalfa field, arms flung wide, spinning in tight circles. Laughter burbled up—a sweet high ripple—faster, faster she spun as goodness strobed out from her.

Eight years old, auburn hair whacked off, she sold it to a wig maker and dropped the earnings in Saint Jude's Poor Box. Ages ten through twelve, she hid food, went without, then snuck out, handing it over to assorted, emaciated hobos.

Great knob jutted from cheek, a raving man stood before Ma as a teen. Reached up, she applied hands to the man's brow. Shower of stars racing through her inner vision, her palms bled heat. Massive swoosh—tumor shrunk to nothing—taint of madness transited into mists, the gent's babbling ceased.

Jolted, awestruck, awareness hit Walker: *Ma, too, possessed divine fingers!*

All things moved her: acuity of light glinting off leaves at dusk to deepen their precious colors; a newborn calf's lick to her palm; dust eddying the wind; Mother's tender looks as Father did his habitual boot stomp before the hearth.

All seemed God-given.

Radiance gone unseen, till one day, as she shoveled shit in the pig shed, God fully opened her up.

You are mine, blasted The Voice of Wisdom.

"Fine," she laughed, "take me!"

Boundaries blurred as aerial spirits whisked about, circulating among the fluid super-sensible realms. Drawn deep into the Mysteries, she could merge at will to commune with Christ, the Virgin Mother, and multitudes of saints.

Injustice—any sort—set her teeth on edge. Always, Ma sided with the underdog, giving comfort to the maligned, the weak, and the ill. She prayed for bullies too—that they be cleansed of the malignant spirits that gripped them.

Each kind act, she glowed more radiant, till an unmistakable halo shaped about her head—a gift she begged God to retract.

Skidded forward in time, the youngest Carmelite nun to ever take vows—family smugly supportive—she became Sister Angelica.

Cloistered, challenged to redeem the world, eagerly the young nun communed and fasted, adored the creak of the kneeler as she knelt to pray, and flooded with rapture as Latin got intoned during High Mass.

Despite bliss, questions churned. "Why, God," she demanded, "did you flood those Dakota farms to destroy all crops? And why, despite prayers to the contrary, did you allow all five Blakely children to die of the pox?"

"Pain....," God boomed, "is required to know true joy." Briefly, she considered this.

"Makes sense, I guess. But still…You needn't make life so tough for us."

Carefully observant regarding matters of Spirit, hours at a stretch, she knelt, head bowed, lost in prayer. Meanwhile, throngs of sparrows warbled, pattering chapel windows; passersby heaved deep, cleansing sighs; and surrounding vegetation shot up several notable inches.

So good was she—so obviously chosen as God's Beloved Conduit—fellow nuns, full-up with jealousy, reported her every infraction—real or imagined. Lift eyes to the cross; she got flogged. Whistle in the fields; other nuns insisted the Father Confessor silence her an entire year. Sneak porridge to the sickly groundskeeper's son; months after, she was made to sup with the hogs.

Onward she prayed, anyhow, "God, please heal my peers' hate and envy."

Habitually her sister nuns scorned heathens and churchgoers alike—the very objects of their arduous prayers—a detail that sorely perplexed her. Ordinary folk, her peers insisted, blasphemed at every turn and weren't to be trusted. In their view, every parishioner, if given a chance, would rob the church blind!

Quite the opposite, she opined: *The church soaked the poor for all they were worth!*

No longer able to abide the surety of the church's embrace, more contradictions sprang to mind. Big sticking point: humans are born and die, then, saved or not, move on to their eternal reward.

Thing of it is, God told her different. Birth and death, heaven and hell are *not* all there is... There's so much more.

God had informed her.

Uncertain if God caused her to stray or if the devil's mischief plagued her, more questions sundered: *Why are non-Catholics, even good ones, damned to eternal hell? Why is the church immensely wealthy when poor folk starve? How can a celibate priest possibly offer sound marital advice? Why are Christians, who claim to bask in God's love, so quick to judge?*

Ground of her essential being slipping, sliding, she questioned all of it.

Why are humans predisposed to evil? And what's the purpose of suffering?

A perplexing oddity cropped up: all deceased, unbaptized newborns got consigned to a slurping, sucking place called limbo. Certainly, limbo appears in Scripture, but surely, He hadn't devised such an unloving concept.

Sadly and surprisingly, God went mute at this juncture, which made her quite wretched.

Seeking to discover the truth, Sister Angelica sought an audience with Mother Superior. "I request permission to leave for a time." The good mother gaped, horrified.

"Have you lost your mind! That's just not done!"

Ever-obedient, Sister Angelica complied. *Wasn't life good anyway?* she tried to convince herself. *Aren't I serving God?*

Rather than abate, dissatisfaction festered.

Unable to abide the badmouthing of parishioners, she disagreed with her sisters ever so sweetly. Regarding Scripture, she argued outright against nonsensical details. "Old Testament Prophet Jeremiah stood in the marketplace to trumpet out God's anguish. So, if my own visions are God given, why is it that I, as a female, am forbidden to teach in public?"

"It's…," Mother Superior spluttered, "simply not permitted!"

Gripped with certainty that God meant her a more generous hearted life, one more connected with humanity, imploring for guidance, she fasted and prayed ceaselessly.

Five years into her stay, as she knelt one day, fingering rosary beads in the convent garden, despite ants busily tunneling her robes and pesky yellow jackets tweaking her ears, there she remained, untwitching, hours on end.

Evening bells tolled, calling all to Mass. Sister Angelica, flung prostrate onto damp earth, gave serious thought to forsaking her goal, but then called out, "Please God, forgive my impatience, but I do all You say, even the silly senseless things—including directions that contradict other stuff.

"I made myself Your bride, gave You my life. I get that You want me to change my path, yet You offer no guidance. Please…I beg You—I ask most respectful—should I stay or should I go?" Quite some time she went on like this, her asking—begging, really—with God ignoring.

Twilight bore down. Wasps ceased to drone. Distant yelp, a dog bark—earth turned chilly, then colder.

A strong. hollow moan boomed from nowhere; might've been the wind, but the wind hadn't blown. "Go!" it roared.

Head lifted, Sister Angelica saw no one. Yet, wind sucked from lungs, she doubled over.

Every speck—pores included—flooding with light, rapture overtook her.

Immensity filling, spreading, she'd never felt the like.

Mysteries unfolded. Whirring, breathy prayers. Gregorian chants. Angels—a chorus—flooded in, offering a peek at God's Will as it gently nestled within her everlasting soul.

"Praise be!" she'd whooped.

Armed with the keenest sense of God's intent, determined to make her mark by doing simple good works, Sister Angelica departed the convent.

Prayerful talents notwithstanding, ill prepared for life outside, trying to make sense of an immense, insane world proved daunting. So she sought help from family.

"God cast you out," her father growled, "so we can't abide you among us."

Swiftly, her mother reached around her father to crumple an envelope into her hand.

Fearing sin's contagion, father slammed the door.

Just then a segment of her soul withered, tore off, and disappeared. So away she went, lost and wandering.

Given God's stark absence, she blocked all joy and pleasure. Should a laugh arise unbidden, she slammed a fist to her mouth. Unable to forsake sorrow and loss, daily her light diminished.

A year into near starvation, she retrieved and tore open the envelope her mother had handed her: a deceased maiden aunt, it seemed, making no judgment as to her altered status, had left her the farm.

So there she'd sought refuge to collect her wits, to find purpose and meaning, and most of all, to reconnect with God.

Past unblocked, Ma permitted her son to view the vast empty silence that followed.

Tumbled back into his body, disoriented, full of wonder, absorbing daybreak's soft blur, Walker sat in the truck and pondered all he'd witnessed.

Was it God's intent that Ma's life went as it had, or could she have used free will to change it?

Chapter Seventy-Eight: Walker

Next morning, after Pa drove off, Walker banged at the porch screen.

Door fumbled open, Ma stammered, "It...it's time." Lack of vigor surrounding her, she groped, wending her way through the debris-filled maze.

Steeling himself, Walker followed.

Slow going up stairs, Ma halted at each step to catch breath.

At the top, Walker took the lead, shoving trash to carve a path, edging down the hall to Ma's bedroom, to make space on the mattress. Ma grappled with her mucklucks; he slid them off and helped her lie down.

Struggled upright, dentures extracted from a glass, she sucked them in place, and settled back.

Walker went to touch her. "Don't!" She recoiled. "It hurts too much."

Heart lurching, he pulled up a crate and sat down to wait.

Each inhale, he breathed with her. Each exhale, he sent her—not life force—but unspent love.

Rather than gift her, each breath—crepitation louder, longer—she gifted him instead. "I sent those visions—always, you wanted to know."

"It's an honor to finally have grasp of you." Unabashed, he grinned.

"I believe you visited me from time to time as well."

"Indeed." Pleasure arisen between them, again, Walker resisted the urge to touch her.

"At one time...," voice faltering, Ma pressed, "as if lifting the phone receiver to find the operator waiting, God was ever at my beckon. Each conversation jetted me straight out of my body from sheer bliss. But according to Mother Superior, I was overly prideful about our connection. I *did* lack proper humility, I suppose. It's what caused later troubles with Pa." Sigh wheezed, she rested, eyes shut.

Her damaged eye—the transparency of egg yolk—throbbed and pulsed.

Horrific damage notwithstanding, Walker, scanning the ravages that once comprised her face, bore witness to the constellation of her every freckle, wrinkle, and mole. All beloved contours gravely saddened, her formerly clear, wide eyes, now limited to a solitary functional one, gazed upon the world with fierce suspicion and wariness. He thought to blurt how much he'd missed her—that the loss had removed an essential chunk of his being.

"Where was I..." Ma used a sleeve to wipe drips from her cheek. Walker sat, attentive, as she got back at it. "When first arrived, this farm was in such disarray, but it helped, some, that I'd been a farmer's daughter. So sunup to sundown, I worked without let-up.

"First season, when hailstones decimated my alfalfa crop, assuming the event as God's clever test of my intent, I laughed idiotically, wrung out my hat, dumped water from my boots, and reseeded that field again. Hard as I labored, though, I couldn't manage alone." Not eager to hear what came next, Walker lit up a smoke and took a long, hard toke.

Ma pushed on. "Pa was once very nice, you know." Walker couldn't fathom it. "Arrived in search of work, he took my shabby holdings into account, and looked me up and down. Back then, I was big boned, skeletal thin, had raw-knuckled mannish hands—nothing much to look at. But I *did* have an expectant air, as if, any second, wondrous things might come to pass. So Pa took me for a flirt, I guess.

"He slept in the barn, worked to make himself indispensable, till eventually he ran the place. For a time we were at ease with each other." Ma cast up a bashful look. "Our eyes caught and held as our hands skimmed, passing food platters. Come evening, we sat by the hearth, toasting out toes, allowing silences. Soon as Pa crept into my bed, though, everything changed. Treating me as if I were farm chattel, he did as he pleased with me. And, well"—Ma dabbed her good eye—"you know the rest."

"Did you try to connect with family again?"

Face contracted, Ma turned to the window to follow a crow in flight.

Perhaps she contemplated the coming day, perhaps her dwindling life. Walker thought she wept, but wasn't certain.

At last, she spoke, "To them I was dead."

Wanting to give comfort, hands wrestled together, Walker stared off instead.

"Stubborn old me, spoiled by past intimacy, I still imagined God would blast back into my life and define my higher purpose. Clearly, however, this wasn't meant to be.

"Was I doomed to live this small life?" She indicated the room, the farm. "Had I misinterpreted His intent for me? Unable to accept my puny existence, I prayed for clarity. Yet, only vast insurmountable emptiness—in the form of perpetual exile—engulfed. Had God abandoned me? That question, never far from my thoughts, was why I stayed absent."

Walker scrubbed his cheeks, pondering: *What have I learned, I who've seen the agony of many?*

That there seems no limit to the misery God inflicts. And that humankind cannot avoid or make the slightest sense of any of it. Throat cleared, he spouted wrote comfort: "I believe God has good reason for everything."

"Makes as much sense as anything else." Eyes shut, Ma seemed to scan within, talking as she did so, "However, it felt as if the God, who professes to forgive, refused to forgive me. I prayed anyway to ease my burden. And I prayed for understanding. No reply forthcoming, I then prayed for peace of mind and…much later…prayed to accept my lot.

"Years into it, as you witnessed, I tried suicide. When that failed, I tried to create a life—narrow as it was. Years now, my misery has simmered, nearly tolerable." Voice trailed off, she lay immobile, scarcely taking a breath.

Walker flared. *Prayers—heaps of them—make no difference. God speaks to whomever He wants, whatever way He chooses, yet mostly He ignores us.*

"Matter of fact," Walker offered up, "since I've hit this rough patch, I've struggled to find God as well."

Ma fumbled upright. Ready to help, he scooted close. "You said you were in a pickle, son, so that's why I've shared. Same as me, you possess great knowledge, but have severe limitations caused by imbalance. What I didn't understand then, but know now—this might help—a life, once given to God, despite detours and self-destructive acts, never ceases its path. I failed to grasp this, but you can trust it as fact."

Both fell silent.

Walker found her hand within his grasp. How it got there, he hadn't the slightest.

Ma's suffering, her misspent life, her inability to touch or to connect drew down upon him. Worst of all, certain of God's abandonment, she'd abandoned herself...and also her son.

His own blunders come to sharp focus, he glimpsed his perpetual sense of exile and his inability to connect, his withholding from Delia, his obsessive need for order—that tidiness might give him control over the uncontrollable—and that his pontificating gave him sway over others.

Ma's flaws and suffering being essential to her salvation—he realized his own flaws and suffering might redeem him as well.

Good eye lifted, Ma's gaze fell upon him.

Much changed since yesterday; no longer at the mercy of anything, she radiated love.

Steady warmth flooding in—joy in him now—finally, at long last, he felt loved.

Walker slid to his knees. "God have mercy upon your soul, Ma... and on mine." Face pressed into hands, he wept.

Ma reached to stroke him. "Dear boy, listen… I've never said so, but you've done me proud."

He tried to speak. She cut in, "I've not been much of a mother, but *did* confer my best to you."

Cheeks wiped, it came to him: Never, had she wanted him to go, but, subsuming her own need, had sacrificed him up to a better life.

"Something's troubled me ever so long; just now I have the answer." Ma chuffed several breaths. "My attachment to God, the notion that He and I had something special, caused my suffering. My prayerful gyrations, the stuff I collected—seashells included—meant nothing but greater attachment. I thought I knew so much, but it was just a wee pinch." Hand lifted with great effort, thumb and forefinger tweezed to indicate a smidgen, she then let it drop.

"And...I must tell you...the man you call Voden...we were nuns together. Also...he helps us."

"That a fact?"

Voden, sensing Walker's imminent departure, tried prevent it. "Go, and you undo everything!"

Quite the tussle ensued, so Walker had retreated on foot, leaving his truck behind.

For one so diminutive, Voden packed quite a wallop; Walker massaged his jaw remembering.

That Voden possessed the same indecipherable aura as Ma's—enormity dizzying, he worked to kink these tidbits into alignment.

Clangs pealed the air. Walker clapped hands to ears. Ma looked to the window and grinned.

"Church bells; I rather enjoy them."

Cacophony deafening, spreading in waves, hitting the floor, the walls, Walker's jaw, his throat—the sounds vibrated, rearranging cells, till gradually, they dimmed.

"It's time," Ma announced.

"Should you tell Pa?"

"Given his take, I'm long gone." Covers flung back, she pulled up taller than ordinary height.

Air wobbling, sucking, it transported them out to the yard.

"I'm glad you've come." Caress to his cheek, Ma moved to depart. Walker reached to restrain her.

She eluded grasp. "You must release me."

Sky cracked open to reveal stillness—immense, eternal—a smoky wisp hovering above descended to engulf the woman he knew as Ma.

Swiftly, she merged and melded with it. "Set yourself free, Mama!" Walker cried, fully fortified.

The future, whatever it held, would now be tolerable.

Chapter Seventy-Nine: Lauren

Three weeks subsequent to Walker's disappearance, Lauren-Son received a whispered phone call. "Come to...," the eerily familiar voice trailed off.

"That you, Walker?" No way was this his voice; it might have been Voden's, though.

"Go to Fort Blunt, above the Laundromat. Tell no one." Abrupt click, the call ended.

Rumpled shirt and coveralls donned, without hesitation or sensible thought, skimpy note scrawled, she wrote, *Gone to find Walker,* then out she rushed and drove off.

Storm clouds squatted, following overhead. Winds kicked up, lightening crashed, and rain pelted, as relief overtook her. *Walker had surfaced!*

Then again, fearing what she'd find—feelings for him shifting, recalibrating—she thought it best to view him as a dear friend in need of help.

But...Had he run? If so, why? Moreover, am I walking into danger, and should I have alerted the authorities?

Even bigger: *am I so stupidly naive to still believe in him?*

If he was fine, she'd insist he turn himself in, also that he get his brain checked.

Hours later, she drove into Fort Blunt, found the Laundromat, parked, raced upstairs, located the room and knocked.

No reply, door tried, hinges creaking open, hotly sour smells assailed as she surveyed the scene. Kitchenette cupboards hung loose. Burnt foodstuffs dribbled from the hotplate to encrust the floor. Overturned chairs lay about, and empty tin cans had been chucked among debris. At room's far end, a rag pile shifted. A muffled moan arose from it.

"Walker?" she called as she crept close. "I've come."

Palpable suffering emanated from that mound—the room seethed with it. And Lauren-Son, who'd witnessed all manner of disturbance, was no way eager to unveil what lay beneath.

Pile stirring, muffled inhuman croaking fell out from it.

She forced herself to squat. Hand brushed across fabric's surfaces, pincer bugs scampered, obscenely, from its folds. Delicately, she lifted a corner. Brackish sickening stench—pus and rot assailing—the blanket refused to budge.

Harder tug, the fabric released. Chunks of blood-encrusted flesh coming with, scabbed-over skin opened and bled. "Sorry," Lauren-Son whispered, "I have to see what's happened."

Up to rummage the kitchen, she filled a pan from the tap, located a suitable rag, then returned to the heap to meticulously dab at torn skin and gradually peel fabric back.

Times, when Walker panted, she ran healing energy into his hurts. As his breaths smoothed out, she reapplied traction to fabric.

Three hours, dozens of fresh pans of water later, every inch of him a laceration, bruise, or gash, Walker released from his shroud.

Riven with agony, his face bore strong semblance to The Angel's new look. Nose bulbous and mashed aside, his eyes—puckers of pain—formed slits, and his right ear had a bite taken. Incapable of grasping a spoon or of making controlled movement, his hands—once such miraculous tools—pained her most. Startling misshapen, all bones pulverized, both lay limp.

Fighting tears, they ran down Lauren-Son's cheeks anyway. "You need a doctor," she urged. Walker shook all over, refusing. "You're badly injured. I can't fix you." He formed a wrenching sound; this too meant refusal.

"Ma, Ma," he croaked and thrashed as if a wild, trapped animal.

"I'm here, Walker," Lauren-Son cooed. "I won't let anyone hurt you."

Climbing onto the mat, she encircled him; he went slack against her, and soon his breath shuttled in and out, relaxed.

He muttered; she strained to hear. "Divine Plan..." Murmuring unintelligible, he went on at length, alternately railing against, then praising God for this and that.

Lauren-Son up and bolted to the restroom to blurt, "Little help here, God!"

Faucet leaking away, it made steady *ploit-ploits.*

"Maybe Walker hasn't lost faith," she screeched, "but how am I to believe Your freakin' Divine Plan when you permit such a mess?"

Vocalization—not her own—sprang into her head. *You expect justice to prevail over the Divine Plan. However...All is perfect, though you think it isn't. Just heal him.* This wasn't Walker's voice but was certainly something he might've said.

"How am I to use healing energies when I'm struggling to believe?"

The voice came again: *He'll heal if you help him.*

"I'm far too pissed!"

Anger's good. Use it to enliven him.

"OK!" She marched back to Walker's side. "Turn on the power!"

Rage-sourced energies churning, one hand slid between Walker's shoulder blades, the other at his chest, using fingertips she scanned down into his body, probing into flesh.

Thudding chaotic oscillations informed that he was near collapse. His heart region being most healthy and warm, she anchored her hands there, emitted a high, spiking, reedy sound, then morphed into a healing conduit. Vibrations then blurted from her fingers to heal and strengthen him.

Two weeks passed. Walker's familiar furrowed brow, his deeply etched crow's feet, and tight, grimace-suppressing mouth, now discernible, the return of his precious self brought slight comfort. Yet, his misshapen hands stayed useless. Frequently, she repositioned them to increase blood flow.

And she fretted, big time. Consequence of aiding and abetting a fugitive looming, her thoughts raced, near intolerable. *Oh, my God, what have I done! I've wrecked my life; I'm so terribly stupid...*looped the refrain.

Day fifteen, Walker opened his eyes. A single tear drizzled his cheek.

Slowly, she traced the wetness. "Sad?"

Blearily, he smiled, sucking back tears. "No. Glad." Swiftly, her heart swooped into her throat.

More waiting and inaction passed. Lauren-Son changed Walker's dressings, fed and bathed him.

Days on end, he sat or lay silent, staring off into some faraway place. He wasn't unconscious, just vacant, seeming to process something immense.

Suspended, separate from time, they did not speak. Mostly, she breathed and then breathed some more. Suffering alongside him, she felt, cemented her loyalty.

Walker, a force for good, still held such power. If he wanted, she figured, he could rise up perfectly mended to set everything right.

So she awaited a sign.

Alert for hints of the miraculous, she listened, attentive, to all creaks and studied the shadows. Swishing flies from his face, she stared hard, hoping something fantastic might communicate itself. Out for supplies, she dissected every nuanced conversation with store clerks.

And then…and then, as she held Walker's bloodstained sheet to the light, she squinted and fumbled. For its tatters bore the precise imprint of his suffering, eye-closed face!

Could blood do that? she marveled. Moreover…*Was this the miracle?*

Put to the test, she soaked the sheet in the sink.

Water inky red—the bloodstains faded into oblivion.

So sadly, perhaps, *Walker was a mere mortal after all.*

Week five, rain pelting outside, Walker cracked open an eye to watch as she ran healing energy into him. "Guess I'll be around a while," he croaked.

She cupped a hand over his. "Care to say what happened?"

"It—it's all…hazy." His words came haltingly. "Knew it was wrong to leave—that doing so would have grave consequences—but had to. Was glad I went; great forgiveness came to pass." Eyes misting up, he stared straight ahead, then said, "I'll tell more later."

Walker left of his own free will—was glad he had!

Repelled, disbelieving, swiftly she bricked a layer of numbness around her anxiety.

Next day, Walker tried again: "I was asleep in the rental truck when unseen hands snatched me. Darkness everywhere, I heard humming—a car engine, men arguing—they'd sealed me in a coffin-like box." Lauren-Son gasped a breath.

Eyes shut, he resumed in low monotone, "A pipe vented air. Couldn't move; I'd been trussed and drugged. Sudden blinding light, lid opened, pain seared my crimped limbs as I straightened them. That's all I recall, until I awoke here."

Near as Lauren-Son could piece together, Walker had attended his mother's deathbed, planned to turn himself in after, but got abducted, beaten unconscious, and left for dead.

Still...His tale seemed so far-fetched, authorities would easily poke holes in it. But maybe complainants' families—the husbands—*had* abducted him.

"It pleases me that you've risked much to come." His tone, like a caress, left her tremulous.

"Isn't this odd?" she asked idiotically.

"What?"

"Me caretaking you."

"It's exactly as is meant to be." His words gave her goose bumps.

Flooded with feeling, she exited into the hall, pressed brow to wall to gather her wits, then returned.

Penetrating gaze putting her more ill at ease, he followed her every move.

Attempting nonchalance as she leaned across to adjust his blanket, her arm brushed his face. Heart pounding at a gallop, a sudden thought illuminated: *I love him...always have!*

Scared to touch him, rather than perform her usual hands-on healing, she sat a safe distance and sent out mental streamers to fix him instead.

Closely, Walker watched her.

Lips feeling fluffy, she had no idea how best to configure her face. "Hey," he said.

"Hey yourself."

Big with joy, he raised up and opened his arms. "Come."

Knowing full-well all would change, she went into them and pushed into his neck.

Woozy with desire, she pulled back to raise a questioning brow.

More words in Walker's eyes than he'd ever spoken aloud—oh, those amazing eyes of his!

Lost in their deep pools, she saw intimacy...and love.

Face suffused with gentleness, he placed a hand over her heart.

Warmth seeping in, fear fading, expansive whoosh, something humongous broke loose; she assumed the same happened for him as well.

He pulled her close to trace her spine. No move pained him; indeed, he seemed to mend.

Sparks flying, thrilling, fabulous, there they clung, beyond words.

She loved him then with all her might.

Boldly, she leaned, lips hovering inches from his.

Mouth tasting like carnations, tongue slid into her mouth, he rewarded her with a sucking kiss—no mere dry peck, but an open-mouthed kiss—one impossible to mistake for that of a friend.

Lips brushing, bodies pressing, onto his mat she clambered.

Pulled back, Lauren-Son emitted an uncharacteristic giggle.

Gusts, hilarity, descended.

Walker laughed, all-out. His whole body shook as he used the mitts of his hands to wipe his eyes.

But, then he turned somber.

Eyes holding hers, voice resonant, he announced, "First off, I've always loved you since forever."

Conveying the same, she gave him a soft look. "I love you too."

"Ahh," Walker fumbled sweetly. "You must understand…"

Finger to his lips, she unbuttoned her shirt, and then shed her clothes.

"Stand so I can see you," Walker commanded, thick in the throat.

Awkward, shy, she stood to slowly pivot, but culminated in a bold spin. "Lovely." His voice came ragged. Indeed, first time ever, Lauren-Son felt without blemish.

Hungry for lips and tongue, she helped him fully disrobe.

Care taken to pleasure her, he stroked her every inch. Then, skin on skin, hips grinding, pressing, he hardened. "I'm afraid I'll hurt you," she protested just slightly.

Walker chuffed her cheek. No need to fear hurting him, the more they touched, the more swiftly he seemed to heal. He *did* pause to ask, "Sure you want this?"

"Nothing else matters," she said, emphatic.

Jarring joy, their bodies collided.

Each touch, she fell further. She felt so loved, could not stop, refused to try.

Arched to meet him, she drew him inside. In and out he moved. Eyes on her face to catch every nuance, his exuberance sharply focused...She sensed all of him, even his violent essence as it rested, tightly coiled.

All body parts fit perfectly. Curling, cresting, falling, onward they tumbled and laughed, uproariously. Walker laughed hardest—maybe more than ever.

Mouth pressed upon mouth, their bellies slipped and slid. He jerked; held her tight. She jolted, let out a long, shivery cry. More than primordial goo transmitted; forever, she'd carry his imprint.

$$\infty$$

Day seeped into dusk, bodies interlaced, they lay face-to-face. She sniffed the familiar smells of him; he felt like homecoming.

Bittersweet, elated, inexpressibly sad—beginning or ending—she didn't know what, Walker skimmed a thumb down her neck and broke into their reverie. "You need to know—"

Lauren-Son cut in, "This was perfect."

Walker inhaled, formulating a terribly important thought. She dreaded hearing it.

Abruptly, he began to cough and kept coughing. "I'm in bad need of a smoke," he spluttered.

"Now?" Something amiss, she checked his face.

"Yes, now." All prickles and withdrawal, as if sad or sorry, Walker smiled oddly.

Perplexed, afraid to leave, she arose and slowly dressed.

"Go!" he insisted. Miserable and grieving, such loss etched his face.

Tempted to rush back, she began to pivot and return. "Now!" he barked. She stared mouth a-gape, then departed.

Door ajar upon return, cautiously Lauren-Son opened it.

Everything askew, site of an awful fracas, blankets torn asunder, windows and dishes broken, Walker was gone.

Chapter Eighty: Lauren

Handcuffed and hobbled, as if a runaway slave, authorities brought Walker back and further charged him with failure to appear, violating bail, flight under the circumstances, and resisting arrest. Claiming most injuries had been incurred before he'd been found, to explain more recent damage, police attested they'd been forced to beat him again.

The *Buena Vista Bee* cited Walker's capture, lauding the Fort Blunt police force for his re-arrest: "The Laundromat landlord bragged that he'd received three months rent in advance in the name of a tenant he'd never laid eyes on," claimed Officer Sherwood. "Figuring something was up, I checked the missing persons nationwide database, and Walker Judson popped up as a fugitive from justice.

"Judson claims he took off to attend his mother's deathbed, but the old man living at his alleged childhood home says he doesn't know anyone named Walker Judson and that his wife has disappeared."

Shortly, authorities summoned Lauren-Son, asking where she'd lit off to. "I went in search of Walker," she insisted.

"Any results?" inquired the detective.

"Nope," she lied, "never found him." Peppered with more questions, she cut in, asking, "Am I in trouble? Do I need an attorney?" Ultimately, she proved so dully disappointing, they dismissed her.

Still, as a minor celebrity in the drama, reporters camped outside Rosalee's house, lolling against curbside cars, chatting, and drinking coffee, waiting till she emerged. Times she tried to duck out, they followed like wasps. "Did you help him run?" "Will you be charged?" "Have you secured counsel?" The faster she trotted, the more rapid-fire they questioned.

Another day's news, she was the headliner: *Healer's Consort, Accomplice? Ms. Lauren Finch,* the article said, *key staff person at The Living Light Healing Center, who claims the defendant cured her of severe scoliosis, an irreversible malady, is speculated to have helped Mr. Walker Judson run from justice.* The article, spread to another full page inside, included a horrid high-school photo and accurately described her role at the center.

Comments interspersed throughout condemned her relationship with Walker. "I don't get the attraction," a former student remarked, "but Lauren Finch had such a hold over Walker that I pity his wife." *Surprise, surprise*, whispered Lauren-Son, *that hold's now mutual!*

Bravado aside, years of training and self-discipline took flight. Confidence evaporating, fearing arrest any minute, she felt fragile, hysterical, and terribly vulnerable. Companion of old—eczema—flared to bubble and drip. Skin itchy, she scratched herself raw. Itch insatiable, she gnawed and chewed.

Prisoners were permitted two half-hour visits a day. Lauren-Son, deemed a *person of interest*, was refused entry. Sadly, no one else went to see Walker.

For fact, Delia never went. Neither did Ardis, nor Sherman. No volunteer or student or former patient ever visited…not one. And Rosalee didn't drive. "I'll take you," offered Lauren-Son, "and can wait outside."

"Thank you very much, but no." Ill at ease, Rosalee studied Lauren-Son's stunned face. "Ah…Do you wish to speak?"

Lauren-Son scraped up a sentence. "I thought you cared, Rosalee. So why won't you see him?"

"I am…ah…I do not know what to think. He is like a son to me, but…"

"You've abandoned him too?"

"No…Well, my back pains me. It is a problem to sit in a car." Rosalee avoided Lauren-Son's gaze.

"Pain or not, you could try!"

"So sorry, but I am engaged in a very big struggle."

"Everyone, including you, who is always so nonjudgmental—even you—have rejected him."

Regarding Lauren-Son's sense of Walker's innocence or guilt, sleeping with him pretty much sealed the deal for her. So now, apparently, he was hers alone to defend and to love.

Phone ringing, Lauren-Son picked up. "So," Spivey hollered over the line, "is you his little sexpot?"

"Nobody thinks of me as their *little* anything. But, he *does* mean the world to me."

"Gal"—Spivey dropped her voice—"that man's married, and you is guilty of interferin', 'cause you stole him from that witchy wife o' his. Furthermore, best make sure you is doing what you want, not Mr. Walker's biddin'. 'Cause that fella's pretty persuasive."

"You have it *so* totally wrong!"

Pause on the line, at last Spivey reached out. "Believe me, gal, I ain't glad to speak o' this."

Lauren-Son switched topics. "Tell me...How's the bone hunt coming?"

"Not so good." Weekly, Spivey sent enthusiastic postcard updates: *Gettin' close! Hot on the trail!*

Except her recent card read: *Trail's thinned out.* "I scoured all Walnut Grove County library and courthouse records, but it came to nothin'. If I could find a body who recalled that day, I might piece the situation together. I've been stayin' with my niece, 'cept my welcome's wearin' thin."

"You set yourself a huge challenge."

"Indeed. But as I see it, my search is part of the healin', 'cause lately, I been feelin' closer to Ozzie and gettin' happier by the minute. An' gal?"

"Mmm?"

"You can't do no wrong, 'cause you're 'bout as sexless as they come, 'cept I fret anyhow."

"Your vote of confidence perks me right up!"

"Glad to help!" Spivey cackled. "Take care. Hear?"

"Yessu-m. Bye...and good luck." As Lauren-Son rung off, it occurred to her that she missed Walker with such longing, it nauseated.

Chapter Eighty-One: Lauren

Day bitter cold, Rosalee, Sherman, and Lauren-Son arrived at the courthouse to hear Walker's verdict. Reporters rushed up, popping flashbulbs, as they scratched notepads and stuck microphones in Lauren-Son's face to pepper her with questions. Heads tucked, veered away from the roistering crowd, the trio plunged into the packed-to-overflowing courtroom.

Gracie Thrip stood to indicate seats up front. "Can you believe this?" she called as they clambered over legs.

Rosalee winced as the women hugged. "You OK?" asked Lauren-Son.

Sherman leaned across to check as well.

Dab to her brow, Rosalee gulped and nodded.

Sherman's longing gaze, coupled with Rosalee's sweet smile back at him, startled Lauren-Son. Having been so otherwise involved, she'd missed their growing adoration.

"Let's switch places," she offered.

Eagerly, Sherman slid alongside Rosalee, clasped her hand, and grinned shyly.

Many past patients, staff, volunteers and students in attendance, matter of fact, Buena Vista's entire populace seemed to cram into seats and crowd aisles.

Hello, Lauren-Son mouthed to Danielle's mother.

Curtly, the woman nodded back.

Danielle nowhere in sight, her heart gave a twang.

Delia, too, was notably absent.

Side door thudded open, all turned, riveted, as Walker shuffled, terribly slowly, to his seat.

"Hsss," several onlookers snarled. Other voices shushed them.

Face less swollen, yet still shockingly rearranged, bandage-swathed hands settled into his lap, he twisted to find Lauren-Son.

They locked eyes. She willed herself not to cry. Then he turned back.

The jury filed in to fidget and to avoid eye contact.

"All rise," called the bailiff.

Judge Attic entered to clap his gavel. "Court's now in session. Today we convene to hear the verdict for Mr. Walker Judson's crimes. Members of the jury, I understand that you reached consensus prior to the defendant's disappearance. Is that correct?"

"Yes, we reached a verdict, Your Honor, sir," replied the foreman.

"Fine, then. The defendant will stand."

Chairs scraped back, Walker and Twain stood.

"Despite aggravating factors," Attic made it known, "specifically, the prisoner's disappearance and the leveling of additional charges, the original decision handed down by the jury has not been altered. So... if you please, the verdict..." The jury foreman leaned over the rail, handed an envelope to the clerk, who carried it to the judge. The judge opened, read, handed it back to the clerk, who returned the envelope to the foreman.

All walls, as if paused to hear the outcome, ceased to creak. Vibrating heat ducts quieted as well. No one moved. Not a rustle. Not a whisper. Eyeballs gyrated, shifting in their sockets, swiveling from the jury, to the foreman, to the judge, then to Walker—who stood, somberly impassive, ashen-faced.

Judge Attic cleared his throat. Rosalee clamped onto Lauren-Son's arm.

The judge nodded to the foreman, who read, "As regards three victims, Mrs. Bernice Trabing, Ms. Gert VanBeck, and Mrs. Betty Jean Cowdry, we find the defendant, Walker Judson, guilty as charged of nine counts of rape and sexual assault." On he droned, specifying each count by act and code section.

Sharp intake of breath, although long braced for this outcome, all circuits jammed anyhow. For nothing prepared Lauren-Son for the word *guilty* as it hit her eardrums.

Eyes questing, his despair nearly imperceptible, Walker sought Lauren-Son.

Brimmed with tears, she tried to send him heaps of love.

Onward, the foreman plunged: "The jury acquits Walker Judson of one-hundred and six counts of sexual assault, involving the complainants, Mrs. Dalrymple Gooch and Miss Melissa Dworkin. We deem those couplings to have been consensual." Carefully enumerating each count, crime specified by code section, despite Walker being exonerated of these crimes, Lauren-Son sickened further.

"May I speak, Your Honor?" Hicks asked at verdict's conclusion.

Permission granted, he launched in, "Given the severity of these crimes and the adverse impact of these dastardly acts on my clients, as well as the perpetrator's willful disappearance, I strongly request that the maximum sentence be handed down."

Claps began. Judge Attic banged the gavel.

Claps thundered anyway. Attic banged, spluttering outrage, but could not achieve order.

"Court dismissed," he shouted above the ruckus. "Sentencing takes place next Friday, May third, at nine a.m. The defendant will remain in jail until that date."

Lauren-Son wanted to shout, to rant, to scream. Rosalee wept; Sherman tried to give comfort.

Voices raised, overlapping, as the crowd bunched up and bore down with devouring intent upon Walker. Lauren-Son moved to protect him, but Rosalee restrained her.

A week later court convened, and Judge Attic invited Prosecutor Hicks to center stage. "I ask the clerk to read a statement." Hicks passed papers to the judge and to Twain.

Facing the courtroom, the clerk read aloud, "Officer Robert Swan states in a letter dated, August second, as follows: defendant, Walker Judson, confessed in sworn testimony, 'I fled because I feared I wouldn't survive if sent to prison. I wasn't coerced, wasn't kidnapped. I just left.'"

Twain popped up. "When taken into custody, my client was not informed of his right to remain silent, so his statement got made under duress due to delirium suffered from his injuries." Twain and Hicks spun off arguing, till ultimately Judge Attic allowed the report, making it seem irrefutable fact.

"Also, I regret to inform"—Hicks removed his glasses, huffed the lenses, wiped them, squinted through, adjusted earpieces, put them on, and then scanned his surrounds—"that the witness, Mildred Sharp, died two weeks ago." Collective groan, the crowd stirred. Hand to mouth, Lauren-Son gasped.

Knives in his voice, Hicks kept on, "That poor woman trusted Walker Judson. So much so, she decided against recommended chemotherapy that might've saved her life. So now, she's dead.

"Mr. Judson...," Hicks went on to note, "is a disrespecter of God and Country. Rather than abide by the law of government, he thumbed his nose at all of us and ran. So I ask, when determining sentence, that you consider his blatant failure to respect rules that the rest of us must adhere to."

Allowing a pause, he stood before the judge. "Your Honor, it's perfectly plain that the defendant, Walker Judson, is a cold, unfeeling man, who, I remind you, performed many dastardly acts. Such violence, coupled with his willful disappearance, make it only fitting that you impose the maximum sentence. In fact, the plaintiffs specifically implore: 'See to it that Walker Judson never lays a hand on another poor, unsuspecting soul to practice his healing techniques again.' As for those helped by his work—this man perverts God's magnificent gifts."

Proceedings tumbled further downhill with Twain's half-hearted protest, "I ask that all pressures brought to bear on my client be considered when Your Honor determines his sentence." Gulp of air, he ramped up a tinge of zest. "Cast from home at an early age, Walker Judson grew, against all odds, to be a man of good works. Point of fact, I've received many commendations in his behalf." Hand claps, a clerk rushed in and out through the doors, until three crates got stacked. "These"—Twain indicated the boxes—"are letters of support. I've never seen the like." Walker blushed and bowed his head.

"As for what occurred after he left his mother, he alleges to have been abducted. We may never know for certain. But given his wounds, some person, or persons, hurt him so badly they nearly killed him." Twain brushed Walker's cheek to underscore the damage. "So now..." Twain paused, motionless. Rosalee chewed away at a cuticle. Lauren-

Son held her breath. "Before court administers sentence, Walker Judson will speak on his own behalf."

Shackles clanking, clothed in orange jumpsuit, Walker shuffled up front and stood, looking about, stunned and dulled.

Sight of him so undefended, so hurt, so humble, a thought popped up: *Would that he could rapture out of here!*

Slowly, he scanned, taking long, intimate moments to lock eyes with each and every one.

"He's a good actor," crabbed an onlooker, "make him sit down."

"Three months ago...," Walker began with a rasp; all strained to hear. "I felt compelled to attend to my dying, now deceased mother. I should have gone through proper channels to secure permission to be with her, but couldn't risk being turned down.

"Truly, I'm sorry for the trouble I caused. I planned to turn myself in after, but then..." Face twisted into a ironic half-smile, he cast about. "I got taken."

Please, God, Lauren-Son prayed, through gritted teeth, *help him speak sense!*

Face tipped to catch sunlit rays, sudden strength gained, Walker stood erect and took up another tack. "My healing methods were revealed by God and...I swear, I would never jeopardize that gift.

"I *do*, however, believe that people misinterpreted some of my actions and I deeply regret this. Most important, I'm sorry for whatever pain I've caused. I have never knowingly demeaned or harmed another being. I know I'm imperfect; some say, deeply flawed. At any rate...I hope you can forgive me." Moved to take his seat, Walker drew to a halt.

"I appreciate that you've made me feel at home in Buena Vista; it meant the world. I love my town and this country." A nose honked. Several wiped eyes. Most hissed and spluttered. "Thank you for hearing me out." Walker nodded to the judge. "I'm done."

Hicks leaned across desktop to blurt, "If you love your country so, how is it that you've never paid taxes—any kind?" Walker blinked, startled, unable to respond.

Twain hopped up alongside Walker. "Objection, irrelevant! I beg you,"—worked to near tears, he swallowed hard—"consider the tremendous good this man has done. Thousands, unable to pay for his services, received them anyway, free of charge. And his generosity actually saved this town. Buena Vista would've gone bankrupt if he hadn't bailed them—you folks"—arms open, he swung them, imploring the crowd—"all of you—out."

Moving to stand before the judge, he made one last theatrical swoop. "All we ask here is a liberal sentence. Please…Do not silence this God-fearing man. Thank you. That's all."

Room gone silent, Twain and Walker resumed their seats.

Prosecutor Hicks gave a final rebuttal. "There's no evidence, whatsoever, to support Mr. Judson's claim of abduction. Point of fact, it's irrelevant. Besides, Mr. Judson admits his disappearance was voluntary. So I demand he receive the severest sentence…nothing less."

Court adjourned, Judge Attic marched out…to return what seemed moments later. "The defendant will stand."

Energy sucked inward, Walker stood but seemed to vacate.

All listened gravely as Judge Attic spoke, "I've taken into account mitigating circumstances, that indeed the defendant, Walker Judson has a bevy of supporters who speak highly of him and that he also has no previous history of criminal activity. Weigh that against the man's willful disappearance and his apparent inability to grasp the gravity of his crimes, and I determine that the defendant, Walker Judson, found guilty of the crimes of rape and sexual assault, is hereby sentenced to eighteen years in state prison."

Cry flung from Lauren-Son's mouth, eyes shut as grief worked its way through, she tried to absorb the news. Overtaken by sweaty nausea, she willed the ceiling to drop down and crush all the room's contents.

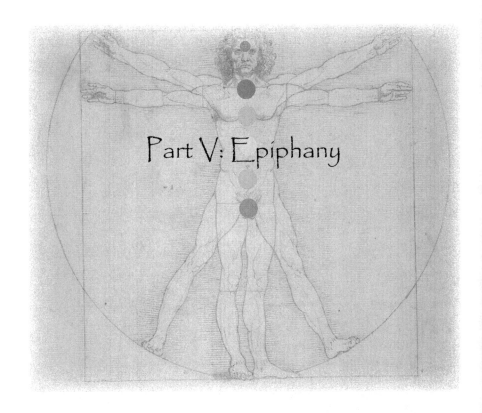

Part V: Epiphany

Chapter Eighty-Two: Walker

Van pulled up to gates of Midway Correctional Institution, a guard stepped out to chat with the driver. He then peered in at Walker, gave a low whistle, stepped back, and waved them through.

Prison air thickly substantial, it clotted and congealed. Guards, emanating distinct, low vibrations, sported crew cuts, wore mirrored sunglasses, called each other *bub,* and gabbed, importantly, into shoulder-clipped, static-laden walkie-talkies. And a steady hum—blaring radios, clacking machinery, water rushing through pipes, banging ventilation, and the edgy pulsations of inhabitants' psyches raised bile in Walker's throat.

Slow, deep breaths, sickness gripped him, and there it remained.

"Strip down and toss your clothes here," a guard commanded.

Walker, bare naked, got doused with chemical disinfectant.

"Shower up and put these on."

Putrid bar of soap and postage-stamp-size towel in hand, Walker stepped into frigid water, showered up, then exited to don regulation prison garb.

"Follow me," came the command.

Ka-chung—metal door slammed shut behind; another snapped open in front.

Pine-Sol scents squeezing Walker's sinuses, eyes watering, wiping them, fiercely, he passed down a corridor, went up several flights of stairs, and exited onto a walkway lined with barred cells.

Silent men lurked in shadows; several stepped up to examine him.

"Home sweet home," the guard announced.

Ka-chung—barred door sprung open, Walker entered a windowless cave. "That's yours." The guard indicated a top bunk. "Chow's at five, so don't be late."

Ka-chung—door banged shut, the guard departed.

"Name's Walker Judson," he addressed the lump on the bottom bunk.

Eye cracked open, the con glared, then flopped over to face the wall.

Cell paced off, the slot measured six by eight feet. Toiletries set at sink's lip, nothing else to do, Walker lay on his cot, arm draped over brow, and gave an appearance of sleep.

Not particularly desolate, a variant of relief overtook him. Point of fact, being in the very place destiny had ever beckoned helped ease the anxiety that had long tugged at him.

Not that he failed to grieve, but life now quickened. Each moment, suffused with meaning, he planned to savor. Beginnings, endings, life, death—all would be treasured.

Ma, he imagined, watched from above. Able to view its entirety, he hoped she grasped his life for what it was: steady, deliberate intent on God's part. Voden too, he now saw, had been integral to The Plan.

A no-brainer, Delia had departed. Long before trial's end, she'd been lost to him.

Unable to summon sorrow about this, mostly he felt empty. Never, had she needed him—not as others did. Oh, she needed attention, craved his touch, but thanks to her shark-like nature, she'd do fine without him.

What made Walker feel valued and therefore inspired to love was the power he held over others. Mostly, he needed to be needed but then resented that need and used that suffocated feeling to fuel his rage. So sadly, since Delia had never fully fallen under his sway, he could never quite love her.

And...In more ways than one, she'd betrayed him. In particular, The Angel had not disappeared. The evening before he'd taken off, in a fit of pique, she'd smashed it to bits. Even now, loss of his beloved Guiding One pierced his heart and remained embedded therein.

And then there was his personal gift...Lauren-Son. As if he were Leonardo daVinci, returned to the Louvre to reassess *The Mona Lisa*— as if he possessed the skill and singularity of focus required to perfect such a masterpiece, and then had the strength, the conviction, to leave it to the pleasure of others—proudly he swelled at thought of her. For one so ordinary, she kept growing stronger, more wondrous.

Ever curious to him had been the gradual unfolding of his life, despite details already known, which continued to delight, to surprise him. Confounded that such happiness could exist with her, a smile stretched his face.

As for that final day in Fort Blunt, he was of two minds. Ashamed of his own lack of clarity and blundering, partly he wished their coupling had never taken place.

Regret squelched, he reminded himself—for the highest good—that too had been fated.

Dark thoughts invaded. Chest achy, oxygen sucked out, Walker believed, momentarily, that he might not make it. For, Lauren-Son, hearing the full truth, would certainly lose all faith in him.

He hated himself for many things. Yet to his mind, he'd committed none of the crimes for which he'd been found guilty.

I've done far worse!

Cell door clanged open. "To your feet!" yipped the guard.

Stepped from his cell, first time in thousands, Walker got counted.

Prison head count served to torment. Daily, every half hour till lights-out, doors unbolted and swung open as inmates frothed from cells into corridors to form a single line and call out assigned numbers in sharp, terse barks. Come nighttime, guards passed by every hour without let up to flash light in each con's face, still counting.

In line with fellow inmates, Walker marched the corridor, went down a flight of stairs to join inmates from the floor below, taking more stairs to merge with the chow line. "Walker Judson," he said, introducing himself to the fellow adjacent.

Clattering utensils, metal trays, raised voices, and clangorous kitchen sounds obliterating articulation, the inmate nodded, grudgingly.

Noise engulfed all. Mess hall floors and walls forming a resonating tureen made yelling requisite. Men sat at bolted-down tables, arms looped around plates, shoveling food into mouths at a rapid rate, gabbing, loudly, mouths full. Amid stink of food, sweat, and of overarching fear, innards recoiling, Walker lifted a tray, as a beefy hasher slopped food onto it. Jellied white bread sandwiches, canned peaches, and frozen creamed corn comprised lunch.

"My, my!" twanged a voice over the din. "What have we here?"

Greeting assumed for another, Walker ducked his head.

As if addressing a larger audience, the voice twanged again. "I mean you, dear Christed One."

Speaker spotted, Walker raised a spated hand. "How do. Name's Judson."

Again, the man called out, "This here preacher man's come to us, heaven-sent."

Accepting this as an introduction, Walker nodded.

The speaker grinned. "Why so bashful, darlin'? I don't bite." Not as a question, but as a command, he added, "Join me."

Off the con sauntered to the far wall, two bulked-up white guys ambling along at his heels, Walker following.

Tray set down, benchmates scooted over, the fellow introduced himself. "Name's Lawrence P. Cotter. The Loon to my pals."

Epiphany – that singular shining moment wherein one grasps matters of great import.

Recognition brimming, Walker studied the narrow, beaky face and accompanying chiseled body of the Adonis who sat across from him, mustered up a grin, and forced himself to relax.

Always, he'd foreseen this. Known the who, the how, the where and when, yet nothing fully prepared him for the finality.

My life, he realized, *is done.*

Chapter Eighty-Three: Lauren

Money borrowed from Mom, Lauren-Son went thrice to the prison, only to be told that Walker was in isolation. Savings low, unable to afford another aborted trip, life slid into a routine. Mornings she made calls and wrote letters on Walker's behalf and sent baked goods to bribe guards for better treatment. Pointedly friendly by phone, she got on a first name basis with several prison staff. Afternoons, terribly drained, she napped.

Walker got one ten-minute phone call per week, so she grabbed the spot. Particularly awkward by phone, he wasted precious minutes clearing his throat as Lauren-Son frantically searched for topics. This day, however, she lit right into it, "Twain's a dope, you know. He should file an appeal, but hasn't done a thing. 'Why bother,' he said to me. 'If I submit one, the judge will just dismiss it.' What made Delia choose him, anyway, and why did you keep him?"

"No need to worry about me," he assured. "Accept what is and, please...Let me go."

"Let you go?"

"You focus on me because you're afraid to deal with what comes next. Drop me...Attend to the unknown, and you'll grasp God's plan for you."

"Forget about God. Heck, I want you!"

"Don't miss me. I'm always with you. And understand...All that's come to pass is precisely as is meant to be." Silence on the line; she jiggled the receiver.

"Walker?"

"My life's fine, so stop trying to get me out. Freedom's merely a state of mind, and inside these walls I'm freer than ever. Presently, my job involves making the most of what little time remains."

What little time remains!

His words chilled.

Prison, it seemed, hadn't diminished Walker. If anything, he drew strength from it.

Chapter Eighty-Four: Walker

Privacy impossible to come by, inmates pissed, shat, and showered for all to see. Worse yet, TVs and boom boxes, heavy laden with base notes, blared constantly, to bombard Walker's third floor cell with noise. Day and night, sounds sharp as knives—deliberately designed to interfere with free-flowing thought—cleaved his brain.

Unable to block it out, he heard all: could even discern subtle and distant chatter. Buildings away—he heard inmates and guards mutter, plot, and scheme. Every dawn, death row inmate, Robbie Renfrow, who resided within farthest reaches of the compound, sobbed softly.

Another challenge beset him. Sly, grotesque, palpably cold demonic entities bubbled up from muck to groan, screech, and saturate prison confines. Reptilian, wormlike, terrifyingly familiar, attracted to the emotionally charged atmosphere, these apparitions of the lower astral soaked into bodies and clung there. Air saturated, snapping, sucking, these monstrosities fed on terror and gobbled up souls.

Seeking to protect all, Walker surrounded himself with an egg-shaped barrier of golden light, then steadily, stealthily, performed remote repair to energy bodies, left and right. Understanding this to be God's futile plan for him—to transmute prevalent dark energy into healthy vibration—he dove in, regardless, to persist, relentlessly.

A week into his stay, Walker trudged along in the exercise yard, solitary and silent.

"Wha'choo lookin' at?" A spectacular mountain of a man deliberately slammed into him.

Walker stumbled, righted himself, then croaked pleasantly, "No harm meant, but I was noticing your limp."

Bulbous of nose, tattooed teardrops spattering one cheek, the con menaced. "You a faggot?"

"No, I'm not." Rubbing his shoulder, Walker hastily took off the direction opposite.

Just shy of forty, mane gone white overnight, this halo, coupled with his insatiable need to look directly into another's eyes, riled fellow inmates. And so, his relatively unmuscled state, along with his intense demeanor and useless hands, made him stand out as a most excellent target.

Blending in meant acquiring a tattoo, losing a tooth—or several—honing skills as a card shark, running drugs, or sexually humiliating a fellow inmate. Moreover, to stay safe, all cons sought to align and hang tight with same-race brothers. Yet, Walker's unwillingness to identify with any group further perfected his role as a victim.

The Loon came alongside chatting amiably, "Best not mess with Baby Huey. Do so, he'll ream you t'other bunghole."

"Appreciate the tip."

"Notta problem." Terrible beauty bounced off The Loon as he beamed, mightily. "At some point, however, I shall take out a helping in trade from your holy hide."

Resistance churning, uncertain how best to compose his face, Walker, seeking to control the jitters, felt a surge of nothingness enter and sweep through to overwhelm.

An acne-scarred inmate, divots to brow and cheeks, approached and spoke in haste, "Word has it you is a sort of medicine man. And, well...I got this puss-filled cyst—it hurts so bad, I can't lean or sit. Sick bay gives me pills, but they don't help none."

"Let's have a look." Shirt lifted, Walker palpated the egg-size lump. And then, time and space compressing, senses delving into flesh, festering gob located, he yanked it up and out.

"Whatever you did, man…" The con rubbed the spot in wonder. "It don't hurt no more."

Glad to resume this familiar role, hoping such deeds might render him more acceptable to God, Walker smiled back.

Eyes-bugging, The Loon looked on amazed.

Out in the yard another day, as Walker discretely performed a healing on an inmate with sky-high blood sugars, The Loon, following his every action with avid interest, sauntered over, then gave the diabetic a shove, demanding, "Take a hike."

No protest or backward glance, off the fellow scurried.

"Lets us take a stroll," The Loon invited.

Along the yard's perimeter, the two went, going past grunting, testosterone-laden, weight-hefting, bench-pressing men.

At fence's far end, a baby-faced con waited. "Say man," he addressed The Loon, "I need help."

"What sort of help might ya'll need?"

"From the library. I tried to read for myself, but don't get the meaning. Fellas say you're smart and might—could—be for hire."

Hand draped, palm side up, The Loon stated his terms. "That'll be three rolls of stamps, a pound of coffee, five soup cans—barley's a must—and a carton of Camels, up front."

"Yes sir! Soon as I can get 'em." The con took off.

The Loon called after, "Get 'em quick, hear? Else I won't help." Hand dropped, he turned to Walker with an elaborate shrug. "Common knowledge, your appeal's gone down the proverbial toilet. And, being as I have a keen desire to help, what say I have at it for you?"

"Very kind. I'll think on it."

Never would The Loon grant favor that did not require a four-fold return. And...Far more than obligation accumulated. For much akin to Walker's propensity to sneak fragments of other's lives, The Loon collected souls.

Chapter Eighty-Five: Lauren

Lauren-Son stepped into the law book-jammed office, located Twain behind a stack of papers, and blurted, "Walker needs your help."

Smile leached from his face, briefly Twain regarded her, then turned away to consult notes.

"What can I do for you?" he asked shortly.

"You haven't filed an appeal."

"Sit. Sit." Twain pointed to a chair. "Good to see you."

"Walker's been beaten several times," she launched in. "He's not exactly an instigator. His hands are useless, so he can't even protect himself. Desperate to get help for him, I tried to convince *60 Minutes* to do an exposé."

"*60 Minutes!*" Twain tilted his chair, amused. "How'd you get such an idea?" Cheeks a-flame, Lauren-Son dropped her gaze.

"The point is"—daintily she crossed her legs—"you need to free him." Twain eyed her thighs.

"I'm pleased to speak with you." He didn't seem pleased, only preoccupied or bored, perhaps.

"Even those claiming to be forever in Walker's debt have lost interest."

"How about his wife, Delia?" Tie adjusted, Twain sat straighter.

"I'd rather not talk about his wife." Mind detoured to their final contact: Delia, hand thrust out, had announced, "I'm so out of here!" Given that the IRS had attached Walker and Delia's assets, with no money coming in to The Living Light, Lauren-Son wondered how she afforded the chunky diamond ring that graced her finger.

"This mess isn't your fault." Delia didn't apologize, but actually thought she had.

Lauren-Son glared at her. "Your shenanigans made matters far messier for Walker than would've been."

"You pathetic, slobbering hanger-on, you have no idea the havoc I've wreaked!" Out Delia flounced, slamming the door.

With Delia and Ardis nowhere to be found, Delia had left a giant swath of debt, and Ardis had jilted a sad, bewildered husband, leaving him with a passel of kids to manage.

Closely, Twain watched her. "So how are you getting on?"

"Never mind me." Legs uncrossed, she came up close; the scent of Twain's aftershave raised bile in her throat. "Resisting arrest...What a joke! Whoever crushed Walker's hands should be accountable!"

Twain shot back, "How could you possibly know what happened?" Lauren-Son squirmed, uneasy.

"Look here, young lady, I staked my reputation on your hero, but he up and left, making me look like a perfect ass. And that's something Old Bertie will not stand for!" Distaste rippling his face, he pressed, "If he hadn't run, they'd have given him a fraction of the sentence, possibly five years probation, max. Bottom line—your darling Walker is no hapless victim. All that's happened is his own fault."

"You're *so* wrong!"

"Hate to burst your bubble, young lady, but Walker Judson is not a good man."

"How can you say that?"

Twain leaned in, confidential. "What about paying me? I received my retainer, but never got a cent after that."

"Delia managed their finances; why not go after her?"

"I don't grovel, miss." Briefcase hefted onto desktop, Twain sorted its contents, added a calculator and pens, rudely signaling annoyance.

She tried again. "Walker has this knack for opening people up. Granted, sometimes he opened a person more than they could handle. But possibly, repressed energies got released, causing a flood of sexual confusion for those women."

Twain laughed, cheerless, horrid. "Oh really!"

"Did you consider that the complainants made this whole thing up? All were so gonzo over Walker; they flocked round, hoping to be singled out...to be treated special. When he failed to reciprocate, they turned against him." The rough equivalent to being gummed to death by a ravenous pack of toothless senior citizens, those women cloyed and pecked. Knowing Walker, that must've crazed him.

"See here—" Finger inserted at his neck, Twain loosened his collar.

Lauren-Son cut in and sought to shame him, "No, you see here! You failed him—we all have! Don't you understand? No matter how ugly, evil, or creepy the person, Walker saw—not human failings, but potential. So sending him to prison is, like, the ultimate test of his unconditional compassion, and we've left him to rot. Ach..." She pressed her temples.

Twain made an indifferent noise. "I'm not the enemy. Surely you grasp that."

"Why didn't you pursue collusion? Miss Wilkins, with her ax to grind, could've planted the idea of abuse. Certainly, that merited investigation."

"There was nothing to it."

"But he was nearly killed by someone trying to silence him..."

Twain put up a hand. "Conspiracy theories: I enjoy them, too! But why go to such trouble, when your man is such a small fry?"

"To make him stop work," she floundered. "Because they couldn't bear his goodness."

"Bah! You grasp at straws." Sigh released, Twain tilted his chair, cupped hands behind his head, and stared at the ceiling.

Shortly, he glanced back and let fly, "In all candor, Walker Judson is an insufferable prick disguised as a saint. Or perhaps a saint disguised as a prick." Hand flip-flopped, lever-like, he mused, "Sainted prick. Pricked saint. At any rate...I have it on good authority there's far more wrong with my client than his nose-diving reputation. I'll tell you what..." Twain shot her a sly look, sifted through desktop papers, and tugged out a file.

"Right off, I hired a psychiatrist who noted Walker to be filled with deep, unquenchable rage, but then advised not to use the information— said it was too damaging." Lauren-Son flinched. "Also"—he scanned papers—"he gave a diagnosis of *fugue* states. Fugue being a form of temporary amnesia that permits one to assault, molest, even to self-mutilate, and then not recall having committed such acts."

People in fugue states, which are prompted by unmet needs of the unconscious, she recalled, commit unseemly acts, then reject those actions from conscious thought. Overall, Walker presented such a disciplined, controlled front. Yet perhaps, on occasion, the rage he sought to suppress may have actually gained the upper hand.

"Arguing *fugue* states," Twain concluded, shutting the file, "might have helped build a case of mental instability, but when I posed it to Walker, he declined."

Aside, he added, "Pity really. It might've helped."

"Can you use that information now?"

"And further waste my time?"

Helpless, drained, Lauren-Son slumped in the chair.

That Twain shared confidential material struck her as inappropriate. Just the same...*Had Walker been unstable all along, or had he suddenly flipped?*

We all, she hastened to reason, *hide dark aspects that aren't necessarily pathological.*

Questions too scary, she sought to suppress them.

Thoughts swarmed anyhow. *The impact he had on others was subtle, insidious...*the thought went on to complete itself...*and therefore, perhaps, more dangerous.*

So was he a sex addict, acting out reckless, inappropriate behaviors without regard to consequence?

Given how deeply Walker had touched her—with such loving tenderness—that view seemed inaccurate.

Stubbornly stupid as it may seem, despite Mildred's death, his conviction, and Twain's damming recriminations, quite simply, she loved him. He was her friend, her mentor, her hero. Everything she liked about herself—all strong, capable aspects—he'd helped to forge.

Besides...Stop believing, and she'd be forced to question everything.

Twain resumed a prior topic. "I'm still puzzled as to what happened to that enormous defense fund. When asked, Walker claimed he knew nothing!"

"Whatever you think, he was no thief."

Twain leveled his gaze at her. "That man's a sly one...a wolf in sheep's clothing. I've met more honest sociopaths. And, based on my dealings with him, Walker Judson has been thoroughly dishonest."

"But I know him..." Brain yelling at her heart, weight of

conversation drawn down, her sentiments began tilting away from Walker.

Twain raised his voice over hers, "Fact is, nobody knows the real Walker Judson, least of all, himself." Fingers drumming the desktop, he smiled such a tiny smile it barely showed.

Chapter Eighty-Six: Walker

As Walker steadily scooped bedsheets into dryer drums, trustees scurried past on errands. Men such as these garnered special privileges by snitching, and several had informed on him for doing healings.

Hopped onto the counter, The Loon drew up a knee and cupped it.

"Down offa there," growled a guard, strolling past.

"Yes, sir!" Ignoring the directive, The Loon passed a cigarette beneath his nose, sniffed, then inserted it between pre-moistened lips and lit up. Smoke trickling from nostrils, he dropped a fresh cigarette in the mitt of Walker's hand.

As Walker fumbled to light up The Loon gabbed away, "Commonly, appeals get ignored and left to marinate. Soon as I file 'em, though, solicitations that have dragged on for years get action. So how about it, then?"

"If you'd been my attorney," Walker said, admiringly, "likely, I'd not even be here."

"That's right!" Slid from his perch, The Loon generously lit Walker up.

Smoke blown sharply upward, Walker savored the nicotine rush. "When vindication *does* come for me, it won't be in the court of public opinion. It'll be from another dimension altogether." Desperate as he was to be free—ambition, hope, future plans fallen away—there'd be no triumphant homecoming. For, never would he collect up his life and begin again.

Calm with that certitude, hand reached up, he gave the sky a pat. "So thanks for your kind offer, but I have to pass." For no one, Walker vowed, aside from God, would ever control him.

"What-*ever*, man!" Cigarette thumped aside, The Loon, calling to another con, stomped off.

$$\infty$$

"Prison rules prohibit all transactions between inmates and guards," the warden informed. "Plain language, Judson, keep doing your rigmarole on anyone, and you'll spend your life in solitary. Understand?"

"I do." Walker nodded solemnly.

Weekly, he got hauled to the warden's office for this exact same chat. Certainly, he grasped the consequences, but—so little time left, filled with the futile compulsion to heal others—unable to cease, even if he wished to, God set this particular course, not he.

Hands pleasantly folded, the warden regarded him. "Let's see"— he counted up—"past four days, you've spent seventy-six hours in solitary, and my boys say you seem to enjoy it."

"In all candor, I do." Walker did not mind the hole; actually, he craved it as the sole place wherein blessed peace and quiet prevailed.

The warden reviewed a file. "I can't figure you out, Judson. Other than time spent in confinement, your behavior is exemplary. But still… Defying rules and such, won't go over well with the Parole Board." Given the purple bands beneath the man's eyes and the perpetual pinch of his brow, the warden cared, mightily, for his charges; worried so, he lost sleep. And, secretly, the good man wished to request a healing from lymphoma, but thought it unseemly to say so.

Yet nightly, Walker sent healing vibes his way anyhow.

"You, Judson, still try, desperately, to hold onto a sense of purpose. I suppose your actions take your mind off the present. Yet, inmates spot that as weakness and, well…" Being seen so clearly took Walker's breath.

Life shrunk to a singular, forlorn obsession, the harder he focused on doing good works, the easier his mind emptied of grief. "It matters not, sir, where I am, or what's happening around me, or how I protect myself. What matters most is what's in my heart." Cheerful despair hung heavily there.

Figuring God had dropped Ma into horrific darkness, Ma assumed she'd displeased Him and, further, that He'd rescinded their past intimacy. However, God thought her strong enough to handle her suffering and trusted that her despair would ultimately strengthen her.

Cast into a similar dark pit, he understood acceptance to be the requisite ingredient to strive for.

"Stay safe Judson. Hear?" The warden pressed a buzzer.

As the guard appeared to escort Walker out, it came to him that souls convene prior to birth—family, friends, even enemies—and sign on for tasks and challenges that enable each being to evolve. One selects parents and life's difficulties beforehand; all parties agree to this.

Knowing full well how this life would pain him, Walker signed on for all of it: his relations with Lauren-Son, his choice of wife and family, his present tribulations, even this interlude with the warden.

His next life, however, *nirvana*—the highest possible spiritual attainment—would claim him.

On way to the mess, Walker noting a short-statured guard keenly watching him from the western tower, paused to inquire, "Who is that?"

His escort swiveled to check, then ogled him. "You lost your mind? No one's there."

Intervals throughout the day, Walker felt watchful eyes upon him: not The Loon's, nor his henchmen, but someone else's gaze. He felt it strongest in the exercise yard and as he passed to and from the mess.

Runty tower guard's shorter-than-regulation height, coupled with Lauren's mention of Voden as still missing gave him pause. According to Ma, she and Voden had shared convent life. Add this to Voden's presence at The Living Light, and Walker grasped that a benevolent thread connected him to this odd man.

Yet Voden's shifting careers—as nun, as healer, and now as a prison guard—failed to explain his purpose here.

Thwack—food splattered. Utensils clattered. A saucer whizzed past, slicing air.

Whoosh—a tray slammed the wall, missing Walker's good ear by inches as he entered the mess hall.

"Moth-ah fu—a!" a con bellowed.

Fists collided. Punches landed on jaws, bellies, arms, shoulders. Curses, howls—benches got yanked up and tossed, and bodies crashed about, as twenty or so African-American brothers went after three slender Vietnamese.

Prison rules being easy to follow, the code of honor among inmates far more complex, prisoners were not classified by severity of crime, but by racial heritage. Much ado made of dignity and strength between same race cons, they assembled into brotherhoods.

Never mind genuine affinity, clans banned tight, obliged to defend a brother's every slight—real or imagined. Ties such as these created bonds of servitude wherein death and destruction prevailed. And, regardless as to the cause of this present fracas, the Vietnamese were the distinct recipients of an ass-whupping.

Hopped onto a table, Walker shouted over the din, "Hey!"

The roomful of cons looked up, bewildered.

Arms extended, as if to embrace—much akin to the aurora borealis, light spiraled steadily out from him.

Cons, staring open-mouthed, slowly relaxed fists, picked up plates, righted benches, wiped each other off, and sat back down.

Point being: as if true brothers, blacks, whites, yellows, and browns freely co-mingled, chatting amiably, while Walker, guards surrounding, got marched back to solitary.

Chapter Eighty-Seven: Lauren

In downtown Buena Vista, as Lauren-Son went about her business, townsfolk passed by, eyes downcast as if navigating potholes, though none existed. Overhearing murmured mention of Walker, she saw eyes roll and faces pucker. As if under quarantine, all avoided The Living Light. And, Lauren-Son, being too distracted, hadn't the heart to stir it to life again.

She *did* transact a somber pharmacy purchase; the clerk shot his head up to smirk, and then acted as if she were an affliction he wished to be cured of. Unfriendly gaze preferable to total avoidance, she stared firmly back.

$$\infty$$

Returned to Rosalee's, the phone rang, so Lauren-Son grabbed it. "It's your mother," the voice said.

"Oh, hey."

"How about you come home?"

"Thanks, but I've got to see this through—whatever that means."

"Why can't you do what you need to from here?"

"Let me think on it."

Good-byes said, Lauren-Son fumbled the newly purchased box open, read the directions, inhaled a giant gulp, and peed on the white stick.

Stick overtaken by distinct pink, the results registered affirmative.

Silent throb of day's afterglow slanted in from the window—the light momentarily orange, quickly faded to purple.

Torrent of emotions—fear, joy, grief—welled up, she stroked her flat belly and felt life.

"Hello," she burbled at her navel, "and welcome."

Chapter Eighty-Eight: Lauren

Again, the phone rang. "Come...Help me search," Spivey pled.

"Sorry, but I have major business to attend to."

"Lordy, girl! I've been bitin' my tongue, but I got to say...You think you're nothin' without that man, only this ain't 'bout him. It's 'bout what God wants, and I say...God wants you to get on with your life!" Spivey sounded as if she might reach through the earpiece to slap her silly.

"I didn't give up on you either, Spivey. So let it drop." She couldn't forsake Walker now, even if she wanted to. "And Spivey?"

"Mmm?"

"What if you never find Ozmond's bones?"

"I ain't gonna fail." She sounded scared she might, though.

"Whatever happens, find him or not, I'd be pleased to help organize a memorial service to put him to rest."

"Gal, that's a good fallback! 'Cept I ain't ready to give up just yet." They bid goodbye.

Lauren-Son called her mother back. "Thanks for the offer, Mom, but I'm not coming."

"What will you do?"

"Try to see Walker again."

Paused outside The Living Light, a distinct sense of dwindling overwhelmed. Potted flowers at the entryway drooped limply, and the donated Mickey Mouse statue, hand raised, greeted no one. Waiting room devoid of bodies, no one venture inside for help of any kind.

Fond memories—feet running upstairs and down, doors slamming, the pace and clatter of friendly folk going in and out, laugher, hugs abounding—surfaced. Walker clapping her shoulder, congratulating for her first full-fledged healing. Danielle's upturned, pain-free face regarding her in wide-eyed wonder. Spivey happily crabbing. Rosalee's gentle, kind ways; the habitual trail of sunflower seeds in her wake. Sherman's achingly sweet rendition of The Beatles' song, *Yesterday*. Voden's quiet, all-seeing presence. The Angel: the serenity it emanated.

Its benevolent face no longer present—grief gusted.

Eyes strong with feeling, Rosalee came to her side. "Please come back to run this place."

Unable to speak, Lauren-Son did a head bob.

Rosalee held out paper sack. "For lunch."

Tuna salad sandwiches reposed inside lovingly dyed her favorite shade—eggplant—Lauren-Son wailed, "How will I survive without you?" Toppled into Rosalee's arms, she clung there.

Pat, pat—went Rosalee. "You will see. All will be hunky-dory again."

Stepped outside, Lauren-Son fired up her car.

Rosalee put up her most chipper face. With no more herbs to dispense, no repairs to oversee, no babies to hold, no one to comfort, no more endless cups of coffee to serve, no Walker, no Voden or Silly, worse yet, no more Living Light—what ever would become of her?

Knock, knock—Lauren-Son rolled down her window.

Rosalee bent and shot Lauren-Son a satisfied grin. "I have you and Sherman. Also...Walker and I are pen pals."

Sherman came up, drew Rosalee to his side, then kissed and hugged her. "No worries," he tittered. "I'll take care of her."

Light caught Rosalee's broad face and Sherman's thoroughly tattooed form. Moment filed into memory banks, adoring their quiet love for each other, with great reluctance, she pushed on.

Chapter Eighty-Nine: Walker

Plain to for all to see Walker now radiated a distinct otherworldly aura. Using resultant awe to best advantage, rumors grew, and myth built; men claimed he bent minds to do his bidding, foresaw the future—altered it to suit himself—and shape-shifted at will.

And so, in a system where disrespect formed the natural order, he garnered the respect of all: guards included. Cons treated him with deference; none dared go at him. And only with great reluctance, did prison officials interrupt his work.

Yet, as with most things neat and tidy, the single exception remained.

Up, The Loon stepped this day to hiss, "If ya'll can fix, then ya'll can mess 'em up, as well. So really...I must learn how to perform your fancy tricks."

Walker paused, considering. *What's the harm? Give this man whatever he wants. Peace will prevail and might stave off the inevitable.*

Protective tenderness, arose as he felt the ancient, hungry, irresistible desire for adulation and power that sucked and tugged, beckoning he and his companion into its vortex. Yet Walker, who valued resistance stalled again. "At some point, I just might show you."

Desperation, rage, terror—skittering The Loon's face, the con produced a glottal noise, spat at dirt, ground the gob, spun on heel, and departed.

Certain forms of suffering exude a distinct odor. Putrefaction—rot—for example, bespeaks of destruction that festers from inside out.

The Loon's suffering—coiled within—stank from the man's pores. Beneath that, an icy clutch—terror—lurked. Walker, on the other hand, smelt his own scent: that of a trapped, wild animal, coyotes circling.

Chapter Ninety: Lauren

Face crinkled with pleasure, Walker stepped into the visitor's cage to placed mitts of hands on the mesh screen between them. "I'm certainly glad to see you!" he enthused. "So...How've you been?"

"Pretty great at the moment." Heart gone berserk, Lauren-Son hated that she cold not touch him.

Hair shockingly white, purple troughs beneath bloodshot eyes, his comforting calm enveloped her.

Percussive booms shattering the room, a palsy tremored him.

Each note, his spasms intensified.

"You OK?" she asked, dying to kiss him.

"I'm fine. But let me hear about you."

"Well..." Much to tell—that she'd missed him dreadfully, that he'd touched her to the core, that she ached to resume life as it had been, that she felt lost and ill-defined, that she had momentous news—instead, she studied his face.

Never, will I tire of seeing you! "Uh..." she faltered. "Rosalee sends her love. So does Sherman."

There they stood, dumb as mannequins.

She sought his eyes; they exchanged grins. She tried again, "Well, ah...I haven't told anyone"—shyly, she lowered her voice—"about us."

Walker held her gaze, then sucked a breath. "There's something else?"

Awkwardly, she shifted. "Yup, there is."

"No matter what happens, understand that you mean everything to me," he encouraged.

Eagerly she cut in, "Always, we were meant to connect, including what happened physically. So now...I'm pregnant."

"Ahh," Walker blinked, fumbling sweetly. "Very good. I'm glad. Happy, actually. It's a, er...A replacement, you see. The precise point of all of this, of...of everything. I hope you..." Gray blanched his cheeks; he smiled too hard, seemed scared, somehow.

"Replacement for what?" Every inch of her flipped into high-alert.

Walker leaned, brow pressed to mesh. "The first one died before birth. It was my task, yours too, to bring this specific soul back." Smile glued in place, she sought his gaze. Walker, frowning a deep furrow, looked away.

"Bastard!" The woman adjacent slammed the screen, sending it a-ripple. "I am so outta here!"

"Shit, man! Shit!" A hairnetted inmate paced, muttering.

A guard appeared, gripped the woman's elbow to escort her out. She threw him off, fished in her pocket for tissue. "I hate youuuu!" she wailed between nose blows.

"So tell me..." Returned to matters at hand, Lauren-Son had to ask, "Did you harm those women?"

Walker's eyes snapped to her face.

Silent a long time, an eternity passed.

"In essence, yes," his voice came, soft, but clear. "But not the way they said."

"Then how?"

"I let them down, caused them to become attached, when truly, I did not care enough. And I neglected to explain all of this..." Vaguely, he waved. "The why, the wherefore of us...to you."

Walker stared another second, then spoke, carefully, "First time I saw you, I knew who you were, then waited for the circumstances that would cause us to come together—it became the single most important thing."

"What was so terrible?"

"You were a pawn," he slowly enunciated. "In other words, I used you."

External sounds dropped away; she went very still.

Jaw muscle jumping, Walker trembled.

"How—what do you mean?"

Walker did a hapless shrug. "Before your birth, before mine as well, this soul that you now carry, was foreordained. We, neither of us, ever had a choice. All of this, including what happened between us, was pre-scripted for the purpose that now resides within you."

Brain split in two—cleaved like a melon—legs, knees buckling, rest of her dragged down, she had to crouch. Mind a-jumble, pain everywhere: *This*, she figured, *would be a fine moment to die.*

Slow in-breath, legs a-wobble, working to stand, finally, she managed to face him. "You see your child, our child, as a replacement for one lost long ago. Does it matter at all that she might be a person in her own right?"

"I thought its conception an obligation, as my path. And...," Walker continued, "I feared telling would interfere with our work." Levelly, he regarded her as if most sincere.

"You handed me such a load of crap about self-empowerment," she spat, "yet never gave me the option to choose?"

"Sadly, I thought I knew best." Walker rendered his face inscrutable.

Full of dread, she forced herself to persist. "What's the real reason you didn't speak up?"

Yawn of silence, he spoke at last, "Truly, I wanted you for myself."

"But wasn't sleeping with me merely God's Divine Plan?"

Mouth open, Walker hesitated, then seemed to decide. "Actually, it was."

"You had no say?"

"I don't think so."

"Walker, that is so asinine! Of course you had a choice. Most always, we do!" Many things she could forgive, but willful deceit was not among them.

"Guard," she hollered, "get me outta here!" Guards upon her, they escorted her out.

Burst through the gate, unable to think—to see—no grace, no poise, nor interest in staying upright, she toppled and lay on hard concrete, hands pressed to face, and went to pieces inside.

Chapter Ninety-One: Walker

Ash flicked into salvaged milk carton, Walker sat smoking on his bunk. Incessant voices, coupled with radio and TV chatterings, spiraled between tiers as he sensed and heard all, including the hollow *thump, whump*—slap of buttocks against thighs, the ecstatic groans and grunts, along with the biting back of pain to endure, of furtive bodies as they rubbed together that impinged upon his ears.

Cigarette stubbed out, ears pressed between palms to block sounds, he flung himself into The Absolute. Mind free, unfettered—the infinite, formless indescribable, wherein all things exist, or do not, these realms being where he preferred to reside these days, places so breathtakingly gorgeous that earth's reality lacked in comparison—a smile lit his face.

A passing guard assumed him to be lost in trashy thoughts, yet triple murderer, Artie Wallbeck, held his attention this night.

"Aieeeee!" Four cells down Artie thrashed, emitting inhuman keenings.

Suck of breath, Walker slowed the man's wild hammering heart rate, synchronized it with his own calm, steady one, till agitation ceased, and his subject snored, steadily.

Deeper, Walker delved, entering the craggy texture and content of Artie's nightmares, wherein horrific, ceaseless beatings suppurated. Pained by such visions, tenderly, sucking, slurping, he spat out haunting memories, and implanted soothing lullabies alongside tender, loving scenes.

Tumbled from The Absolute to reenter his own body, he heard Artie sigh, content. In time, he foresaw that this nasty brutal character would grow kinder, gentler.

How ironic, Walker thought, *that I'm permitted to alter the trajectory of this man's life, but not my own.*

Barring the ability to change things, tremors intensifying, he awaited redemption. Yet emptiness yawned before him to obliterate all public memory of his life's good works. And so, back into eternal vastness he slid, and there he sought to dwell until summoned.

Chapter Ninety-Two: Lauren

No idea where she was going or how she got there, Lauren-Son found herself parked outside her childhood home. Riotous flowerbeds encircling the tidy lawn, no matter how often she came and went, this quiet suburban street, this house, with its white paint and green trim, remained safely unchanged.

Car exited, she cut across the yard to enter the kitchen.

"Thank God you're OK!" Mom helloed. "When you called you just panted. I've been terrified something had happened!" Talcum powder and soap scenting all, in her mother swooped to give her daughter a fierce squeeze. "Let's see you, sweetie." Head lifted, Lauren-Son swiped at her cheeks. "What ever is the matter?" Mom raised a hand to soothe; Lauren-Son flinched and stepped away.

"I'm a huge mess."

Mom wrung her hands. "What's this is about?"

"Give me a second!"

Mom retreated to the kitchen, clanked silverware, banged a bit, then called out, "Cream or sugar?"

"Don't care."

Eyes moist, Mom returned, tray of gingersnaps, pot of tea, cups and saucers in hand. All else gone awry, she always claimed a cup of tea as life's best antidote to every travail.

"Let's sit." Mom indicated the dining table.

Vapor steaming, liquid poured into dainty china cups, placed upon saucers, with cream added, Mom stirred in a precise heap of sugar for Lauren-Son, passed it, and then settled into a chair. "There now!" She exhaled an expectant grin.

"I am *so* ashamed!" Eyes downcast, busily Lauren-Son examined her hands.

Tick-tock, tick-tock—mantle clock puttering away, the silence went on and on.

Head back up, noting her mother's concerned gaze, she pressed her palms into her lap.

Chair pushed back, Mom came around to encircle her. "Oh honey, how can I help?" As gently as possible, Lauren-Son peeled her mother off.

Eyes shut, working to compose herself, realization stabbed... Unless willing to speak with Walker again, he'd never know their child. "So..." she announced, "you were completely correct. I've just learned that my perfect life has been a giant sham."

"Oh no, honey." Mom cut in, eagerly radiating love. "Think of all the good you've done! I *did* always think Walker was...ah...troubled, though."

"Crazy, you mean?"

"Not exactly."

"Well...I certainly do have a lifelong affinity for lunatics!" Bluster aside, she began worrying.

Walker's stability, morality and truthfulness in question, perhaps crazy genes also ran amok inside her as well. *So how will our collective lunacy impact the child to come?*

"Do you want to talk about it?"

"Guess I'm not ready."

"I'm here when you need me. The important thing is that you know how much I love you." Mom's hand crept out to touch hers.

Rare occasions, when unable to be home to greet Lauren-Son after school, Mom filled the Crockpot with soup and taped a photo of herself to the lid. *Turn me on,* read the instructing note on the tape recorder.

Push of the button, Mom's voice chirped: "Hi, sweetie! Hope you had a nice day. Serve yourself; it's split pea. Play an hour, then do your homework. And, honey, don't forget those birthday thank-you notes. If you need me, I'm at Ruth Martin's at Davenport-four-oh-six-five-three. Bye-bye. Love you."

Eagerly, impatient, she'd await Mom's return. They'd review the day's highs and lows and share everything. *Can I replicate such comfort for my child?*

Overtaken by weariness, she closed the subject. "Think I'll go rest."

"Will you stay?" Mom inquired.

"If it's OK."

"Of course! You're welcome as long as you like!"

Slowly, Lauren-Son mounted the stairs to her childhood bedroom.

Door shut, back flat to the wall, a vast chasm opened where Walker and The Living Light once resided. She slid into a crouch. Unable to figure how she'd ever stand upright, she took in her surroundings.

Years back, Mom painted the dresser, applying a flock of cream-colored doves to its drawers. An abandoned robin's nest, a jar of colored bits of ocean-tumbled glass, leaves she'd pressed and strewn about, and her special rock pile—favorites she'd collected, since forever, and had been loath to toss—her most treasured possessions, now seemed so ridiculously senseless.

Karmic whiplash—destiny marching steadily one direction, but then, without rhyme or reason, an abrupt turnabout—that's how her life felt.

She'd assumed she'd known Walker, but had been terribly wrong. Walker's uncensored compassion, his goodness, his immaculate hands—all of it a huge sham—she'd only seen him as she wished him to be. He'd kept secrets, lied about his true interest in her, then betrayed her.

She also had to marvel: *Stupidest thing I ever did was sleep with him!*

Slid out flat, sharp head bang to the floor, she waited to feel something.

Her eyes stayed dry, so did her heart. She felt nothing—nada—zilch.

Stomach roiling, abruptly, she sat upright, trying not to puke.

No tears, though...would've been a relief had they come.

Walker tolerated his precognitive skills with alleged modesty and reluctance, claiming the wish to remain ignorant of such details. Yet all along, fully cognizant of this so-called Divine Plan to borrow her womb, he'd kept that tidbit undeclared.

"I don't try to know future events," he'd once announced, "the information just comes. Next week you'll buy Converse All-Stars, but then immediately regret it. I could speak up now to spare you the bother, but you'll insist on buying the shoes anyway.

"What I *see* isn't imagined or guesswork. If you saw as I do, you'd go mad. Truth be told, I'd far prefer any other challenge."

Pity and concern for Walker fallen away, what he'd done defied decency and logic!

Mom knocked, then entered to sit alongside. Lauren-Son shot her a baleful look. Mom reached over to squeeze her hand. "Somehow, we'll get through this."

Fighting tears, Lauren-Son stared at the ceiling. "I can't yet speak of the biggest part."

Chapter Ninety-Three: Walker

Walker gazed down at the graveyard. A tumult of souls, those lost, none at ease, who lingered there—called out in unison: *Help us find peace!*

Up The Loon sidled, fingers threaded through mesh, to smirk. "Like what ya'll see, Preacher Man?"

"Some days this view's peaceful." Silent a moment, the men pondered the scene below. Most gravestones stood upright; some had toppled, and all marched, steadily, up the slope.

"Jimmie the Bean," The Loon elucidated, "who trims the weeds, says no names, only prisoners' numbers grace those older markers. Seems the logbook got destroyed in a fire, so no one, not even the good warden, knows whose remains rest beneath which headstones. Perhaps no pity, seeing as we all go back into the void from whence we come."

"What else do you know about that place?" The cemetery, a preoccupation of late, tantalized Walker.

"Hear of the *Great Flood of 1879?*"

"Can't say as I have."

"Story goes, record-high floodwaters drug caskets from earth, disgorging corpses so's they bobbed along like tops in swollen, raging waters—musta been quite the sight!

"Over there's the original graveyard." The Loon pointed to a trough-like depression farther down the slope. "Being that the first site was subject to flooding, prison officials re-interred all remains and moved 'em to higher ground. Hear tell, to spare bother, authorities then commingled about five hundred bodies into a single mass grave. Careless-like—as if tossing a salad—they heaped body parts together, mixing a Jap's leg with the skull and ribcage of a nigger's." He gave the fence a shake, sending it a-quiver. "That ain't right!

"Nowadays, however, even in death, all races get segregated.

Spicks loll along that side perimeter. Chinks, all kinds, get relegated to the lower wall. Niggers situate in the bottommost section. That there highest part"—The Loon used his chin to point—"is for whites. Dagoes reside in the best-groomed subsection. And someday, we too will rest thereabouts. You n' me, snugged up close for all eternity—it captivates my mind!"

"Years ago"—Walker paused to straighten his denim cuffs—"while visiting a pet cemetery, I found an immense grave marker that read: *Beloved Alfonso: More than just a duck.*"

Eagerly, The Loon awaited the punch line; Walker shrugged. "I just hope the same is said of me. *Walker Judson: More than just a healer-gone-bad.*"

"Yo—my man!" Both men looked up. Across the way a chubby con jerked his head, signaling.

The Loon stretched his extreme biceps. "Duty calls."

Moved to leave, he looked back cheerily. "It still remains my keenest desire to have ya'll teach me, and I aim to have my way." Off he swaggered across the yard. Walker watched him go. The Loon paused, selected a rock, chunked it overhand and knocked a bird from flight.

End's approach upon him, worldly connection steadily loosening, Walker did not fear death's aftermath, for he'd taken a thorough peek at the other side. Point of fact, he ached for it. He *did* fear the arduous process of getting there: the precise way his end would come.

So, he reluctantly steeled himself. For death, the how, the where, the why, being requisite—its pull called him home.

Clot of bugs blundering into his face, skimming the surrounding razor wire, atop the thirty-foot fence, his vision came to rest upon the short-statured guard in the western tower's parapet. Their juxtaposition brought the ever-watchful serenity of The Angel to mind.

As if Sherman had joined him, a thrush hopped onto a gravestone to flutter wings and warble, sweetly. Easily, he conjured Rosalee by his side, arms wrapped round his waist, emitting lovely giggles. Then there was Lauren-Son...Try as he might, he failed to conjure her.

I hate you! she'd screamed those final righteous words. How he lamented the loss of her!

His many failings he could live with, but estrangement from this one—his heart's desire—bunched his chest, near intolerable.

Terrible weight of her judgment—her falling out of love, her hatred—he grasped, perfectly.

I've made grievous mistakes. I've denied the afflictions of my own psyche, projecting them onto others in the form of illness and disease. As a result, I've tricked folks into carrying my rage so that I seem to manifest only goodness and light. But my rage overflowed anyhow. As a result, I've hurt many.

Emptiness overtook him. Hunger invaded. Hunger for intimacy, for closeness, and for circumstances to be different. No amount of awareness or insight could save him. He had freewill all right, but being long-wedded to The Plan, his fate seemed sealed.

Good works all but forgotten, his life would serve to warn others: *Beware of Hubris!*

Still, he wished to reshape how he'd be remembered. The more insightful might see his failings as part of his sacrifice. After all, as the yogi had informed, next life he'd incarnate as a bodhisattva: a mortal committed to a life in service.

Face tipped to the sun, breezes rumpling hair, his soul flew free, winging out beyond the fence to Buena Vista. As ever, he admired the town's fierce tenacity, for, at God's command, it clung fast to the steep, unwelcoming slope. He then thanked every tree, building and mineshaft that resided upon it. In particular, he thanked The Living Light—the refuge it gave him.

Brring, brring—the yard buzzer called him back.

Becalmed, yet deeply empty, Walker stepped in line. Cons regarded him, quizzical, muttering among themselves.

"Say there, Preacher Man," The Loon called out, "what else do the dead say? Just a bitty bit of time before ya'll join 'em?" Walker's heart thumped wildly.

Chapter Ninety-Four: Lauren

Morning arrived; Mom knocked. Lauren-Son opened her mouth in response, yet no words exited.

"Rosalee's on the phone, honey. She'd like to speak with you."

Lifting, straightening, collecting disparate pieces of herself, without a hello, she announced to her friend, "I refuse to have any more to do with Walker."

"You were his strongest ally, but now you hate him?" Rosalee sounded terribly hurt.

"Let's just say, I discovered a couple major things I don't care to forgive."

"You expect perfection, but Walker is just a man."

"Too true, Rosie. He's a very bad man with a huge hole in his heart!"

"Why do you say that?" Rosalee riled.

"Believe me, he is!" Viciously, Lauren-Son categorized Walker's many faults, yet neglected to declare what happened between them or to divulge her current state, till she eventually ran out of words. "Bye now, and please—leave me be."

Spivey called next to crow, "Found Ozmond's bones!"

"Wow, and where?" Lauren-Son tried to enthuse.

"As guessed, in Harperville. Sheriff's wife—now 'bout a hundred plus years old—says she gave her husband conniptions when she took Ozzie's body after the hangin', cleaned him up, real good, and buried him in the family plot.

"Hew-hew-hew," she cackled, hard. "Just now, the sheriff and Ozzie is buried, side-by-side. Ain't that a picture now?

"Yesterday, I bought a coffin; sheen's prit' near the exact color o'

Ozzie's skin. Paperwork's been a heap o' trouble, but I can't take him without it."

"For fact, they're his bones?"

"It's you that put me to the notion; even if I bring back the wrong ones, it don't matter, 'cause I'll be lovin' up and puttin' some soul to rest."

"You forgive us whites?"

"It helps some—the sheriff's wife takin' him in like that—but I ain't bullyin' myself into forgivin'. When the good Lord says so, I'll be done.

"So"—Spivey shifted tone—"how're you doin', gal?"

Sigh heaved, Lauren-Son, bit back tears. "Not great, actually."

"Mr. Walker, same as all o' us, was capable of great good, 'cept he let his nasty self take charge."

"I too got carried away. So now I hate myself."

"Years ago," Spivey saw fit to say, "I asked them hospital folk to remove the chunk o' my brain, the part that held memory. When they said no, I worked hard to block all feelin'. So, I 'preciated most that The Foundation, gave me safe refuge from myself. See...I thought I was a powerless victim. But, lately, I see that I ain't.

"You ain't either, gal. The Living Light gave you asylum, too, 'cept it's time for you to git free from it. If I learnt one thing, it's that you can't run away from your sorry 'ole self. The only way out is to dive straight on in and face your problems."

Misery required her undivided attention, so presently Lauren-Son held fast to wallowing. "Just now, I'd like to sleep, oh, say, for a century."

"That's just plain stupid, 'cause you have that other bitty life to consider."

"What? How could you know?"

"Spivey don't need no eyes to see how it is with you."

Rung off, bewildered, Lauren-Son retreated to bed.

At dawn, hazy light peeked through curtains as Lauren-Son dangled in the perfect, netherworld between sleep and awake. A dog barked. Sprinklers clicked on and putted away. Mind calm, clear, no troubles flooding in, she stretched and sat.

Recall hit. Then panic. Heat fanned out from her chest, heart banging, back she tunneled into covers.

Get up!—she insisted but failed to budge.

Anger gouging all kindness from her heart, she dove in to thoroughly enjoy loathing Walker. He'd used his work as his sole source of fulfillment to compensate for what he was not—a whole, balanced person. No longer as initially thought—actually, his sorrow was smoldering rage. His kind acts merely sucked folks into dependence. His reticence wasn't loneliness; it served as cover for his many secrets.

Walker's pulpy face and pulverized hands appearing in her mind's eye, a rogue thought flitted through: *If he could fix and rearrange bodies, couldn't he also break bones and rip apart tissue—even tear open an aneurysm to kill in an instant?*

Realization hit: *He'd faked his own abduction, beat himself up, then suckered all into believing others had done it!*

Never mind the absurdity that his hands could do no harm; he'd done unforgivable things; many suffered as a result. "I'm transferring spiritual energy," Walker explained the times he'd pinched clients.

Ways he controlled her: paying her rent, not paying it; his not so subtle disapproval of Arvin; how he'd groomed her to teach but merely used her as his tool; his demand that she keep quiet about Mildred Sharp. His special treatment of her...and of Melissa. The many ways he'd sidelined Delia. Her constant fear of failing him. Ach...Her lunatic faith, trust, devotion to him overwhelmed!

Walker's dark side being so artfully hidden, what about my own willingness to ignore it?

Onlooker silence permits continued victimization. So indeed, as Walker's complicit sidekick, never had she given serious thought to question or to refuse him. Actually, she made excuses for his questionable acts and looked the other way.

Indeed, the more she turned against Walker, the more she had to turn against herself. For she too was culpable!

As she lay there tripping over regrets, she sensed Walker blindly crashing about, trying to reach through to her.

Firmly, steadily, she blocked him. Yet, she felt him jab, poke, and nip at her innards.

"Get out," she yelped. "I hate you!" A light caress traced her jaw.

Eyes pinched shut, mind made vacant, Walker's eyes—those intense, deep pools—appeared.

"Your next job,"he warbled, "your most important task, is to create a new self: one who refuses to follow, idolizes no one, is completely independent, doesn't conform, and takes full responsibility for all that's created. You'll make a fine example for others. So hang in there, don't give up—however long it takes." Words jamming her brain, they nestled in hair follicles, burrowing deep into crevices of gray matter. "And when your new, fully empowered self blossoms, something wonderful will come."

Slid off the mattress, she knelt to pray. "God, I haven't been too receptive of late, but please, make Walker leave me be!" Eyes raised, checking, fingers raked through scalp, arms examined, she looked down at herself. Hands held to light, she inspected her palms and then the backs.

No light emanating, she dropped them, relieved.

"Mark me now," boomed a voice. "All that's happened was meant to be."

"Get out," she shrieked. "Wherever you are, Walker Judson, listen up…" Fumbled to her feet, she shook a fist. "Never again will I act from blind faith and subservient denial. My days as your lame-brained, suck-up, hero-worshiping personal slave are done! And, whatever future I create for this child and for myself—to help others, to speak out against your kind—is mine, not yours!"

Blinding flash sundering her senses—familiar scents, tobacco and mint, spewing the air—tears flooding her eyes; she wiped them, fiercely. Chest constricted, in serious pain, given the hollow diminishment felt, the being known as Walker Judson had just departed.

Chapter Ninety-Five: Walker

Searchlights strobing, a guard strolled along the tier, blurting light into each con's face. Bars automatically locking behind, he let himself out of the cellblock.

Darkness drawn down, breathy sounds surrounding, Walker's cellmate on the overhead bunk flapped lips, snoring. Water burbling, a distant latrine flushed. Proudly, a rookie guard clomped to show off new boots. Quarter mile away, mass murderer, Robbie Renfrow stirred and groaned. And the self-important assistant warden plotted his upcoming day.

Why sense all this, or grasp matters beforehand when not permitted to intervene? He wondered the trillionth time. *Moreover, if my farsightedness gives a glimpse of the loss to come, why not barter my soul to change it?*

One thing he *did* know. *Time was precious, and little of it remained.*

Four a.m., covers flung back, Walker stood and flicked the light switch.

Dim yellow glow casting a long shadow, Regis groaned and flopped to face the wall.

"Sorry," Walker apologized.

Regis Fulbright, small-time pro boxer, aggrieved at his wife for overcooking his eggs, cold-cocked her clear into the next world. Yet still, he lamented, loud and often, "A three-minute egg's mo' betta than a four-minute one."

Regis, an advanced syphilitic, did not request to be healed of it. His arthritic, gnarled knuckles and crimped hands of greatest concern, daily he pestered Walker to fix them.

Given the multitudes of bunions to alleviate, the hemorrhoids to shrink, blood pressure counts to pare down, and impotencies to make turgid, bunking with Walker had been a hard won prize for Regis.

Breath decidedly rank, Walker went to the sink, turned on the spigot, brushed his teeth, spat, slurped water, gargled, and spat again. Next, he washed his face and underarms, toweled dry, carefully combed his hair, and then went to stand at the bars.

Pleasant memories surfaced: the tart crunch of a Gravenstein apple; Ma's conch as it whispered tales; the first time he saw light emanate from treetops and stretch far into the sky, then those trees mentioned Gaia and spoke of earth as a precious living, breathing being.

Realization that he'd given his life to fraudulence—memories, not his, but those snatched from folks he'd treated—flared.

Bent double with shame, he arose, then shuffled back to his bunk.

Disgraced, highly fallible, times during and after the trial, he hoped, even prayed, that God might smite him. Truth be told, in this lifetime, unable to take the ultimate step as a bodhisattva; to subsume his ego in order to attain unity with humanity's suffering—such a strain to pretend to be wise, strong, gracious, good, kind—he'd hoped to be made better by just faking it.

But still, that was not where God condemned him. And, being that no forgiving communication indicated otherwise, God *did* condemn him.

Fumbling, he lit a cigarette and scanned the cell. His Royal typewriter, his last remaining worldly possession, fallen to disuse on account of his hands, rested on a shelf. Last evening, he'd divested himself of the Book of Psalms, giving it to Regis. For Regis, lacking any religious bent, coveted anything that Walker touched.

Five a.m., still dark, growing lighter, languid snores, interspersed among coughs and sleeper's groans, wafted between tiers. Cigarette extinguished in the sink, it gently hissed. Walker re-combed his hair, then sat back to wait and to imagine dawn's advent.

Prison windows too high or non-existent, he'd never seen the sunrise since arrival: an event sorely missed. Within prison confines, muddied light entered without keenness as the sun rose to dapple the bottommost tier. An hour from now, scant sunlit slivers would peek, albeit briefly, through top tier cellblock windows: an event he greatly appreciated.

Today, however, he would not bear witness.

Time and space warped, eddying; a vast desert scene appeared. A crowd on its feet—thousands—pulsed forth as a wee girl-child reached out to heal and bless them each. Winds kicking up, sand abraded ankles. Clouds thinned, parting. Numinous bliss emanating, lighted shafts penetrated all present, and then Lauren-Son and Ma materialized.

Magnificent to behold, eyes perfect, nose straight, skin smooth, Ma's face bore no concavity nor telltale scarring. Arms flung wide, round and round she began to spin. "Join me!" she beckoned to Lauren-Son, to the girl-child, and to Walker.

And so, four humming tops spun.

Movement above catching attention, they drew to a halt. "Oh my," gaped Ma.

Violets—an infinity—splattered earth. As raindrops might, soft florets—azure, cobalt, aqua, periwinkle and navy—fell round them. Walker reached out; one wafted, weightless, into his hand.

Falling slowed to a drizzle, gradually it ceased.

Lips pressed to every cheek, Ma kissed, then beamed upon them. "Together at last!"

Scene fading to nothing, Walker sat at bunk's edge. Grief, desire, loss, pain, overwhelmed. Appreciating all he'd learned from Lauren-Son—that profound happiness actually could exist, he had to marvel: *Such a wondrous woman she's become!* Never dull, always bright—growing more so—as his truest gift, she'd burrowed into his very marrow, moving him past life-long separation.

Their closeness, having his heart's desire, then desecrating it by overriding her need for truth...he'd destroyed the very thing he'd forever sought. Love...pure and simple.

Enraged by his own behavior, no right to reach out to overcome her reproach, the loss of her constricted his throat.

Yet...Gradually, persistently, this wondrous, tender new life shot forth. Fiercely, urgently, it clung and grew. It being the point of all, his life had not been a total loss.

Footsteps approached; he checked his watch.

Cell door clanged open. "Your pal sent me," the guard announced.

Stepped onto the gangway, Walker thrust out his wrists. The guard shook his head. "No need."

Searchlight roving as they went along the tier, men lurked in the shadows, knuckles of hands gripping bars as he passed. Artie Wallbeck stepped up to whisper, "Thanks, man."

Down the stairs, heavy set of doors unbolted, Walker traversed a long hall, went through more locked barred doors to enter the library.

Respectful incline of the head, the guard departed.

The library, exclusively for inmate use, housed a collection of dog-eared law books. A deeply etched table, assorted names and initials carved into it, graced the room's center. "My, my!" Leisurely, sinuous, The Loon sauntered forth. "Preacher Man's come to pay little old moi a visit!" Walker's heart made swift descent from chest to belly.

Sharp metal extracted from waistband, delicately balanced between thumb and forefinger, The Loon gave it a lick. Blood spurting onto shirtfront, hand splayed, shiv thrust down, he impaled himself to the tabletop.

Shiv yanked up, swiftly, he impaled the other hand. Walker flinched each time. "How am I doing as a sainted one?"

Hands on display, blood poured steadily onto the table, pattering the floor as The Loon fixed Walker with a stare. "I'm asking, real respectful-like...Teach me."

Reached out, Walker touched the right hand's bloody spot. "Consider yourself taught."

The hole failed to cleanse itself. The laceration did not recede or form a tidy scar. It *did* continue to bleed, messing table and floor. "You do the other," Walker instructed.

Face creased into a frown, The Loon spluttered, "You mocking me?"

"You already have the ability to heal."

"Nothings fixed."

"Fixing's not always visible."

Up, The Loon sidled, nose to nose. "Teach me," he hissed, spritzing Walker with spittle. "Else I rip out your heart!" Walker searched the man's face.

Truly, he understood The Loon's fear, felt his pain. "You're a healer—always have been. But you must only do good, not evil; if abused, the gift is rescinded."

"I am asking polite," The Loon enunciated, real slow. "Show me how to fix my hands."

Walls tilted, careening. Steam hissed as it traversed pipes. Machinery whimpered and hummed. "I just did," Walker calmly repeated.

Door slammed in the corridor; the world went silent.

Never did The Loon's yellow-irised eyes blink. Walker held steady, felt no sorrow, no anger, and no more fear. The Loon heaved a sigh, rolled up sleeves to expose extreme biceps, tucked his shirt in, eying Walker all the while. "I'm terribly disappointed. So, ya'll know how it's gotta be."

"It seems, dear fellow, you're nominated to do the deed. For that… I'm grateful."

Door come open behind, The Loon looked past Walker, quizzical.

A low, purring voice spoke, "'Tis Voden Fucols, Boss."

Walker's heart soared. "Thanks for coming!"

"Wouldn't have missed it." A watery, transparent version of Voden Fucols came to Walker's side. "By the way"—lips puckered, Voden made kisses—"Ma sends her love."

"Ah, so! Still, I'm not clear, though. Are you her angel or mine?"

Shiv juggled hand-to-hand, The Loon cast fretful glances between Walker and the vacant airspace.

"Mr. Fucols serves as a familial angel assigned to your lineage for, what seems, all time. Way back, he served as your Ma's convent confidant. Presently, he belongs to you, posed as a prison guard: albeit an invisible one. Once, he stepped out of line to act as the nut-job, Oswell Nothnagel, for Lauren. Soon he shall guide your daughter, as well." Candy bar plucked from thin air, Voden unwrapped and munched it down.

Eyes bugging, increasingly confused, sensing a presence, yet unable to see it, The Loon tensed, apoplectic.

"Initially," Voden continued, "you experienced the angelic essence embodied within the statue, but its inanimate state proved rather limited, so the person of Voden Fucols arrived. Silly, a lesser angel-in-training, came along as well. For a time, The Angel and Mr. Fucols were symbiotes.

"Alas, The Angel went rogue, insisted on summoning you to your mother's deathbed; Mr. Fucols thought it ill-advised. Why God permitted it, Mr. Fucols is now able to grasp." Light illumined Voden as he cast Walker fond looks. "For one so thoroughly opposed to the notion of choice, even Mr. Fucols has gained knowledge vis-à-vis such matters during this earthly tenure. Therefore you, Boss, may choose death or may opt to step into the unknown."

Walker jerked into a hacking cough.

Patiently, The Loon waited.

Coughs escalating, gasping for breath, Walker emitted a tone no human had previously issued forth. Entire body a-tremble, cells, molecules busily rearranging—the room, all books, the chairs, the walls, The Loon, who waited impatient, began vibrating, as well.

Sudden sign of the cross made, The Loon collected himself, then shrugged, apologetic, "Hate to interrupt, Preacher Man, but you and I have business."

Quick up-slash, he plunged the shiv into Walker's chest.

Massive thud, shock of pain, air punched from lungs, Walker stumbled, grabbed The Loon, and leaned heavily into him.

Locked into a tender near-kiss, The Loon held onto him; Walker gave off a gentle smile.

Hands slick with blood, eyes full of fear, The Loon shoved Walker and lurched off.

Drops of blood scribed Walker's front. Rivulets trailed his armpits, ran down pant legs to pool at his feet. Terrible slowness, his knees collapsed to drag him down. Heart palpating wildly, the lucid segment of his brain registered peace, not fear.

Voden, cradling Walker's head in his lap, soothed, "We shall leave momentarily."

Gust of air, prison walls, ceiling included, vanished to reveal an immense star-dappled sky.

Low moan emitted, feathers fluffing, softly flapping, Voden's wingspan unfolded.

Breath and life leaching out, body severing from its soul—wings engulfed, lifting off—to carry this Beloved Soul—one recently assigned to Walker Judson—to meet the dawn.

Body dissolved to merge with The Radiant All, outward-pitched waves elevated the vibration and frequency of the eternal universe.

Chapter Ninety-Six: Lauren

Three months later, Lauren, as she'd resumed calling herself, answered a knock at Mom's kitchen door. There a young woman, swathed in saffron robes, stood.

Taken for a Hare Krishna, Lauren moved to give her the brush-off.

"Surprise!" tittered a familiar voice. "I was asked to come see you."

Noting the enormous eyes and perfectly sculpted neck, joined to meet flawless clavicles, Lauren peered out to ask, "Melissa?"

"Correct! Recently, I joined a Zen community." She did a modest pirouette.

"You're a Buddhist?" Lauren gaped. "Uh...Care to join me? I'm about to have lunch."

"Yes, I'm a Buddhist, and yes, I'd love lunch." *Scritchslap, scritchslap*—Melissa stepped inside, discretely sliding eyes over Lauren's belly bump.

"What brings you here?"

"Walker was the closest I've known to a living saint, and sadly, rather than carry the lessons from my time at the ashram, I threw myself at him. Never mind that he had a wife, I was sure sleeping with him would make me whole. When he refused, I wanted to hurt him. So, perfect timing, when the trial came up, I joined in."

Plate thunked before her guest, Lauren-Son sat across. "You didn't have an affair, then?"

"It was only wishful thinking."

"How messed up is that!" Amazed, glad, confused, Lauren reached across to grab Melissa's wrist. "Any idea if he actually harmed those other women?"

"Put it this way," Melissa leaned in confidential, "before the trial, Ardis set up a meeting with those other so-called victims. Being that she never acted without Delia's say-so, and since Walker had just rejected my advances, I tried to get included, but they shunned me."

"Jeeze! Did they include Mildred Sharp?

"I wouldn't know."

"Do you suppose they set Walker up?"

"Possibly, but why."

"Because he'd let them or maybe to get him out of the way." Teeth achy from clenching, she dropped Melissa's wrist. But then—seeking to control her own hands—she crimped them in her lap.

Up they crept anyway to rearrange utensils.

Perhaps she'd pay Walker a visit to ask about this and about countless other matters. But then she remembered...There could be no final cleansing conversation.

Face constricted, Lauren's voice broke, "I understand that Walker's dead." And she felt like crying for about a zillion years.

Melissa's chin quivered. "I accused a man of doing things he never did and helped send him to prison. That's why, though painful as hell, I wrote Walker weekly, even visited twice. Also, I offered to try to get the verdict overturned, but he refused. My last letters got returned unopened. Can you believe, he even insisted he forgave me and that all of it would've happened anyway. Plus, he insisted you'd help me—that we could help each other."

Skimmed through several facial calisthenics, Lauren settled for a grimace. "Surely you're mistaken. Walker wouldn't dare send anyone."

Skimpy shoulder shrug, Melissa persisted, "This was no mistake." Fidgeting with prayer beads, she passed them through her fingers at a torrid pace.

Lauren sat back, mesmerized. "First an ashram, then Walker, now a Buddhist—what's with the need to subjugate yourself?" Face squinched, Melissa considered this; Lauren pressed, "You haven't gained insight. Instead, you glom onto yet another fanaticism to repeat those exact same mistakes."

Grimly, Melissa nodded. "It's like a familiar, well-worn groove. Try as I might to climb out, I keep falling back in."

"What's wrong with us? Why hand ourselves over to be remade? Spiritual moochers is what we are!"

"Actually, I'm a seeker."

"That's just *so* sad!"

"You blame me?"

"I've been a seeker too." *Difference between us*, Lauren thought loftily, *I'm trying to learn from my mistakes, while you repeat yours.* "Look...To a degree, I'm recovering from the same problem. Given what Walker did to me, I have trouble believing in anything. But you... you still want to believe.

"The difference is that I now choose to be in charge. Life is not done to us; we permit it." Not sure she fully believed this, she wanted to. "Bottom line...We've both given up power and must reclaim it."

"As a fledgling nun, I'm celibate," Melissa said, smugly, "which keeps me out of trouble. And I have this wise Buddhist teacher who helps me."

"I've grown highly allergic to gurus!"

"Oh..." *Scritch-scratch*—Melissa went for the door and scraped a box—firmly trussed in strands of colored twine—inside. "Walker said this would arrive and that I was to bring it to you"

Wads of newspaper unwrapped, hundreds of seashells inside, hands run over shell's surfaces—keyhole limpets, a nautilus, abalone shells, periwinkles, scallops, and unidentifiable others—none bore the slightest chip or dent.

Note located, it read: *Compassion—is all we ask. That...and a trip to the seashore.* Given the loopy scrawl, Walker hadn't authored it.

"Walker specifically said to hold the conch to your ear...that, somehow, it would explain all."

Cabbage-size shell lifted, it immediately whispered: "Your daughter determines our fate."

Senses swelling, Lauren felt the sylph-like presence of a nun; proximity, so tangible she could've reached in through the veils to touch her rough, woolen habit.

Unceasing bliss, God's favor shone upon the woman. Fade to a scruffy farm, to utter ordinariness, that same woman hefted buckets of slop and bales of straw and longed for communion with God. Silence and suffering prevalent, she underwent self-reproach and bewilderment. Clearly, however, Lauren understood the blessing: what the woman mistook for exile had been the way forward.

Another image, softly focused, formed. That of herself in an auditorium before a large audience, beneath a banner that heralded: *Lauren Finch, Guru Buster*.

Melissa looked at her shyly. "Walker said to tell you…'There are no victims. Consequently, when you access your full potential, you'll make many mistakes. And for that, you too will be forgiven.'"

"He said that?"

"Yup."

Meal done, they went to the door. "Do you forgive him?" Melissa inquired.

Lauren offered up, "Not sure, but you've certainly given me plenty to consider."

Moved to leave, Melissa turned back. "One last thing…Walker said you should keep an eye out for Voden—that he now belongs to that which you've created." Eyes skimming her belly, she limped off.

No longer falling to pieces, there Lauren stood, lost in thought.

Overtaken by soft slackness, the gelatinous mass—the new forming being—bumped gently within its embryonic sac to make purposeful contact.

Fingertips to mouth, Lauren gave them a kiss, then rubbed at her navel.

Whoosh of wings, The Angel—or Voden, perhaps—embraced her.

Sorrow lifting, grace entered. And hope, fierce unnamable, traveled the tips of her toes to illumine all cells. Senses keen, mind unfettered, clarity came. Odd as it seems, she thanked Walker's inability to contain his rage and grief for sparing her his same fate. Oh, she had work to do, a ton, but this moment marked the start.

Wings unfolded, spanned to full size, she lost her body and truly remembered how to fly!

Chapter Ninety-Seven: Walker

Light skimmed the room and fell onto Lawrence P. Cotter, formerly known as The Loon, who sat surrounded by inmates listening in rapt attention, as the con bestowed loving kindness upon each of them.

No stab of envy, no desire for power, Walker, warmed by a deep sense of satisfaction, felt ever so glad to be alive and to be ordinary. For, finally, at long last, he was truly himself.

That day in the library, death did not actually take him. The tale, as previously told, unfolded in all its precise detail as he'd always envisioned. Yet, that road was not the one he'd chosen.

Everything stayed precisely the same till subsequent to Voden's revelations, when the scene had radically diverged. Walker's hacking cough had morphed into a primal maw, whereupon an unfamiliar feeling, a groan, a laugh, a sob, arose from deep within to issue forth. Collected upon a momentous wave, it spewed out to enfold and knock The Loon and Walker into each other's arms precisely the moment Walker issued the words, "I freely give you all of it."

Before the two men could right themselves and regain their senses, the diaphanous creature known as Voden Fucols had departed.

The Loon stood, stupefied, as Walker explained that he'd conferred his power—the ability to perform healings, the capacity to foresee the future, the magnetism to attract others—unto him. Naturally, he'd warned of the burdens: the loss of self, the inability to form intimate connection, being major deterrents.

Unforeseen by either man, years hence, The Loon, a strong healer, doing great good for countless others, would be skewered for failing to heal an inmate.

Eyes shut, Walker now grinned. For, having given himself the option to choose, he had chosen. So now he'd grow old and become a mere footnote.

How he enjoyed this newly birthed self; one he'd gladly inhabit till then end of his days!

Had he ever actually dwelt within the shadow world between reality and illusion; had he truly been able to bi-locate, existing in two places at once; had his hands actually glowed, searingly hot; had he seen the particulars of the future; and had he actually dwelt in the shadow world between reality and illusion?

None of that mattered. For having stepped into the unknown, he saw the world anew. A world where he knew nothing, whatsoever. And that was just fine with him.

Epilogue: Jessie

Lauren strapped Jessie, her three-year-old, into the car seat, set the seashell-filled backpack on the floor, and then drove off.

This trip got set in motion the day Jessie hefted the conch, peeked inside, held it to her ear, then, head thrown back, giggled, hysterically. "Shells want us to take them to mad water," she'd declared.

Jessie drowsed as Lauren navigated low-lying fog and looped along switch-back canyons. One particular S-curve brought her spine to mind; her hunchback and its miraculous straightening. So naturally thoughts of Walker surfaced.

Some time back, Rosalee called to report him as alive, yet much changed. Shocked, amazed, Lauren took up tentative, awkward correspondence to give him news of Jessie.

As if an achy phantom limb, she missed him. Still hurt and angry, she did not like, trust, respect, or admire him, but prayed that he stay safe. With no further urge to deify or to demonize him, mostly these days she thought of him as a complex mix of deep goodness and huge flaws.

Regarding her part: she'd had an urgent need to hand her autonomy over to him, and he hadn't entirely obliged. Rather than take charge herself, afraid she could not succeed without his help, she'd made him responsible for her life, relying heavily upon him, counting on him to be all things she was not. Times she'd tried to emulate him, he'd insisted she be herself. Also, he'd encouraged her to take the good he had to offer, toss out the bad, and be responsible for her choices. So possibly, he hadn't failed her; she'd failed herself.

Air smelling of brine, she parked, shed shoes, slung on the backpack, hefted the groggy child onto her hip, and made her way down the rocky path, heading toward the curvaceous coastline.

Wriggled from grasp, Jessie held her hand. Seaweed pods crunching underfoot, winds whipping up, they came to the flat strand where gulls shrieked, flapping wings. Jessie squealed and ran, calling after them.

Lauren squatted, opened the backpack, hailed her daughter back, and handed over a shell. "What's supposed to happen with these?"

"Watch me..." Off the child rushed to place the pilot shell in the sand and then return.

Lauren handed over others. Careful to avoid kelp and beach detritus, setting each shell out of reach from breaking waves, Jessie placed them as obtrusively as possible. Then the duo retreated to the dunes to watch.

Beachcombers arrived, heads down, scrutinizing. "Look, a perfect sand dollar!" The woman held her trophy aloft. "Found one too, a keyhole limpet," called another.

Chubby hand pressed to mouth Jessie suppressed a giggle.

More walkers caught up. Heads briefly together, they examined their treasures, then scattered.

A lone jogger bounded up, yelped, trotted back, jogged in place, lifted a shell, inspecting, glanced up, then down the strand, hopping all the while. Shell stuffed into pouch, he then loped off.

Best saved for last, Lauren handed over the conch.

Lifted to her ear, Jessie gravely addressed it, "Uh-huh, I promise." Off she scurried to set it at water's edge, and then she returned to crouch.

The next wave took it.

Jessie sighed, content. "I did good, Mama?"

Lauren pulled her daughter to her. "Indeed you did!"

Sand drizzled through fingers, Jessie, embraced within Lauren's lap, watched the ocean, offset against darkening sky, as the sun slid off the horizon. Sky deepened to crimson, to orange, then to lavender, and then darker still, it faded to purple.

Spotting an eligible stone, the child scrambled to heft and run fingers across its surface. Rock slid into coverall pocket, she declared, "Next we visit Papa." Gripping Mommy's hand, they headed home.

Acknowledgements:

Many thanks are due to: Dorothy Wall, Lydia Bird, Michael Ray Brown, and Paul Dinas for their early, sometimes repeated, edits. A huge heap of gratitude to Michelle Caplan for her several, insightful edits and brilliant direction.

To my dear friends who endured my pestering for input: Robin Heywood, Mark Cohen, Jill James, Jim Webster, Pamela Boyd, Ace Allen, Abbe Bates, Joanne James, Ellen Morse Weston, Blythe Bulmore, Dian Burke, and Jeff Hawkins. Thanks so much to Michael Paris for his gifted photographic eye. Oh, and thanks to my buddy, Morgan Taylor, for his expertise regarding legal and criminal matters.

I thank Ellen Bass' writing group, and Keith Raffel, for his input as to the ins-and outs of the new, very changed world of publishing. Beyond words, I thank my personal angel and dearest friend, Deborah Allen, for our many healing conversations.

To my other dear sister of blood and bone, Anne Wallace, who read more versions of the book than anyone. And thanks to much of the rest of my family who either edited repeated reads or endured my frets: Dick Strubbe, Bill Strubbe, John Strubbe, Jason Strubbe, Shiloh Klepp, and Nikolas Strubbe. I thank my deceased mom, Jane Carle Strubbe, for her deep love of words and for expanding my vision as to the possible. And my deceased dad, John Adrian Strubbe, for his quiet courage to push on each day in the face of suffering and adversity.

Credit and thanks to Carolyn Myss for her story about Padre Pio, to my friend, Barbara Selfridge, for her short missive about my father's death, and to Tom Wolf for his book, *A Man In Full,* which helped shape this novel's prison mess hall rumble. Thanks to John Grisham for his trial expertise and prison scenes. And to all authors whose amazing works helped me improve my writing skills.

Once again, and most of all, appreciation to my beloved hubby, John Wittenberg, who lived with, and endured nearly a quarter of a century's worth of my obsession with this topic.

Author's Biographical Note

Janice Strubbe Wittenberg is author of the non-fiction book, *The Rebellious Body: Reclaim Your Life from Environmental Illness or Chronic Fatigue Syndrome* (Plenum Publishers, 1996). *The Worship of Walker Judson* is her first novel. As a registered nurse, she spent over thirty years working in mental health. Today, she resides in Aptos, California with her beloved husband, John, two superb cats, hosts several beehives, and tends a flock of hilarious chickens.

Visit the author's website:
Strubbe-Wittenberg.com

Made in the USA
San Bernardino, CA
27 April 2014